Acclaim for Nicholas O'Connell's *Storms of Denali*

A powerful and addictive read, *The Storms of Denali* will sweep you in like an avalanche on the south face of the mountain herself. A vividly written tale about a climb up an unforgiving mountain, O'Connell's novel teaches us what an adventure story is really about—attempting the top is only part of the game; finding one's way home is what makes the true hero."
> —Garth Stein, author of the bestseller *The Art of Racing in the Rain*

This book is a page-turner. Nick O'Connell clearly knows a great deal about mountain climbing and how to couple this knowledge with a compelling and gripping narrative. There's plenty of tension and drama in *Storms of Denali*. It will be entertaining and engaging for readers even if they don't know much about climbing.
> —David Guterson, author of *Snow Falling on Cedars* and *Ed King*

Storms of Denali will be a great study for those who wish to climb high and a thriller for the "armchair mountaineer."
> —Lou Whittaker, author of *Memoirs of a Mountain Guide*
> and founder of Rainier Mountaineering, Inc.

Nick O'Connell has portrayed the risks, joys, emotions, and hard labor experienced during the ascent of North America's most frigid mountain. In his novel he displays a full comprehension of these varying experiences and dangers that may be encountered in surviving Denali.
> —Fred Beckey, climbing legend and author of
> *Fred Beckey's 100 Favorite North American Climbs*

Nick O'Connell has crafted a remarkable story of risk, death and survival on Denali, the coldest big mountain in the world. Every reader—climber or not—should find this account of a difficult and dangerous ascent both absorbing and mesmerizing. There is a short list of memorable works of fiction about climbing. *Storms of Denali* deserves to be among them.
> —Jim Wickwire, one of the first two Americans to summit K2
> and co-author of the memoir *Addicted to Danger*

An extraordinary novel. Through verisimilitude and candor..., O'Connell plumbs the motivations, risk, and nuances of an ordinary climber's life. The mounting tension, deft characterizations, and sun-burnt realism of *The Storms of Denali* transport the reader more vividly than any other book about the mountain.

—Jonathan Waterman, author of
In the Shadow of Denali and *Running Dry*

The Storms of Denali is a genuinely engaging novel with not only the suspense and superb pacing we expect from a good adventure story but vividly drawn characters and a fascinating, detailed portrait of the culture of mountain climbers as well. Nick O'Connell's first novel is both a thrilling ride and danged satisfying read.

—Charles Johnson, author of the
National Book Award-winning novel *Middle Passage*

Whether you're an experienced climber or an armchair mountaineer, you're going to enjoy the read. Nick's taken his experience as a mountaineer and his expertise as a writer and delivered a great story, told very well.

—Phil Ershler, International Mountain Guides director and author of
Together on Top of the World, made the first ascent of Everest's north side

The Storms of Denali captures the odd magic created from the hardships, sublime beauty, and pure adventure encountered while climbing Denali. This is a great story, written by an author clearly familiar with the Denali experience. The story tackles some of the calculus that leads climbers to push themselves and risk their very lives in an effort to bring beauty and balance to their existence. Destined to become a classic in North American climbing fiction.

—John Race, longtime Denali guide and director
of the Northwest Mountain School

STORMS OF DENALI

STORMS OF DENALI
NICHOLAS O'CONNELL

UNIVERSITY OF ALASKA PRESS · FAIRBANKS

University of Alaska Press
P.O. Box 756240
Fairbanks, AK 99775-6240

ISBN 978-1-60223-183-2 (cloth); 978-1-60223-184-9 (paper); 978-1-60223-185-6
(electronic)

Library of Congress Cataloging-in-Publication Data

O'Connell, Nicholas.
The storms of Denali / Nicholas O'Connell.
    p. cm.
 ISBN 978-1-60223-183-2 (acid-free paper)—ISBN 978-1-60223-184-9 (acid-free paper)
—ISBN 978-1-60223-185-6
 I. Title.
 PS3615.O37S76 2012
 813'.6—dc23
                              2012005523

Cover design by Kristina Kachele
Cover photos by Alec Turner

This publication was printed on acid-free paper that meets the minimum requirements
for ANSI / NISO Z39.48–1992 (R2002) (Permanence of Paper for Printed Library
Materials).

Printed in the United States on recycled paper

Dedicated to my wife, Lisa Lynn Sowder

PROLOGUE

The storm caught us in the open, halfway down the southeast ridge of Denali, the highest and coldest mountain in North America. The wind gusted furiously, sandblasting my face with ice pellets and knocking me to my knees. I hunched against the slope and watched our 9 mm red Perlon rope levitate off the snow as if it were obeying a conjurer's trick. Then the gust subsided, and the rope returned to the ground.

I stood up and stumbled forward, following Wyn as he staggered down the curving, heavily corniced ramp of crusty, wind-scoured snow with patches of blue, bulletproof ice. The descent presented no great technical difficulties other than dizzying exposure, but it took an enormous act of will to keep walking. Last night's bivouac at 19,000 feet had completely fried my brain.

Placing my feet carefully, I reminded myself that most mountaineering accidents happen on the descent. One slip, one screwup, and that would be it. I thought of my wife and son back in Seattle. I remembered them standing in the doorway of our home, Jill's eyes dark and angry, Andy clutching his stuffed frog. I tried to fix this image in my mind, but their faces blurred, expanded and contracted like the figures in a fun-house mirror.

The rope tugged against my harness.

"Sorry!" I yelled and kept moving. It was about a mile to the end of the southeast ridge, but the snow was maddeningly unpredictable, sometimes offering a stable platform, other times collapsing beneath my plastic boots.

Wyn broke trail 150 feet ahead. Like a bird dog on a leash, he tugged constantly at the rope, urging me forward. Despite his impatience, it was a relief to have him leading. As on so many other climbs, I depended on his strength to pull us through. Nothing seemed to stop him.

As I watched his yellow parka bobbing hypnotically down the ridge, my right crampon caught on a chunk of ice. I tripped and tried to jam my ice axe into the slope, but my frostbitten hands couldn't apply any pressure. Picking up speed, I rocketed headfirst down the slope.

The rope jerked tight against my waist. I flipped over, hit a patch of soft snow, and came to rest on my side. I lay there for a full minute, panting. Slowly I got to my knees, looked around, and brushed the snow off my face. Other than ripping the elbow out of my parka, I was okay. I sucked the thin, bitter air through my compressed lips and tried to regain my composure. Blood pounded in my temples. My heart hammered wildly. I waved up at Wyn. He was still in self-arrest position, his legs spread-eagled against the slope, the pick of his axe buried into the ice.

We exchanged a long look; neither one of us had to say anything. I owed him. Step by exhausting step, I regained the top of the ridge, expending energy I would desperately need later. Then I fell in behind him, riveting my attention on the snow in front of me.

Every step brought us closer to base camp. We crouched against the slope when the wind threatened to knock us over. Stood up when it died down. I tried not to think about the danger, nor the condition of our partners behind us. I simply put one foot in front of the other, over and over again. After what seemed an eternity, we reached the end of the ridge. Clouds soared up the south face, obscuring our descent route. The storm was building.

Scraps of mist sailed by, lowering the visibility to several hundred feet. I got compass bearings on the jagged, white pyramids of Mount Hunter and Mount Huntington to the south. Clouds gathered behind them like an enormous anvil.

Clutching the map with my frostbitten hands, I used the edge of the compass to sight a line from each summit to the southeast ridge. The intersection of the lines was our present position, if my calculations were correct. By the time I glanced up to double-check the bearings, clouds had already covered their summits. I'd always prided myself on my route-finding ability. Now it would be put to the test.

I looked back up the slope to where Al and Lane descended behind us. Their progress was agonizingly slow. Al went first, walking pigeon-toed, taking a few steps and then stopping. Lane followed behind, keeping Al on a short leash.

"C'mon!" Wyn shouted up at them. I looked at my altimeter watch: 8:35 a.m. Precious minutes were ticking by. I was frantic to keep moving, but we had to wait for Al and Lane. It was a cardinal rule of climbing: keep the group together. An invisible rope bound us to them.

I tried to unbuckle my pack, but my hands felt like blocks of wood. Using my knuckles, I managed to release the buckles, lowered the pack to the ground, and collapsed on top of it. A toxic cocktail of chemicals churned in my gut. For the last few hours, I'd been fanta-sizing about eating my last square of chocolate. Now I took it out of my pack, turned it over in my black insulated mittens, and popped it into my mouth. It was as hard and brittle as shale, but it softened on my tongue. I ate it slowly, savoring every bit. It soothed my stomach, but now I had no food left. We *had* to get back to base camp soon.

Wyn sat down next to me. The last few weeks had taken a toll on him. His face was creased and sunburned, his lips scabbed, his breathing fast and shallow. His food was gone; he'd eaten his last lemon drop for breakfast. He took a swig from his water bottle and handed it to me. I drank deeply; we had to keep hydrated. Food was optional. Water was essential.

"Which way?" Wyn asked, pointing ahead.

I carefully unfolded the map, making sure that the wind didn't rip it out of my hands. The blue topographic lines gathered in a knot, indicating the steepness of our descent route. I studied the dark patches of rock and the white patches of ice, looking for a way through it. Right or left or straight? A simple decision, but our lives hung in the balance.

"Straight," I said finally, "keeping to the snow."

He looked at the map. "Are you sure we're here?" He pointed to the spot on the summit ridge where the lines met.

"Yes," I said, nodding. "Got a compass bearing on Hunter and Huntington."

"How could you triangulate?" he asked, looking toward the summits now obscured by clouds as gray and thick as wool.

"I took bearings before the clouds moved in."

He nodded and handed the map back to me. "Look. They're almost here."

Turning around, I watched Al and Lane stagger toward us. When they arrived, Al bent over his ice axe and tried to catch his breath. His lips were blue and trembling, his breathing labored and erratic.

Wyn went over to help him.

"I got him," Lane said, keeping a tight grip on the rope. His blond mustache was caked with ice, his skin red with cold, his large back stooped from the effort of short-roping. As a firefighter and mountain rescue volunteer, he was used to dealing with emergencies, but he was acting increasingly irrational. Perhaps he had altitude sickness, too.

"Which way?" he asked.

"Straight," I yelled.

He shook his head. "Right. We need to go right."

I took out the map. "The map says straight."

He seemed to have trouble focusing on it. "Need to get down fast. South face."

"No way," Wyn shouted. "It's way too steep."

"Rescue operation." Lane's speech was becoming garbled, his judgment questionable.

"That's crazy," I said.

"Have to try," Lane said. "Helicopter. Air-vac."

"There's no helicopter!" I shouted. "No air evacuation. Remember?" We'd radioed at the bivouac. Kim, the base camp manager, had made it very clear. No helicopters would fly in this weather. I beckoned him forward. "This way."

Lane looked at Al and motioned to the right.

"Straight!" I shouted, but the wind snatched the words away.

Lane moved to the right. Al followed behind him. They stumbled off into the mist, heading toward the sheer south face of Denali.

THREE MONTHS EARLIER

ONE

On a rainy night in early March, several months before, I stopped in at the 5.10 Tavern, a big barn of a place on the north side of Capitol Hill in Seattle. The 5.10 doesn't look like much from the outside, just a faded brick facade overgrown with English ivy. A neon ice axe and coil of rope blinked above the entrance, providing the only clue it's the epicenter of Seattle climbing.

Pulling open the heavy wooden door, I caught a whiff of beer, French fries, and the faint tang of gymnast's chalk, which climbers use to dry their hands before attempting to scale the tavern's big chimney. The smell brought back memories of the times I'd hung out here in my twenties, living the life of a climbing bum, scarfing half-eaten hamburgers from the plates left behind by well-heeled customers.

The place had changed little over the years. Telephone cable spools still served as tables. Nails protruded from the rafters. Fiberglass insulation peeled off the ceiling. Boards were stacked against the back wall. It looked like the 5.10 was permanently under construction.

I scanned the crowd for Wyn Mitchell, my former climbing partner. He had called and asked me to meet him here at 9 p.m. I hadn't seen him in four years, since our botched attempt on the West Buttress of Denali. I was psyched to see him again. Wyn could be aggravating, but his enthusiasm was contagious.

As I looked around for him, I noticed a photo had been added to the gallery above the bar. In addition to Sir Edmund Hillary, Reinhold Messner, Chris Bonington, John Roskelley, and Jim Whittaker, there was a shot of Wyn, with his wild blond hair, angular jaw, and gap-toothed grin. He leaned against his ice axe, the jagged summit of the Petit Dru in the background. He'd achieved his apotheosis: he'd become one of the gods of the climbing galaxy.

Wading through the crowd, I ordered a pint at the bar. I didn't see any luminaries, just the 5.10's regular crowd—working stiffs from the neighborhood, several older guys in pile jackets reminiscing about the Golden Age of Cascade climbing, and a group of gaunt, young, hard men who wore tank tops to show off their biceps and talked earnestly about gear, routes, and upcoming climbs. While snow fell in the Cascades, they bragged about all the hard climbs they were going to do—all from the safety of the great indoors.

I staked out a booth in back where I could sip my beer and keep an eye on the entrance. When Wyn left for Yosemite, California, four years ago in his green VW van plastered with climbing stickers, I wasn't sure when I'd see him again. Inseparable through high school, college, and early adulthood, it seemed our paths had finally diverged: his toward extreme climbing, mine toward marriage, family, and a real job.

Once he left, my life began to change, and fast. Jill and I got married, and a few months later, Andy was born. To support the family, I switched from part-time to full-time at Alpine Gear, an outdoor equipment retailer. When Hal, the owner, offered me a chance to buy into the business, I accepted. I still got out into the hills occasionally, but I didn't have time for serious climbing.

I looked at my watch: 9:20 p.m. Wyn was late, as usual. I thought about heading home, but I decided to give him five more minutes. I passed the time watching the nightly chimney climbing competition.

The tavern's twenty-five-foot stone-and-concrete chimney looks like something in a ski lodge. Rusty, the owner, named the place after the chimney's rock climbing rating—5.10—formerly the top end of the scale, five indicating the need for a rope to do a move safely, and ten the rating on a scale of difficulty that begins at one and goes up to an unbelievably hard 5.15. To drum up business, he promised a free pitcher of beer to whoever could scale it. But the 5.10 rating didn't pose much of a problem for a competent climber, so the contest cut into his profits. He tried to discontinue it, but everybody griped so much that he gave up the idea. Instead, he hammered off all the easy holds. Now you had to be a virtuoso to do it. It was supposed to go at 5.11c, but, rumor had it, Rusty's latest alteration had made it even harder.

That night several climbers were giving it a try. Many of them I knew from the store, where they bought the rock shoes with sticky rubber soles and bags of chalk attached to the back of their belts. They were a determined bunch and for good reason: no one had climbed it since Rusty's last "alteration" a month ago.

Al McKenzie, a customer and Boeing engineer, gave it a go. Thin, dark-haired, with sleepy eyes and black-framed glasses held in place by an elastic band, he looked like a large stork. But he quickly moved up the chimney, grimacing as he clawed at the rock for some semblance of a hold. Despite his appearance and awkward style, he was a formidable climber. I'd climbed with him before and had watched him solo a vertical waterfall as if it were a stepladder. He was fanatical about his "tools," as he called his ice climbing equipment, carrying them around in an aluminum briefcase. His mastery of ice didn't translate to the chimney, though. He peeled off, landing on the foam pad Rusty had installed on the advice of his insurance company.

Then the gaunt, young, hard men took over. They reminded me of myself at that age—brash, opinionated, and totally committed to the sport. They considered me hopelessly out of date, a traditional or "trad" climber, as they liked to say, who couldn't compete with what they were doing in rock climbing, which was true. They barely acknowledged me when they came into the store, listening with amused tolerance to my advice about gear. This didn't stop them from asking me for pro discounts, however, which I refused. I had to make a living, too.

A blond guy with big biceps went next. He tried to muscle his way up, grasping the holds so hard it looked like they'd break. He grunted and pressure breathed like a steam engine, his face turning red and his eyes bugging out. He tried to overpower the rock, not bothering to use balance or finesse. Still, he gutted it out to the crux, grasped a pebble embedded in the concrete, but couldn't support his weight with it. When he hit the floor, the whole place shook.

"Freight Train," his friends chanted. He grinned, shook his head, and went back to his booth for a swig of beer. No shame in falling off that route.

Then Wyn walked in. He checked out the chimney and then spotted me in back. He moved quickly through the crowd, nodding to a few people. The group of young men watched him walk over to my table.

When he got to my booth, he grinned and clapped me on the shoulder. "Great to see you, John."

I grasped his husk of a hand. It was like shaking hands with a wood rasp. "Let me buy you a beer."

I ordered another pint and returned to the booth. He pulled off his blue down parka and checked out the chimney climbing competition. Everything Wyn owned was held together with duct tape, from the sleeve of his parka to the toe of his blown-out running shoes. He'd ripped out the armpits of his purple T-shirt and torn the knees out of his faded blue jeans, which were held up by a piece of nylon webbing.

But the unkempt clothes and wild blond hair couldn't hide his overall fitness. He had the build of a greyhound—barrel chest, arms knotted with veins, and long, muscular legs. There didn't seem to be an ounce of fat on him. He may have dressed like a bum, but he was one of the best climbers in the world.

"You need a new wardrobe," I said, setting down a pint. "Who's sponsoring you? Goodwill?"

"That's good, John."

"We'll put you on the payroll—while we still have one."

"What's wrong?"

I raised my eyebrows. "Mountain Mart."

"Cheesy name."

"They're a discounter. They're eating our lunch."

He made a dismissive gesture with his hand. "But you've got the expertise."

"I *had* the expertise." I leaned back in the booth.

"Say," Wyn's eyes widened. "Why don't you bankroll my next expedition? In exchange, I'll represent you."

Now this was an idea. Wyn's endorsement could boost our sales. "You've certainly become . . . famous."

"What do you mean?"

"Take a look."

He turned around to look at the mug shot above the bar. "Oh, that," he said wearily. There were lines underneath his eyes, a tracery of veins across his nose and cheeks. It wasn't just sun exposure.

"What about you?" he said, his intense blue eyes boring into me. "How's life? How's Jill? Andy? What is he now, two?"

"Four." I pulled out a photo and suddenly felt the gulf between us. I'd become such a dad.

Wyn took the photo in his big, rough hands and glanced from me to it. "He looks like you."

"You think so? I think he looks like Jill. He *loves* to climb." I put it back in my wallet.

"Just like his old man," Wyn said, winking. "When are we going to take him out?"

"Not just yet."

"Don't want him to repeat the idiotic stuff we used to do?"

"No."

"John, you're a hypocrite."

"No, I'm a parent."

"Same thing."

"Exactly."

Wyn laughed. As someone totally committed to climbing, he had little time for long-term relationships, or marriage. He had no trouble meeting women, but these infatuations lasted no longer than the next expedition. Women fell in love with him, but Wyn never returned the favor. He had a coldness about him. He was always preparing for the next climb, and the next, and the next.

"What about Jill?" he asked. "I'm surprised she let you out of the house."

"I still get out," I said defensively.

"Does she know you're meeting with me?"

"Why should that matter?"

Wyn smiled slyly.

Who was I kidding? Of course it mattered. Jill was the reason for the rift between us. Shortly before we left for Denali, Jill became pregnant. I still went on the trip, but my attention was divided. When a storm moved in on summit day, I turned around, 1,000 feet from the top.

That was our last trip together. I told myself I'd made the right call, given the circumstances, but I wondered. We'd *almost* climbed Denali. I massaged the tip of my left pinky finger, turned hard and callused by frostbite. It was my consolation prize.

"So how was Europe?" I asked, eager to change the subject.

"Europe?" His grin vanished. "I did some amazing routes—the Bonatti Pillar of the Dru, the Central Pillar of Freney..."

"Yes, I got your postcards," I said. These were the classics of the alpine world—long, steep, committing routes on which some of the world's most famous climbers had inscribed their names. I used to pore over pictures of them, memorizing the lines, figuring out the belay stances, strategizing about equipment, alternately excited and frightened about the prospect of getting on them. We'd planned to go to Europe the summer after our attempt on Denali, but once Andy was born it was out of the question. A sea of jealousy welled up out of nowhere. "It must have been fantastic to do those climbs."

"It was," he said philosophically. "I wished we could have done them together."

"What happened on the Eiger?" I asked. I'd read an account of it in the climbing mags, but I wanted his take on it.

He turned to watch another climber fall off the chimney. "What's wrong with these guys?"

"Rusty hammered off another hold. It goes 5.11c now—supposedly. Nobody's done it yet."

Wyn picked at a scab on the back of his hand.

"So what about the Eiger?"

He stared into his beer glass as if he were looking for inspiration. "My partner fell."

"I heard. Weren't you roped up?"

He nodded. "I was belaying him up the ice hose near the top. A rock hit him. He lost his balance. The rope caught him but he kept falling—all the way back down the face."

"Why didn't the rope hold him?"

"He didn't fasten his harness." Wyn flicked a beer coaster back and forth with his fingers. "Hans didn't pay enough attention to details."

"Jesus. I'm sorry."

Wyn massaged his face. "He bounded down the side of that face like a rag doll."

I was silent. I didn't know what to say. "How did you get off the face?"

Wyn bit a hangnail off his finger. "I soloed the rest of the route."

The north face of the Eiger was one of the most dangerous climbs in the Alps, a treacherous mix of ice, snow, and rotten rock. "You must have been scared shitless."

"What was I going to do? I'd passed the Hinterstoisser Traverse. I was committed."

The name made me shiver. The traverse was named after Anderl Hinterstoisser, a brilliant German climber who'd led his team across it. The traverse proved the key to the upper part of the route, but it was a death trap as well. When a storm moved in, Hinterstoisser couldn't reverse course. He slipped and fell to his death. His three companions also perished. Thereafter, climbers referred to the Eiger North Face as The Wall of Death.

There were only a handful of climbers in the world who'd soloed the face. Wyn had joined very elite company. But he was almost apologetic about it. It seemed that his partner's death had cracked the hard shell of his personality.

"So that's why you left Europe?"

"That and because nobody wanted to climb with me. They said I was jinxed."

I'd always thought this was a bum rap against him. Now I wondered. "So why did you come back to Seattle?"

"Friends," he said. "Family."

"Family?"

We both laughed at that. Wyn was always feuding with his family, who didn't approve of his vagabond lifestyle.

A pair of climbers walked past our booth, trying not to stare at Wyn.

"Can you keep a secret?" He took something from his jacket. He spread out the map, making sure that no one else was watching. His index finger traveled through an area of tightly bunched topographic lines, indicating a near-vertical face. His finger stopped at the 20,320-foot summit of Denali.

"Take a look," he whispered. "It's a route worthy of Reinhold Messner." The celebrated Tyrolean mountaineer had been Wyn's hero since high school. Even Wyn had heroes.

He pushed the map toward me. It was folded and refolded, creased and recreased. He had pored over it, studying every detail.

I scrutinized it. It had been hard enough to attempt Denali via the West Buttress, the easiest route. This line was twice as long as the Eiger North Face and 7,000 feet higher. It looked *brutal*.

I pushed the map back to him. "There's nothing there."

"Look again, John." He pushed the map back to me. "If it were obvious, it would've been done by now."

He took a pencil, marked an X on the Southeast Fork of the Kahiltna Glacier, circled it, and wrote BASE CAMP in big, bold letters as if he were explaining things to a child. The pencil then traced a route up the immense glacier, found a hollow, and wrote CAMP I. It crossed the glacier and stopped at a point on the southern flank of McKinley: CAMP II, FACE CAMP. Then it began to rise.

"That's the tail end of an avalanche chute," I protested. "Tons of snow and ice will funnel through there. It'll be a bowling alley—with you and your partner as the pins."

The pencil stopped. Wyn smiled indulgently. I didn't want to upset him, but neither did I want him to do something crazy. I'd been through this before with him. I'd listened to many of his brilliant "visionary ideas." Some of these resulted in fantastic climbs—some of the best moments in my life—standing at the summit of Mount Rainier after a lightning-fast ascent of the steep Liberty Ridge route. But others had turned into scary epics, including a climb of the north face of Mount Index where I'd dislodged a block the size of a television set and severed our rope.

"John, take a *careful* look." He tapped the pencil on the map. "We'll follow the ridge right above the chute." He pointed to the so-called ridge. "Sure, there might be some rock and snow fall in the chute, but above it, very little. Now, I admit there are sections we'd have to hurry through."

"Who's 'we'?"

He ignored my question. The pencil resumed its climb. It rose up the side of the peak and paused on a ridge near 10,000 feet: CAMP III.

"We'll have to ferry a few loads up here," he said. "Then we should have some good ice climbing to Camp IV at 12,000."

In spite of myself, I got drawn into the route. The pencil wound its way through a labyrinth of crevasses, seracs, hanging glaciers, and avalanche chutes, neatly sidestepping most of the objective hazards without deviating more than necessary from the vertical. I could see CAMP V coming up: a shallow basin at 15,000 feet.

The pencil continued its unrelenting climb, as if all of this were preordained. It moved horizontally to avoid a particularly steep pillar, and then, emboldened, shot straight up through a gap to 18,000 feet, and the merest hint of a shelf: CAMP VI.

"Summit camp," he said. "From there, we'll take this couloir to the top."

The pencil eased its way up a long, broad ridge to the summit of North America.

"Bingo." He drew a little flag at the top.

I whistled with fear and admiration. In many ways, the climb seemed a product of Wyn's personality, shunning the obvious lines in favor of the steep and extreme ones. And yet there wasn't the gratuitous exposure or objective hazards I would have expected. The route certainly seemed difficult, but it didn't seem like a suicide mission.

"It looks fantastic." I pushed the map back to him. "It'll be all over the climbing magazines."

He scrutinized me, waiting for more.

"Go for it, Wyn."

"I'll need a partner." He leaned back in the booth and looked at me out of the corner of his eye. "Interested?"

I took a sip of beer. I'd let him down gently. I'd think of others he could ask. "No way."

"Why not?"

"Oh, nothing important. Just my job, wife, child."

"So what? Take a vacation."

He was right. I hadn't had a vacation in almost two years. Not a real vacation, just a day or two here and there. I didn't need to go into that. That would just make it easier for him to talk me into the climb.

"Why me, Wyn?"

He grinned. "You've been up there, John. You know what it's like. You know what to bring, what to do. And . . ."

"And?"

"I can trust you."

"What do you mean?"

Wyn shook his head as if to clear it. "You won't forget to buckle your fucking harness. You won't forget to put in a decent anchor. You won't make some bone-headed mistake that will get us both killed."

I nodded. I'd always prided myself on my ability to climb safely and competently, even in dangerous conditions. That's what made us such a good team. He provided the drive, energy, and ambition. I provided judgment, direction, organization, and a measure of caution. Together, we'd completed some incredibly difficult climbs, including a winter ascent of Mount Fairweather when I got us back down in the middle of a blizzard using only compass bearings. He might be able to dream up an improbable line like that one, but I liked to think that without me he'd have a hard time following it. Frankly, I was flattered. He had his pick of all the young, hard men and here he was asking an old, washed-up climber like me to join him. I could feel my resolve eroding.

"When does all this take place?"

"June."

"June?"

"It'll be easy to plan," he insisted. "I've already got most of it organized." He showed me some scribbling on the back of a bar napkin.

"Please," I said. "That's not planning."

"You don't need a spreadsheet."

I restrained myself from mentioning how often he'd forgotten his harness or climbing helmet or sleeping bag because he didn't have a checklist. I looked at my watch: 10 p.m. I had to get home. "Who else are you going to ask?"

"Just us two." He clapped me on the shoulder. "Like the old days."

"Wyn, I appreciate the invitation, but I can't do it." I started to get up. "I've got too many commitments. Ask one of these guys around here."

"No?" Wyn smiled. "Don't you want a shot at . . . redemption?"

"That was a cheap shot."

"C'mon," he said, grinning. "We need to go back. We need to knock it off."

I shook my head. "Things have changed."

"Need to talk it over with Jill?" he teased.

"Yes."

"Need to work things out?"

"What's your problem? What is it?"

"Okay," he said, holding up his palms. "You're married. You've got a family. You've got responsibilities. I didn't mean it."

But of course he did. He enjoyed twisting the knife.

"How's Andy doing?" he asked.

"He's a dynamo."

"Just like his dad."

"You're so transparent." I got up to leave. "You'll have to come by and see him."

"Jill doesn't like me."

"Yes, she does. She just thinks you're egotistical and irresponsible."

He rolled his eyes. "I need to grow up. I need to get married. I need to do something with my life."

The guy with the white-blond hair came over to our table. "Are you Wyn Mitchell?"

"I am."

"Lane Fredrickson." They shook hands. "The guys say you can climb this chimney."

"Do they?" Wyn grinned. "I don't know if I can. I heard Rusty worked it over with a chisel."

"It's thin," Lane said, fingering his goatee. "But if anyone can do it, you can do it. Care to give it a try?"

"I'm pretty out of shape." Wyn pinched his stomach. There was nothing but skin.

Lane set a pitcher of beer down on the table. "This pitcher says you can't do it."

Wyn appraised him. "You're betting I can't climb it?"

"Yes, sir." Lane nodded. "We've been trying for a month to climb it. We want to see you give it a shot."

Wyn's eyes were cool and amused. "Hard to beat free beer, but I don't have my shoes."

"I'll get you some."

"Screw it. I don't need them."

Wyn got up from the table. He walked over to the chimney and peeled off his socks and shoes. The other climbers gave him room. Stretching his legs and arms, he examined the wall, pantomiming each move as he imagined his way up. He began climbing in his bare feet.

The bar fell silent.

He quickly ascended the lower chimney, moving from hold to hold as if they were rungs of a ladder. He stopped below the crux and leaned out to study it. He explored the wall with his right hand. Nothing. He moved the left hand up, feeling the surface for a knob, pocket, or pebble. Nothing. He spotted a big jug hold farther up, but it looked blank in between. He could jump for it, as some others had tried to do, but that wasn't Wyn's way. He leaned out again and noticed something. He placed his hands on either side of a bulge in the rock and pushed them together. He inched his way upward.

A murmur went through the crowd. No one had attempted this move before. There was surprise and wonder in the eyes of the other climbers. Why hadn't they thought of it?

Wyn reached up and grasped the jug hold. He held on with one hand and shook out the other. He changed hands and repeated the process. Five feet left to go.

He pressure breathed, forcing air through compressed lips to bring oxygen to his lungs. Then he resumed climbing. Instead of proceeding directly up the last five feet, he traversed right to a small crack. It barely accepted the tips of his fingers. His T-shirt grew dark with sweat. The harder he worked, the more he sweated. Three feet from the top his fingers slipped out of the crack. He forced them back in. They slipped out. He shoved them in. He was struggling now, pumping out fast. He teetered on toeholds, twenty feet off the ground. If he fell now, he'd risk breaking a leg.

Wyn kept his cool. He willed himself back onto the wall. His fingers were bleeding, but he inserted them back into the crack. He winced as he got his toes in as well. That proved the difference. He rose up the crack. He worked slowly, painfully, deliberately, not risking any sudden movement that might throw him off balance. It must have been agony, but he kept climbing. Finally, he reached up and rang the big Swiss cowbell at the top.

The place went wild. People shouted and toasted each other. Rusty, the owner, tossed his bar towel in the air.

Wyn paid no attention. Trembling and soaked with sweat, he avoided the exit rope adjacent to the chimney and performed the even more difficult feat of down-climbing the route. He did it with uncanny concentration, ignoring the pain, the exhaustion, the cheering, and focusing only on the tiny holds in front of him. When he got down near ground level, he jumped lightly to the floor. Lane handed him the pitcher of beer.

"Bravo," Lane shouted, pounding him on the back.

Wyn wiped the sweat from his face with his T-shirt. The young men crowded around. They pumped his hand. They clapped his shoulder. They wanted a piece of him. How had he done the move? What was his next climb? Did he need a partner? All the commotion provided the perfect excuse to leave. No more talk about a new route on Denali. I didn't need that kind of trouble in my life.

TWO

The rain danced off the road, sluiced down the gutters, and blurred the windshield of my Jeep Cherokee. Another low pressure system squatted over the Seattle area, bringing in wave after wave of wet winter storms. This time of year, systems lined up off the north Pacific and marched through the Puget Sound area, knocking down trees, eroding hillsides, washing away houses. A dark Scandinavian gloom settled over the region. It was no surprise Seattle had one of the highest suicide rates in the nation.

Keeping a firm grip on the steering wheel, I followed the twists and turns of the road up the west side of Queen Anne Hill, dodging one fallen Douglas fir limb after another. I'd driven this route so often I felt like a rat in a cage. Sometimes I'd take a different side street just to add variety to my life.

As I drove, I turned over Wyn's invitation. The idea of climbing Denali certainly intrigued me. I had no illusions about Everest or K2 or

Kanchenjunga. That wasn't in the cards. But Denali was possible. We could fly to Anchorage and take a ski plane to base camp. With good weather, it would take us three weeks to get to the top.

If I wanted another shot at it, I had to try it soon. I was thirty-five and counting. My responsibilities at home and work were increasing. But did I want to go with Wyn? And did I want to attempt such a difficult route? As usual, Wyn had rattled the comfortable little cage I'd constructed for myself.

All the lights were out on our block. Tree branches littered the sidewalk. I parked in front of our place, a two-story, cedar shake bungalow perched precariously on the edge of a ravine.

A gust of rain drenched me as I dashed to the front door. I peeled off my jacket, hung it up in the hallway, and kicked off my wet shoes. After fumbling around in the utility closet for a flashlight, I walked into the living room.

"Is that you, honey?" Jill called from the couch.

"Be there in a minute." I poured myself a glass of wine and brought it out to the living room, now freshly painted in Damson Plum. Two candles on the coffee table illuminated the high ceiling and a big bay window that overlooked Puget Sound. The flickering light revealed the tasteful simplicity of the room—tatami mats on the floor, scroll paintings on the side walls, and simple wood furniture in the dining room. The house was an expression of Jill's personality: clean, elegant, and uncluttered. My "junk" was relegated to the basement. Andy's toys were concealed behind a bamboo screen in the corner.

As I sat down on the couch, she moved next to me and kissed me on the cheek. Was this a truce? She wore a purple cashmere sweater, jeans, and my wool hiking socks. "Why are you so late?"

"Just finishing up at the store," I said.

"This late?"

"And I stopped for a beer."

Putting my arm around her, I tried to pull her closer. She inched toward me but stayed tense. Jill had an edge about her, a hint of what

I called her father's Wing Commander personality. She liked to be in charge, and since I liked to be in charge, we quarreled. Even after four years, we were still working out the boundaries of our marriage.

When we met six years ago in a climbing course, I had no idea that I'd marry her. I preferred girlfriends who were pals, tomboys who liked to go climbing as much as I did and didn't draw my energies away from the crags. Jill wore pearls, drank bourbon, and spoke scathingly about current events and politicians she'd come to know through her father's navy career. As a climbing bum, obsessed only with the next hard route, I felt outclassed.

She had been born in Galveston, Texas, but had lived all over the world—Okinawa, Japan, the Philippines—before her dad was assigned to Naval Air Station Whidbey Island in Oak Harbor, Washington. Her dad was an A6 Intruder pilot who specialized in night missions off aircraft carriers, one of the most dangerous kinds of military aviation. He flew twenty missions in the Persian Gulf and was disappointed when the war ended because he had wanted to fly more. Afterwards, the navy transferred him to Oak Harbor with the idea of easing him out of combat flying and into administration. He had resisted this in every way short of insubordination. On his last training mission, his jet surged off an aircraft carrier and promptly lost power. He punched out, but he was not high enough for his chute to open. He fell like a stone into Puget Sound.

"Who did you meet for a beer?" Jill asked.

"Wyn."

"Wyn?" She sat up. "I thought he was in France."

"No, he's back in the States."

"What's he doing here?"

"He's staying in Seattle for a while." I took a sip of wine. "I hope this storm lets up."

"He's not planning another climb, is he?"

"Wyn's always planning another climb."

Jill turned to face me. "What is it?"

"Denali."

Jill nodded as if she expected this. "And he wants you to go with him, right?"

"He asked me, yes." It was a relief to have it out in the open.

She hugged her knees. "What did you tell him?"

"I told him no."

She turned to look at me. "But you're thinking of going, aren't you?"

"Well, I haven't ruled it out."

"John, he'll chew you up and spit you out." She moved to the other side of the couch. "You'll be fodder for his next slide show."

"Wyn is my friend." I put the wine glass down on the table. "Besides, I may not have another chance. If we have another baby…" This had been the subject of many discussions lately. Jill was pushing for a second child.

"How long would you be gone?" She slumped back against the couch.

"Three weeks." I delivered the line as nonchalantly as possible.

"Three weeks!" Her shoulders rose and fell, absorbing the shock.

I knew it was a stretch, but I hadn't had a real vacation in four years. Then again, neither had she. In some ways the last four years had flown by, but in other ways they had seemed like an eternity.

"What about me and Andy?"

"My mom will help out."

She sighed loudly and deeply. "God, I can't believe we're having this conversation again."

"Listen." I put my arm around her. "Things at the store have really been getting to me. Mountain Mart is killing us. There's a lot of stress. I *need* a break."

"But why can't we just take a family vacation?" She raked her hands through her hair. "What do you need to prove?"

"I'm a climber, Jill." My voice was rising. "It's *who I am*."

"You're an *idiot*," she said, getting up from the couch. "I can't believe we're going through this again. Why can't you take up golf, for Christ's sake? What about Ping-Pong? Checkers? Chess? Badminton? Parcheesi?"

"Jill?" There was no stopping her now.

She picked up a pillow and threw it at me. I caught it in midair, but it knocked over my glass, spilling wine on my pants.

"You're just like my goddamned dad. You *never* learn." She held her head in her hands. "You're going to get yourself killed!"

"No, I'm not."

"How do you know that?" She faced me. "Do you want Andy to grow up without a father?"

"Of course not."

"Well, it could happen." She was pacing now. "It happens all the time. Afterwards they interview friends who say, 'I'm glad he died doing what he loved to do.' Bullshit! They never talk to the wife. It's the wife who pays the price."

"Jill, it's just a climb."

"You're not listening, John." She hugged herself. "You're not a free agent anymore. You can't just *leave.*"

I tried to put my arm around her, but she twisted away.

"You're putting it all at risk—our marriage, our family, everything. You understand that, don't you?"

"Of course I do," I said, but I really had no idea.

"I'm going to bed." She shook her head. "I can't deal with this."

Grabbing one of the candles, she spilled wax on the table, swore, and stomped up the stairs to our bedroom.

I sank deeper into the couch. Rain rattled against the bay window. A fog horn sounded in the distance. The lights from the container ships glistened in the harbor. The railroad cars coupled and uncoupled; their metal brakes screeched, hissed, and squealed. The sound of dripping came from the kitchen. I could tell from the pitch of the sound that the bucket was almost full. I'd put it in the middle of the floor to catch a leak in the roof. Picking myself up off the couch, I took the bucket into the kitchen, emptied it into the sink, and put it back on the floor. I thought of how much my dad enjoyed fixing things like this. He was a mechanical genius and had worked his entire career as a Boeing machinist. A month after retiring with full benefits, he dropped dead of a heart attack. No puttering around the house. No playing with the grandchildren. No afternoon trips to Home Depot.

I went in to check on Andy. He was lying on his back, spread-eagled on the bed. His head was turned to the side and his mouth was agape, a line of drool pooling on the pillow. He was breathing softly and evenly, with a beatific expression on his face. I stared at him for a long time, thinking of all the trouble and joy he'd brought me. Then I covered him with a blanket, kissed him on the forehead, and went upstairs to bed.

The dripping woke me at 6 a.m. I sat up in bed and looked out the window at the gray early morning light. Rain pelted against the pane. Jill was asleep on the other side of the bed, snoring softly, her back turned toward me. I burrowed back under the down comforter, put my hand around her waist, and tried to fall back asleep. Drip. Drip. Drip. Throwing off the covers, I put on my jeans and sweatshirt and went downstairs. The bucket was overflowing. I emptied it into the sink and mopped the floor. I donned my raincoat and rubber boots and stepped outside.

Climbing the aluminum ladder with a can of roofing adhesive, I felt something in me quicken. At the top the ladder teetered. The ground swam below me. Adrenaline pricked the back of my neck. Touching the side of the house, I steadied the ladder. The old sense of mastery flooded over me, a feeling as dangerous and addictive as a narcotic. The sensation of ascent.

Fir limbs littered the flat tar roof. I cleared them off and found a pool of water where the roof sagged. Removing moss, leaves, and fir needles from one of the downspouts, I drained as much of the water as I could. The roof needed to be repaired, but for now, I applied a thick coat of roofing adhesive. It was dirty, sloppy work. Afterwards, I blew on my hands, stomped my feet, and watched a ferry cut a wide, white wake across the gunmetal surface of Puget Sound.

By the time I got back inside, the smells of breakfast filled the kitchen. Jill stood at the stove in her purple kimono, the weight of her breasts pressing against the silk. She turned the bacon, stirred the pancake batter, and dipped her finger into a jar of plum sauce to taste it. This was her Saturday morning ritual. Over the years, her family had moved so much that they relied on customs like this to keep a sense of continuity. Like most rituals, it had to be performed in a certain way—only *homemade* plum sauce would do, even though it required several days of round-the-clock effort—but the enactment of it reminded her of the time her family had lived in Japan.

"How's the roof?" she asked, flipping a pancake.

"Better." I looked up at the ceiling. The dripping had stopped—for now. "Where's Andy?"

"He's still asleep." She poured more batter into the pan. "Should we have someone take a look at it?"

"I already did." I washed my hands in the sink. "I got a bid for $10,000."

Jill winced. She kept track of the finances, which was helpful, but it gave her more control than I liked. "We should get a second one."

"Definitely." I poured myself a cup of coffee. "We can't afford ten grand."

"No, but we need to get it fixed." She pointed the spatula up at the stain in the ceiling. "Do you want me to call someone?"

"No, I'll do it."

"We *have* to fix it before we remodel the kitchen."

I rolled my eyes. Remodel, a four-letter word. "Jill, we just finished remodeling the living and dining rooms."

"The floor is hideous, John. People will think that we're blind."

"I don't care what other people think."

"Obviously." She went back to the pancakes.

Taking my coffee out to the dining room, I scanned the newspaper. The economy was tanking. Consumer spending had slumped. I fingered the newspaper, trying not to look at the business page.

Jill came out of the kitchen and handed me a plate of pancakes. "Why do you look so worried?"

"Things are slow at the store," I said, putting the paper down.

"And you still want to climb Denali?"

"Hal can handle things while I'm gone," I said. "Besides, I'll get product knowledge."

"Product knowledge?" Jill nearly choked on her pancake. "You could get that climbing Mount Rainier."

"It's not the same." I shook my head. "I've been losing customers because they don't trust my advice. I don't do hard climbing anymore." I stood up and started to clear my plate. When Wyn had suggested the route, I had refused. But now there was no going back. The pathogen had entered my bloodstream.

She put her hand over her mouth as if swallowing something hard and bitter. "Sit down." Her lower lip trembled as she blew her nose with a Kleenex. "We're not done here."

I sighed and sat back down, hating myself for putting her through this again, but unwilling to back down.

She spoke slowly, deliberately, barely keeping her emotions in control. "If you go, you have to promise me three things."

"What are they?" I crossed my arms, surprised that she'd thought through the terms of her concession.

"First, you have to take along at least two other guys. I don't want you going with Wyn alone. Four is the minimum for that kind of climb. You've said so yourself."

This would complicate things, but I'd considered it myself. "I'll have to talk to Wyn about it. It may be hard to find the other guys."

"Do it," she said, pulling her kimono tighter.

"Okay."

"Second, one of the guys has to be a doctor or a medical professional."

"It's not that easy—"

"I don't care." Her voice was flat, declarative. "Find someone."

"I'll see what I can do."

"Third, finish the climb so we can get on with our lives," she said, massaging her temple. "I know you have to do this. It's part of who you are."

I took her hand, marveling at her understanding.

"Just get it done," she said, withdrawing her hand. "I don't want to go through this again."

I nodded and looked away, a wave of self-loathing overwhelming me. What was I doing? Risking my marriage for a climb? I felt unworthy of the sacrifice she was making, but I just couldn't help myself.

She leaned forward and stared at her wedding ring, as if expecting to find an answer revealed in the clear middle of the cut diamond.

The door was open. I just had to step through it. I went over and hugged her. She tensed. I touched her breast. She pushed my hand away. "Not now."

THREE

It was an early Saturday afternoon when I drove down to the 5.10. Mount Rainier towered behind the steel and glass office buildings of downtown Seattle like an immense, inscrutable deity. On clear days like this, the 14,410-foot peak, a dormant volcano, dominated the local horizon, dwarfing cities, freeways, and the web of human culture that had grown up around its base. "The Mountain," as Seattleites called it, appeared rarely in the spring. Its appearance was a good omen.

The back door of the 5.10 was propped open with a mop and bucket. The smell of stale beer filled my nostrils. My feet stuck to the floor as I walked past the chairs stacked upside down on the cable spools. A waitress was cleaning up from last night.

"Can I get you something?" she asked, her ponytail bouncing behind her.

"A glass of water, thanks. Is Wyn here?"

"Yes, he's in his 'office.'" She winked as if we had an understanding about Wyn's crazy behavior.

I spotted Wyn in a booth in back, surrounded by his papers and a laptop. Wyn read over his notes and collated his photos for the next slide show, his principal way of making a living.

He scribbled on a yellow legal pad, his lips compressed in concentration. He had the manner of an executive at a Fortune 500 company, even though his "desk" consisted of a booth in the back of a bar.

He looked up and gestured to the bench. "Have a seat."

I sat down and leaned back in the booth.

"So is it a go?" he asked, finishing up his writing. "Will she-who-must-be-obeyed let you out of the house?"

"It's a go."

"Yes!" Wyn pumped his fist. "Did you have to beg?"

"Shut up."

"Okay, but seriously, any concessions?"

"She wants us to take two other climbers."

"What?" He slammed his palm on the table.

"She thinks it'll be safer."

Wyn scowled. "That'll screw everything up. We'll have to totally change our approach to the route."

The waitress brought a glass of water for me and a pint of beer for Wyn.

"This is why I could never be married." He shook his head. "Do you want me to talk to her?"

"I don't think it would help."

"You're probably right." He tapped his pen against the table.

"She wants one of these guys to be a doctor or a medical professional."

He sipped on his beer. "So there's no way Jill is going to back down?"

"Well, it's not like what she's saying is without merit," I said. "Having a party of four in the Alaska Range is not a bad idea. And I wouldn't mind having a medical professional with us."

"But speed is safety." Wyn rapped the table with his knuckle. "I want to do it alpine style in one push. If we have four climbers, we'll likely have to do it in stages."

"That would be fine with me."

"We'll be on the route a lot longer." Wyn leaned over the table toward me. "More objective danger. More gear to haul. More things to go wrong."

"But we'll have more margin for error in case anything happens— crevasse fall, avalanche, rock fall, altitude sickness."

Wyn didn't seem impressed by the dangers I'd just catalogued. "Any idea about who to ask?"

"I've got some names." In truth, I'd been calling around. It was difficult to assemble a team on such short notice, even with the incentive of a new route and Wyn's star power. It came down to two possibilities: Al McKenzie, a veteran ice climber, and Lane Frederickson, a talented but inexperienced climber who was a firefighter with extensive medical training. They were already partners, which was a plus.

"I took the liberty of inviting them down here today," I said. "They should be here soon."

"Did you tell them about the route?"

"Only that it was a first ascent on the south side of Denali."

"Good." He touched the blue stone on his necklace, an amulet blessed by the head lama of some monastery high in the Himalayas. "Have you climbed with them?"

"I've climbed with Al."

"Is he strong?"

"He's determined. We did the first ascent of The Dagger together."

"I heard about that." Wyn said, fingering his resume. "How did it go?"

I told him the story. We started at 6 a.m., in the darkness. Al led the first pitch up the five-hundred-foot pillar of ice located near Banff, in Canada. Al was precise about his placements, picky about his tools. He figured out every angle before he went for something. But once he went for it, he didn't back down. He was dogged. He got good pick placements despite the ice, which shattered easily. It was exhausting, nervy climbing, with little protection and few places to rest. We summited at 6 p.m. in the dark. Al didn't seem fazed at all. I was gripped.

Wyn scratched the wispy, albino whiskers on his chin. "So you'd recommend him?"

"Yeah, I would. Once he gets his teeth into something, he won't let go."

"Any hesitation?" His eyes narrowed. "Tell me now."

"He's deliberate."

"Are you saying he's slow?"

"Not exactly slow, but not as fast as you or me on an alpine route."

"That's critical." Wyn made a notation on his legal pad. "What about his friend? What's his name—Lane?"

"I don't know him well, but he's supposed to be strong, and he's got medical training."

Wyn drummed his fingers on the table. "Anybody else?"

"Nope." I took a sip of water. "Do you have any ideas?"

He tapped his pen against the table. "I'll make some calls."

Al and Lane walked in.

Wyn rose to shake their hands. "Gentlemen, have a seat."

They slid into the booth. They were an unlikely pair. Al was tall and lean, a marathon runner. He had dark hair, black-framed glasses, and an Adam's apple that bobbed when he spoke. He wore a blue oxford shirt, khaki pants, and scuffed, black wing tips.

Lane stroked his blond goatee. He had white eyelashes, white eyebrows, and a white-blond crew cut. He looked like some kind of Norse god. The scanner on his belt squawked with static. "Sorry." He turned it down. "I'm on call."

"Thanks for meeting with us," Wyn said. "Did John tell you about the route?"

"He said it was a new route on the south face." Al cleared his throat. "But the south face's pretty much been climbed out. What did you have in mind?"

"You've done your homework," Wyn said.

Al pushed his glasses up with his index finger. "I want to know what I'm getting into."

"Let's hear about your climbing experience first," Wyn said.

"I did The Dagger with John," Al said, nodding at me, and then rattled off his other climbs—the Weeping Wall in Banff, Bridalveil Falls in Telluride, Black Ice Couloir on the Grand Teton—some of the most difficult test pieces in North America.

"How about rock?"

"I can lead 5.11."

Wyn's eyes crinkled with amusement. "At sea level and 60 degrees, right."

Al shrugged. "It would be harder up high, of course."

"Any high-altitude experience?"

"Aconcagua—last year."

"Which route?"

"The Polish Glacier."

"How'd you do?"

"I got up it," Al said, grinning. "But I was beat."

Wyn frowned. This was not a particularly difficult route, but at 22,500 feet, Aconcagua qualified as a high-altitude climb. "Why do you want to do a route on Denali?"

"I've always wanted to do a first ascent on a big peak." Al blinked his heavy-lidded eyes. "It's the next step. I've always wanted to do the big D."

Wyn nodded. "Lane, what was your hardest route?"

"Liberty Ridge on Rainier."

"Why?"

"It didn't exactly go according to plan." Lane glanced from Wyn to me as if gauging our approval. "It was supposed to be a snow climb, but we ran into ice."

"That's an understatement," Al said. "It was a skating rink. Some pitches were totally run out. We weren't able to put in much gear. But Lane's an animal. He didn't freak out at the thirty feet of vertical water ice on this one step. I had to front-point on hinged crampons in floppy leather boots."

"That was nothing," Lane said. "I had to follow with two ice axes—no tools."

"Once we got off the ridge, the clouds rolled in." Al rubbed his hands together, relishing the tale. "We set up camp on Liberty Cap. It blew like a son of a bitch. I got hypothermic setting up the tent. Fortunately, Lane got some hot drinks down me."

"Standard operating procedure," Lane said.

"It says here you've done some mountain rescue work," Wyn said, pointing to the resume.

"Yes, sir." He stroked his goatee. "Two years running."

I nodded approvingly. Perhaps Lane could help rein in Wyn's blitz-krieg style of climbing. I wouldn't be the only one applying the brakes.

Al pushed up his glasses with his finger. Lane rolled his shoulders. They glanced back and forth between us, awaiting a verdict.

"You learn a lot from climbs like that," Wyn said. "Want anything from the bar?"

They shook their heads. As I got up to let him out, Wyn took me by the arm. We walked over to the other side of the 5.10. "What do you think?" he asked.

My feelings about them wavered. Al was pushing forty and was so fastidious I wasn't sure I wanted to spend a whole month with him. Lane seemed likeable, but it was hard to tell how he would do higher up on the mountain. Still, he seemed capable, and he did have the medical training. Despite my questions about group dynamics and their high-altitude experience, their consent would make the climb possible.

"Let's invite them," I said. "We can do the climb in stages, not one push. That way we'll all have a chance to get acclimated."

Wyn fingered the amulet on his necklace. "I'd like to have a more experienced crew."

"I don't think we're going to find one," I said, leaning over the bar. "If we want to do the climb, I think we have to ask them."

Wyn shook his head. "I'm not ready to do that."

I put my hand on his shoulder. "I've put a ton of time and effort into getting my wife and business partner to sign off on this thing. I want to make it work."

Wyn frowned. "It's not my fault that your wife insists we bring two other climbers. That's your problem—not mine."

"It's your problem if you want me to go," I shot back.

"Okay," Wyn said. "I just want to see who else might be interested."

"You've got a week," I said. "After that, we either invite these guys or we call it off."

"Whatever you say, John," Wyn said, returning to the booth.

"We still have a few more candidates to interview," Wyn said, looking back and forth between them. "Are you guys interested?"

"Count me in," Al said, pushing up his glasses. "But I'd like to know what route you're planning to do."

"Can't tell you right now," Wyn said. "But I'll put you down as a yes. How about you, Lane?"

"Yes, sir," he said. "But I need to know ASAP if it's a go."

"I'll let you know within a week," Wyn said. "Thanks for meeting with us."

Everyone stood up. Wyn and I shook hands with them.

"Don't worry," Wyn said after they left. "I've got a big, black book."

"Get back to me quickly." I wagged my finger at him. "Don't leave me hanging."

"I'll be in touch," he said, getting into his van.

FOUR

It was 10 p.m. and still light when our jet touched down at Anchorage International Airport. The setting sun gilded the city's drab downtown office buildings, catching their windows on fire and painting the surrounding Chugach Mountains in a dull, red glow. In the twilight, we loaded our gear into a big, yellow taxi and drove north.

After passing through a rash of Wendy's, McDonald's, and Burger Kings, we entered suburbs of prefab houses, trinket shops, and gas stations. These gave way to thickets of Douglas fir, black spruce, alder, and willow bogs. The trees crowded in on all sides, as if ready to swallow the highway.

The driver attacked the road, slaloming around the corners, accelerating on the straightaways, attempting to pass every car and truck on the way to Talkeetna, the jump-off point for climbers flying in to Denali. Wyn had told him to get into town ASAP so we could get the earliest flight into the base camp. He had taken him at his word.

"Whoa!" the driver shouted as we narrowly avoided a head-on collision with a car.

"Slow down," I told him.

He shrugged and eased up slightly on the accelerator.

Wyn shot a glance back at me but maintained a death grip on the front dashboard.

As the taxi careened around a corner, I lurched into Al, who lurched into Lane. The cab reeked of Al's b.o. and Lane's aftershave, reminding me I was going to be with these guys for a month. Rolling down the window, I felt the evening air rush through my hair. It smelled of pollen, fireweed, and the manic growth of the high arctic summer. I drew a deep breath. Despite my guilt over leaving Jill and Andy, it was a relief to have the trip underway.

"You're doing the big D, aren't you?" the driver said, grinning. He was a gnome of a man with a bald head, a bushy beard, and a gleaming gold tooth.

"Yes," Wyn replied.

"Watch your step," he warned. "I drove a guy out this morning."

"What happened?" Wyn asked.

"Broken arm. Multiple contusions. Frostbite," he said. "He took a tumble on the West Buttress."

"Why didn't they medivac him out?" Lane asked.

"This is Alaska," he cackled. "Sometimes I'm the ambulance service."

As if to prove this, he floored it, trying to rocket past another RV. He braked at the last second when a car appeared in the oncoming lane.

"Be careful up there," the driver said sagely. "It's dangerous."

"So's the road," Wyn said dryly.

The driver just chuckled. As we approached a rise, he swerved to the side. The engine sputtered, coughed, backfired, and shuddered to a halt.

"Why are we stopping?" Wyn asked. The plan was to get up to Talkeetna by dark. It had already been a long day.

"Thar she blows!" the driver said, opening the door. He chuckled and walked over to a patch of fireweed to take a pee. We piled out of the cab. In the distance loomed the Alaska Range—Foraker, Hunter, Huntington—three of the biggest, steepest, iciest peaks in all of North America. Above them rose a higher, farther peak. It was not pointed like the Matterhorn or Everest, but broad and wide and spiked like the back of an ice dragon. A high scum of clouds ringed the summit, signaling an incoming front.

"There it is, gentlemen," Wyn said, taking out his topographical map. "You can see the bottom half of our route." He got a gleam in his eye as he pointed it out. Whenever I saw that look, I instinctively wanted to apply the brakes. At 20,320 feet, Denali was mesmerizing from this distance, but I had no trouble remembering how miserable it could be. The peaks in the Alaska Range rise so abruptly from the tundra they create their own microclimate, attracting hellacious storms from the Gulf of Alaska. Conditions can quickly turn ugly, from a sunny day to a raging gale in hours. Still, I couldn't help feel a tingle of excitement at the sight of it.

"You guys are lucky," the driver said, zipping up his pants. "She doesn't usually show herself."

We piled back into the taxi. Now we knew what we were up against. It was no longer an abstraction, a tangle of topographic lines on a map, but a high, cold, and dangerous objective. We rode in silence the rest of the way.

WELCOME TO BEAUTIFUL DOWNTOWN TALKEETNA, read the hand-painted wooden sign at the entrance to town. The taxi bumped and lurched down the one-lane, potholed road, the only paved street in the cluster of log-cabin-style buildings. Talkeetna looked like it had been recently hacked out of the wilderness, with many of the houses built from the fallen trees. Blackberry vines and alder crowded in around the edges of town as if they were trying to reclaim the land that was rightfully theirs. We were nearing the end of the road, one of the last outposts of civilization before the vastness of the Far North begins.

We passed log houses with corrugated metal roofs, backyards full of old washing machines, refrigerators, microwave ovens, stereos, mattresses, broken-down cars, and disassembled airplanes, their rusting parts strewn around them.

The driver honked at a dog asleep in the middle of the road.

"Move it, mutt!" he shouted.

The dog slowly got up and walked over to the edge of the road. The driver stopped in front of a log cabin with antlers over the door. He helped unload our gear on the grass. "Take care," he said, cackling again. Then he floored it and disappeared in a cloud of dust.

A grizzled husky dozed on the cabin's doorstep. The town seemed to be a kind of retirement home for sled dogs. Wyn stepped over the husky and knocked on the heavy wooden door.

"Come in," a voice boomed. Wyn opened the door. The bush pilot, Miles Nelson, beckoned us into his office. He wore black jeans, a black T-shirt, and a blue handkerchief over his head that gave him the air of a pirate. He had a phone in one hand and a cigar in the other.

According to Wyn, Miles had flown a helicopter in Vietnam and was shot down three times. After the war, he moved here and started flying climbers and sightseers into Denali. He was known for daring and impressive stunts. Last year, he had landed a small plane at 14,000 feet on the side of Denali and brought down an injured Korean climber. He had a reputation for being crazy but competent, the best bush pilot in the business, and the resident expert on Alaska mountaineering.

"Don't give me that crap!" he yelled over the phone. "Just get the goddamned parts!" He slammed the phone down. "My peak season and they can't get parts for my planes."

"Remember me?" Wyn extended his hand. "Wyn Mitchell."

"Of course I do." Miles stood up and shook his hand. "I flew you in to the base of Moose's Tooth three years ago. You're a regular star now."

Wyn couldn't help smiling. He introduced the rest of us. Miles picked up a box of oily airplane engine valves and motioned for us to sit down on the couch. The shelves around the wood-paneled room were stacked with charts and aviation manuals. Combat ribbons hung from a frame above his desk, his sole effort at interior decoration.

"How does the weather look?" Wyn asked.

"Iffy." Miles waggled his hand back and forth, roiling the layers of smoke that filled the room.

"What's the earliest we can fly in?" Wyn asked.

Miles expelled a cloud of smoke. "I'll get you guys up there ASAP, but a couple parties are ahead of you. The forecast calls for more snow up high. If it clears, and that's a big if, I could have you in by—say—tomorrow afternoon." Another cloud of smoke. "Soon enough?"

"The quicker, the better."

"That's what everyone says. I'll do my best, but I can't promise anything. Be ready to go by that time. I don't want to have to drag you out of the bar."

"We'll be ready," Wyn said. "Where should we stay?"

"Camp in the front yard if you want," he said. "That'll save you money and make it easier for me to round you up. You can put your gear in the shed out back. I've got a safe for your valuables. Oh, make sure that you have some netting. The mosquitoes are big up here. The Alaska state bird."

We all laughed. He was the kind of guy you wanted to please.

We pitched our tents on his lawn, Wyn and I in one tent, Lane and Al in the other. It was past midnight by the time we finished and still light outside. I wanted to go to sleep, but Wyn insisted on going down to the Fairview Inn for a drink.

Opening the screen door, we walked into a knotty-pine paneled room with wooden benches, a dartboard, and a counter bristling with beer taps. The menu on the wall was in English, Japanese, French, German, Korean. The place was internationally famous—with climbers at least. Wyn went to the bar and came back with a pitcher of beer and four shot glasses of whiskey. He handed them around.

"To the summit," he toasted.

"Yes." Al touched his glass with Wyn's.

"We're going to knock the bastard off." Lane joined in.

"Hear, hear," I added, clinking glasses. "Let's hope the weather cooperates."

"I can always count on you, John," Wyn goaded. "The voice of reason."

"Screw you, Wyn—someone has to be."

"Just kidding." He knocked me on the shoulder. "Don't take it personally."

"I won't, but if the weather goes to shit, I'm going to make the same call I made last time."

"Yeah." Wyn's eyes narrowed. "I bet you will."

Al and Lane looked back and forth between us, as if unsure of how to take this.

I downed my shot of whiskey. It stung to have him make fun of me in front of the others. Maybe the fame had gone to his head.

"So what's the plan?" Lane asked. "What do we do tomorrow?"

"Inventory," I said, taking back control of the conversation. "We need to make sure we've got everything. If we're missing anything, we can buy it here."

Lane glanced over at Wyn to see if he had anything to add.

"John's right," Wyn said. "We'll do a quick shakedown. Can't afford to forget anything. When I was on Trango Tower last year, we got hit by a storm halfway up. The ropes iced up. We couldn't go up. We couldn't go down. I thought we were screwed. Luckily I brought enough chow to wait out the storm. It took us two days to rap back down."

"That long?" Al asked.

"It's a huge peak," Wyn said. "Have you seen it?"

"In photographs."

"It's awesome—20,000 feet tall and straight as an Egyptian obelisk."

Al and Lane leaned closer to listen. Al quizzed him on the technical details while Lane slapped him on the back. They hung on his words. They ordered a second round. I left him to his latest disciples.

As I walked along the main street in the semidarkness, I looked up at the eerie light in the northern sky. The trees and vegetation were familiar, but the perpetual twilight gave the place a creepy, other-worldly feeling.

It was a relief to crawl into the tent and close the flap behind me. As I undressed, I wondered if I really was getting too old for all this. Had I become a fuddy-duddy more interested in safety than climbing? As I crawled into my bag, my feet brushed up against something small and hard. I fumbled around for my headlamp and shone the light on the object. It was one of Andy's green plastic frogs. It was a reminder, a talisman, a good luck charm. Jill must have put it there. I put it back in the bag, pulled the hood over my head, and soon fell asleep.

The sun was up and the grass was bright with dew when I poked my head out of the tent at 8 a.m. Wyn was passed out in the sleeping bag next to me, so I walked down to the Roadhouse, a Talkeetna institution with hewn log walls, a sitting room full of couches and oilcloth-covered picnic tables, and a wood stove and a pile of kindling in the corner. The clientele wore plaid shirts, blue jeans, and Stihl chainsaw hats. Faded posters of Denali covered the walls.

I ordered the "Mountain Man" breakfast—a prodigious heap of eggs, bacon, hash browns, toast, and the restaurant's signature cinnamon rolls—all this washed down with as much coffee as I could drink.

While I waited for the waitress to bring my breakfast, I glanced at the *Anchorage Daily News*. There was a front-page story about the number of climbers killed on the peak this year. The death toll had risen to six: four Japanese and two Germans. I put the newspaper away.

Wyn showed up at 8:30 a.m., eyes bleary, hair tousled, face covered with blond stubble. He blinked his eyes, yawned, and rubbed his face.

"Rough night?" It was hard to keep the patronizing tone out of my voice.

"Good for morale." He rubbed his eyes, coughed, and cleared his throat. "Group dynamics. Team building. Why did you leave so early?"

"It was 2 a.m."

"Are you ready for the nursing home yet?"

"Not quite yet," I said, laughing. This was one of our standard jokes. If either of us complained about aches or pains, the other always suggested a trip to the nursing home. It was a way of enforcing the "No Whining" code common to climbers.

"Good." Wyn picked up the menu and stared it as if it were written in Sanskrit. He hailed the waitress and ordered two large orange juices. He chugged them in succession and then ordered the rest of his meal.

"So you had a chance to talk to Lane and Al," I said.

"Yeah," he said. "They're decent guys."

"But I wonder how they do up high."

"That's the test," Wyn said. After last night's conversation, I sensed that Wyn was hedging his bets, grooming Al or Lane as my replacement in case I bagged out this time, too.

Wyn's breakfast arrived, and he started chowing down. We wouldn't be seeing this kind of spread anytime soon. Lane and Al stumbled in around 9 a.m., looking haggard and hungry.

"Any news from Miles?" Al asked.

"Not yet," Wyn said. "But the weather looks good. Probably today or tomorrow."

"Good," he said. "I can't wait to get up there."

"But there's no beer up there," Wyn said.

"I've given up drinking beer," Al said.

"Since when?" Wyn asked.

"Since last night."

"We'll see how long that resolution lasts."

After breakfast, we went back to the tents to sort our gear. Lining up the packs and the boxes of extra gear, I conducted the inventory, checking off items on a spreadsheet I'd run from the store's computer. Logistics were crucial on this kind of climb, especially now that we planned to do it expedition style, establishing camps and moving up slowly. Expedition style played to my strengths—patience, organization, and steady, methodical progress—though Wyn's greyhound metabolism likely would bridle against it.

Given our party's composition, there were many reasons for climbing it this way. It would allow me to get back into shape and sharpen my climbing skills before we made a dash for the top. It would offset Lane's and Al's lack of experience at altitude and give us a greater margin of safety for storms and route-finding errors. Finally, it would provide us time to come together as a team. I only hoped that Wyn wouldn't have second thoughts about it.

"Three expedition tents?" I called out to Wyn, who searched for the gear.

"Check."

These were light, durable two-man tents with reinforced seams and poles that could withstand winds in excess of 100 miles per hour, not unheard of on Denali. The tents were expensive but were the key to surviving the route. I got them below wholesale from the manufacturer, one of the many favors I'd called in to make this climb possible.

"Two gas stoves with spare parts?"

"Check."

The stoves had to perform flawlessly. We would cook all of our food on them and melt all of our water from snow.

As we went through the list, I kept track of the weight, a critical factor on the climb. There were no Sherpas in Alaska. We had to carry everything on our backs or in the plastic sleds we'd drag behind us on our way up the lower glacier. Anything superfluous would have to go.

"Two climbing ropes?"

"Check."

"Fixed line."

"Check," he said, holding them up with disdain. If he'd had his way, we would have done the route in one quick push without fixed ropes.

I moved down the list: ice screws, pitons, and camming devices to keep us secured to the face; steel crampons with aggressive front-points for hard ice and snow, aluminum snowshoes for the lower glacier, ice axes and ice hammers with banana picks to penetrate steep ice. We couldn't afford to forget anything. Even a small omission could spell disaster.

Once we accounted for the group equipment, Wyn distributed the meals. He used a Swiss Army knife to slit the top of a large cardboard box containing plastic bags of food. Dinner consisted of Top Ramen with chicken, powdered tomato soup with cheese, and Tuna Helper. For breakfast, orange drink, instant oatmeal, and powdered coffee. Each of us chose our own lunch and dessert fare. The goal was clear: light, easy-to-fix meals, with lots of calories—taste was a secondary concern, according to Wyn.

"Do we have this every night?" Lane grumbled, hefting a packet of Top Ramen. "It tastes like cardboard."

"It's loaded with salt," Wyn said. "You'll love it."

Lane shook his head.

Wyn shrugged and inspected the packs to make sure that everyone had brought all the necessary equipment and nothing more. He was adamant about this. I'd seen him do his "gear check" before: he would ridicule unnecessary equipment.

All of our sleeping bags passed inspection. They weighed five pounds apiece and would keep us warm down to 40 below zero. Ditto for the down parkas, Gore-Tex jackets and pants, plastic mountaineering boots with inner boots, and Cordura overboots with foam-rubber soles.

He went through Al's pack, zeroing in on the six different picks for each of his three ice tools. He dumped three of the picks on the ground.

"Wait a minute," Al said, picking them up. "Those are my latest designs."

"What do you mean?" Wyn said.

"I made them myself," Al said, adjusting his glasses. "I'm field-testing them."

"Field-testing?" Wyn examined one of the picks. "You won't need it up here. Trust me."

"I'm taking it anyway," Al said.

Wyn shrugged. "What's this?" he said, picking up a harmonica.

"For singing around the campfire."

"Okay," Wyn snorted. "But you'll have to carry it." He kept rummaging. He pulled out a GPS. "Do you need this?"

"Wouldn't go climbing without it," Al said. "It'll tell us our exact position. See, it picks up the signals from these satellites..."

"I know how it works," Wyn said, tossing it back in the pack. "But it's not always reliable."

Al started to say something but thought better of it. The rest of Al's equipment got the stamp of approval.

Then Wyn went through Lane's pack. Lane took out his medical kit, a black nylon bag containing group first-aid equipment.

"What's in here?" Wyn asked, holding up a plastic vial.

"Halcion," Lane said. "For sleeping."

"Vitamin H," Wyn said, grinning.

"Decadron for acute mountain sickness and edema."

"Check."

"Percocet for pain." Lane shook it. "This is great stuff."

"Hope I never have to find out." Wyn examined the container.

The rest of the medical kit included ibuprofen, antibiotics, bandages, suture kit, thermometer, adhesive tape, antiseptic ointment, moleskin for blisters, and a host of other treatments. This was the most complete first-aid kit I'd seen on a climb. It was a relief to have Lane along.

Wyn pulled out a coil of thin black rope from Lane's pack.

"What's this for?" He held up the black static line, a coil of rope as thin as a clothesline.

"It's a 100-meter static line for rescues."

"We've already got static line and climbing rope."

"I think we should bring it," Lane said. "I've been in lots of rescues. It's incredibly useful."

"How about this?" Wyn held up a yellow folding fiberglass board.

"Rescue litter."

"Leave it." Wyn tossed it on the grass. "We can improvise one."

Lane picked it back up. "It's essential," he said. "You brought me along for my medical and rescue expertise. I think I should make the call."

"Speed is safety," Wyn said. "Lose the static line or the litter. We can't take both. Look at all the other crap we have to carry." He gestured to the pile of group gear and the huge overstuffed packs.

Lane rolled his shoulders. "With all due respect, your safety record doesn't exactly inspire confidence."

Wyn bristled. "My partners died because of *their* mistakes. Not mine." Wyn walked toward Lane and spoke directly into his face like a baseball manager to an umpire. "That's what I'm trying to prevent."

"Okay," Lane said, backing away. "I'm not accusing you of anything. I'm just saying there may be a better way."

"How would you know?" Wyn said, his face reddening. "You've never climbed at altitude."

"Okay, the litter goes." Lane spoke in a short, clipped tone. "But don't complain to me when we have to haul somebody's ass down the glacier. You may be the climbing leader, but I'm the rescue leader. If we get in a rescue situation, my word goes."

"Just do what I say and we won't need a rescue." A smile played on Wyn's lips. "Trust me."

"Whatever you say," Lane said mockingly.

"Thank you."

Lane tossed the litter into the pile to be left behind. No one said anything. Wyn was being overbearing, but he was right; we needed to strip things down to essentials. Each of us would have to carry one hundred pounds of equipment, half of it in our internal frame packs, the other half trailing behind us on a plastic sled. Any additional weight would make the trek into base camp unbearable.

After cramming our gear into the packs and duffel bags, we dumped them in the back of Miles' shed. He had flown one group of climbers in already. He would be returning for the next group soon. Wyn suggested we head back into town to play basketball, his attempt to smooth things over. There was a hoop attached to a telephone pole just off the main street.

It was late morning, and the weather had warmed up. We peeled off our shirts. With his broad shoulders and muscled biceps, Lane looked like he could heft a piano. Al was tall with a wide wingspan. Wyn bounced the basketball, flexing his tightly veined arms. I was the Michelin man of the group, sporting a ring of fat around my waist.

Since Lane and Al were the tallest, they agreed to play on opposite sides. I teamed up with Lane, Wyn with Al. Lane was about Al's height, but stronger and more aggressive. On offense, he set hard screens on Wyn, springing me for open jump shots I mostly missed.

Wyn's game was all hustle and scrappiness, but he couldn't match Lane's height and quickness. He drove inside, got bottled up, and then kicked it back outside to Al, who had a sneaky set shot that was hard to stop. I tried to crowd Wyn, but he ran circles around me. When I backed off and tried to use my height and weight to keep him out of the paint, he drove by me. Lane backed me up. He had a great sense of anticipation. He'd block out Al and at the last second leap up to swat Wyn's shot into the bushes. He seemed to play with particular relish after the pack inventory. When one of my jump shots bounced off the rim, Lane elbowed Wyn out of the way to get the rebound, hitting him in the jaw.

"Sorry," Lane said. "You okay?"

"Yeah," Wyn said, massaging his jaw. "Don't worry about it."

A few minutes later, we broke up to eat lunch and run errands. I walked back to Miles' place to shower. Later that evening, we went to the West Rib for burgers and fries, likely our last dinner in Talkeetna. The mood was subdued until Lane ordered a pitcher of beer and shots for everyone. Slowly the talking and joking returned. After a beer and a shot of Johnny Walker Red, which Lane insisted I drink, I left to call Jill. Fortunately, I got the recorder. I didn't want to get into an argument or hear a summons to return home. "I love you," I said to the machine. "I'll call later. Give Andy a kiss for me."

The sun was still in the sky, but I walked back to the tent to go to sleep. It had been a long day. A mosquito got inside. I tried but failed to catch it. I lay back on my sleeping bag and looked up at the yellow fabric, still aglow in the perpetual twilight. Questions crowded my mind. Could I keep up with the rest of the team? Could I keep them from killing each other? Did I have a realistic shot at the summit? To get there, I'd have to put it all on the line this time. No holding back. The mosquito made the mistake of flying into a corner. I killed it with a quick grab. Then I poked my head outside. The clouds were dissipating. A high pressure system seemed to be moving in. Things looked auspicious for tomorrow.

Someone was shaking my shoulder. "John, wake up," Wyn said. "Time to go." The light was bright through the tent fabric. My watch read 6:15 a.m.

Wyn stuffed his sleeping bag into a nylon sack. "We're up next."

"Damn," I said, sitting up. "I was hoping for breakfast at the Roadhouse."

"I took care of that." He handed me a cinnamon roll. "One for you, two for the others. Right out of the oven."

"Good work." I pulled on my long underwear and started packing.

Wyn explained that Miles wanted to fly the two of us in first. The plane could carry only two passengers and their gear. Then he'd return for Lane and Al. We hauled our packs and duffel bags out to the orange Cessna 185, which was parked on the edge of the runway behind his cabin. Miles was gassing it up through a hole in the top of the wing.

"Morning," he hollered. "We lucked out with the weather."

He was wearing black pants, combat boots, and a green camouflage jacket. A pair of mirrored Vuarnet sunglasses hung from a string around his neck. He slurped a cup of coffee as he directed us in loading the small plane. "Just shove it in there," he said. It was hard to believe that we could get all the gear into the plane, but he didn't seem concerned.

After loading the gear, we sipped coffee and ate our cinnamon rolls in the cold while he checked the instruments. I examined the skis attached to the plane's wheels. Miles would lower the skis as we approached the glacier, allowing the Cessna to land on the snow.

"All aboard," Miles said. Wyn crawled in first and found a place behind Miles. "Hey John, grab those branches, will you?" Miles asked, pointing to a pile of fir boughs on the runway.

"What are they for?"

"You'll see."

I picked up the boughs, which were fragrant and sticky with pitch. Climbing into the cockpit, I tried to put the boughs on the floor, but there was not enough room. So I kept them in my lap. Buckling my seatbelt, I smeared pitch on my pile jacket, but I didn't care. We were on our way.

Miles primed the engine, turned the key, and the propeller sputtered to life. He adjusted the power until the engine ran smoothly and the prop feathered nicely. Then he gave it some gas, and the plane lurched onto the gravel runway. A blue delivery truck blocked his access to the middle of the runway.

Miles opened his window and shouted. "Hey, Stan, get your goddamn truck out of my way."

The driver waved and pulled the truck off the runway. Miles taxied the Cessna around and pointed it down the dirt and gravel runway. At the end loomed the power lines above the Fairview Inn.

"Hang on," Miles shouted above the noise of the engine. He shoved the stick forward and opened the throttle. The plane bumped along, picking up speed. The Fairview Inn was coming up fast. I looked over at Miles. His jaw was set.

Finally, he pulled up on the stick and the heavily laden bird soared smoothly into the air, easily clearing the top of the inn. We circled the town and headed north toward Denali. As we rose higher, the horizon widened out around us. The channels of the Susitna River looked like a huge braid of cables. It was big and shallow and clouded gray with glacial debris. The tundra on either side of the river was so green it almost hurt my eyes. It was pocked with bogs, streams, and small lakes, remnants of the glaciers from the last ice age. This was a glimpse into what the earth must have looked like 10,000 years ago when the big glaciers melted and vegetation broke out on the earth, bringing herds of bison and the bands of human beings who hunted them. We were going back to a time when civilization was just a veneer on the planet, as thin and fragile as lichen on a granite boulder.

The sheer expansiveness of the country oppressed me. It dwarfed any sense of the human scale. There were no artifacts of civilization. No cities. No power lines. No water tanks. We were a long, long way from home. We were entering a vastness unfathomable to someone who had never been out of the Lower Forty-eight.

The plane headed for the crystalline world of the Alaska Range, its summits sheathed in clouds. The land rose underneath us as we passed over the foothills. The green of the tundra gave way to the ugly brown snouts of glaciers, fractured ice falls, deep blue crevasses, and then the white purity of the glacier itself. The plane's engine whined as we flew higher. Miles pulled up on the stick, but the plane barely climbed. It was close to its ceiling.

Ahead loomed One Shot Pass, a V-shaped notch in the ridge. We had to clear this to get to base camp.

"Damn." Miles jiggled the stick in frustration. We were still below the pass and yet the airplane couldn't seem to climb much higher.

"Anything we can throw out?" Miles asked.

"What are you talking about?" Wyn replied.

"It's going to be close," Miles said. "Any cargo we could jettison?"

"Hell no!" Wyn said.

"Okay," Miles said, nonplussed. "Guess I'll take other measures." He pointed the plane straight toward the pass and pulled up on the stick as far as it would go. The plane barely budged. We were closing in on the snow and shattered rock below it. Ahead, the massive face of Foraker bulked in the background.

"Hang on," Miles said. He rolled the Cessna over on its wingtip so that we soared through the pass vertically. My stomach flipped over. We cleared the pass with several hundred feet to spare. A jumbo jet could have made it.

"Whew," Miles said, wiping his hand across his brow.

Wyn rolled his eyes.

Miles laughed at our worried looks.

Very funny, I thought.

The Cessna plunged down from the pass and into the inner gorge of the Alaska Range. Miles banked right and headed up the enormous Kahiltna Glacier, a super-highway of ice.

It was a cold, harsh, inhospitable world, but it was impossible not to be overcome by the beauty of the place—the clarity of the air, the creamy, airbrushed appearance of the glacier from above, the sharpness of the crenellated ice ridges, and the outsized architecture of the range itself. I pressed my nose to the Plexiglas window, taking in some of the biggest and steepest peaks in North America. But they were dwarfed by the colossus in front of us—the immense, wide mass of Denali, the local Athabascan name meaning "The Great One." The satellite summits reflected further glory on the big D, a soaring expanse of ice, snow, and rock. I tried to get a look at our line on the south face, but it was easier to see from the other side of the plane.

Miles banked back and forth along the glacier. He flew close to the peaks and laughed at our groans. After he'd had his fun with us, he headed for the landing strip, a flat area on the southeast fork of the Kahiltna. The bright red, yellow, and blue dots grew in size until I could pick out the individual tents clustered around base camp. It was like coming home.

Miles got on the radio and asked about landing conditions. The light was flat, so he decided to make a pass over the runway first.

"Toss those boughs when I tell you," he said.

"Okay," I said, wondering if this was another trick. I opened my window. The cold air rushed in.

"Now!" he ordered.

I tossed out the first bough. It fluttered down like a large, green feather, landing behind us on the glacier.

"Again!" he yelled.

I tossed a second bough.

He circled back for another run. On his signal, I dropped the third and fourth boughs.

"Why did we do that?" I asked.

"Depth perception." He grinned, his teeth yellowed from cigar smoke. "I don't enjoy crashing."

Miles brought the plane sharply to the right and made a half circle around the huge amphitheater. The Cessna passed close to the ice-plastered flank of Mount Hunter and headed for the runway.

"Hang on," he said.

Leveling the wings, he aimed at a space between the fir boughs, which stood out clearly against the flat gray light. The plane's skis came down beneath us. The little Cessna rocked and swayed as it neared the surface of the glacier. The right ski caught first, jarring the plane. Miles fought to get the wings level. Then the left ski hit, righting the plane's balance. The Cessna skimmed lightly across the snow and came to rest just outside the canvas hut of the Base Camp.

"Unload that stuff quickly," Miles said. "I want to get your buddies before the weather changes."

I jumped out of the plane and sank up to my knees in a small crevasse.

"Oh, yeah, watch out for that crevasse," he said.

"Thanks a lot."

I probed the crevasse with an ice axe. Fortunately, it was shallow. I grabbed the duffel bags and packs as Wyn handed them out of the plane.

"Back in a jiffy." Miles closed the door and turned the plane around. I felt a twinge of abandonment as I watched the orange Cessna taxi and take off down the glacier. It grew smaller and smaller until it disappeared behind the huge, icy flank of Mount Hunter. We were finally at base camp. We were committed. There was no going back now.

FIVE

Ice crystals glittered in the thin, bitter air as I dragged my duffel bags across the runway. Dropping the bags in front of the Weatherhaven shelter, I sat down to catch my breath. We were only at 7,200 feet and already I was having trouble breathing.

Mountains shot up on all sides of base camp: the steep, ice-plastered flanks of 14,570-foot Mount Hunter to the south; the immense, glittering triangle of 17,400-foot Mount Foraker to the west; the massive south face of Denali to the north. I was smack dab in the middle of the greatest hits of North American climbing.

As I caught my breath, I watched an avalanche release on the face of Mount Hunter across the valley. Like a slow-motion waterfall, it started at the top of the peak and cascaded down a dizzying array of ridges, steep faces, and wildly fluted snow-covered ridges before ending in a thunderous roar at the base of the glacier. Hunter's north face was a lot like the route we were planning to do, only half as long.

After dumping his duffel bags next to mine, Wyn went over to the door of the base camp manager's Weatherhaven hut. There was a lawn chair in front and empty beer bottles and cans of Chevron Blazo fuel strewn out back. It looked like a typical Alaska camp located in the middle of a glacier.

"Hello." Wyn tapped on the door of the hut.

"Just a minute," someone yelled from inside. A tall, slender woman emerged from the hut.

"Wyn!" She gave him a big, wet kiss.

Wyn stepped back surprised, but pleased. "Kim, I thought you went back to school."

"I did," she said, releasing him. She wore a white quilted down jacket, blue sweat pants, and a pair of running shoes. She was sexy in a well-scrubbed, outdoorsy way. "I just work summers now. What about you?"

"I was in Europe—climbing." He cleared his throat.

"I heard you *soloed* the Eiger."

"Well, some of it." Wyn scratched his nose.

"That's awesome," she said. "Why didn't you send me a postcard?"

"I was traveling." He shrugged. "You know how it is."

"Yeah, I've heard that before." She gathered her blond hair in a ponytail and tied it with a piece of red fluorescent surveyor's tape. She had brown eyes, freckles, and a darkly tanned face with patches of pink skin on the bridge of her nose. "What are you doing back here?"

"Planning to do Denali." Wyn motioned over to me. "With my friend, John."

She smiled at me and then went back to quizzing Wyn. "Which route?" She gave him an appraising squint as if she was used to seeing lunatics and that he was guilty until proven innocent. As base camp manager, it was her job to radio weather information to the bush pilots and the Talkeetna Ranger Station. She organized the flights in and out of base camp, answered questions, and kept things running smoothly—no easy task. Her unofficial job was serving as the sanity check in the less-than-mentally-sound community around the base camp.

"What have you heard about the south face?" Wyn asked.

"Several parties have done the Cassin, but nothing else. There's a lot of snow up there."

"Good. Not as many crevasses."

"Lots of avalanches, though." She pointed to where the topographic lines on our map gathered along our proposed route up the East Fork of the Kahiltna Glacier. "The slides travel across the entire valley."

The distant roar of an avalanche made me flinch. She touched my arm. "Don't worry," she said. "It's miles away."

Her smile was dazzling; she must have had guys hitting on her all the time.

Wyn ignored the avalanche and kept talking. "Has anybody done the American Direct?"

She shook her head. "Too much objective hazard."

"Where?" he asked, holding out the topographic map. "Show me."

"Here." She indicated the slope of the south face. "It's the main funnel for snow, ice, rocks, and avalanche debris." She prodded the map for emphasis with her thin, tanned, well-formed fingers. "And watch out for crevasses. The new snow covered a lot of them." She handed the map back to Wyn. "I'd consider doing another route if I were you. How about the Cassin? Or the West Buttress?"

"Thanks." Wyn folded up the map. "We tried that before."

"Did you climb it?" she asked.

"We got close," Wyn said, avoiding looking at me.

"Maybe you should go for it," she said, looking back and forth between us. "It would be safer."

For me, it would be a worthy achievement, but there was no way he would go for it. No guts. No glory. No material for his slide shows.

"Thanks, Kim," he said, folding up the map.

"My pleasure." She smiled. Her teeth were small, even, and perfect. "Be safe."

"Don't worry," Wyn said.

"Stop by later on for a beer," she said. "I'd like to hear more about Europe."

"Will do."

"You, too, John." Then she turned and went back into the hut.

We walked back to our duffel bags. "What a babe," I said.

Wyn nodded.

"What happened with her?"

"Long story." He indicated the small rise behind the hut. "Let's camp near the top of the hill. It's too crowded down here."

"Did you hear what she said about the conditions?" I asked. "Maybe we should consider doing the West Buttress."

"Kim hasn't been up there," Wyn said. "I got a look at it from the plane. The ridges didn't look that bad. Besides, the West Buttress is old business."

"Not for me." I stopped and looked at him. "I've thought about it a lot."

"Have you?" he said, appraising me.

"Maybe we should finish it off."

"It's a cow path," he said, dismissing it.

We carried our duffel bags up the small rise behind the hut. As I fought for breath, I began to wonder about the wisdom of doing a new route. But like a greyhound after a rabbit, Wyn had locked onto it. I knew from past experience it would be hard to dissuade him. This was both the advantage and drawback of climbing with him. Once he committed himself to something, he wouldn't let it go until he finished it. I'd have to make a strong argument if I wanted to deflect him from his purpose. As we passed a blue dome tent, someone called out to him.

"Hey, Wyn, what's going on?"

"Scott," Wyn said. "Long time no see." They shook hands. Scott was tall, bearded, and hairy; he wore red insulated overalls and a New York Yankees baseball cap.

Wyn introduced me.

We shook hands.

"How's the guiding business?" Wyn asked.

"Can't complain," Scott said. "Got another group of clients to the top and not one of them killed me."

"How's the route?"

"A slog," Scott said, taking off the cap and running his hands through his greasy hair. "What route are you planning to do?"

"It's a secret." He put a finger to his lips.

"You can tell me."

"Okay, a new route on south face."

"Where?"

"The complete American direct," Wyn whispered.

"Thought it had been done."

"Not the last bit. They avoided the rock climbing at the top."

Scott whistled. "Sounds hairball. Mind if I tag along?"

Wyn glanced over at me. "We've got a...good team. We're pretty well set."

"Well, some other time." Scott shook hands with us. "Hey, good to see you guys. Stop by and see us later on."

"Will do," Wyn said.

As flattering as it was to bask in Wyn's celebrity, I began to understand that my role was contingent. Wyn wanted to ace this new route, and if I or Lane or Al couldn't keep up, he wouldn't hesitate to dump us in favor of someone like Scott. He was promiscuous in his partners.

We moved past the other tents clustered around base camp. A group of three climbers sat outside the tents on foam pads, basking in the sun like large, brightly colored lizards. They were not a particularly attractive collection of humanity. They were "outgoing," meaning they had already spent three to four weeks without soap, a shower, or attention to hygiene. Their clothes were stained with food and filth. Their hair was matted and greasy. Their faces were smeared with sunscreen. Their beards were ratty and overflowing. They smelled like animals at the zoo.

By contrast, we were "incoming." Our clothes were clean, our energy level was high, and our stench relatively low. I would have liked to camp with the rest of the climbers, just for the camaraderie, but Wyn wanted solitude. We carried the heavy duffel bags up through the snow toward the top of a small hill a hundred yards away from the tents.

"It's quieter up here," Wyn said. "We won't have people waking us up all the time."

"Whatever you say," I said, grunting my way up the slope. It took us a second trip to get all of our stuff up to the top of the hill. From there, we had a panoramic view of the base camp and a clear perspective on Denali. It looked so far away it seemed to belong to another world. As I vacillated between dread of the climb and elation at being up here, Wyn's confidence made it easier for me to believe that we could knock it off.

I started stomping out a platform for our tent. Wyn stopped me.

"Wait," he said. He took out a bottle of whiskey. "A peace offering."

"To who? The Goddess of the Hearth?"

"That would be Jill." He laughed. "No, to the gods of Denali." He splashed some whiskey into the snow.

"Not too much," I said. "Don't waste it."

"Don't worry," he said. "Now we can proceed."

"Shall we hold hands and chant?"

"Humor me," Wyn said. "We've got plenty of whiskey."

I waited impatiently while he completed his nutty ritual. After leveling out a platform, we erected our red four-season tent. Again, I needed to sit down and catch my breath.

Unpacking our duffel bags, we put the foam pads and sleeping bags inside. We began the ritual of making a home, colonizing a harsh and inhospitable place. It was reassuring to fall into the old rhythm of unpacking and preparing the camp. It made the landscape feel familiar.

Life really was simpler up here. There were no worries about what to wear, what to do. Once you knew the routine, you simply repeated it.

And this kept you on track when the wind started gusting, the snow started falling, the air thinned out. Then simple tasks like lacing up your boots provided all the challenge that you needed.

Wyn had all this down. He had an economy of motion and purpose that I'd always admired. He never seemed to hurry but always was the first one out of camp in the morning. Right now, he was sorting his equipment. Whereas the rest of his clothes were worn and ragged, his climbing equipment was in perfect shape. He tested the sharpness of his ice tool against his thumb and then put it back in the duffel bag.

"I got you out of the house, didn't I?" he said, his eyes twinkling.

"You sure did," I said, taking in the panorama of peaks. "I just hope my marriage survives it."

"I wouldn't worry about it," he said nonchalantly. "Jill will come around."

"I'm glad you're so sure about it." Sitting on my foam pad, I took in the scenery. The sun had burned off the fog of early morning. The air was amazingly clear. I could see for miles with remarkable resolution. The sun rose over the south face of Denali. It was only about ten miles away as the crow flies but more than two miles higher than us.

Wyn took out the binoculars and glassed the south face, a wide-open bowl split by an indistinct ridge. "There *is* a lot of snow. Take a look."

With the binoculars, the features of the climb came into focus—the lower face was obscured, but the middle and upper parts of the face stood out in steep and graphic relief—the spiral couloir like a wide toboggan run gaining access to the middle ridge; the broken, rocky ground above it ending at the base of a granite buttress; the steep, three-tiered structure of the buttress, the flat "football field" near the top of the second tier, an ideal camp; the towering third section; and finally, the summit ridge. It made me sick to contemplate the whole of it, so I tried to break it down into discrete problems. This was the way to avoid getting psyched out.

"You want to stay out of the gullies," he said. "That's the secret of climbing in the Alaska Range. Most of them are avalanche chutes."

"I know, Wyn." I put the binoculars down and went back to unpack my gear.

A few minutes later, he yelled, "Look! An avalanche on the south face!"

I grabbed the binoculars and glassed what looked like a tidal wave tumbling down the south face. It started near the summit ridge, picked up steam, and roared down the gulley to the right of our route. It looked like it was moving in slow motion, but it was probably traveling at hundreds of miles an hour.

"Kim was right," I said. "There's tons of snow up there. But at least our line didn't get hit too badly."

"See," Wyn said, applying some sunscreen. "I'm not a total kamikaze after all."

"That remains to be seen," I said dryly.

I went back to unpacking. After putting my sleeping bag and gear in the tent, I heard the drone of a plane. A tiny, orange speck emerged from behind Mount Hunter. It banked to the right and headed for the runway. The nose of the plane lifted, and the speed slowed as its skis made contact with the snow. It skidded softly toward the base camp hut.

We walked down the hill toward the runway. The door of the Cessna flew open, and Lane jumped out.

"Let me out of here," he yelled in mock outrage. "That guy should have his license revoked." He stopped and surveyed the mountains around him. "Damn."

Al unfolded his long, bony limbs and emerged from the plane like a stork. "Geez," he said, pushing up his glasses with his index finger. "This is great."

We helped them unload the plane.

"See you in a month," Miles yelled above the roar of the engine. "Y'all take care up there." Miles pronounced the words slowly and seriously as if it were a benediction. Then he gave us a thumbs-up, gunned the engine, spun the plane around, and took off down the runway. The plane rose quickly before waggling its wings—one last good-bye.

We carried their gear up to our campsite. As Lane and Al set up their tent, I brought out some freeze-dried Turkey Tetrazzini for dinner.

"Put it away, John." Lane produced three plastic shopping bags and took out four New York steaks, eight ears of corn, potato salad, blackberry pie, a half gallon of vanilla ice cream, and two six-packs of Budweiser. "We can eat well the first night." He shot a look at Wyn. "Especially when we don't have to carry it."

"Fantastic," Wyn said, eyeing the steaks. "Save the Turkey Tetrazzini for later."

Lane gave Al the job of boiling the water for the corn, something that would be easy. While Lane and Al started dinner, Wyn and I sat around on our foam pads and sipped whiskey. I blabbed about how excited I was to do the climb, psyching myself up for it. I was alternately depressed and ecstatic to be here, a typical attitude before a big climb.

Gas stoves roared in the tents below us. The smell of tomato soup wafted up to us. An occasional laugh broke the silence that filled the amphitheater.

"How would you like your steak?" Lane asked in the tone of a waiter at a fine restaurant.

"Medium," I said.

"Medium rare," Wyn said.

Lane nodded and went back to the stove. He had constructed a countertop out of snow, with two stoves resting on top of it, and room for his spice rack and spatulas. He dropped two steaks into the pan. They sizzled and gave off a rich, fatty odor that made my stomach growl. Lane had a rapt, introspective look as he turned the meat. He seemed to be retreating back to what he knew well to avoid being cowed by the surroundings. There was little of the bravado he had exhibited back at the 5.10 Tavern. Al seemed similarly subdued, dutifully taking orders from Lane, but not saying much. Wyn seemed to be the only one who was relaxed: he filed his crampon points, whistled Beethoven's Ninth Symphony, and breathed deeply, as if the air up here were purer and more exquisite than that at sea level.

A few minutes later, Al called us to dinner. He handed out ears of corn and the potato salad.

"Good job on the corn," Lane said to Al. "It's only a little overcooked. You'll make sous chef in no time."

"I thought I was sous chef," Al grumbled.

"You can barely boil water," Lane growled. "You'll have to work up to Top Ramen."

"No place to go but up," Al said.

"Are these okay?" Lane handed out the steaks. "I can put them back on if you want, but I hate to overcook a good piece of meat."

Sitting down on our foam pads in a circle, we passed around butter, salt, and pepper.

Wyn cracked a beer. "To the chef." We clinked beer cans.

I sipped my beer and marveled at the scenery. Stars glistened on the pastel blue horizon. My anxiety about the climb diminished with the food, camaraderie, and the glow of the midnight sun.

"How long have you been a firefighter?" Wyn asked Lane.

"Four years." Lane cut a piece of steak and chewed it meditatively.

"You like the work?" Wyn asked.

"Love it," Lane said.

"But it's dangerous, isn't it?"

"Just like climbing, right?" Lane took a swig of beer. "It can be dangerous, but that's part of the job. Couple years ago when I was just getting started, we got a call from the south end. House fire. Routine. But when we got there, smoke was pouring out of the place and blue flames shot out of the roof like a blowtorch. Someone was screaming from inside the main floor. I saw this little girl pressed up against the wall inside.

"I started running toward the front door, but my partner caught me. 'Too dangerous,' he said. 'Ruptured gas line.'

"'Where?'

"'On the roof.' He pointed to the blue flames.

"'Who'd put a gas line on the roof?'

"'Too dangerous,' he said. 'Evacuate.'

"When I stood my ground, he said, 'Get your ass out of here! That's an order!'

"'Bullshit,' I said. I'm a by-the-book guy, but sometimes you have to go with your gut. 'She's going to die if I don't.' I tried to push past him, but he grabbed me and held me back while the rest of the crew got the pumper truck going. By then the heat was so intense no one could have survived it."

Lane finished chewing the steak. "We found out later the blue flame *wasn't* a broken gas line. It was a kind of insulation that produces a blowtorch effect. If my partner had read the literature instead of the latest *Playboy*, the little girl would still be alive. Her mom had gone to the neighbors to borrow an egg. She turned on the stove too high. She poured oil into the pan. It flared up and started a grease fire." He studied his beer can and then crushed it. "Won't let it happen again."

There was a long silence. Wyn brought out the topographical map.

"Let me give you guys a rundown on what's up for tomorrow." He spread out the map on a foam pad and explained the plan: Tomorrow, Day 1, haul half of our gear up the Kahiltna, taking a right up the East Fork, caching the gear at 8,000, and returning here. Day 2, retrace our steps, taking the rest of the gear, and camp at 8,000. Day 3, move up to 9,500, cache the gear and head back. Day 4, move up to 9,500. Day 5, carry all the way up to Face Camp at 11,500, and come back to 9,500. Day 6, head up to Face Camp. It was ten miles from the landing strip to Face Camp and 4,000 feet of elevation gain.

"That's not a lot of mileage or elevation gain," Al pointed out. "We could easily do more."

"We need to take things easy," Wyn replied. "I don't want anyone coming down with altitude sickness."

"Fair enough," Al said. "But weather's a factor, too. As long as it's clear, I think we should get as much hauling in as possible."

"We don't want to rush." Wyn pointed to the map. "We'll try for here the next night. It's about five miles up the glacier. If everyone does well, we'll see about moving quicker."

Al pushed up his glasses but said nothing more. It was hard to know whether this had appeased him.

"Sounds good to me," Lane said. "You're the man."

"Thanks," Wyn said, seeming pleased his authority wasn't going to be questioned again. "Tomorrow, we'll hit the road early. We want to get up to the next camp before the snow turns to mush. Otherwise, we'll have to wear snowshoes. Let's say we get up at 3:30 a.m."

"3:30?" Lane asked.

"Yeah, 3:30." Wyn nodded emphatically. "No worries about darkness at this latitude." He took his plate over to the cooking area. "Great dinner, guys. Our turn tomorrow night."

Wyn started up the stove and began boiling water for the dishes. I went back to the tent for the steel wool pads. Al took out his harmonica and began riffing away. At first, I couldn't catch the tune. Then I recognized it: "Rawhide." The doleful notes echoed off the peaks, filling the amphitheater with an eerie, mysterious music. Al wasn't the most accomplished musician, but the sound of the instrument made the desolate landscape feel more like home, just as it must have for cowboys gathered around the campfires of the old West.

At 3 a.m., I woke and stuck my head out of the tent. It was cold and clear, the surface of the glacier glazed with ice. This would make our first carry much easier as it would provide a stable surface for our feet. I dozed in my sleeping bag until the alarm pulsed at 3:30 a.m. Wyn woke with a start.

"What?" He looked around the tent, blinking his eyes. "Shit, I was dreaming I'd fallen off the Eiger." He rubbed his eyes, sat up in his bag, and combed his unruly hair with his hand.

I put on my pile jacket. Still groggy from the lack of sleep, I pumped up the stove, opened the valve, and watched the gas pooled in the metal cup below the burner. Turning my face away, I flicked the lighter and ignited the gas, which made a small whump. It burned fiercely, the flame rising, and then diminished. I opened the valve and a blue flame blossomed in the center of the burner. The stove roared. I put a pot of water on to boil. Soon we'd have instant coffee and oatmeal.

Already Wyn was loading the sleds with gear. He packed cans of white gas, bags of food, and climbing equipment. He put more of it on his sled than on mine. I didn't stop him. I still wasn't sure about my level of conditioning. I didn't want to overdo it.

Al coughed, and Lane swore softly in the other tent. A high, gray cloud lingered above Mount Foraker, but overall, the weather looked good.

The light was pale, ethereal, almost spiritual in quality. It satisfied a yearning so deep I couldn't name or explain it. Everything up here was far removed from the clamor and din of everyday life back in Seattle.

After Wyn finished loading the sleds, I put my lunch, spare clothing, and the rest of my gear into my pack. I hefted it—thirty pounds at least, a reasonable weight for the first day, considering I'd also be dragging a sled like a draft horse.

Putting on my seat harness, I went down a mental checklist before venturing onto the glacier. Climbing rope tied in an overhand loop and clipped into locking carabiner. Check. Biner gate screwed shut. Check. Sled tied directly to the rope so it won't pull me down if I fall into a crevasse. Check. Jumars with spring-loaded metal teeth to grip the rope and get my ass out of crevasse ASAP. Check.

"Okay?" Wyn yelled out.

"Okay!" I yelled back.

"Move out," Al said. He and Lane were right behind us. We descended past the Weatherhaven hut and onto the glacier. A few other climbers were up cooking breakfast, but we were the only ones on the move. My throat felt raw from the cold, but it was good to get under way.

Our objective was to get down to the Kahiltna Glacier, ascend it for a couple miles, and then take a right on the East Fork of the Kahiltna. Our plan was the classic one for high altitude: carry gear up to a higher camp, and then return to the previous camp to sleep. That was the best way to acclimatize.

My crampons crunched on the snow as we descended Heartbreak Hill, so named because it was the last incline up to base camp. The sled scraped and slid along, hitting me in the back of my plastic boots. I had to knock it out of the way to keep it from tripping me.

Despite the annoyance of the sled, I relished the feeling of movement. This was my first real exercise in several days. I inhaled the cold, pure air, exhaling a long, white beard of breath. It was exhilarating to get back into the life of the body. This is what I missed back at the store, my workouts sandwiched in between customers, inventories, and meetings with sales reps.

The Kahiltna Glacier flattened out when we reached its main fork. The pack dug into my shoulders and hips. The sled dragged. The rope went taut between Wyn and me. I hurried to keep pace and maintain the correct distance. If too much slack gathered in the rope, it would be difficult to self-arrest. Strict rope technique was essential for safe glacier travel.

As the broad, bright slope of the Kahiltna Glacier undulated upward, I had to hustle to keep up with Wyn. He followed the well-beaten "cow path" up the glacier, the main route used in climbing Denali. We passed the remains of a recent camp—the melted hummock of a windbreak, the flat spot for the tent, the discarded spaghetti, and the snow stained with urine and feces. The appeal of the East Fork became immediately clear. Once we were up there, we'd have the place pretty much to ourselves.

The West Buttress route got so much traffic it was hard to consider it wilderness, which made it easy to forget its danger. I watched the rope, making sure not to allow too much slack. Even though lots of climbers used this trail, I couldn't trust it. As the sun rose, it opened crevasses and weakened snow bridges. The bridges could be solid in the morning and collapse by afternoon.

We hopped across our first small crevasse. It had polished, blue ice on its sides and exhaled a cold breeze that felt like icy breath.

A few minutes later, we ran into another party coming back down the glacier. They moved slowly across a snow bridge over a large crevasse. The leader was dragging something behind him on a sled. It was long and thin and wrapped in the blue rain fly. It was too big for the sled and pulled him off balance. He yanked and pulled at the sled, trying to keep it from falling into the crevasse. We stopped and waited for them to cross.

"How's it going?" Wyn asked.

The guy dragging the sled didn't answer. He stopped, coughed, and tried to catch his breath. He was tall, with broad shoulders, a graying beard, and bushy eyebrows caked with ice. His left hand was bare and covered with purple frostbite blisters. His face was white, his eyes dark sockets of exhaustion.

"My wife fell into a crevasse," he gasped. He bent over and coughed for several seconds. Then he regained his composure. "Couldn't get her out." He started hacking and doubled over with the exertion. Then he wiped his eyes with his sleeve. By this time, the two other climbers caught up with him. A man and a woman. Their faces were ashen, their mouths agape.

Wyn helped the guy take off his pack. "What happened to your hand?"

"Fuck it!" He wiped the tears from his eyes. "I don't give a fuck about it!"

Wyn ignored him. "Do you have any extra gloves in here?"

"Somewhere." He sat slumped on the snow. "Doesn't matter."

"Where?"

"Bottom compartment."

I unzipped it and took out a pair of wool mittens. "Put these on."

The guy tried to do this, but his hands were too stiff.

"They're screwed," he said shrilly. "Totally screwed."

Wyn put the mittens on for him. "Now let's get some hot drinks into you."

"No thanks." He stood up abruptly. "How far to base camp?"

"A mile or so."

"Do you have some water?" He breathed hard, trying to regain his composure.

Wyn took out his water bottle and let him drink. He spilled most of it over his face. He handed the bottle to his companions.

"You really should let us—"

The guy shook his head. "Got to get out of this...shit hole." He coughed again and pulled angrily at the sled.

He got the sled moving and kept going. I watched the dark cargo slide by. The sled wobbled and fishtailed behind him, scraping and bumping and throwing him off balance, overloaded with something it was never intended to carry. It was hard to believe this was happening. All of the justifications I'd mouthed about climbing being no more dangerous than driving on the freeway came back to haunt me as the mealy justifications they really were.

The couple filed past us without saying anything. They continued to Lane and Al, who turned to talk to them. Then they kept going, a bleak procession back to base camp.

"Let's take a break up ahead," Wyn announced. He made his way across the snow bridge, keeping the sled out of the crevasse. A hundred yards later, he probed the surface of the glacier with his ice axe for crevasses. When he was satisfied it was safe, he brought me up. Lane and Al joined us.

"Everyone okay?" Wyn asked, hands on his hips.

No one replied. It was hard to know what to say. Wyn didn't seem especially shocked by the dead body, but Al looked like he was about to get sick.

"We should have tried to help them," Lane said, taking off his pack.

"I tried to," Wyn said. "They wanted to keep going."

"We should have insisted," Lane said. "They looked like they were in shock."

"What were we going to do?" Wyn raised his palms. "Tackle them and tie them down?"

"Sometimes you have to," Lane insisted. "For their own good."

"I guess." Wyn sat down on his pack and drank from his water bottle. Then he went around and checked the knots and rigging of all the sleds. Satisfied, he went back to his pack. "Let's hydrate and get something to eat. We'll take a right turn up ahead."

Lane and Al looked at each other but said nothing. Lane shook his head, breathed deeply, and adjusted the laces of his boots: he probably saw situations like this all the time. Al retreated into himself, adjusted his fogged glasses, fiddled with the buttons on his altimeter watch, and munched on a chocolate bar. The stakes were now clear.

I took several deep draughts of water the consistency of a Slurpee. Even though I kept it in an insulated container, the water was close to freezing. After cracking a brittle square of chocolate in my teeth, I stood up. My mind reeled from the sickening way the overloaded sled fishtailed across the snow.

"Saddle up." Wyn lifted his blue internal frame pack above him and lowered it onto his shoulders. Lane stood up and got ready to go. "Be careful up front."

"No worries," Wyn said. Then he began moving, the sled scraping along behind him. He zigzagged up the glacier, deftly running his sled over and around the small crevasses, scanning the ground, focusing on the sights and sounds of his surroundings. He had a preternatural alertness—all his senses seemed to come alive up here.

Even though we'd encountered a dead body twenty minutes ago, Wyn kept his cool. It was both creepy and calming. No matter what kind of problems we encountered, I could count on him to get us through.

At the confluence with the East Fork of the Kahiltna, Wyn diagonaled right, leaving the main trail behind. Now the real work began. My lungs burned. My calves ached. The sled jerked and pulled me off balance.

Wyn moved upward like a machine. He pulled at the rope and looked back at me to see what kind of progress I was making. I tried to establish a rhythm, but Wyn's constant pulling on the rope threw me off. I didn't want to say anything—I didn't want to be the weak link—but finally I couldn't take it anymore. "Slow down!" I yelled.

"Sorry," he said. He slackened his pace for a few hundred yards but then picked it up again. Wyn had an incredible energy level. He had to keep moving, whether on a climb or in the rest of his life. Now he was straining on the rope like a hunting dog on a leash. I tried to go as fast as I could, but I didn't want to get totally exhausted. If I just kept a good pace for the first week, I'd gradually get back into shape. Still, it was humiliating to slow down the group. Lane and Al were right behind me.

Lane was a specimen. He had a broad, muscular chest, bulging arms, and huge, tree-trunk legs. His only weakness was his pacing. One minute he was right behind me, pressure breathing like a locomotive. The next minute he'd fall back several hundred yards. It was irritating.

In my vanity, I got sucked into competing with Wyn and the others. Instead of telling Wyn again to slow down, I tried to maintain the pace. My pulse raced. My breath came light and fast. My body tried desperately to cope with the altitude. I forced myself to breathe rhythmically. It wasn't enough.

By the time I reached the camp, I felt dizzy and nauseous. I dumped my pack, unclipped from the rope, and collapsed on the snow. Stars circled around my head like electrons around a molecule. I chugged the first water bottle and took out another one. *Hydrate, hydrate*, I told myself. By the time I got half of the bottle down, my eyes were regaining their focus, but my head still throbbed.

Lane threw his pack down next to me. "This is awesome," he said. "I can't believe the size of the peaks."

Wyn nodded sagely. "If you think the views are good now, just wait." He pointed up the valley of the East Fork where the steep, icy walls narrowed. "They get better and better."

"I'm glad we're doing this route," Lane said, pointing out the glacier ahead. "It's great to get away from the main fork." He kicked at the snow. "I feel sorry for that woman. I see too much of that on my job."

"I know what you mean," Wyn said, probing the snow with his ice axe. "I've seen more than my fair share of it."

While they talked, I forced myself to eat and drink. I stared dully at the sun coming up on Mount Crosson, a perfect triangle of a peak with a delicate scrollwork of snow on its eastern flank. I knew on some level it was a beautiful sight, but the throbbing in my head made it hard to appreciate.

To my relief, I wasn't the only one suffering from the altitude. Al wasn't exactly hopping around. He took out a stick of pepperoni and chewed it slowly. He had to take a breath between bites.

While Al and I rested, Lane and Wyn dug a trench in the snow and filled it with the food and other gear we'd carried up here. Lane piled the snow back on it and marked it with bamboo wands tied with surveyor's tape.

"Bury it deep," Wyn warned.

"Roger," Lane said, tamping the snow down with his shovel.

"Shake and bake." Wyn stomped his boots like a horse getting ready to move.

I got up slowly, my back stiff from carrying the pack. I wanted to rest, but we needed to get back to base camp. It was 7:30 a.m., and already the sun was softening up the snow. My first few steps punched through the surface.

I smeared more sunscreen on my face and draped a blue handkerchief over the back of my neck, tucking it into the rim of my baseball hat to keep it in place. I must have looked like a soldier in a Third World country's foreign legion, but at least I wouldn't get scorched.

After I clipped back into the rope, we descended quickly, the sleds skipping along behind us. With no weight in our packs, we quickly reached the main fork of the Kahiltna. Then the sun and the exertion began to take their toll. My head pounded. My vision blurred. A migraine spread through my skull. It was all I could do to keep moving.

The climbing rope began coiling in front of me, but I didn't bother to stop and look up. I figured Wyn was preparing to cross an easy snow bridge and soon would be paying out the rope. I kept moving, allowing twenty feet of it to collect. Then I stopped and looked up. Ahead, Wyn went to his knees as if searching for a lost contact lens.

Why is he stopping? I thought, irritated. I was anxious to get down to a lower elevation and get out of the sun.

"Falling!" he yelled.

I dove to the snow, jammed the pick of my ice axe into it, spread-eagled my legs, and dug in my boots. I kept my eye on the coils of rope next to me. If he fell any farther, he could travel twenty feet before my self-arrest would catch him. The impact would rip me out of my stance.

It looked like he had broken through with his legs, but had used his ice axe to keep from falling all the way in. Bracing his arms on the surface of the snow, he slowly removed one leg, then the other. He pivoted onto his stomach and crawled back toward me. When he was about ten feet away from the crevasse, he stood up. Unbuckling his pack, he sat down on it and wiped his forehead with his sleeve. His face was dripping with sweat. "Why did it take you so long to go into self-arrest?" he yelled.

"I didn't think you were in trouble," I said, getting up from my stance.

"Self-arrest first, ask questions later," Wyn said, grimacing. "Read the signs!"

I nodded, chastened.

"Christ, what's all this slack in the rope?" He pointed to the coils. "I'm glad I *didn't* fall."

"Sorry," I said, getting back up. "I wasn't paying attention."

"I guess not." He stood up and put his pack back on.

I felt stupid, chastened. Experience was not enough. Climbing demanded total concentration. If I wanted to be more than a liability, I needed to get my head back into the game.

"What's wrong?" Lane asked. "Why are we stopping?"

"Crevasse," Wyn said. "Watch your step."

Lane looked from one of us to the other, trying to figure out what had happened. He cupped his gloves and yelled back to Al, "Crevasse!"

Wyn probed the snow with his ice axe, finding solid ground a few yards to the left of where he'd fallen. Then he kept going. I waited for the slack to come out of the rope and then started walking, determined not to commit another blunder. Wyn was so competent I tended to doubt anything could go wrong with him in charge.

The hole he'd punched through the roof of a crevasse was as wide as a manhole cover. His legs must have dangled in empty air for a good minute. No wonder he was so angry.

When I got to the far side of the crevasse, I checked the locking carabiner attaching the rope to my harness. It was unlocked. Shit! I'd forgotten to lock it up after we'd dumped the equipment at the cache. If the carabiner had opened accidentally, the rope wouldn't have caught Wyn. He'd have fallen all the way to the bottom.

Wake up! I berated myself. *Get a fucking grip!* This was not a hike up Mount Si. Small things could have huge consequences. Wyn could have plunged to the bottom of that crevasse. There would be a brief description and analysis of his death in the *American Alpine Journal*'s yearly accident report. Other climbers would shake their heads. "His partner was an idiot," they'd say. "He forgot to lock his 'biner. Can you believe it?"

The rope snaked along the glacier. The white surface looked safe, stable, predictable, but it was anything but. Despite my headache, I stayed vigilant.

Soon, we were chugging up Heartbreak Hill. My calves screamed. My head throbbed. I just wanted to get into my sleeping bag and pass out. When we pulled into base camp, most of the other climbers were up and milling around. There was no sign of the group with the dead body. They must have flown out.

At the front of our tent, Wyn stopped and un-roped. Lane and Al walked over to their tent. After everyone had a chance to dump their gear, Wyn called a meeting. He sat on his foam pad, his mirrored sunglasses reflecting back at us.

"We had a close one back there," he said in a clipped, matter-of-fact voice. "I broke through the snow bridge and almost fell into that crevasse. I was lucky. It could have been me on that sled we saw earlier today." He worked his jaw back and forth. "You've *got* to self-arrest in a situation like that, even if we're not sure what's happening."

Lane and Al looked puzzled, as if they didn't know why they had to endure this lecture. I rocked back and forth on my pack, scalded with humiliation, staring at the snow.

"You've got to pay attention. You heard about my buddy, Hans, on the Eiger? He was a brilliant climber. Brilliant! But he didn't tie into his harness. The next thing I knew he was plunging headfirst down the ice hose. He left a bloody smear all the way down the Eiger."

He let that sink in and then resumed. "We've *got* to get our heads into this climb."

No one said anything. Lane puffed his chest out and stretched. Al shot me a sympathetic look. They walked back to their tent and coiled their rope. I went inside our tent, took some ibuprofen and lay down. It felt like someone was pounding a nail through my forehead. A black cloud of self-loathing came over me. Who was I kidding anyway? There was no way I could do this route. I couldn't even self-arrest properly. I shouldn't be up here at all.

I lay in the tent and tried to get some sleep. It must have been eighty degrees in there, but at least I was out of the sun. Wyn went down to the other tents to talk to Kim and his guide friends. I could hear them laughing and joking. He was probably inviting Scott to take my place on the climb. I couldn't care less. In fact, it would be a relief. Then I could abandon the climb.

My eyes felt better when I woke. I rubbed them and put duct tape around the sides of the sunglasses to reduce the glare. The sun was so intense up here that even the darkened lenses and leather side shields of my mountaineering sunglasses couldn't block all of the light. I hoped the expanded side shields would help.

Taking the spaghetti out of the duffel bag, I started dinner. At least I could get that right. In short order, I had the sauce bubbling and a pot of water boiling for the pasta. Uncorking a bottle of Chianti, I called the others to dinner.

There was plenty of spaghetti for everyone—even Lane and Wyn had their fill—but the wine didn't go very far. We supplemented it with a bottle of whiskey. While Wyn and Lane yakked about climbing, I talked with Al about his job at Boeing. Al and I had a lot in common. We were the only ones who'd been married in the group. I sensed we shared a common desire to keep Wyn's more hare-brained ideas under control. Though I'd climbed with Al before, I hadn't spent a lot of time with him. The expedition could serve as an opportunity to become friends.

"How do you like the lazy B?" I asked.

"I hate it," Al said, forking the spaghetti into his mouth.

"What's wrong?"

"Meetings," he said. "No one can do anything without a meeting. They need to meet before they decide to wipe their ass."

"That company's huge," I said. "We have only two full-time employees, and we have a hard time keeping on track."

"It's a joke." Al slurped another noodle. "Every time I turn around my lead is telling me what to do. 'Faster! The customer is waiting! Don't worry if the circuitry needs a redesign. Slap it in! Patch it up!'" Al shook his head. "I want to go off on my own. Design climbing gear."

"Good luck," I said. "There's a lot of competition."

Al shrugged. "I'm almost forty. I figure it's time to start up my own company."

"It's an adventure," I said, shaking my head. "My business is getting squeezed by Mountain Mart."

"But I've got some great ideas," he said, his eyes lighting up. "You could sell them in your shop."

"What are they?"

"Ice Nine," Al said excitedly. "A new line of ice climbing gear."

"Cool. When do you come out with your prototype?"

"Within a year." He rummaged around in the pocket of his parka and took out three forged ice picks that looked like the beaks of predatory birds. "I don't want to be critical, but your selection of gear is too generic. If you want to beat Mountain Mart, you have to carry the latest stuff. My line could put you over the top."

"We'll see." I stood up to get some more spaghetti. I appreciated his enthusiasm but doubted a new line of ice climbing gear could get us back to profitability. As much as I admired his climbing ability, I found Al's personality off-putting. It was irritating to hear him criticize our inventory, something I prided myself on. Still, I tried to keep an open mind. I had to be open to new ideas if I wanted to turn the business around.

Meanwhile, Wyn and Lane were talking climbing.

"What peaks would you recommend in the Alps?" Lane asked. "The Eiger?"

Wyn shook his head. "Too much objective hazard. I'd do Mount Blanc and the Matterhorn. Get a feel for the place first. It's a whole other world—the huts, the guided parties, the history. The climbing is plenty hard—but you can call in a helicopter if you get in trouble. Not like up here."

It was annoying to see how chummy Lane and Wyn had become. Lane was the new protégé. After dinner, they played catch with a plastic football. Al riffed on his harmonica, the notes echoing off the glacier. I tried to call home, but I couldn't get through. I put the cell phone back in the case and walked down to the landing strip.

The last flight of the evening was coming in. The Cessna skidded across the glacier and came to a halt. Another group of climbers jumped out. I fantasized about getting in and flying back to civilization.

Following the path to the end of the runway, I surveyed the panorama of mountains surrounding base camp. Their brooding, mystical quality came to the fore in the endless twilight of the Alaska summer. Despite my anxiety about the climb, the silence and indifference of the peaks calmed me. They put me in touch with a timetable so different from the one I was used to, a timetable measured in millions of years, rather than weeks, days, hours, minutes, seconds. Many things still troubled me: I remembered the overloaded sled bumping and sliding along the glacier. Why was I risking my life to ascend a hunk of ice and rock when I could be home with my family? I had no answers, so I put them to the peaks. Their very vastness seemed a kind of response. The mountains returned nothing of the human. For once, I was grateful for that.

A religious peace settled over the place. Wyn was right. It would be good to get away from the crowds on the West Buttress route. Tomorrow, we'd move up to the cache, leaving the crowds behind.

A breeze started up. Putting my hands in my pockets to warm them, I slowly trudged back to camp, mindful not to step into a crevasse. There was great beauty here, but also great danger. It was hard to separate the two.

SIX

By 4 a.m., pale rays of sun lit the steepled ridges of Mount Foraker directly south of us. There were a few high clouds to the south, but the weather seemed to be holding. My altimeter watch read 7,200 feet. The air temperature was forty degrees. This was our third day on the hill. The plan was to haul the rest of our gear up to the cache. We were leaving base camp behind, cutting the umbilical cord. I hoped I hadn't made the wrong decision in sticking with the expedition.

Lane dug a hole in the snow outside the tent. Inside, he placed a big pot of beef stew he'd made the night before. "It will be waiting for us when we get back," he said, covering it with snow and marking it with a wand.

Such a gesture impressed me, even though I now felt I was competing with Lane for Wyn's approval. Wyn stomped his plastic boots and stared up at the stars. He waited for Al to fix his crampons, then we took off, following yesterday's footsteps, which were faint and melted out. I forgot my worries about the climb and tried to move quickly and efficiently over the snow.

At the main fork, we took a break and hydrated. Al and Lane caught up with us a few minutes later. Wyn lectured everyone about crevasse rescue—then we kept going. He gave a wide berth to the hole where he'd punched through yesterday. Then we crossed the snow bridge where we'd met the party with the dead climber. I could still see their grief-stricken faces, the husband's blistered and frostbitten hand, and hear the ugly scraping of the overloaded sled. Trying to suppress the memory, I felt the rope come taut at my waist. I tensed, thinking Wyn had fallen. But he turned around and looked back at me, wondering why I was slowing. I motioned for him to keep moving, so he turned around and diagonaled up onto the pristine East Fork.

We entered a sublunar world of icefalls, broken rock, and faint stars. In this white wilderness, the world was reduced to elemental simplicity—black rock, dazzlingly white snow, and the merciless sun that would soon fry our faces, burn our necks, and bake our brains.

The glacier was silent except for the sound of our breathing and the scrape of the sleds over the snow. My lungs expanded as I began to feel the results of yesterday's acclimatization. But Wyn's pace began to wear on me. My breathing came faster. My stamina faltered. Just when I thought we'd reached the top of the last ridge, another loomed ahead. I needed to rest, drink, and eat some food.

Wyn glanced back, noticing the drag on the rope, and took a break. When I caught up with him, I looked at my altimeter watch: 8,200 feet. At this height, we were higher than many other summits I'd notched. While waiting for Al and Lane, I drank deeply, trying to down a minimum of four quarts a day to acclimatize. I didn't relish a repeat of yesterday's crushing headache.

A few minutes later, Lane and Al joined us. Al flung his pack down and collapsed on a rock. He swept his greasy, black hair back with his hand and took a drink from his water bottle. His crampons were finally staying on his boots: a minor victory. Lane breathed in and out, deep and steadily, like a bellows. He seemed unbothered by his heavy pack.

While they rested, Wyn and I got ready to move again. It was nearly 6 a.m., and we needed to reach Camp 1 by 8 a.m. It was 800 feet higher and a mile farther. If we rested too long the snow would soften up. Wyn paced back and forth, hitting the snow with his ice axe. Time to move.

As we rose higher, the sky became a deep blue-black, as if we were looking into outer space. The sun appeared from behind the mountains. It reflected off the snow, seeming to hit from everywhere at once. With the tape added to the leather side guards, my glacier glasses shielded my eyes and functioned like blinders on a draft horse. Keep marching.

Regulating my breathing, I managed to keep up with Wyn. We topped a rise and spotted the bamboo wands marking the caches. I tried not to look at them. *Step by step*, I told myself. *Keep it together*. My heart pounded like a jackhammer, but I maintained my pace. Then I was there.

As I approached the cache, a Hershey's candy wrapper skipped across the snow.

"Ravens," Wyn said disgustedly.

Taking off my pack, I picked up a punctured plastic grocery bag. Pieces of chocolate, foil, and paper fell out.

"Lane should have buried these deeper," Wyn said. "I told him this would happen."

Only one chocolate bar was left. They'd also eaten a couple of dinners. We might have to begin rationing some of our food, not a good idea on a climb like Denali where you needed to take in as many calories as you could. "I just wish they'd eaten those freeze-dried eggs you brought."

"Those are good," Wyn insisted. "High in protein."

"Low in taste."

We dug out the rest of the cache. The ravens also had pillaged a pound of butter, leaving a tattered wrapper. Lane would be pissed about that. He was planning to make beef Stroganoff tonight.

We pulled out the rest of the food, fuel, and several stuff sacks filled with clothes. Lane's and Al's gear was sopping wet.

"Rookies," Wyn muttered. "I told them to wrap their clothes in plastic."

After emptying the cache, we used our ice axes to probe the snow for hidden crevasses, then took the wands from the cache and marked out a safe 100-feet-square perimeter. This would allow us to walk around without falling into a crevasse.

As we finished up, Lane and Al arrived in camp. The sun had softened the snow, making the going difficult. After they dropped their packs and untied from the rope, I broke the news about the cache.

"Frigging birds," Lane said.

Wyn was fuming. He handed Al the stuff sack full of sopping clothes. "Next time, wrap these in plastic before you put them in the cache."

"Sorry," Al said. "I should have known better."

Fortunately, the sky was clear. It was 10 a.m., and the temperature was starting to warm up. After we'd set up our tents, Lane and Al strung a clothesline between their ice axes. They hung up their socks, shirts, underwear, and pants, hoping the sun would dry them out. Wyn and I read and napped inside our tent while Al and Lane prepared supper.

"Hey!" Lane hollered.

I stuck my head out of the tent to see a swift black shape explode from the frying pan. Lane wheeled and threw his ice hammer at it. Improbably, the hammer hit it. The big raven flew in an erratic, wobbling circle, its wing broken. Lane chased after it with an ice axe.

"Watch out for crevasses," I shouted after him. "You're going beyond the perimeter."

The bird landed on the snow a few hundred feet away. It flopped around, staining the snow a brilliant red. Lane threw his other ice axe at it, missed, and then chased it. The raven tried to fly away, but Lane caught it and wrung its neck. It flapped, squawked, and finally went limp. He carried the bird triumphantly back to camp.

"Anyone have a recipe for raven?" he asked, holding it up.

The bird's black feathers were ruffled and speckled with blood. It was an impressive bird, with a huge black beard, gleaming dark eyes, and large fleshy talons. It was covered with lice. Lane threw it down when he saw this.

"Get it out of here," I said, uneasy about the dead bird. "Go throw it in a crevasse."

Wyn emerged from the tent. "What's going on?"

Lane pointed to the bird.

"Why did you kill it?" Wyn asked.

"Payback."

Wyn examined the bird closely, felt the point of its talon. "Well, it's too late now to do anything about it. Bury it in a crevasse. Don't kill any more of them. The Athabascan Indians considered ravens tricksters. They're sacred birds."

"What do you mean?" Lane said. "It stole our chocolate and almost ate our dinner."

"If we dig our caches deep enough, they can't steal it." Wyn grabbed the dead raven by the foot. "John, can you tie in with me?" We roped up and walked over to a crevasse a few hundred feet away. Tossing the bird into the crevasse, Wyn mumbled a few words. I made the sign of the cross. We walked back to camp in silence.

"Dinner's ready," Lane announced. Al ladled the noodles onto our plates. Lane poured sauce over the top of them.

"*Bon appetit*," Lane said.

"What?" Al asked.

"It means 'Eat well' in French."

Al grunted. "*Bonjour* to you, too."

Wyn and I nodded but said little. The raven's death had subdued us. As we ate dinner, another raven landed on a rock one hundred yards from camp. I wondered if this was the dead bird's mate. It perched on the boulder, cocked its head, and watched us eat.

"Krraaak," it called and flapped its wings. It gave me the creeps having the bird watching us. Lane threw a snowball at it. The bird flapped off, but then returned to its perch. It kept its vigil until dusk, then flew away.

Later, clouds moved in. The temperature dropped. As I lay in my sleeping bag, I tried to imagine what Jill and Andy were doing now—probably having dinner, a bath, a *Cat in the Hat* book. Then my thoughts drifted back to the raven—its bright, malicious eye growing vague, glassy, opaque.

Snow fell most of the night. By morning, it had covered all of our gear. Temperatures were in the twenties. The wind was light enough to bring the wind chill down to ten degrees, but not enough to keep us in camp.

After getting dressed, we prepared a breakfast of cereal, raisins, and powdered milk. As we ate and sipped coffee, we listened to the light tick of the snowflakes against the nylon fabric of the tent. A loud fart came from the other tent.

"The Stroganoff is taking effect," Wyn said dryly.

"Yeah," I said, trying to laugh. My head was pounding, and my nose was running. It was either altitude or a cold. Or both. After breakfast, I asked Lane for Vitamin C from the first-aid kit. Then Wyn loaded up the sleds, again putting most of the stuff sacks full of food, climbing gear, and other equipment on his. I didn't stop him.

Wyn tied into the rope and sled and got ready to go. Al and Lane were right behind him. They were in high spirits, laughing, and thoroughly enjoying themselves. They seemed to be acclimatizing well, as if they were on a day hike, not on an expedition to a high arctic peak. I dreaded being the weak link again. As usual, Wyn and I moved out first. We stomped through a layer of light, squeaky powder.

"Watch out for crevasses," Wyn shouted back at the rest of us. "This snow will conceal them."

"Roger," Lane said.

The valley narrowed as we headed toward the base of the south face. Peaks stood out in stark relief like immense, chipped arrowheads. The roar of avalanches boomed and echoed ominously around the valley. Most of them were far away, but they put me on edge, and maybe Wyn, too—he stayed in the middle of the glacier, avoiding the ice and snow-spackled walls of Kahiltna Peak to the north.

As we climbed higher, the new snow deepened. It looked lovely and peaceful, a land of confectioner's sugar, but it could easily hide a crevasse. Wyn moved carefully, scanning the terrain for a depression or fissure that might indicate a crevasse. He probed the snow occasionally with his ice axe but didn't find anything. Lane and Al had crept up behind me, sniffing our trail like huskies.

Despite Wyn's deliberate pace, the altitude began to get to me. I moved slowly, as if underwater, causing Wyn to jerk the rope. I was acclimatizing slowly, holding up the group. I had a headache, nausea, dizziness. I'd never had a bout of altitude sickness like this before. He turned around to see how I was doing. I knew by the set of his mouth that he wanted to move faster, but he didn't say anything. Instead, he turned his attention to the snow conditions.

A loud report in the distance signaled the onslaught of another avalanche up the valley. Tons of snow broke off the side of the cliff and cascaded down onto the glacier. The debris traveled across the glacier and up the other side several hundred yards in front of us. The resulting wind dusted us with a fine mist of snow. The tiny crystals made me sneeze.

"Wyn, should we turn around?" I yelled.

"No, we need to pick up the pace, John," he said.

I nodded. I felt too tired to push the point. A few minutes later, we climbed up and over the avalanche debris. It looked like enormous frozen curds of cottage cheese. My pace slowed as I picked my way through chunks of ice as big as refrigerators. My head felt like an over-inflated balloon.

"Can Al and I go ahead?" Lane called to Wyn. "We have to move faster."

"Just don't get out of sight," Wyn said. "Is your sled rigged properly?"

"Of course." Lane walked by me.

Al clapped me on the shoulder as he passed. "It's just like a marathon, buddy. Take it slow and easy."

I nodded and yet felt patronized. Wyn frowned as they moved ahead. He hated to relinquish the lead. "Watch out for crevasses."

Al raised his ice axe in reply. They moved steadily up the valley. They obviously relished the chance to prove themselves by getting out front. I couldn't blame them. Besides, I wouldn't be holding them up.

Lane and Al set a brisk pace up the headwall of the glacier. This was the last steep section before Face Camp where the real technical difficulties began. It would have been easier to follow the glacier right up under the base of the Cassin Ridge, but so much avalanche debris was releasing it would have been suicidal. Instead, Lane took a page from Wyn by following a line up the center of the glacier. The angle of the ice rose steeply, making climbing arduous, but the conditions were safer. As the glacial ice buckled, it created a complex web of crevasses. Lane wove between them, picking a line that avoided most of the objective danger.

There was no way I could keep up with them. The balloon in my head kept getting bigger. I kept my feet moving, slowly but steadily. I was almost to Face Camp. I fantasized about getting into the tent, burrowing into my down bag, and falling into a catatonic slumber.

As the glacier steepened, I focused just on the snow in front of me, not bothering to look ahead to see how close we were. Al and Lane's path ascended the snout of the glacier, zigzagging dizzily upward. My lungs burned. My body ached. My head felt ready to burst.

I leaned over against my ice axe. It felt like someone was playing a pipe organ inside my head. Why was I busting my ass to climb this stupid peak? What was I trying to prove? I rested and caught my breath.

"John, can we pick up the pace?" Wyn shouted. "We need to get up there before the glacier softens up."

"I'm going as fast as I can," I said.

"I thought I told you to get in shape," Wyn said.

"I didn't have time," I said.

Wyn shook his head in disgust. He turned around and walked back to me. "Here," he said, dumping his pack. "Let me carry some of that gear."

"I don't need help, Wyn," I said. "I can carry it."

He ignored me, taking three gallon fuel cans from my sled and lashing them to his.

"I'm not your client, Wyn."

"I never said that you were." He hoisted his pack. "I'm just trying to solve a problem."

So that's what I was now—a problem. Who was I kidding? I might as well turn around right now. But I didn't have the energy. So I kept going, putting one step in front of another, closing in on the high basin that would serve as Face Camp. The last mile seemed endless. When we reached their tent, I un-roped, helped Wyn set up our tent, crawled into my sleeping bag, and fell asleep, totally spanked.

SEVEN

Snow sagged against the red fabric of the tent. Knocking it off, I unleashed a cascade of hoar frost from the tent walls. It landed in my hair and on my neck. Shrinking back into my sleeping bag, I glanced at my watch: 4 a.m. I must have slept through dinner. The pounding in my head had eased, but I still felt shot. I was ready to hang it up. I just didn't think I could keep up with the others. But how would I break it to Wyn that I wanted to bail? I turned it over in my head, finding no easy way to do it. At 5 a.m., I started up the stove and made coffee.

Across from me, Wyn's blond hair looked like a bird's nest. The stubble on his chin had grown thick and ragged. He snorted, rolled over, and propped his head with his hand.

"Want some coffee?" I asked him.

"Yeah."

I handed him a cup and sipped my own. "How does the weather look?"

"Should be okay," he said. "We can rest up today and then head up the face tomorrow."

"Wyn," I said, hesitating. "I'm not sure I want to keep going."

"What?"

"I'm pretty wasted," I said. "I'm not sure I can keep up."

"Give it time, John," he said. "You'll get there."

"But I was dead weight yesterday."

"You've always taken a long time to acclimatize," he said philosophically.

"But what if I don't?" I asked. "I don't want to get altitude sickness up on the face."

Wyn blew on his coffee.

"How about we do the West Buttress route to acclimatize and then head up this route."

"That's bullshit, John," Wyn said. "We've had this discussion before. We don't have time to do both routes. You told Jill we'd be back in a month."

"I'm just not sure I can do this route," I said. "I think it's out of my league."

"Of course you can do it," he said. "You're going with *me*. You're giving up before we've even started."

"I'm just trying to be realistic," I said.

He grunted dismissively. "You're psyching yourself out."

"What do you mean?" I said. "What about yesterday?"

"You'll get there." He knocked me on the shoulder and gave me the big Wyn gap-toothed grin. "I've got confidence in you, buddy."

Unzipping the sleeping bag, I pulled on my Gore-Tex pants. My back still ached, but I wasn't breathing as hard as yesterday. Outside, clouds had dissipated, providing clear views of the full extent of the face, ringed by remote, fantastic, snow-spackled peaks. With its jagged peaks and baroque flutings of snow and ice, it looked like the throne room of the mountain gods.

I brought out my foam pad and coffee. Wyn came out and sat down next to me. He took out his binoculars and glassed the route.

"How does it look?" I asked.

"I think it'll go," he said, adjusting the focus of the lens.

"When have you ever said a route wouldn't go?"

He shrugged. "I guess I'm an optimist."

"You guess?" I laughed. "When it comes to climbing routes, you're a Pollyanna."

"So what are you?" he asked. "A pessimist?"

"A pragmatist," I said, sipping the coffee. "I just don't want to get my ass kicked."

"You can't always help that," he said, laughing. "Besides, epics make for great slide shows."

"As long as you survive them."

"There is that."

We passed the binoculars back and forth, watching the pattern of avalanches and rock fall, trying to get a feel for the safest way through it.

The south face of Denali represents one of the biggest prizes in American climbing, an immense canvas on which elite climbers painted their vertical masterpieces. If we pulled off this route, it would add yet another notch to Wyn's career and put me in pretty select company, too. I had no illusions about surpassing Wyn, but this route would serve as the capstone of my career, as long as it didn't kill me.

I knew Al also wanted it bad. He had done dozens of hard frozen waterfalls and one high-altitude ascent—Aconcagua. Now he'd try to put the two games together. The route would put him on the map as a serious ice specialist at altitude and kick-start his gear business. Outsiders might care less about our route, but within the climbing community, it would be huge.

Lane, new to climbing, didn't seem to grasp the alpine significance of the route, but I hoped it would bring out his inherent competitiveness—with himself, with Wyn, with the mountain. If he could harness that, it would propel him to the top, despite his lack of experience. If it overwhelmed him, it might destroy the team and our expedition. But I didn't think that would happen. The ascent would mark him as an up-and-comer on the local scene. With his medical training and overall strength, he could parlay the ascent into invitations to join Himalayan expeditions. Like the rest of us, he had a lot riding on the climb.

Sitting back on my foam pad, I glassed the south face—a massive wall of ice, snow, and clean orange granite. Many famous climbers had inscribed their names here. To our left, the Cassin Ridge, a jagged rocky spine, split the face in two. Climbed in 1961 by the famed Italian Riccardo Cassin, the Cassin Ridge is on every top climber's tick list. To the right of it, a smaller, broken, indistinct ridge shoots up the face. This ridge forms the bulk of the American Direct route, climbed in 1967 but still considered one of the classics of the mountain, even harder and more prestigious than the Cassin. We would climb part of this route on our way to the top, but would open up new ground lower on the face, and then ascend the last three rock buttresses below the southeast ridge. On peaks like Denali, you could seldom establish a completely new route. Previous climbers had taken the best lines. It took someone with Wyn's eye to find new routes and figure out how to climb them. If we could pull off this ascent, we would become part of mountaineering's pantheon.

Lane and Al emerged from their tent, blinking and rubbing their eyes. They spread their foam pads out next to us and sat down to take a look at the route, glistening in the sun. Now everyone had a chance to wrap his mind around it.

"Whoa," Lane said. "It's steep."

"Yeah, but it's foreshortened from here," Wyn said. "It's not as bad as it looks."

Lane scratched the stubble of his beard.

"Look at that avalanche," Al said as a slide cascaded down the face, falling to the right of the American ridge we had chosen as our line of attack. The slide poured down the snow slopes but missed the ridge, dusting it with some powdery snow. Just as Wyn had predicted, the top of the ridge got little debris, although it was swept on both sides by avalanches. It looked like a reasonably safe line up an incredibly dangerous face.

We were now at 11,400 feet, directly in line with the American ridge. There was no easy way up it, and no easy way to retreat from it. Rising 8,000 feet above us, the buttress presented a challenging mix of fifty- to sixty-degree snow and ice slopes and near-vertical sections of granite. Because of its southern exposure, the ice had melted and refrozen, forming a bulletproof surface that gleamed like stainless steel. As intimidating as this looked, I knew that such slopes would take ice screws well and provide a stable surface for our crampons.

The main problem was avalanches. Snow falling up high would bond poorly with the hard ice, triggering regular avalanches. Most of the debris passed to the right of our ridge route, but smaller avalanches occasionally hit close to our line. Our best chance of avoiding them would be to climb at night and hole up in bivy spots during the day.

I stared at it, trying to piece together the route with the arrows and lines Wyn had marked on the photograph. The route was intimidating, but it didn't look like a suicide mission.

"I think it'll go," I said, echoing Wyn's assessment. As soon as I'd said this, my stomach went queasy.

Lane grabbed the glasses. I could tell by the way he kicked the snow with his boots and squinted up at the route that he had his doubts about it. "Shit," Lane said, shaking his head. "It's full on."

"It's not that bad." Wyn came up next to him and pointed out the route. "See, there's the line we want to take. It starts out at the base of the ridge. It goes left up that snow ramp."

Lane whistled and handed the glasses back to Wyn. Then he went inside the tent.

"The start won't be too difficult," Wyn said, seeming not to notice Lane's departure. "I'm more worried about the next section. We'll head straight up from there, moving through that mixed ground. There will be lots of gear placements in the rock section, but there could be some rock fall."

"I'd prefer to place gear in the rock," Al said, clearing his throat. "I'm not crazy about snow anchors. They can melt out."

"Right," Wyn said. "That could be a problem on the lower section."

"Should we fix that section or just move through it?" Al asked.

"We should fix it," Wyn said, eyes riveted to the route. "I don't see any way around it. We still need to acclimatize. We have no idea what might hit us when we're up there."

"Isn't that the truth," I said, remembering our last attempt on the peak. "We got spanked by the weather. We need an exit strategy."

"So let's fix the first half of the face with static line," Wyn said. "We can do a modified expedition style, putting in a camp or two, working our way up step by step, and then shoot up the rest of the face alpine style." He slapped his palms together. "How does that sound?"

"That'll mean a lot of load carrying," Al said. "A lot of jumaring."

"Do you have a better plan?" Wyn turned to study him.

"Not really," Al said. "I like the idea of doing it alpine style all the way, but it's so damn big." He glanced toward their tent and lowered his voice. "And for the sake of Lane's and . . ." he hesitated and thought better of saying my name. "We might want to take it slow."

"How about you, John?"

"Given our party, that seems the best approach." I liked the idea of getting accustomed to the exposure and altitude on the face. Doing the peak alpine style straight through to the top just didn't seem possible for me.

"So we have a consensus?" Wyn asked.

"Except for Lane," I said.

Al flashed a grin. "Lane will come around."

"Great," Wyn said, putting down the glasses. "Let's get on it."

I took the binoculars and glassed over the route. "I can't believe nobody's done it yet."

Wyn laughed. "Maybe nobody else is dumb enough to try it."

—

When we left camp at 2 a.m., the face was silent. The only sounds were the crunch of our crampons and the rhythm of our breathing. My stomach knotted up as we approached the face. Wyn was out front—probing occasionally with his ice axe, alert for rock fall or avalanches. Our view of the lower half improved as we got closer to the base of the route, but the overhanging bulge of the ridge obscured the upper face. I focused on getting up to the bergschrund, a fissure in the glacier near the base of the face.

The air was cold and still. We had been lucky with the weather so far, but I hoped a big storm didn't hit us high on the face. Taking another step, I noticed an occasional rock imbedded in the snow. No stones fell now, but they would probably start up during the warm part of the day. Another reason for climbing at night.

The rope tugged against my harness. Wyn was moving again. I hurried to keep up with him. I was acclimatizing pretty well, and I was beginning to get my strength and endurance back. But my stomach still bothered me. A few minutes later, I stopped and retched.

"You okay?" Wyn asked, looking at his watch. He probably was kicking himself for agreeing to take me on the trip.

I nodded and wiped my mouth with my glove. Pressure breathing steadily, I regained my composure, drank some water, and sucked on a lemon drop. Then I kept going.

As the face steepened below the bergschrund, Wyn kicked the front points into the ice. He took an ice screw, hollowed out a spot in the ice with the adze of his axe, and then threaded in the screw. He did this quickly and efficiently. No wasted motion. No hesitation. It was reassuring just to watch him. He attached a sling and carabiner to it and clipped into our rope. Now we had protection in case of a slip.

A hundred yards below us, Al and Lane zig-zagged up the glacier. Lane carried the large spool of static line, which he'd volunteered to haul. He was breathing hard but didn't seem too bothered by the weight. In load carrying, he found a way to contribute.

The rope tugged me out of my reverie. Wyn moved up the slope and reached the bergschrund. He moved left, stopped, and looked around. He moved back to the right. He kicked loose some ice chips, which flew back down toward me. One of them glanced off my helmet.

"Hey!" I yelled.

"Sorry!" he said.

He moved back to the left and sunk another ice screw. "On belay," he shouted. I moved up behind him, kicking the front of one crampon into the snow and keeping the other crampon flat on the snow, a modified French crampon technique. I alternated feet to keep from exhausting myself. My rusty skills were coming back. Finally, I reached the small ledge near the bergschrund.

"Take a look at this view." He made a sweeping gesture with his hand.

I dumped my load next to his, clipped into the anchor, and looked back down the face. Our red tents were mere dots on the glacier below.

As Wyn had suspected, a small hollow in back of the bergschrund accommodated most of our gear. This was a perfect staging area for the route ahead. Enlarging it with my ice axe, I ensured we had plenty of room for our equipment.

A few minutes later, Al emerged from below the lip of the bergschrund. He wore a haggard expression. He breathed raggedly and moved listlessly. Lane was right behind him.

"You should have waited to come up," Wyn chided him.

"We were tired of waiting," Lane said.

"Clip into the anchor," Wyn ordered. "You can dump your gear after John finishes chopping."

I cleared out the ice chips with my snow shovel.

"That was a bitch," Lane said, handing me the static line. "Reminded me of the fire training academy."

I shoved the spool in the back of the hollow and arranged the rest of the gear. Then we dangled our legs over the edge of the bergschrund for a few minutes to let Al catch his breath. Passing a liter of water back and forth, we ate squares of chocolate and took in the amazing scenery.

The steep triangles of Mount Hunter and Mount Foraker stood out in glistening relief as the morning sun lit up their flanks. Moments like this made all the risks of the sport worthwhile.

After returning to advanced base camp around 7 a.m., Wyn wanted to do one more carry. The face had been silent, and we never knew how long we could count on good weather up there. If we got one more carry in, he argued, we'd be in position to start climbing the face. I didn't have the energy to disagree with him, so we loaded up for one last haul.

As we approached the face, I stashed my jacket, because I was getting too warm. When we got under the face, a rock flew by, just missing me.

"Rock!" I yelled at Wyn.

He raised his ice axe in acknowledgment. Lane and Al were right on our tail. As I looked back toward them, I noticed something out of the corner of my eye. A puff of white exploded near the top of the face. It moved in what looked like slow motion. A large avalanche had released. We were near the base of the arête but could be caught in the debris.

"Run!" I shouted.

Wyn looked up and started sprinting to the left of the ridge. Lane and Al were right behind us. They started running, too. The slide sounded like distant thunder. It rocketed down the upper face, heading for the gully to our right. The rumble grew deep, strong, ominous. I kept tripping on my crampons, falling, and getting up again.

The slide sounded like a 747. The blast of wind flattened me. Wiggling out of my pack, I covered my head with it. Snow cascaded down the face. The world went white. Ice crystals stung my nostrils. I burrowed deeper under the pack. The roar passed over me like a visitation. Bracing for the impact, I felt shards of ice glance off my leg. I curled up in a ball, staying under the pack until the rumble subsided. A cloud of powder snow, fine as flour, hissed around me. Standing up, I had trouble getting my bearings. The world had gone white.

"Wyn!" I yelled, yanking on the rope. "Where are you?"

"Here!" I followed the rope toward him. He was in self-arrest position at the end of it.

"John, you okay?"

"I think so."

"What about Al and Lane?"

"I don't know," I said. "Come back down to me."

Picking my way through the debris, I spotted Lane's red parka. He was lying on the snow, his ice axe dug into the surface. I couldn't tell if he was hurt or not. "You okay?" I asked, helping him up.

Lane spat snow out of his mouth. "I'm alive."

"Where's Al?"

"Back there," he said, pointing. "He got swept up into the avalanche. We need to get to him quick."

We followed the rope under avalanche debris, around several chunks of ice and across to the other side of the chute. We found Al on his back behind a large block of ice. He was panting hard and trying to sit up.

I went over to him and helped him up. "Al, are you okay?"

He couldn't speak; he just kept panting. I checked his pulse. It was fast and light. He sat with his arms on his knees and shook his head.

Wyn and Lane caught up with me. "Is he okay?"

"I don't know," I said. "He won't talk."

"Al?" Lane shook him by the shoulder. He grabbed his pulse. "He might be in shock."

Al's face was dusted with snow, his glasses were knocked askew, and his lip was bleeding. He coughed and spat out a long rope of blood.

"Let's get him out of here," Wyn warned. "There may be another slide."

We dragged him out of the path of the avalanche. Sure enough, another slide came down a few minutes later, inundating the area where we'd stood. We put a down jacket on Al and gave him some water. He pushed up his glasses with his index finger. "Thought I was a goner."

"Where's your pack?" Lane asked.

"Ditched it," Al said. "It was dragging me down." Al took another swig of water, exhaled loudly, and rapped his knuckles on the bright green plastic helmet. "Glad I was wearing this."

"How did you get out of the slide?" Wyn asked.

Al stopped to take a breath. "Swam. Got up to the surface, and then to the side." He turned to Lane. "I owe you."

"Returning the favor," Lane said.

We all sat there shivering. We wanted to rest, but we needed to move. There would be more avalanches coming down the face. We couldn't relax, not even for a minute.

"You're one tough bastard," Wyn said, slapping Al on the shoulder. "You, too, Lane."

Al nodded and slowly rose to his feet.

Lane grinned fiercely and shook his fist at the peak. "We're going to knock you off!"

As if unimpressed with the threat, the face released another slide. It was smaller than the previous avalanche and dissipated before it reached us, but it reminded me of the precariousness of our position.

EIGHT

While Lane bandaged Al's lip, Wyn and I searched for his pack. The snow had set like concrete. If the slide had buried any one of us, it likely would have been our tomb. I removed one chunk, then another. Even with insulated mitts, my hands grew cold and clumsy.

Taking a break to catch my breath, I watched Wyn digging systematically in an ever-enlarging circle like a terrier searching for a bone. As the sun rose higher, the face released a barrage of snow, ice, and stone fall. The rocks whizzed past my head like dark, malicious bees.

"We need to get moving," I said.

"Not without his pack," Wyn said.

"We should get him out of here," Lane said, finishing up with Al. "We could all get hit by another slide."

"Just a minute," Wyn yelled. "He can't make his carries without that pack."

A small rock glanced off the top of my helmet. "I don't care!" I shouted. "We'll figure out something. Let's go!"

A volley of rocks pelted us. Wyn covered his face with his arm. He stood up, reluctantly giving up the search.

I led down slope, pulling Wyn away from the face. Al hobbled along at an agonizingly slow pace. The crack of another slide put me into overdrive, sprinting as fast as I could. Seconds later, I turned to see the slide inundate the spot where we'd searched for Al's pack.

As we emerged from the shadow of the south face, the temperature climbed from the low teens to the seventies. The sun turned the snow-spackled walls of the cirque into a giant reflector oven. Sweat trickled down my face, stung my eyes, and drenched my pile underwear, but I didn't bother to stop and shed my parka. I just wanted to get as far away from the face as possible. Fear made my mouth taste like cardboard.

After slogging the last hundred yards to camp, I dumped my pack and pulled off my parka and pants. I had to sit and pressure breathe for several minutes to stop the throbbing in my head.

"We were lucky," Wyn said. "It could have been worse."

"Yeah, we could've gotten killed," I said.

"Now we know the path that avalanches take," he said calmly.

"But the avalanche wasn't supposed to hit that side of the ridge."

"The mountain had other plans." Wyn shrugged. "I made a mistake."

I kicked off my crampons in disgust.

He looked at me tolerantly as if I were a disobedient child. "If we travel at night, we'll be fine."

"How can you be so confident?"

"We had no problem until the second carry," he said, squinting up at the route.

"This is crazy, Wyn." I rocked back and forth on my foam pad. "I can't justify the risk."

"Then go home," he said blandly. "But if you bail, you can forget the slide show."

"Are you threatening me?"

"No, I'm being realistic. No one is going to watch a slide show of a trip that didn't get beyond advanced base camp."

"Of course, but..."

"If you really want to do this..." Wyn looked away from me. "You have to put it on the line." Then he looked back up at the face. "There's a reason no one else has done this route. It's damned hard. No one is going to give it to you. You have to take it."

"That's easy for you to say," I said. "You don't have a wife and kid at home."

He laughed. "Despite rumors to the contrary, I have no interest in committing suicide."

"You pay your money..." I said.

"And you take your chance," he said matter-of-factly. He stood up, stretched, and walked down to meet Al. He put his arm around him and helped Lane bring him up the last few hundred feet. Al's breathing was fast and shallow. After I helped him untie from the rope and take off his harness, he collapsed in the snow next to the tent. I removed his crampon straps and then his boots. Lane helped him into the tent. He came out a few minutes later.

"He's okay," he said. "I took his pulse."

"Did he twist his knee?" Wyn asked.

"We'll see," Lane said. "Right now, he's just scared."

"Understandable." Wyn brought a mug of tea to the tent. "Hey, Al, want something to drink?"

There was some rustling around in the tent. Al's haggard face appeared at the door.

"Thanks." He took the mug and went back into the tent. The rest of us huddled around the entrance, drinking tea, catching our breath, and looking back up at the face. Sunlight slanted across it, revealing a broken ridge of ledges, overhanging rock, and hard, blue water ice. A crooked line began to appear, threading its way through the bowling alleys of avalanches and rock fall. Slides continued to hiss down the face, racing across the wide, steep open areas, yet mostly missing the narrow path we would have to follow.

I tried to commit the various sections into memory—the avalanche-swept lower face, the mixed rock and ice climbing of the middle face, the pure ice climbing above, and finally the rock buttresses that guarded the summit ridge. It would be difficult and dangerous, especially on the lower half, but it looked possible. If we climbed at night past the avalanche chutes, we could proceed fairly safely. It was a vertical distance of 6,000 feet, through some of the wildest terrain on the planet.

Wyn glassed the face with his binoculars, checking and counterchecking his observations with his map and photographs. "Sorry," Wyn said. "Thought we'd be okay to make that last carry."

"It's not your fault," I said. "No one knew."

"But we could have guessed," Lane said, an edge in his voice. His cheeks were red and his nose was peeling. "Al almost bought it. He lost his pack. I think we need to reevaluate our decision-making process."

Wyn put the binoculars down. "What do you mean?"

"You dictate too many of our decisions," Lane said, chewing a piece of gum. "We need to work by consensus."

Wyn stared at him. "I'm fine with you guys having input, but you don't have enough climbing experience to make the call."

"I'm not talking just about climbing experience," Lane said. "Remember, you brought me along for my medical and rescue knowledge."

"Yes, but you don't have enough *climbing* experience to evaluate risk," Wyn countered. "That's what we're talking about."

"It's not as simple as that." Lane let out a small derisive laugh. "There's more than one way to solve a problem."

"Not always." Wyn stared at him. "Sometimes there's only one way, and sometimes you don't have time to talk about it. Sometimes you simply have to act and trust in the experience of your leader." Wyn looked back up at the south face. The ice glistened in the full glare of the midday sun. The ridges bristled and beetled over us, gleaming menacingly.

"From now on, we'll climb at night," Wyn said. "That okay with you, Lane?"

"That would be an improvement," Lane said, avoiding looking at Wyn. "If we move in the middle of the day, we're going to get hammered."

"What about up high?" I asked. "We may need to climb during the day, especially on summit day."

"True," Wyn said. "But up high there will be less avalanche danger. I'm talking about the lower face."

"It will also be really cold up high," Lane said. "The snow should be stable."

"Maybe," Wyn said. "Depends how it bonds with the underlying layers. We'll reevaluate the conditions as we go. Any questions?" Wyn looked from me to Lane. Wyn was shorter than both of us, but he had an intensity that made him difficult to oppose. I nodded. Lane raised an eyebrow. The mutiny was quelled, at least for now.

"Can you guys stop arguing and get me some more tea?" Al emerged from the tent, blinking his eyes, and limping slightly. Wyn poured hot water into his cup. "Shit, what a headache. I feel like Humpty Dumpty."

"You're lucky you aren't," Wyn said.

Al pushed his glasses up with his finger. "Glad I took swimming lessons."

"What do you mean?" I asked.

"When the avalanche hit, I started dog paddling," he said, grinning.

"What were you doing?" Lane asked incredulously.

"Dog paddling," Al said, as if it were the most obvious thing in the world. He furiously mimed the motions with his hands. "That's what got me through."

We were so wired from the near escape we laughed as if he were Jerry Lewis. There was something ludicrous about imagining Al dog paddling through this huge avalanche, his sleepy eyes and long, basset hound face barely staying above the debris.

I wiped the tears from my eyes. Wyn covered his mouth with his hand. Lane coughed, trying to get enough air to keep laughing. Al looked innocent, as if he didn't know what the hilarity was about.

"Al, you're one lucky dog," Wyn said as the laughing subsided.

Al grinned as if he were personally responsible for his luck.

When I looked back up at the mountain, the graceful tracery of a mare's tail cloud had appeared over the peak.

"It looks like a front is moving in," Wyn said, looking in the same direction. "Now that we've gotten our swimming lessons, why don't we build some walls around the tents?"

After finishing the tea, we got to work. My back ached, but I helped Wyn stomp down the snow next to our tent to compact it. Taking out the aluminum snow saw with serrated teeth, I cut the snow into bricks the size of cinder blocks. I handed the blocks to Wyn, who built a three-foot-high wall to protect the tents from high winds. I had to stop to catch my breath and keep my temples from throbbing, but at least I was starting to acclimatize. Wyn waited impatiently for me.

"Keep going," he said. "That storm's coming in."

Sinking the saw into the snow, I fashioned another block. Before I had a chance to recover, he was back. He had a way of turning the simplest tasks into competitive events. I wasn't going to ask him to slow down. I'd match his pace. I cut another block for him. The deeper I went into the snow, the easier it became. Slice one side. Pressure breath. Slice other side. Breath. Finish sides. Breath. Slice the bottom half. Breath. He was waiting for me when I finished the block. My head started spinning, but I wouldn't stop. I wanted to prove something.

"Don't I get a coffee break?" I handed him another block.

"You're a salaried employee." He smiled indulgently, took the block, and placed it along with the others. "You'll get your stock options."

"They're probably all underwater."

He began chinking the gaps between the blocks. This allowed me to catch up. When he came back, I was ready with another block. By mid-afternoon, the wall was finished. I hoped it would be enough. Winds had been clocked at more than one hundred miles per hour on Denali.

After dinner, we sat in the vestibule of the tent and watched clouds race across the face, rip apart, and then reform. They seemed to chase and catch each other, then disintegrate, form, and reform, with endless variations. It was mesmerizing to watch, even though they heralded a storm. The temperature plummeted. Snow started falling. Shivering in my down parka, I got into my bag and went to sleep. At 11 p.m., I woke to hear the tent flapping so hard I thought it would shred. But the fabric stayed taut and durable; the snow walls took the brunt of the wind.

I tried to go back to sleep, but to no avail. Tossing and turning, I fretted about the route ahead. How would we get above the bergschrund, essentially a giant crevasse? How could we avoid avalanches on the lower face? Would we be able to work our way up the middle of the face? How would I perform on the rock buttresses below the summit ridge? It was too much to contemplate.

The storm raged throughout the next day. Winds gusted to probably seventy miles per hour. Snow accumulated and flattened the sides of the tent. Wyn darted outside periodically to shovel it off. I took my turn a few times but stayed in the tent most of the day, reading *Don Quixote*, a book I'd started reading in college. I figured it would be appropriate for our journey, the ultimate quixotic quest.

I enjoyed reading about the improbable Don Quixote and his sidekick Sancho Panza, but then the pace slowed and I put down the book. Sitting up in my sleeping bag, I looked around at the interior of the tent. It was heaped with socks, pile jackets, mittens, double boot liners, packages of food, granola bars, water bottles, and climbing gear. It reeked of sweat, farts, dirty socks, food, gasoline, and sunscreen, all mixed together into an aggressive, offensive odor.

The outside world didn't intrude much up here, which in some ways was great. No phone, no email, no bills. We were locked in a bubble. There was nothing other than the 8 p.m. radio call to bring us news of the outside world, and it was only about the weather. No tanking economy, wars, famine, or starvation. But there was nothing else, either. The yellow walls of the tent began to close in on me. It was small to begin with, but now it felt claustrophobic.

Wyn sat up in his sleeping bag reading *Thus Spake Zarathustra*.

Another gust of wind hammered the tent. I put on my down parka, opened the door, and stepped out into the gale. The wind almost knocked me over. Struggling to maintain my balance in my down booties, I dialed our home number on my cell phone. Nothing. No response. I considered trying again but didn't want to wear out the batteries: we might need the phone in an emergency. The wind whipped across the surface of the snow, creating ground blizzards that came at me from every direction. I felt trapped. I considered going over to Lane and Al's tent but didn't want to posthole through the two feet of new snow.

I crawled back into the tent.

"Any luck?" Wyn asked. He was being conciliatory, which I appreciated.

"No," I said, stowing the phone in my pack. "Not yet."

"Try up higher. It'll be clear as a bell."

"I hope so."

"Are you worried about them?"

"Not really, I just miss them."

He went back to reading his book.

Burrowing into the sleeping bag, I took out my wallet photo of them. I admired Jill's green eyes and how they looked as if they were spaced too close together. Andy had buried his head into Jill's shoulder and smiled shyly at the camera. I stood in the background, my arms around both of them, grinning like the proud father, the patriarch, the family man—with little hint of the conflicts that lay beneath this perfect, airbrushed portrait.

The photo made me think I had the best of both worlds. While I'd married and veered off the climbing fast track, Wyn had taken the other direction. In the intervening years, he had hardened into a caricature of himself—there were creases in the corners of his eyes, sun damage on his nose, wrinkles around his mouth, and a sore left knee that he claimed could predict the weather. All of the peaks, the partners, the deaths, and the effort had taken their toll on him; he looked older than thirty-five.

Wyn put down his book and took out his chessboard. "How about a game?" he said.

"Why not?" I said.

I played the match without conviction and quickly paid for it. I took his bishop, which exposed me to his queen. Three moves later he checkmated me.

"Play again?" he asked.

I agreed, even though I didn't really want to. The wind punched and battered the tent; we wouldn't be doing any climbing today. He thrashed me in the next game. I got angry. I used to beat him at chess, but like so many other things, I didn't have time to play anymore. Still, I agreed to a third game. Wyn was a sucker for the quick, lightning strike. If I showed more patience, I might win.

"Do you think you'll ever get married, Wyn?" I asked, making the opening pawn move. I knew this question would distract him.

"Doubt it," he said.

"Why?"

"It makes people into fools." He grinned, advancing his pawn.

I frowned.

"Not you, of course, but a lot of people."

"Thanks a lot," I said,

"You asked me," he said.

"What ever happened with Kim?" I said, using my pawn up to counter his.

"We hung out together for a couple months, but then I went to Patagonia. Everything was great until I headed out the door." He massaged his cheek with his hand. "She begged. She pleaded. She threw all of my climbing gear out on the lawn and stomped on it." He laughed. "She thought she could change me."

Then he took my knight. The bastard had lulled me into feeling sorry for him and neglecting the game.

I swore softly, determined to pay attention.

"She's great," he said, studying his next move. "I'm probably an idiot not to marry her."

"So you'll just keep climbing?" I scanned the board, seeking a weakness.

"Why not?" he said, advancing his pawn. "I'm like a shark." There was a trace of wistfulness in his voice. "I have to keep moving."

"You'll never settle down?" I asked, moving my rook into position on the side. I planned to use it to take one of his pieces if he tried to quickly checkmate me.

"I despise that term," he said matter-of-factly. "It reminds me of settling into the grave. But who knows? Maybe I'll become an investment banker like my dad. Make tons of money. Buy a mansion on Lake Washington."

He scratched his beard and advanced his bishop deep into my half of the board. He held onto it and said, "Check."

I was waiting for this and took the bishop with my knight. Wyn often overlooked the lowly knight.

"Why didn't I see that?" He thumped the sleeping bag. "That was so obvious. John, you're so predictable."

"So are you." Slowly, patiently I broke down his defenses, until finally I checkmated him with a pawn, the ultimate in humiliation. Wyn knocked the board aside. He went outside, shoveled the snow off the tent, and then came back in.

"Play again?" he said, picking up the pieces.

"Not right now." I felt another headache coming on. I wanted to rest, but Wyn kept up the conversation. It was a repeat of many long, circular arguments we'd had over the years. However, I did sense some softening in his position. Perhaps the deaths of his partners had got him thinking about his own mortality.

"Why do you like being married?" he asked me.

"It's a whole new life," I began. "It's not a substitute for climbing, but something else entirely."

"Don't you ever feel trapped?" he asked.

"Of course I do," I said. "I feel like a piece of taffy, pulled in all directions at once."

"That's good?" Wyn picked up his Swiss Army knife and opened the blade.

"I like the variety of it. Climbing gave me that for a while, but I used it up. I was never as driven as you."

"You could have been if you'd stayed with it."

I shook my head and lay back against my sleeping bag. "There were too many other things I wanted to do."

"You have to choose," he said, folding and unfolding the blade. "You've got to simplify. You've got to cut away the things that get in the way of your goals."

"But simplicity is boring," I said. "This tent is simple, and I'm already getting sick of it."

"At least it hasn't collapsed." Wyn sat up in his sleeping bag. "Simplicity makes ambition possible. Without it, goals slip away. Mediocrity prevails."

"It doesn't have to," I countered. "Life should be in balance."

"Not if you're pushing the extremes," he said. "There's nothing balanced about it. Look at Beethoven, Picasso, Faulkner, Messner—none of them were *balanced*. They were obsessive." He used his hands as blinders to make his point. "They were totally committed to what they were doing."

"Yeah, but they had wives, families, pet dogs."

He snorted dismissively. "Have you ever read their biographies?" he asked. "They didn't exactly practice family values. Faulkner ignored his daughter. When she called him on it, he said in so many words, 'No one ever heard of Shakespeare's daughter.'" He grinned wickedly. "How's that for family values?"

"What about his daughter?" I said, shaking my head. "How do you think she felt?"

He shrugged his shoulders. "Excellence requires sacrifice. No one likes to hear it, but it's true. You don't accomplish things because of your race, color, background, or because you're nice to people, but by effort and talent." He stopped to let that thought sink in. The gleam in his eye looked slightly demented. His speech was becoming pressured. "When I'm focused on a goal like getting to the top of this peak I won't let anything get in the way of that. If it does..." He snapped the blade shut.

Wyn's tirade had sucked the air out of the tent. The yellow walls felt narrow, constricted, and excessively bright. After taking a drink of water, I got back in my sleeping bag. "Where did you come up with this philosophy?"

"Look at this knife." The blade glinted in the light. "It's the ultimate in simplicity—function reduced to its purest form. Sharp, curved, perfect for cutting." He touched the blade with his finger. "I enjoy just looking at it."

"That sounds like something out of that Nietzsche book."

"Partly," he said.

"You don't really believe all that crap, do you?" I asked.

"Not all of it," he said defensively. "But a lot of it's true. That which doesn't kill you makes you stronger. Only the strong survive. That's what's happened with my partners."

"Don't you believe in morality?" I asked.

"I do," he said. "But with conditions."

"What do you mean?"

"Have you ever heard of situation ethics?"

I nodded.

"Do you know what they are?"

"I guess that means you make a decision based on the circumstances."

"Precisely," Wyn said, slapping the book with his hand. "That's the way I look at morality. Remember after the Eiger climb when all these imbeciles criticized me for not saving Hans?"

"I remember."

"You wouldn't believe the second-guessing," he said, shaking his head contemptuously. "'Why didn't you help him?' 'Why didn't you do something?'" he asked, mimicking the accusations. "There was nothing I could do. Nothing. It was his fault that he didn't tie into his harness. And yet they all but accused me of killing him."

"So there was no way you could have helped him?" I said.

"No," Wyn said. "It was his mistake. Pure and simple."

"But you knew he wasn't an experienced climber?"

"Are you playing devil's advocate?"

"I'm just asking. It seems like a pattern. Several of your partners who died were less experienced than you. Is that why you lobbied against Al and Lane?"

"Yes, it is."

"And what do you think of them now?"

We spoke in whispers, even though the storm would have made it impossible for them to hear us.

"The jury's still out," he said, sitting cross-legged. "We'll see how they do on the face. If they can't keep up, we'll have to decide."

"They've come a long way," I countered.

"But if they get in trouble up high." His blue eyes narrowed. "We'll have to decide..."

"Situation ethics."

"Exactly. There will only be so much we can do for them."

"So you'd just cut 'em loose."

"If I had to." He snapped the blade back into the knife.

"Survival of the fittest and all that?"

"Something like that," Wyn said.

"That seems selfish to me."

Wyn pursed his lips. "That's the way it is. There comes a point when you have to decide, when it would be suicidal to continue to help."

"Would you risk your life if I got into trouble?"

"Of course," he said. "And you'd do the same for me. But if it was certain that I'd die because of it, I wouldn't do it. And the same for you. I'd want you to save yourself. I wouldn't want Jill to become a widow and Andy to lose his father."

"I don't understand that," I said. "Even if there was a chance, I'd have to try. If I didn't, I couldn't live with myself."

"You'd learn to," he said, snapping the knife. "The rules are different up here. You do what you have to do." His face looked old, crinkled, resigned. "If that means cutting the rope to save yourself, you cut the rope."

The storm continued throughout the next day. The smell inside the tent made me nauseous. I *had* to go outside. Putting on my down parka, pants, and boots, I went outside to dig out the tent walls. When I stepped outside the vestibule, the wind nearly blew off my pile hat. Shoving it back on, I steadied myself and grabbed the snow shovel. My legs wobbled from the lack of activity, but it felt good to stretch them. I cleared the snow off one side of the tent, then the other. Afterwards, I was still breathing normally. I was starting to acclimatize.

Glancing up at the face, I caught a glimpse of the jagged buttress. It looked steep and foreshortened. I almost wished I hadn't seen it. I went back inside the tent.

It was 4:30 p.m. Time to get ready for tomorrow. I got out my rigid crampons and made sure they fit the boots. I didn't want them coming off when I was front-pointing up the face. Fitting them to my boots, I filed them until they felt sharp against my finger. Now they would bite easily into the hardest ice, making climbing possible on the sections of near vertical ground that we'd likely encounter tomorrow.

While I sharpened my ice tools, Wyn walked over to Al and Lane's tent. A few minutes later, he returned.

"We're on for tomorrow," Wyn said.

"How's Al's knee?"

"He says it's better," Wyn said, zipping shut the tent. "In fact, they wanted to join us."

"That's great."

"Al doesn't have his pack, remember?"

"I can loan him my summit pack."

"It doesn't have enough capacity."

"So what did you tell them?"

"That we'd take the first lead. Al didn't like it, but he agreed. He's hungry, which is good."

"How about Lane?"

"He thinks he knows more than he does." Wyn shook his head. "He told me we shouldn't go up tomorrow, that the avalanche danger was too great."

"What do you think?"

"I've been watching the face," Wyn said. "It's been swept clean by avalanches already. We'll have to be careful, but I think we'll be okay."

"Lane knows a lot about rescues."

"But not much about snow conditions," Wyn said. "We're close to the ceiling for most helicopters. The trick is to *avoid* the accident in the first place. He'll have to keep his ego in check if he wants to do that."

"Is that how you've managed to survive?"

Wyn's blue eyes glittered with amusement. "Let's just say I'm hard to kill."

"That sounds like hubris."

"It's the truth." He primed the stove. "Now, let's melt some snow. We'll need to have plenty of water for tomorrow."

The face was eerily quiet the next morning. I woke at 2 a.m. and looked outside. The cirque was cold and still. The storm had blown itself out.

"Let's get moving," Wyn said, pulling on his parka.

After a breakfast of instant coffee and oatmeal, we headed out, glad to be moving again. The plan was to establish the first camp somewhere on the face above. Since we were the first to attempt the line, we'd get a chance to play explorers.

The face loomed above. Everything was silent save for the crunch of our crampons against the windblown snow. The temperature was below zero, and the snow seemed stable.

Wyn veered farther to the left of the buttress this time, keeping his distance from the avalanche chute. We moved quickly through the danger zone. I flinched when a rock tumbled down. My shoulders tensed, waiting for the sharp crack that signaled an avalanche.

By the time we reached the bergschrund, I was breathing hard, relieved we'd made it through. As the sun rose, we drank some water and shared several small, brittle squares of chocolate. Clearing away the snow, I found our gear intact in the back of the crevasse. I picked up the static line and shoved it into my pack. This would serve as a fixed rope on the lower half of the route, giving us an escape route if another storm moved in. We could simply rappel down the line and return to camp. No sweat.

Wyn took out his ice hammer, ice axe, and a bandolier of slings, ice screws, pitons, and nuts to protect himself from a fall. Leaning back to scope out the route, he squinted up at the jumble of ice and rock above him. Then he tied into the red kermantle rope and ratcheted in two eight-inch ice screws for an anchor. After I put him on belay, he drove in the pick of the ice axe, testing the hardness of the snow. Then he buried both picks into the surface as smooth and white as porcelain, kicked in the front points of his crampons, and rose up the face.

He headed for a gap in the schrund. Right below it, he put in an ice screw, attached a sling to it, and clipped into the rope. Then he wiggled into it, wiry, decisive, and quick. He walked up his crampons, kicked them in, and then repeated the process. He worked quickly and meticulously, hanging off his tools to keep from torching the muscles in his arms. It was classic monkey hang technique.

"Good job," I shouted up at him, keeping the rope running through my belay device. My mood soared; maybe we'd get up this damn rock pile after all.

Wyn kept going. He didn't appear to be exerting himself, even though the slope was a good seventy degrees. The tiny picks of his axes and the front points of his crampons kept him from falling. The axes traced short, compact arcs, biting easily into the surface. He knew exactly how far to put them in for a solid placement. He didn't overdrive them so he didn't have to work to get them out. I payed out the rope as he worked his way up the first pitch.

When he disappeared around a bulge in the snow, I heard nothing for a few minutes. A shower of ice chips ricocheted off my helmet.

"Off belay!" he yelled.

"You're off!" I said, taking the rope out of my belay device. Then he pulled the rest of the rope back up to him. Now it was my turn. Putting on the pack with the spool of fixed rope, I waited for him to secure the climbing rope to the anchor.

"Okay," he yelled. "You're on!"

"Climbing!" I placed the jaws of two metal jumars or ascenders on the rope. Then I tied a section of rope to each of them, and then made a loop at the lower end for each of my boots. Sliding the first jumar up the rope, I brought my right foot with it. I did the same thing with the other jumar. I gradually moved up the rope, alternately raising one jumar, weighting it, then pushing the other one higher. My pack was heavy and awkward, but I moved faster than if I had had to climb the pitch. Jumaring was a compromise of Wyn's ethics—he would have preferred that each of us climb every pitch—but I had argued for it. It would allow us to move much faster.

As I jugged my way up the pitch, I admired his skill in leading it; it was a lot harder than it looked from below. I paid out the static line behind me, attaching it to the ice screws he had sunk into the hard snow to protect the pitch. I was breathing hard by the time I reached the belay stance.

"Nice lead," I said.

"Thanks," he said, beaming. As always, Wyn came alive when he climbed. He could be petulant and judgmental when stormbound in a cramped tent, but when he got out on the sharp end of the rope, his spirits soared.

While he secured the static line to the anchor, I took the rack from him and examined the route ahead: a steep snow slope veering to the left. My pulse quickened as I contemplated the lead. It wasn't as steep as the last pitch, but it was seventy-degree ice. I hadn't done such hard climbing in years. I took several deep breaths to calm myself.

"Are you sure you're up for this?" Wyn asked.

"I'm fine," I lied, feeling my stomach do a flip-turn.

"Okay," he said, putting me on belay.

"Climbing," I said dully.

"Climb on," he said. "One step at a time."

I drove one axe into the slope. It took easily. There was something incredibly satisfying about the thunk of a good placement. It made me feel solid, protected, safe. The snow was perfect, just like Styrofoam. This boosted my confidence. I drove in the other axe, which was just as secure. I kicked in the crampons. Everything seemed solid.

"See you up there," I said.

"You're all over it," he yelled, paying out the rope.

I repeated the process. My axes and crampons held, but I overdrove them and had to work to take them out of the snow. I was too scared to proceed as effortlessly as Wyn. I made progress but worked too hard. The thin bitter air took its toll. Looking back, I saw Wyn twenty feet beneath my boots. My arms and legs shook. This was too far to go without a placement. Grabbing a six-inch ice screw off the rack, I rotated it into the slope. Sinking it in as far as possible, I looped a sling into the eye, clipped the sling into a carabiner, and clipped the carabiner into the rope. Any fall now would be short.

"Relax," Wyn said. "You're doing fine."

I breathed deeply to regain my composure. With the first screw in, I regained some confidence. I moved up, trying to forget my fear and concentrate on the climbing. *Establish a rhythm. Don't hurry. Move deliberately.* I kicked in the right crampon, then the left. I sunk the right axe, then the left. I moved up and repeated the sequence. It was exhausting, but I made progress.

Ten feet later, I put in another screw. I was really sewing up the pitch. I wanted to be as safe as possible, even if I sacrificed speed. Wyn was probably exasperated with my pace, but to his credit he didn't say anything. The screw went in easily. I clipped into it and moved past it.

As I front-pointed up the steep snow, my left calf began cramping up. As I put my weight on it, it spasmed and threw me off balance. For a split second, I was falling. Then my axes held. Heart pumping wildly, I madly kicked my crampons back into the slope and tried to recover. Visions of tumbling back down to base camp made my head swim. I deliberately avoided looking down and instead made sure that I had solid placements. My calves screamed with the effort, but I kept going, using French crampon technique, placing the bottom points rather than the front points into slope, a much less fatiguing technique and only possible on a less than vertical slope like this one. This eased the strain on my calves but required that I bend my foot back at an awkward angle. I alternated techniques, using one or the other depending on the steepness of the pitch and the tiredness of my feet and calves.

Finally, I reached a good belay stance. I barely had enough energy to get two ice screws into some blue ice and tie into them. Then I backed them up with my ice hammer and ice tool, clipping them into the anchor. I glanced at my watch; I'd climbed the pitch, but it had taken almost an hour, way too slow for a climb like this one.

"Off belay," I yelled wearily to Wyn.

"You're off!" he replied.

I pulled up about twenty feet of climbing rope until it went taut.

"That's me!" he yelled.

I tied the rope into the anchor.

"On belay!" I shouted.

"Okay," he yelled. "Climbing."

Wyn jugged up quickly, paying out the static line as he went.

"Good lead," Wyn said. "You're back into the game."

"I don't know about that," I said. "I felt pretty shaky."

"Hey, you did what you had to do." He tugged at the anchor. "A little slow, but no problem."

"I'm the tortoise, you're the hare."

"Does that mean you'll beat me in the end?"

"We'll see." I handed him the rack.

"Rock and roll," he said, taking off. He cleared the end of the snow ramp and headed straight up the face. He reeled out fifty feet of rope before putting in an ice screw. That was Wyn all over. He was so solid that he didn't bother to protect a pitch as much as I did. Still, it worried me. I glanced down at the anchor. If he fell, it could rip out.

But of course he didn't fall. He danced up the slope like a ballerina, moving effortlessly from placement to placement. Not only were we making progress, we were breaking new ground. No one had ever climbed this slope, a rare experience on a mountain like Denali. As I watched Wyn sail up the route, joy welled up in my chest. No one could ever take this away from me. No customer at the store could ever say that I didn't qualify as a climber. Not after a first ascent. On Denali, no less. Our achievement may have seemed trivial to an outsider, but within the mountaineering world, a new route on Denali was pure, unadulterated platinum.

After jumaring up to him, I took the next lead, a mixed pitch of sixty-degree snow and ice. I worked slowly and methodically up the snow, putting in two-foot pickets every twenty feet. I didn't try to move fast; I knew I couldn't match his pace. I just tried to regulate my breathing and keep from getting scared shitless. We were now far enough up the face that the exposure was extreme. When I dislodged a chunk of ice, it bounded all the way back down to the base.

I shuddered and kept going. My calves screamed as I front-pointed up the last thirty feet below an alcove. Then they started cramping. My arms spasmed. Gritting my teeth, I clawed up the last ten feet and collapsed onto the shelf.

After catching my breath, I got in three ice screws for an anchor. I checked and rechecked them. They were embedded in blue ice. They seemed like they could hold a freight train, but since I'd climbed little over the last few years I didn't trust my equipment. Finally, I yelled to Wyn to take me off belay. He came up and prepared to lead the next pitch through ice that look like Swiss cheese.

"Would you mind not running it out so much this time?" I asked. "It makes me nervous."

"You think I'll fall?" he asked, grinning.

"It could happen."

"No way." He traversed left around a pillar of rock and then straight up a short section of ice. He worked cautiously but continuously, hooking his tools into the honeycombed surface, carefully kicking in his front points so as not to shatter it. I was glad I wasn't leading the pitch. Thirty feet up, he put in the first piece of gear. The tension in my neck eased. Whether for my sake or not, he placed more protection. We were now almost 1,000 feet up the face.

The sun was coming up. Soon the roar of avalanches would resume. We were like Cinderellas at the ball. Wyn quickly led up the rock bulges to the left, a broken pattern of small buttresses interspersed with snow and ice that allowed us to avoid the avalanche chutes to the east. This route skirted the larger avalanche gullies on the face. We still were vulnerable to rocks and smaller slides, but the line looked safer.

I took the last lead, even though I was exhausted. I didn't want Wyn accusing me of being afraid. It was a classic mixed pitch, with water ice and steep granite outcrops. At first, I stayed on the ice, as I could move up it quickly. Then I tried the granite, testing its texture and solidity. Every mountain's rock has an individual character, and

Denali's granite was no exception. Even with my heavy gloves on, I could easily grasp its edges, sink my hands into the cracks, and grip its holds. I moved slowly but steadily, savoring the hardness and coarse friction of the rock. For a few moments at least, I forgot my fear of the face. The sensation of ascent flowed back into me. Reaching a small alcove beneath a granite face, I drove in a piton. It rang as clearly and sweetly as a church bell. Clipping into it, I brought Wyn up.

"Camp 1," Wyn declared.

"Just in time." I motioned over at the sun coming up behind the east face of the peak.

The ice bench tilted sharply downhill, so we hacked away with our ice axes to level it. The carbon steel tools glanced off the ice without making much of a dent, but we kept going. Nothing could dampen our enthusiasm, not even bulletproof ice. After a half hour, we'd gouged out only a few inches, but we kept at it, racing against the clock. We had to set up camp and get down before the sun hit the face. Slowly, the ice yielded to our pounding. My arms had turned to jelly by the time we'd managed to clear a platform just big enough for our tiny two-man tent. Whoever slept on the downhill side would have a buttock perched over the abyss.

We unfolded the tent, inserted the poles, and anchored it to the slope with ice screws. Wyn drove a piton into a crack in the rock above us and tied it into the tent. The ping, ping, ping sound made me smile. Camp 1 had been established.

After stocking the tent with food, stove fuel, and the spool of static line, we got ready to rappel. In the next few days, we'd return with the rest of our gear. For now, we had to get our butts back down through the gauntlet of the avalanche zone. Still, I couldn't help smiling. We'd made great progress. We were on our way.

I handed Wyn the static line. "After you," I said.

NINE

After completing the last rappel, we plunge-stepped down the snow slope, moving quickly through the bowling alley of the lower face. I spotted a slide releasing high on the upper face right before we crossed the avalanche chute. We took cover behind a rock outcrop and watched it thunder down a big chute far to our left. It slalomed around towers, overwhelmed ridges, and swept away rocks and glacial debris. Then it exploded at the base in a cloud of snow as fine and white as powdered sugar.

We kept going, unwilling to rest until we got a safe distance from the face. Wyn led up the hill toward camp, easily outpacing me. I had to stop and hyperventilate to catch my breath. I bent over and put my hands on my knees. All in all, I was pleased with my performance on the face. I might not be as fast as Wyn, but I was steady. And if I kept getting stronger, I could come close to matching him as a partner.

When I caught my breath, I trudged up the last few hundred yards to camp.

Lane and Al were waiting when we arrived back in camp. Lane helped me off with my pack, while Al peppered us with questions. Al seemed more animated than I'd ever seen him on the trip. He seemed to have recovered from the avalanche. He was like the old Al, the one who ate up vertical ice.

"It was awesome climbing," Wyn said, pointing back at the route we'd just done. "John ran right up that face."

I sat on my pack, not having enough breath to reply.

"What was the ice like?" Al asked.

"Styrofoam, steel plate, and this hollow, cheesy stuff," Wyn said. "You have to pick and choose your placements."

"How did your tools work?" Al adjusted his glasses.

"Great."

"Did you use a banana pick?" This was a steeply drooped pick, with a slight recurve at the tip to stick in hard, vertical ice.

"Definitely."

Al nodded quickly to each of Wyn's replies. He rubbed his hands together rapidly and hopped around as if he couldn't contain his enthusiasm. "How about Camp 1?"

"It's not exactly the Hilton," Wyn said. "But it'll do. How's your knee?"

Al massaged it. "Better."

"Don't take a chance unless you're sure," Wyn warned. "I did that with my knee, and it took me six months to recover. It still bothers me."

"Don't worry," Al said, shaking his head. "It's okay."

"We'll take the next lead," Wyn said. "Once your knee is okay, you can go out front."

"No need to wait." Al pushed up his glasses with his index finger. "Lane and I are ready."

"One step at a time." Wyn kicked skeptically at the ground in front of him.

"You haven't exactly followed that philosophy in your own climbing."

Wyn laughed. "You calling me a hypocrite?"

"Not exactly." Al looked away. "I just want a chance to get out front."

"You'll get it," Wyn said. "Don't worry about that."

While they talked, I crawled into the tent. When I woke up several hours later, my head throbbed and my joints and muscles ached like I had the flu. My feet and legs cramped up from the front-pointing. I downed a couple of ibuprofen with a gulp of water and took a nap. When I woke up Wyn was outside the tent glassing the face.

"Hey, John, I think I found a site for the next camp." He thrust the binoculars through the door of the tent.

I slowly got out of the tent and examined the slope. "Are you sure?"

"See the cleft between two huge granite towers?"

I handed the binoculars back to him. "I see it."

"That's our goal for tomorrow," he said.

I held my back and winced. "I need a break."

"How're you feeling?"

"Shot."

Wyn frowned and bit his lip, obviously disappointed that I didn't share his enthusiasm. He never seemed to tire once he locked on to a climb. The goal of the summit seemed to give him more energy than before. But I wasn't going to jeopardize my shot at the summit by pushing myself and getting sick. I sometimes tired of my Mr. Safety role, but I needed to play it if we wanted to get to the top—and back.

"Let's send Al and Lane on a carry," I suggested. "They need a turn out front."

"You think so?" He scratched his beard and shot a look toward their tent.

"Al's a good climber," I argued. "He's psyched; you could see it in the questions he asked. And I sold him on this trip because I told him he'd do some leading. Besides, the ropes and anchors are already in place. It should be easy getting the stuff up to Camp 1."

"I guess you're right," he replied. He stood outside the door of the tent, his hands on his hips, his face creased with thought. "What the hell? Let's give 'em a shot at it."

Wyn and I cooked dinner while they packed. I dumped dried tomato sauce and mushrooms into a pot and mixed it with water. As it simmered, I added dried onions, parsley, and cheddar cheese. Soon, a delicious smell wafted around me.

Sitting on my foam pad, I stirred the sauce. It took forever to cook at altitude, but I was in no hurry. It felt luxurious to rest and recover, letting Lane and Al take the lead. As the temperature dropped, I shoved my hands into the pockets of my down parka. Cold weather meant safe conditions up high, making their carry a lot easier.

When the water boiled, I dumped in the spaghetti.

"Don't overcook it," Lane cautioned as he looked up from stuffing his sleeping bag into the pack.

"Don't worry, chef."

Lane insisted on tasting it. When it was *al dente*, according to his specifications, I drained it into the snow. Then Al, Wyn, and Lane stood in line as I filled up their plates. I dumped the sauce over the spaghetti and dusted it with Parmesan cheese. Back home it would have been an unremarkable meal, but here it tasted like three-star restaurant fare. We ate silently and diligently, wolfing it down before it cooled. Occasionally, Al or Lane would look up at the route.

"How are you guys feeling?" Wyn asked.

"Good," Lane said, twirling the spaghetti on his fork. "I'm almost packed."

"How about you, Al?"

"Psyched," he said, and wiped his mouth on his sleeve.

"How's your knee?"

He flexed it. "Okay."

"Remember, go up to the camp, drop the gear, come back down," Wyn said, looking at Al.

"What if we're feeling good?" Lane said. "Can we put in Camp 2?"

"Don't worry about that," Wyn said. "Just get the kinks out. You can lead next time."

"We're not just pack mules," Al cut in. "We're just as capable as you guys of leading."

"Let's get something straight," Wyn said, putting his fork down. "John and I will do the leading initially. I don't want any *problems.*"

Al swallowed hard and adjusted his glasses, keeping a poker face about his intentions.

Lane finished chewing his spaghetti. "Whatever you say."

"Good," Wyn said, gathering the plates. "You guys get ready. We'll clean up."

Wyn's remarks seemed reasonable to me. His experience and stature clearly made him the leader, and as leader, he was entitled to make such decisions. Besides, he wasn't being an asshole about it.

Wyn and I scrubbed the pots while they got ready. After the dishes, I sat down outside our tent, sipped a cup of cocoa, and watched them finish packing. Al displayed the same fussiness with his packing as he did with his leading. He took a bag of food, stuffed it in the lower compartment of the summit pack, stepped back, appraised its position, then took it out again and put it in the upper compartment. He scowled, scratched his head, then took it out, put it in the lower compartment, and left it there. He cinched the strap tight around the lower end of the pack.

His sun goggles went from the top flap of his pack to the lower compartment to the side pocket and finally back to the top flap. He was taking a lot of extra gear, but I figured that this was his fastidious personality.

Lane, on the other hand, shoved everything into his pack, stood back, appraised it, picked it up, and shook it out again. With his broad shoulders, he tossed it around as if it were a toy. His cheeks grew red with exertion. He seemed rattled by the route ahead.

"How cold will it be up there?" he asked me.

"Below zero."

"Should I bring extra clothing?"

"No, you'll be moving fast. Just take a parka for the belays."

He breathed deeply, getting stoked for the route ahead. "How about a sleeping bag?"

"You won't need it."

"Al said I should take it."

"I wouldn't," I said.

"It's not that heavy." Lane just shoved the sleeping bag into his bloated, overstuffed pack. He was so strong he probably wouldn't notice the extra gear.

Al made last-minute adjustments to his gear. I crawled inside the tent and got into my sleeping bag, relieved they were heading up. I'd recuperate while they stocked the high camp. We'd swing leads back and forth, each team supporting the other, the way it was supposed to be. Everything was going to be okay.

Around 2 a.m., I heard them stomping their feet and cursing the cold. Al swore as he put on his crampons. I burrowed deeper into my sleeping bag, a delicious cocoon of warmth. It must have been below zero outside. Hoar frost clung to the inside of the tent like the inside of a freezer. Outside, the face was likely silent and frozen. When I woke again at 7 a.m., Wyn had the binoculars trained on the face.

"There they are," he said, pointing to a place low on the face. "They're not making very good time."

He handed me the binoculars. I played with the focus and found a red dot and a purple one above the bergschrund. They were brilliant specks of color among the monochrome immensity of snow and rock.

Al was leading. Lane was right behind him. I glassed above them. They still had a long way to go to make it to Camp 1.

I gave the binoculars back to Wyn.

"What's taking them so long?" he asked. "They won't be back off the face before the avalanches start."

"They took heavy packs," I said. "They even carried sleeping bags."

"Sleeping bags!" he yelled. "If you carry that much crap you'll bivouac for sure."

He took out the radio and turned it on. It hissed to life. "Al and Lane, over. Can you read?"

No reply.

"Al and Lane. Can you read?"

No reply.

"They must have turned off their radio," he said, turning it off angrily. "We'll have to try later on."

A gust of wind blew up the glacier. I shivered and went back inside the tent. I tried to read more of *Don Quixote*, a good antidote to the seriousness of the climb. When I got up, Wyn was still glassing the route. He checked and rechecked the map, referred back to the face, trying to memorize every detail. He was fanatical in his preparation. He was always on the job. He had no other life. I both admired and pitied him for this.

Eventually, he came back into the tent and read for a while. The morning passed quickly. Around noon, the sun hit the tent. We went outside and lounged around in our long underwear on our foam pads. For lunch, we had stale Wheat Thins and Swiss cheese and summer sausage. The sausage immediately caused me heartburn. It reminded me that we were getting high; I always had trouble digesting fatty foods at altitude. I'd have to go easy on them, even though they were essential to high-altitude climbing. In many ways, you eat your way to the top of Denali.

Trading the binoculars back and forth, we tracked their progress. They were making better time now. But they still hadn't reached Camp 1. There was no way they could make it back down today.

Wyn grew agitated. He couldn't stand being in a support role. He paced around the camp, snorting, and shaking his head. "I don't have a good feeling about this," he said, kicking the snow. "They're going to get themselves killed if they don't pick it up."

"They're right below the tent," I said. "They should be up there soon."

"I hope so," Wyn said. "They're sitting ducks for anything that comes off the face."

Wyn kept pacing, looking up at the face, checking the weather. He wore a circle around the perimeter of the tent. There were no clouds in the sky, which agitated him even more. We had to make the best of the weather window. If we squandered it by getting behind schedule, we would be SOL.

Around 1 p.m., the radio crackled to life.

"Wyn and John, over. This is Al."

"Al, what's going on up there?" Wyn demanded.

"It was a grunt getting up here." Al spoke slowly, pressure breathing between sentences. "But what an amazing view."

"Any rock fall?"

"We got dusted by a small avalanche."

"Anything hit the tent?"

"Negative," he said. "You guys did a good job."

"How's Lane?"

"Lane's great," Al said, sucking on air. "He's jumaring very quickly."

"Okay, but you're in deep shit. You can't risk coming back today, and you've got no bivouac gear."

"Negative, we've got sleeping bags, a stove, and food."

Wyn clenched the radio as if he were going to break it. "Okay, wait till early tomorrow and then head back down."

"Negative. We're going to keep going, over."

"What?" Wyn yelled. "Get your butts back down here!"

"We're feeling fine," Al said. "No need to rush."

"Al, get back here," Wyn spoke slowly and distinctly.

"Negative," Al said. "It's our turn to lead."

"Al—"

"Sorry," Al said sarcastically. "We're not total idiots. We can lead. If we left it up to you, we'd be jugging the whole frigging mountain."

"You're wasting the good weather," Wyn yelled hoarsely. "You're moving too slowly."

"You remind me of my boss at Boeing," Al said, laughing. "Over and out."

"Damn." Wyn clicked off the radio, made as if to throw it, thought better of it, and put it into the pocket of his parka. He stalked around in his red long underwear, railing at Al and Lane. "Those morons will probably get themselves killed." He started packing. "I'm going up there and bringing them back down."

"Give them a chance," I said, standing up. "If they blow it, we'll take over again. Let's not totally alienate them."

"Well, they're alienating me," he said, the cords standing out in his neck. "And if we don't take advantage of the weather, we're not going to climb this peak."

Wyn had a point, but they did, too. They needed a turn out front. In some ways, I was relieved they'd taken the lead, even though I didn't like the way they did it. Already, I could feel the ache subsiding from my elbows and calves, the tightness easing in my back and shoulders. With another rest day, I'd be ready to lead again.

Wyn, of course, didn't need any rest. He trembled with nervous energy. He insisted on melting water and making dinner, Tuna Helper, of course, for the fifth time this trip. He boiled the noodles into the consistency of paste and burned the sauce, making it a bitch to clean the bottom of the pot. The argument with Al was obviously eating at him, making him curt in his replies. When I complained about his cooking, he replied that it didn't matter how it tasted. "It's the calories that count, John," he said.

With the temperatures near zero, we hit the sack early. Wyn expostulated Nietzsche's theory of morality as the defense of the weak against the strong. I didn't have the energy to rebut him and dozed off as he went on and on, arguing and finally agreeing with himself.

At 3 a.m., I poked my head out of the tent and spotted what looked like their parkas, tiny dots of red and purple against the face. You had to give them credit for going for it. I went back inside and fell asleep. At 5 a.m., I got up and glassed the face. They were a couple of leads above Camp 1. Very slow progress.

The face was still in shade, making it look dark and ominous. I reveled in the silence and tried to block out the looming confrontation with Al and Lane. Taking the green plastic frog from the bottom of my sleeping bag, I wondered what Jill and Andy were doing. Probably sleeping. I ached to pick up Andy. I wanted to put my hand around the curve of Jill's hip. I returned the frog to the top flap of my pack. By the time Wyn got up, the water was boiling for coffee.

"How are they doing?" Wyn asked.

"They're making progress," I said, handing him the binoculars.

Wyn trained the glasses on the face. "They're coming down. I just hope they can make it all the way."

"How far did they get?" I asked.

"Hard to say. A few leads above the camp. Maybe they'll recognize their limits now."

I handed Wyn a cup of coffee. He kept the binoculars and raked them up and down the face. "We'll head up tomorrow," he said. "We'll have to make up for lost time."

"That means heavy packs," I said.

"We don't have a choice now." He kicked at the snow.

"Triumph of will," I said, pointing to my temple.

"Laugh if you want," he said tolerantly. "It's the truth."

Several hours later, Lane and Al trudged into camp. They plunged wearily through the snow, slipping and sliding and punching through the slop. When they got to their tent, I went over to help them with their packs. Wyn didn't bother.

"How far did you make it?" I asked.

"Three leads," Al said triumphantly. "My climbing picks worked great."

"We broke new ground," Lane said, saluting us with his ice axe.

After they had a chance to drink some water, Wyn approached them. "We need to have a meeting."

"Why?" Lane said. "What's there to discuss?"

"There's a lot to discuss," Wyn said. "We've got to work together as a team or we're not going to climb this peak."

Al frowned.

"I'll brew up some tea first," I said.

Al and Lane retreated into their tent. Wyn loomed over the stove like a predatory bird while I boiled water. He crossed his arms, paced, and brooded, talking to himself as if psyching himself for a speech. A few minutes later, I brought tea to them. "Wyn wants a powwow."

"I need to take a nap," Al said. "I couldn't sleep on that ledge."

"Listen," I said. "I don't blame you for wanting to lead, but we need to discuss how you do it."

"This is just like Boeing," Al said, adjusting his glasses. "When in doubt, call a meeting."

"No, it's not," I said. "There's a lot more at stake here."

"I agree," Lane said, sitting up in the tent. "We need to sort this out. We need to work together. But we need our shot at the glory, too."

"You'll get it," I said, pouring tea into their cups. "I'm on your side. I want you guys to swing leads with us. I want to climb this peak *together*."

Lane nodded.

"Every time we talk Wyn comes on like Mister Hot-Shit-Know-It-All," Al said, his armed crossed. "I'm getting sick of it."

"He is one of the best climbers in the world," I said.

"You've got a point there," Lane said.

"I don't care who he is," Al said, spitting out the words. "I took a month off work to do this climb. I don't want to be anybody's personal pack mule."

"It looks like we do have something to talk about."

We gathered outside the tents. We sat down on our foam pads in the snow, Al and Lane on one side, Wyn and I on the other. Since I was the one who brought everyone together, I spoke first.

"Good work leading," I said, looking at Al and Lane. "It was great to have you guys out front. We all have to contribute if we want to climb this thing." I looked up at the face, now dazzlingly bright in the morning sun. "Like the rest of you, I've given up a lot to be here. I left my family and my store to do this climb." I looked around at them. Wyn bit his lip and bided his time. Al hunched over his foam pad, his Adam's apple bobbing as he sipped the tea. Lane rubbed the albino whiskers on his chin. "I have a lot riding on it. I don't want to screw it up."

I kicked at the snow with my boot. "I've been on a lot of trips, mostly with Wyn, but also with you, Al. We've had disagreements, but we've always worked things out. That's why we've succeeded."

I paused to let my words sink in. "And that's why I'd like to hear your side of the story, Al."

Al swallowed hard. "It's pretty simple," he said, avoiding looking at Wyn. "I just want more time out front. Like John, I took a month off of work to be here." He rubbed his hands together and blew on them. "I've done a lot of hard routes." He glanced over at Wyn, who appraised him through mirrored Vuarnets. "I want to do this climb as a leader rather than a follower. I want to be able to say, I climbed Denali, not, I jugged it."

"Okay," I said, playing the part of the talk-show host. "Lane, do you have something to say?"

He nodded and cleared his throat. "As a firefighter, I'm used to being part of a team," he said, fiddling with his altimeter watch. "That's what keeps your butt from getting burnt. I have no problem with a hierarchy." He looked around at us. "We've had our disagreements. I wanted to bring that litter. Wyn disagreed. I went along with that, even though it would give us a margin of safety. I bowed to your climbing expertise."

Lane leaned back on his foam pad, warming to the topic. "Teamwork is essential, but so is leadership. A good leader solicits and receives input from the rest of the team. It's more of a democracy than a dictatorship. So far, this expedition has mostly been a kind of benevolent dictatorship. This was fine at first, but now we've proved ourselves." He pointed up at the face. "I know you think we were slow, but we did three hard leads and got back down before things warmed up. Al and I certainly aren't your equals, but we need to be partners on the team."

Lane breathed deeply. "A strong team includes all of its members. The leader uses them to the best of their abilities. And if he isn't doing that . . ." Lane stroked his beard. "You begin to wonder if someone else might be better suited to the job."

"Are you saying that you want to be the leader?" Wyn broke in.

"Let him finish," I said. "You'll have your say."

"Fine," Wyn said, dismissing me with his hand.

"That's it," Lane said. "I'm done."

"Your turn," I told Wyn.

Wyn stood up. "Let's get one thing straight," he said, looking from Al to Lane. "I never planned that you guys should be pack mules. But I've had a lot of guys die around me. It's made me super aware of what can go wrong. I wanted to give you a chance to gain confidence in your technique. If you go slowly, you have a better chance of doing it safely."

He shoved his hands into the pockets of his pile jacket. "Now if that's dictatorship, so be it. I'm glad you think it's a benevolent dictatorship, but finally, I don't really care what you think. There are times when you have to be brutally honest, and this is one of them. I've learned in climbing that if you're delusional, you're going to get killed. It may happen sooner, it may happen later, but it's going to happen."

Wyn stared at Lane and Al. "It's fine to have goals and dreams, but someone has to have contact with reality." He paused to let his words sink in. "Al, I respect your credentials, but you've never climbed at altitude. You haven't performed well on the expedition so far." Wyn paused, took a deep breath, and crossed his arms across his chest. "From my perspective, you guys are a liability, not an asset, especially when you're in front. It was a bone-headed decision to climb above Camp 1. You wasted an entire day of good weather stringing up three lousy leads."

"Wait a minute," Al broke in.

"Let him finish," I said.

"Pardon my candor," Wyn said, bowing in mock deference to Al. "It's what's helped me survive. It was John's idea to bring you along. He did it to convince his wife to let him go on this climb. You're both decent guys, but if you weren't here we'd probably be up and down by now and enjoying a pitcher of beer back in the Fairview Inn in Talkeetna."

"Stop," I said, waving my hands. "That's not true." Wyn's honesty was going to totally alienate them if he wasn't careful. His temper was going to blow it for all of us. "Listen. I *wanted* to bring you guys on the climb. It's made the expedition a *lot* safer. If we'd gone into a crevasse, you'd have saved our butts."

Al blinked rapidly. Lane glanced at me out of the corner of his eye. Their distrust was blossoming. They nodded tolerantly as I continued, but I could tell their suspicions had grown: maybe I was just using them to get up the peak so I'd have a slide show to bail out Alpine Gear. They may have even believed we'd rehearsed all this, my good-cop act calculated to soften Wyn's bad-cop behavior.

"Listen," Wyn said, looking at Al and Lane. "I'm the leader of this expedition. We need to discuss these things and come to some agreement before we do anything. I want your input, but in the end, I'll make the call."

Al rolled his eyes. "Suppose we don't agree with you. Do you expect us to go along with you anyway?"

"Yes!" His voice cracked. "I'm trying to do what's best for the group.

I want to climb this route and get everybody back safely." Wyn sat down on his foam pad.

"Okay, Wyn," Lane said. "We'll abide by your decisions—as long as we agree with them. We reserve the right to disagree."

"That's fine," Wyn said. "But let's talk about it beforehand. If you make another move like your 'lead'"—he paused to let the sarcasm come out—"you can consider yourself fired from this expedition. You can slog your way up the West Buttress route like everybody else."

Lane started to say something but shook his head instead.

"John and I will do the next lead," Wyn said. "Then we'll see how it goes. If you guys are moving fast and kicking ass, then you'll get the next one. Okay?"

"Okay, whatever," Al said.

Lane nodded curtly.

They got up and went back to their tent. The trust had been broken. It would be difficult to repair.

TEN

The moon rose in the sky as we trudged out of camp. It was a comforting sight, reminding me of early-morning drives to the store, when the city was sleeping, and I was on my way to work. As the angle of the slope steepened, the air grew thin, the sky blue-black, and the full moon appeared as clear and brilliant as a newly minted coin. It seemed like we were leaving the earth behind and climbing into outer space.

Despite the creaking and shifting of my sixty-plus-pound pack, I moved steadily toward the face. It was a relief to leave behind the tensions with Al and Lane. Breathing in the cool, clean air, I felt energized and yet mindful of the enormous task ahead. Because Al and Lane had moved so slowly yesterday, we'd need to reach the base of the spiral couloir, a third of the way up the enormous face. If we didn't make it there, we'd have to bivouac in an area swept by avalanches.

Wyn stopped up ahead. I checked my watch: 2:10 a.m. We were right on schedule. He kept moving again, slowly making his way toward the fixed ropes. The super-cooled air irritated my nose: I sneezed and heard the echo around the amphitheater. The face was eerily quiet.

At the hollow of the bergschrund, Wyn set up a boot axe belay and brought me up. Dumping the pack, I took a swig of water and ate a piece of chocolate. In the moonlight, Foraker looked like it was bathed in silver. As I ate and drank, I hoped that Wyn would volunteer to head up the fixed ropes first.

"You're on," he said, leaning over.

"Are you sure?"

He nodded, turned away from me, and vomited on the snow.

"Are you okay?" I said, standing up.

He motioned me back as he brought up all of last night's dinner. He leaned over the snow, shaking, shivering, wracked with convulsions. Finally, he wiped a bit of vomit from his mouth with the sleeve of his parka.

"Should we head back?" I asked.

He shook his head and leaned over, getting the last of it out. I handed him the poly bottle. He tried to drink, gagged, but got some of it down. He sat down on his pack. I helped him put on his down parka and gave him a piece of hard candy. "You okay to lead?" he croaked.

"I think so." I looked at the steeply ascending line of fixed rope. For a brief moment, the full absurdity of what I was doing hit me. I was entering a world of steep ice, sheer rock faces, and meat-locker temperatures. Who would dream of spending their vacation in such a place? Only nutcases like me. My shoulders tensed. I looked away and considered heading down, but if I did, we'd have to relinquish the lead to Al and Lane. We'd piss away another day, precious time on a peak like this. If I wanted the summit, it came down to decisions like this one.

Hoisting the pack, I cinched the waist belt tight to keep the weight on my hips. Then I took out the jumars, clipped them to the rope, untied the slings, and put my feet through the end loops.

"I'll take a look," I said.

Wyn tried to nod but a spasm of dry heaves bent him over. I waited until he was finished and then put my weight onto the static line.

Jerking my way up the rope, I thought of the conversation I had with an insurance agent several months ago. I wanted to reinstate the climbing rider on my life insurance policy. I reassured her that modern equipment took all the risk out of climbing. She saw through this bullshit and made me pay for it, charging a hefty annual premium to cover death while mountain climbing. But I laughed now. As much as I liked to see myself as different from Wyn with his one-dimensional obsession with the mountains, I had to admit, I was much the same.

At 7 mm, the static line looked about as sturdy as a clothesline, but it was strong enough to hold a small car, provided rock fall hadn't damaged it. Clearing the ice off the line, I slid the other jumar up. I was on my way.

The face steepened. A ramp of snow led up and to the left. Fortunately, the face was quiet—no rock, ice, or snow fall. I got into a rhythm. Left jumar. Breathe. Right jumar. Breathe. It was agonizingly slow. When I tried to increase my pace, the cold air irritated my throat and sent me into a spasm of coughing. I stopped and popped a butterscotch candy into my mouth.

Looking down, I saw I'd covered only fifty feet. I kept going, heading up the snow ramp to the left. At the end of the first rope, I clipped the pack into the anchor and caught my breath. "I'm off!" I yelled to Wyn, who was shivering at the belay below.

While he ascended the fixed rope, I massaged my arms and looked down at our tents. Still no sign of Al or Lane. I hoped they would stay put today and not try to leapfrog us. Wyn arrived a few minutes later, huffing and puffing.

"How's it going?" I asked.

"Okay," he said robotically, his eyes half-closed, his mouth agape. I helped him off with his pack.

"What's wrong?" I asked, putting my hand on his shoulder.

"Something I ate." He waved me off. "Just keep going."

I took a deep breath. So this was how it was going to go. I couldn't rely on him to lead anything today. It worried me to see him so weakened. I needed him at full strength if I had any chance of climbing this route. But I put this out of my mind. "Okay," I said doggedly. "I got it."

Wyn didn't acknowledge me, just sat with his head on his knees, conserving his energy, suppressing the occasional dry heaves, retreating into himself.

The pack seemed heavier this time. Stamping my feet, I started up, not even bothering to look above. It was 3 a.m. The sky gleamed with stars. If I could suck it up, we would be up to camp in another couple hours.

After the argument with Al and Lane, I relished being alone. I drank in the power of the mountain, the depth of its silence. I felt rejuvenated, as if a new person was emerging from the harried, divided life I had led over the last five years. I had to concentrate on only one task: getting myself and my partners safely up this mountain.

Ascending the ropes with a full pack put great strain on my forearms and feet. My left ankle ached from the exertion. I kept going, keeping a pace I hoped I could maintain throughout the day.

On this fixed rope and the four to follow, there was no Wyn to clear the ice off the static line. No Wyn to holler encouragement. No Wyn to lead by example. It made me appreciate just how much he did without making a big deal about it. I chugged up the line, losing track of time. I stopped occasionally to pop a candy in my mouth. There was no sign of the yellow tent under the big overhang, only the thin black static line, leading up. Always up.

The pack threw me off balance as I fought my way through the rock band, the front points of my crampons sparking off the gray-orange granite. It was awkward to move through this section, harder to stabilize myself than when ascending snow. I had to stop and breathe deeply until I felt better. I was getting really tired now. The straps of the pack cut into my hips and shoulders. My forearms were shaking with exhaustion. I reached the end of one rope and carefully transferred the jumars to the next one. *Concentrate*, I told myself. *No mistakes.* A small blunder could prove fatal. Keep the jumars on the line. Stay clipped in at the belays.

I ticked off the pitches. I was getting close now. As the sun rose above the horizon, rocks began to loosen. Ice chips bounded down the face, harbingers of avalanches to come.

A rock buzzed by my ear like a killer bee. I picked up my pace. The angle eased and then shot up a snow slope to the right, ending beneath the big overhang. The tiny, yellow tent stood out like a beacon among the rock and snow. I moved faster, eager to dump my load. When I reached the top of the rope and clipped my pack into the anchor, I let out a whoop.

The tent, however, was full of snow. I got down on all fours and swept it out, finishing as Wyn appeared.

Despite my fatigue, I helped him off with his pack. Neither one of us said anything about the role reversal; we just accepted it, like the old days. I made sure that both of us were clipped into the anchor before we got into the tent. From now on, we'd seldom go anywhere without being clipped into a rope, an awkward but necessary part of life in a vertical environment.

Taking out his sleeping bag and pad, I gave him the more spacious upper berth. He got into it without saying anything and promptly went to sleep. Then I got into my bag, trying to get comfortable even though half my butt was over the abyss. I reminded myself about the six ice screws that anchored the tent in place; they would hold a minivan. It was 6 a.m. The avalanches would start up soon. But for now we were safe. We were in our camp. That was enough.

At 10 a.m., I sat up in my sleeping bag and took out the CB radio for the morning call.

"This is John, over."

"Roger, John," said Al.

"We're in Camp 1, over."

"Great..." Static drowned out the rest. We were in line of sight with them now, but the CB still had trouble transmitting. It made me realize how little we could rely on it to communicate with the outside world.

"How're you guys doing, over?" I asked.

"Fine." Al coughed. "We'll be up tomorrow."

"Good, let's touch base tonight. The ledge is too small for both of us. If the weather's bad, I don't want all of us stuck here."

"Roger."

"And, Al, you might want to zip up the tent next time." I tried to keep my tone free of accusation. "It was full of snow."

"We shut it, John."

"It was open when I got here."

There was a long silence as Al took in the criticism. It did little good to chew someone out over the radio. I'd save that discussion for when they got up here.

"How come you moved so slow up the fixed ropes?" Al asked.

"Wyn had stomach problems."

"Is he okay?" Al's voice rose with concern.

"He's better," I said, looking over to where he was sleeping.

"What's your plan?"

"We'll head up the fixed ropes tomorrow, then lead up to Spiral Camp."

"That's a lot of climbing," Al said. "We put in three fixed ropes in a day."

"I know," I said pointedly. "We're hoping to do better."

"Sure you don't want us to take over?"

"Let's talk at 8 p.m."

"I think we could move faster."

"Thanks, Al."

Al was delusional, but at least he was hungry. I didn't mind him jockeying to get out front as long as he kept the good of the entire team in mind. There was nothing wrong with conflict as long as you harnessed it to climb the peak.

Around noon, Wyn crawled outside of his sleeping bag, filled a pot with snow, and brought it back into the tent. Coughing and wheezing, he hung the small propane stove from the top of the tent with a chain, turned up the gas, and lit the burner. The stove cooked slowly, but this contraption allowed us to cook inside the tent without spilling water.

Now that Wyn was feeling better, I let him take charge of cooking. After the water boiled, he threw in some chicken soup, stirred it up, and poured me a bowl.

I sat up in my sleeping bag and spooned the broth into my mouth. There was a piece of paper floating in it. I handed the bowl back to him. "Waiter, there's toilet paper in my soup."

"Sorry," he said sheepishly. He had obviously taken the snow from the area designated for the latrine. He fished a piece of toilet paper out of it. "There," he said, as if that would fix everything.

I was so hungry, I ate it anyway. We were really groveling now. Manners degenerated on the climb, but there were limits. Toilet paper was over the line. I hoped it didn't set off yet another round of barfing.

Wyn drank a little broth but couldn't keep it down.

"You want it?" he asked, holding it at arm's length as if he couldn't get far enough away from it.

"Sure." I took it and drank it. We stayed put through the middle of the day, resting and staring out at the vast panorama of the Alaska Range spread out beneath us. The huge pyramids of Foraker and Hunter dominated the near horizon, but beyond them I caught glimpses of the lakes and streams of the tundra. From this distance it was just a blur, a tantalizing reminder of the world we'd left behind.

Avalanches roared over the top of us and dusted the tent with snow. They sounded like jets taking off from Sea-Tac. But since none did any damage, I began to ignore them.

At the 8 p.m. radio call, we heard a climber had been killed on the Orient Express. This was an icy chute on the west side of the mountain popular with Asian climbers—hence the name. The Koreans in particular had a reputation for recklessness as they often climbed without proper gear or acclimatization.

"Those guys are crazy," Wyn said, shaking his head. "It's almost like they want to die."

"I doubt it," I said. "They probably just slipped."

"No, they push it too hard," he said, leaning on his elbow. "They don't take enough equipment. They ignore bad weather."

"Sounds a lot like us," I said, rocking back on my foam pad.

Wyn dismissed this talk with a wave of his hand. "We're completely different." Despite Wyn's rationalizations, the news brought home the danger for all of us.

The weather report had called for clear skies for the next day or two. Wyn and I decided to keep going. We radioed Al and Lane to let them know. They agreed to head up the next day. Since Al didn't have an overnight pack, he'd have to jerry rig the day pack. This would reduce the amount of time we could spend on the upper face, making speed essential.

Turning off the radio, we sat around a candle lantern, the closest thing we could get to a fire on this high, cold face. The flame flickered over us, providing little warmth but a lot of comfort. Instinctively, we tried to warm our gloved hands in front of it. The tent was a tiny island of warmth and light on the vast, cold face.

"Do you think it's wrong for me to be on this climb?" I said, cupping my hands together.

"You're asking me?" Wyn said, incredulously.

"I just want another opinion."

"I think you have to put it all in the balance," he said, pursing his lips. "You've got to live your life. You can't let people dictate what you should or shouldn't do with it. If this is what you want to do, you should go for it."

"But do you think it's irresponsible, now that I'm a dad?"

"No way," Wyn answered, as if the answer was obvious. "Not according to my calculus. You have to be careful. But if you buy it, you buy it, whether it's up here or driving on I-5."

"You're not like the parents in Andy's preschool class," I said, chuckling at Wyn's iconoclastic attitude. "When I told one of the moms I was planning to climb Denali, she looked at me like I was crazy."

"Don't let other people's expectations prevent you from getting what you want out of life," he said, staring at the candle. "My dad tried to do that with me. He's still trying." He laughed. "He thinks I've wasted my life."

"My dad was never that way," I said. "His idea was to get a good job at a place like Boeing. Get married. Have a couple kids. Putter around the house. Be content with that. He never understood my restlessness."

"It's okay to be restless," Wyn said, raising his voice. "It's better than boredom."

"Or quiet desperation." I looked into the flame, brooding. "I wish I was content to work fifty hours a week, spend time with Andy, volunteer at the daycare, go to Hawaii on vacation, and get the best possible no-smoking rate on the life insurance policy. But I've tried to live that life, and it suffocated me."

"You see." He knocked me on the shoulder. "We're not that different."

"I never said we were," I said. "Only I got married and you didn't."

"There is that," he said, grinning smugly.

"I went on to mastering the Diaper Genie, while you went on to climbing El Cap."

"I just followed my dreams," Wyn said quietly. "That's all I've tried to do."

After packing, we headed up the face, leaving the tent for Al and Lane. It was 2 a.m. and ten degrees below zero. Wyn went first, following the static line up through a mixed band of snow and rock. He tested the line before attaching his jumar to it. I kept him on belay—just in case—we still weren't sure of Al and Lane's ability to fix ropes. It held.

"Bomber," Wyn yelled back—the rope was safe. He clipped into the next one and moved up. Shivering, I started up, relieved to get underway. I was amazed at how many anchors Al had placed. There were way more than necessary; no wonder it had taken them so long. But at least they were reliable.

It was much tougher going today. We were at 14,000 feet, close to the elevation at the top of Mount Rainier, and hadn't taken a rest day to acclimatize. Now we were paying the price. I felt like I was moving through a fog. My temples throbbed, exaggerating the difficulty of jumaring. Wyn wasn't moving much faster. I had no trouble keeping up with him.

Working our way up the second fixed rope, we emerged right below the top of the ridge. This was one of the most dangerous sections of the entire route. We were close to the massive funnel of the south face, the path of the biggest avalanches. Even if they didn't hit us, the wind and debris could snuff us out like insects at a picnic. And if the big slides didn't get us, the smaller ones might.

It was eerily beautiful—the snow, blue ice, and graying rock illuminated by the faint light of stars. The ridge rose above us like a flying buttress on a Gothic cathedral. For now, the face was quiet.

Wyn continued up the third fixed rope. Near the top, the anchors came a lot less frequently. I put Wyn back on belay as he front-pointed up the hard snow. The slings were awkwardly tied, but the ice screws, pickets, pitons, and other placements were solid. It looked as if Lane had put these in. He was learning his trade.

The third rope ended at the base of a rock wall, smaller and not nearly as well protected as Camp 1. Here, we paused to regroup before leading the next section. As we got higher on the face, the panorama kept enlarging—range upon range of mountains, glaciers, and snowfields. It looked like a landscape from the last ice age. Wyn ate a Snickers bar, his first food in a day. A rime of ice covered his beard, eyebrows, and blond hair. Aside from his green helmet, he could have been a stone-age mammoth hunter.

The wind started blowing, sending gusts of powder snow skipping over the rocks. He took off his mittens and blew on his hands. He stomped his feet and shook his arms. With so little fat on him, he was particularly susceptible to cold. As long as he kept moving, he was okay, but when he stopped, he started shivering. His face was lean and emaciated; his lips were split and scabbed by the sun. He sat on his pack, sipping some water, gathering his strength.

The water in my poly bottle was so cold it made my mouth hurt. The pieces of chocolate shattered as I bit into them. If I waited long enough, I assumed Wyn would lead the pitch, but he kept sitting, craning his neck, trying to see what was beyond the rock wall.

Our goal was to get to Camp 2, a ridge of snow right below the Spiral Couloir, a long, protected funnel in the middle of the face. It should provide enough room for both teams to camp safely. But it would be a grunt getting there. We'd have to keep a strenuous pace all day long and probably into the night. If we didn't get there, we'd have to camp in an exposed and highly dangerous spot. So far, we'd played it smart by climbing at night, but now we'd have to chance it. It was a calculated risk.

"Your lead?" Wyn said.

"Sure," I said nonchalantly. I was disappointed he didn't want to take the lead but tried not to show it. "I'll have a go."

I lifted my pack, racked the gear, and took a look at the next pitch. It was a short, vertical step of rock and then a ramp of hard, blue ice. I'd climbed pitches like this before, but never above 14,000 feet. I broke it down into sections, took a deep breath, and started up. Working my way up a crack, I slotted in a Friend, a spring-loaded camming device that would hold the rope if I fell. As the angle steepened, the climbing became harder. Cursing and swearing, I clawed my way up the crack, my crampons scraping across the rock like fingernails across a blackboard.

At the top, I twisted a screw into the blue ice, enjoying the squeaking sound it made as it penetrated deep into the surface. Burying it up to the head, I clipped a carabiner to it and attached it to the rope. A small victory.

Now that I had my protection in place, I took aim at the next section, a hard and featureless ramp of ice. This route had everything— rock, snow, hard ice, altitude. If we did it, the bragging rights would be huge. I kicked my right crampon into it, but the points bounced off. It was like trying to climb a steel plate.

I scanned the blue surface and found a whitish seam that looked softer. Kicking my right crampon into it, the front points barely penetrated it. That would have to be enough. I did the same with the picks of my ice axe and ice hammer. Only a few placements would do; most of the surface was like steel. Looking carefully, I found tiny pockets, holes, and seams. I moved up my right axe. Then my left. I repeated the sequence, scanning the opaque, blue surface for weaknesses. I was ten feet above the ice screw and feeling good. I was getting back into the life.

I glanced down at Wyn, who shouted encouragement. I nodded and went back to work. Willing my axes and front points into the ice, I ascended to right below the vertical step. Spotting a baseball-sized cavity, I sunk my left axe into it. Solid. Then I moved up my feet. With three points in the ice, I took an ice screw off the rack and started to place it. At twenty feet above the last point of protection, I needed to get something in. Fast.

As I unclipped it, a small avalanche hit me. I pivoted wildly off the left axe, swinging backward like a barn door. The ice screw bounded down the face. Fear surged through me like an electric current. The snow twisted me backward. I fought to keep my crampons in, contorting my body like a pretzel as I clung desperately to my left axe.

Powder snow filled my mouth, suffocating me. *I'm off!* I thought, but somehow I clung to the face. Finally the avalanche subsided. Swinging wildly, I tried to sink my right axe. It glanced off the ice. I tried again. No go. My left arm was cramping up; I had to get something in or I'd fall forty feet.

I spotted a pocket of white ice. I drove the axe into it with all my might, hearing a solid thunk as I nailed it. Shifting my weight to the right axe, I took the pressure off my throbbing left arm. Thank God. I looked up ahead. I still needed to get something in. Another avalanche could hit at any minute.

Unclipping another ice screw, I sunk it into the hard, blue ice and threaded it in. Before I could clip it, more powder snow sloughed over me, knocking a carabiner out of my hand. It bounded crazily down the face, screaming and whistling like a banshee. My heart was pounding.

As the snow slowed, I clipped another carabiner and sling into the rope. If I fell now, the rope would catch me. Fighting panic, I wiped the sweat from my forehead. My heart pounded, but I kept moving. The angle eased, but the ice was still hard and polished like onyx. Finally, I found a small alcove for the belay. Two ice screws made it solid.

It took me several minutes to collect myself. Breathing deeply, I tried to recall all the reasons for climbing this bastard. It would help the store, my reputation, all that crap. But finally, it was hard to exactly say why I wanted it. I just did. For now, that was enough. I called for Wyn to come up, keeping him on a tight leash all the way. With no avalanche sweeping the gully, he seconded the pitch quickly.

"Great lead!" he shouted. "That was a total horror show." He laughed and knocked his mittens together. "I got a picture of you hanging off that left axe. Just wait till we put the slide show together. You'll be the hero."

"John's bold deeds," I said. "The world's shortest book."

"Don't underestimate yourself," he said, taking the rack. "I would've had trouble leading it."

"I'm just glad I got through it," I said, shaking my head. "This route is intense."

"See?" His eyes were wide with excitement. "I told you so. Remember our conversation back at the 5.10?"

"I remember." I wiped my nose with my glove. "You made a great sales pitch."

"You were ripe for it," Wyn said, grinning. "I could tell."

I took a swig from his water bottle. "What do you think about those clouds?"

A scrim of high clouds appeared from the south—the weather direction. We were still a long way below Spiral Camp.

"No worries," Wyn said, waving aside my concern. "They won't bring a storm—yet."

I frowned. "I hope you're right. I don't want to bivy up here."

"We won't if we move fast," he said. "I'm going to keep going. Okay?"

"You feel good?"

"You inspired me." He winked. "I'll stay just to the left of the ridge crest. Keep your butt cheeks crossed."

I nodded. We'd been in this situation so many times before that we didn't need to discuss it. We both knew we were taking a chance, but it was necessary to get to the face. We were in this together now. It would be very difficult to retreat from Spiral Camp. In fact, it probably would be easier to climb the rest of the face.

Thirty yards above me, Wyn hammered in a piton. The rising ping, ping, ping of the hammer sounded like wonderful music: a well-placed piton was almost impossible to pull out by accident. He reholstered the hammer, moving slowly and carefully around boulders and up small snow chutes. He was sure and economical in his movements, but slower than usual.

After he had tied off the static line, I jugged up the pitch. As soon as I reached the top of the fixed rope, he was off again. We were moving together, making steady progress up the broken ridge. The rhythm of climbing together returned. After so many years, we were nearly equals again. My confidence soared.

Then I heard a sharp snap above us on the face. I looked up past Wyn to see a boulder the size of a car detach itself from a cliff. The boulder tumbled end over end in what looked like slow motion. It crashed and boomed down the face above us, bounding high and setting off subsidiary rock slides.

"Rock!" I screamed.

He pressed himself tight to the face. The boulder rocketed toward us. I dove into the snow behind a small rock. The boulder would obliterate me if it hit my stance. I tried to make myself as small as possible.

The rock thundered toward us, shaking the ground when it hit. I looked up once and then buried my head. It landed a hundred feet to my left and exploded into fragments, which pelted around me.

The rope pulled me forward, ripping me out of my stance. Wyn must have fallen. Suddenly I was exposed. A golf-ball-sized rock glanced off my helmet. I buried myself deeper into the snow. A volley of pebbles rattled off my helmet. When they stopped, I stood up and surveyed the damage. Stones were imbedded in the snow around me. One had ripped the cuff of my pants. But none had scored a direct hit.

The air was filled with granite dust. It smelled like brimstone and fear. I was unhurt but shaking from the near miss. Wyn was still dangling from the face.

"Wyn, you okay?"

"Yeah," he moaned. "I smashed my finger."

"How bad?"

"We'll see. You okay?"

"I just about shit my pants," I said. "Does that count?"

"No," he laughed.

I thought Wyn might back off, but he got back up to his stance and kept going. He reclimbed the section where he'd fallen. He stuck his head over the top and peered around like a gopher, making sure that another cascade of stones wasn't headed his way. Then he swung his right leg over the top and disappeared.

Several minutes later, he shouted for me to come up. When I reached his stance, he clapped me on the back. "Look at this," he said, showing me where a rock had hit his finger, causing a deep, purple bruise.

"Is it broken?" I asked.

"I don't think so," he said, shaking it. "But it hurts like hell."

"Do you want me to lead?"

"Would you mind?" He winced and put his glove back on. I could see it hurt him more than he was willing to admit.

"Okay," I said, trying to sound nonchalant. In truth, I was tense, jittery, and paranoid. My legs were spasming. I was cold and getting colder. "Do you think we should keep going?"

"Of course," Wyn said. "If we stay put, we're dead meat. Just look up there." He pointed toward the series of seracs, ice fields, and avalanche chutes that ringed the south face. Soon debris would thunder down them.

Racking the gear, I started moving. "Wish me luck," I said.

"You got it."

By the time he caught me at the belay, his finger had stopped throbbing. He led the next pitch. We climbed through the early afternoon and into the early evening. We saw each other on the belays, but each of us moved in his own world. A large avalanche raced down the face to our right, dusting us with some light powdery snow. A small rockslide pelted down to our left. We barely noticed.

As Wyn predicted, the ridge afforded some protection. It divided the immense face, providing a narrow, sketchy path through the chaos of ice, snow, and rock on either side. It wasn't much, but it was enough.

We stopped only for a few minutes at a time. We didn't want our muscles to cramp up. We kept slogging. There was nothing else to do.

A scattering of stones ricocheted down the snow slope above us. I winced and increased my pace. Wyn put in fewer and fewer anchors, trying to move fast and minimize our exposure.

Shadows lengthened across the face. The stone fall slowed. The world grew silent, save for the ping, ping, ping of Wyn's piton hammer. We'd been going continuously for almost twenty hours. I was beyond tired, yet my adrenaline kept me focused. I belayed Wyn up the slope, and then jugged up behind him.

He racked the gear quickly. His face was ashen, deeply lined. Ice covered his beard. "Spiral Camp," he said, pointing to the top of a large snowfield. "Almost there."

I nodded dumbly, running on autopilot.

Putting him on belay, I forced myself to check my knot, locking carabiner—all the links in the belay chain. I discovered I hadn't locked my biner. Again.

I didn't bother telling him this, but I watched as he slogged up the slope. After what seemed like hours, I heard, "Off belay, John!"

By the time I arrived at the campsite, I was nodding off. Wyn helped me clip into the anchor. I took off my pack and clipped it in, too. Neither of us said anything. We knew what to do.

I got out my snow shovel and started digging a platform for the tent. I was so tired I could barely stand up. We dug side by side, stopping to catch our breath. All I wanted to do was lie down, but I didn't want to disappoint Wyn. Gradually, we enlarged the platform, perched on a steep slope near the bottom of the Spiral Couloir.

As a level spot emerged, I took out the tent. Wyn came over to help with it. The wind tugged at the fabric, threatening to blow it back down the face. We spread it across the platform, anchored it with pickets, and fitted the poles into the sleeves. I had to stop several times to warm up my hands. Hoar frost had coated our clothes, eyebrows, beard, and hair.

"Why don't you get inside?" he said, after we put the last pole in place. "Your weight can anchor the tent."

Thanks a lot, I thought. My contribution had been reduced to nothing more than ballast. But it was a relief to sit down, and I knew I was more than just dead weight. I'd helped him, and now he was helping me. I'd not only kept up with him, I'd equaled and sometimes surpassed him. If not for my efforts, we'd never have reached this spot. This was what partnership was all about.

Spreading out my foam pad and sleeping bag, I fought to stay awake. *Get your crampons off or they'll shred the fabric*, I told myself.

Trips often came down to moments like this: tasks that in other circumstances were trivial became almost insurmountable. Warming my wooden hands, I flicked away the ice and tugged on the buckle. It gave. I stowed the crampon next to the tent door and went to work on the other one.

Outside the tent, Wyn cursed as he drove a picket into the snow. What a relief it was to climb with him. Despite his lack of interpersonal skills, he was a generous, selfless partner and a climbing machine.

After anchoring the tent, he unzipped the door and stuck his head in. He moved like an automaton, having done this so many times that he hardly seemed to think. He took off his crampons and boots, setting them to the side of the door. Then he hung the stove from the ceiling. Taking out the cook kit, he filled a pan with snow, poured water in it, and set the pan on the stove. Soon the tent warmed up.

A few minutes later, he handed me a cup of Top Ramen. It tasted better than any meal I've had in my life. I would've eaten it even if it had toilet paper in it. Putting the bowl to my lips, I drank greedily, burned myself, and spilled it over my parka. Forcing myself to sip more slowly, I felt the warmth spread to my throat, esophagus, and stomach.

We had made it. For now, at least, we were safe. We had moved continuously for almost twenty-four hours. We had dodged rock fall, avalanches, and all the mountain had thrown at us. We had come together as a team. Through great risk and effort, we had put ourselves in position to finish the climb. The lower, more dangerous half of the face was behind us. After a few more days, we might even top out on this thing.

ELEVEN

The wind rose in the night. Violent gusts shook and battered the tent, threatening to fling it off the mountain. I burrowed deeper in my sleeping bag, praying the ice screws and pickets would hold. The tent was top-of-the-line, designed to withstand winds in excess of eighty miles per hour, but gusts of 120 miles an hour had occurred on Denali. Some of these storms had literally blown climbers off the peak.

The wind died down, then roared back, hammering away at the tent, straining the fabric, bowing the poles, tugging at the anchors. All this noise made it difficult to sleep, despite my exhaustion.

By morning, I had a splitting headache. Snow had collapsed the sides of the tent. The tiny chamber was as narrow as a crypt.

"Wyn?"

"Huh?"

"The tent is collapsing."

"Yeah?"

"Would you mind digging it out?"

He sighed.

"I did it last time."

He sat bolt upright, put on his parka and boots, grabbed the shovel, and disappeared through the door. Cold air and snow blasted through the opening. Reaching up, I shut the door of the tent. I heard him swear as he fought the wind and blowing snow. The shovel scraped against the tent fabric. Gradually, the tent sprang back into place.

"A front's coming in," he said, returning.

The weather radio confirmed it. A storm was blowing in from the Gulf of Alaska. The snow would load the slopes, making an advance or a retreat difficult and dangerous. We'd have to sit tight, at least for now, and suffer through it. But our supplies were dwindling. The ravens' raid on the cache had put a serious dent in our reserves. And since Al was only carrying a daypack, our margin was even slimmer. We had enough food for a week, but storms regularly pinned parties down for that long. All the seemingly minor mistakes were catching up with us.

Avalanches went off like cannons around us. Slopes released with a distant boom, then roared down the face, coming frighteningly close.

Every slide made my headache worse. It felt like someone had my head in a vise and was slowly tightening it. I had pushed too hard. Now I was paying the price. My temples throbbed. My vision was blurred. My lungs labored to get enough oxygen to my brain. I felt exhausted and despondent. I just wanted to go to sleep, but the noise and headache made it impossible.

I took some Tylenol with Codeine and immediately regretted it. I got up quickly from my bag.

"What are you doing?" Wyn asked.

Putting my hand over my mouth, I got halfway through the door before I puked up the remains of last night's chicken soup. It splattered over the tent fly and the snow in front of it. Sitting on my knees, I vomited up noodles and dried peas, enduring wave after wave of nausea. Finally, the dry heaves waned. I wiped my mouth with my sleeve. It was hard to focus on anything. I felt dizzy and lightheaded: was this the onset of high-altitude pulmonary edema? I scraped the vomit off the tent fly. In the cold, it came off easily.

"You okay, John?"

"Great," I said, suddenly pissed at him. "How do I look?"

"You look like hell." He handed me some Pepto-Bismol tablets. Chewing them quickly, I collapsed into my sleeping bag. The world began to spin. My breathing was rapid. Then slow. Rapid. Slow. I wanted all of it to just go away. I wanted to be home with Jill. I needed to take her out to dinner. We hadn't been out on a date in a year. Maybe that was part of the problem. I thought about Andy and what we'd do together when I got back. I would teach him to play soccer, the game Wyn and I had grown up playing. I'd steer him away from climbing. I fell asleep resolved to do this.

Wyn nudged me on the shoulder. "Drink this," he ordered, handing me a cup of mint tea. I propped my head up with my elbow. I sipped gingerly, not wanting to burn my mouth. I breathed deeply, trying to slow down my racing pulse.

Sitting up, I checked my pulse again. It was elevated. This could be a symptom of pulmonary or cerebral edema, a deadly high-altitude illness caused by ascending too quickly. Victims often didn't recognize the symptoms until it was too late.

Flipping through the first-aid manual, I read that blue lips and fingernails meant lack of oxygen in the blood, a potential sign of edema. I checked my fingernails for a bluish tinge. Sure enough, it was there, but was it edema or simply the cold weather? It seemed difficult to distinguish ordinary complaints from more serious ones. Coughing was supposed to be another sign, but I had none of the crackles, gurgles, and wheezes typical of pulmonary edema. Taking out my compass to check my color, I barely recognized myself in the mirror: I looked wild, hunted and weather beaten, but my lips were pink and peeling—not blue. Still, there was a fine line between edema, or HAPE, and ordinary mountain sickness.

"Do you think I have HAPE?" I asked, pressure breathing to get the words out.

He examined my eyes and lips and then shook his head. "I don't think so," he said. "But I'll keep an eye on you. Rest. Drink. That's key to preventing it."

Finishing my tea, I pulled up the hood of my sleeping bag, telling myself everything would be okay. Finally, I fell asleep. When I woke in the afternoon, Wyn shoved another cup in front of me. I felt like I was nailed to the tent floor. It was all I could do to drink, crawl outside to pee, and retreat back into my sleeping bag. By the early evening, my headache had eased but my breathing remained labored. Wyn made tea and got up to check on the weather.

At 8 p.m., he picked up the radio.

"This is Wyn, over."

"Roger, Wyn, this is Al, over."

"How are you guys doing?"

"Okay, but I don't like this storm."

"Are you guys at Camp 1?"

"Roger, we made it up here yesterday."

"How's Lane doing?"

"We're both ready to go."

"Are you planning a rest day?"

"Negative. We're heading up tomorrow."

"I'd advise against it," Wyn said. "The slopes will be loaded."

"We need to keep up with you," Al said. "We don't have a lot of food…"

"Didn't you hear the weather report? It's supposed to storm for another day or two."

"We heard it."

Wyn paused and shook his head. "Just watch yourselves. Play it safe."

"Funny to hear that coming from you."

"It's true."

"But we want to get back out front."

"When you guys are ready, you can have it."

"You keep saying that."

"You guys have to step up."

"That's what we're planning to do."

"Okay." Wyn rubbed his face. "Start early. Pull the ladder up behind you."

I got a sick feeling in my stomach. If they pulled the ropes, we were committed.

"Are you sure?" Al asked.

"Yes."

"That will take forever." His voice cracked. "Then we'll have no way down."

"Leave a few fixed ropes across the traverses if you like. Pull the rest. We may need them higher."

Al sighed. "We'll try."

"Let's talk tomorrow at 8 p.m."

"You got it." Wyn turned off the radio. "Hope they stay put during this storm."

I nodded. "Al seems to be getting desperate."

"At least he's determined," Wyn said, scratching his chin. "You've got to give him that."

Wyn went back to reading. I forced myself to finish the water bottle. Then I put on my parka and went out the door. Windblown snow hit me in the face; it was harsh and abrasive as sand. Scooping up some snow, I brought it inside and got the stove going. Soon we had chicken soup. Then I went outside for more snow. I spent the rest of the evening melting snow and rehydrating, checking and rechecking my fingernails for the bluish tinge.

The storm continued off and on throughout the next day. The yellow walls of the tent began to close in. I read the first-aid manual and stared at the wall of the tent. The tedium of being tent-bound began to set in. My coughing got worse, a dry, hacking cough that left me wheezing and red-faced.

Wyn took out a map, examining our route. It was the same map he'd brought to the 5.10, but now it was falling apart. We were at 15,000 feet, midway up the face, but still had 5,000 feet to go. We were a long way from the summit.

I started to ask about the couloir ahead, but a bout of coughing overcame me.

"Could you put a lid on that?" he said, wincing.

"On what?"

"That cough," he said, throwing the map down. "It's driving me nuts."

"Sorry," I said, coughing again. "I can't help it."

"At least cover your mouth."

"I will if you stop biting your fingernails."

"I can't help it."

"Yes, you can."

"No, I can't. It helps calm my nerves."

"Well, I can't help coughing either." We both fell silent. I pretended to go to sleep. It was unsettling to have to wait up here while the storm continued, not able to go up or down. As long as we were moving, making progress, our mood was good. But when we stopped, frustration built.

"How about a game of chess?" Wyn asked.

"Okay," I said nonchalantly, eager to win one from the bastard. I was so mad that I concentrated hard, even though it made my head throb. I managed to hold even with him through most of the game. Near the end, he foolishly exposed his Queen. I took her with a pawn he had overlooked—a triumphant move for me. A few moves later, I checkmated him. Then I lay back down in the sleeping bag, exhausted.

"Let's play another," he said, putting the pieces back on the board.

"No, I've got to rest."

"You're afraid I'll win."

"That's it."

He unzipped the tent door and poked his head outside.

"How does it look?"

"Better, but it's still blowing pretty hard," he said, closing the door.

Listening to the flapping of the tent, my mood alternated between dread at our position and optimism about getting to the top. Would I have the strength to make it to the summit? Would I chicken out like last time? Should I try to descend now, before they pulled the fixed ropes? I checked my fingernails: still blue.

"Here." Wyn handed me a cup of tea.

I thanked him and took it. Shortly after I'd finished the tea, he took out the chess board.

"How about another game?" He grinned.

"Okay."

This time I let him win. It was a peace offering. Wyn was so competitive that it bugged him if he lost at anything, even something as trivial as a chess game. He seemed very pleased with himself.

"What are your plans after this climb?" he asked, putting the board away.

"First I want to get up *this* thing," I said. "Then I'll get back to Seattle, see Andy and Jill, and put the store back in order."

"Sure, but after that?"

"I don't know. Why?"

"Do you want to know a secret?" Wyn glanced from side to side as if someone could overhear him. "I've got a lead on a permit—for the big E."

"Really?"

"Don't tell anybody," he said, grabbing my arm. The Wyn paranoia again.

"Which route is it?"

He rubbed his hands together. "It's this very cool variation on the West Ridge." He drew an imaginary line in the air. "Straight up and down. Just like this route."

"Cool."

"Are you interested?"

"You want me to go to Everest?" I sat up in my sleeping bag.

"Sure, why not?" he said, his eyebrows rising with surprise. "You've been kicking ass up here."

"Well, for one thing, it would be the end of my marriage," I said, shaking my head. "Jill would never go for that."

"You might be surprised," Wyn said, ever the optimist. It was obvious why he wasn't married. In this department, he really didn't have a clue.

"Besides, we haven't even climbed this thing."

"I know, I know, I'm getting ahead of myself." He waved aside my objection. "Forgive me. Are you interested?"

"Of course I'm interested, but..." I looked around at the dirty clothes, empty Top Ramen packages of soup, used tea bags, and Hershey's wrappers. I hadn't changed my underwear in a week. I hadn't bathed or showered since the start of the trip. My hair was oily and dark and matted. My cheeks were caked with sunscreen and peeling skin. My face had turned so dark that I looked like a Bedouin. The rest of me smelled like his camel.

Wyn looked and smelled even worse. He considered personal hygiene a luxury on climbing trips and paid only as much attention to it as necessary. The only exception was his toenails, which he clipped with studied fascination as if he couldn't believe such marvels were grown by his own body. On Everest there would be three months of this, plus exponentially more danger.

"There are other guys I could ask," Wyn said, sounding miffed.

"Let me think about it," I said, getting up for some snow. It seemed bad form to be thinking about another climb when we hadn't finished this one. Besides, I didn't want to even imagine all of the horse-trading I'd have to do to get away for three months. Outside, the clouds had disappeared. The wind still buffeted the tent, but the storm was blowing itself out.

"Guess what we're having for dinner?" I said, returning with a pot of snow.

"Top Ramen?"

"Pasta with puttanesca sauce."

"Really?" Wyn looked puzzled. "Where did you get that?"

"Wait and see." I boiled the Top Ramen, took out a can of sardines, poured the oil over the noodles, and counted out the fillets. "Voila."

Wyn rolled his eyes, but he ate the sardines. Each of us got exactly five. Unfortunately, the sardines proved too much for my stomach. I nearly puked on the first one. I gave the rest to Wyn, who eagerly wolfed them down. I regretted not getting the protein, but I didn't want to throw up. The altitude was taking a toll on my health. My body was deteriorating. A gash on the back of my hand still wasn't healed. The spare tire around my waist had disappeared. My ribs stuck out underneath my biohazardous underwear.

While we ate, we listened to the evening's radio forecast, our only real contact with the outside world. The forecast called for clearing weather. Afterwards, we tried to raise Al and Lane. No luck. Perhaps they were moving below us or had simply forgotten to call. I stuck my head outside the tent. The wind was dying down.

"I wonder if we should head back down and try to find them?" I asked.

"Are you kidding?" he said. "We have no idea where they are. If they don't call by tomorrow, then we'll go looking for them."

He tried to call again but got nothing but static. We went to sleep, turning off the radio to save on batteries.

My thoughts drifted back to Jill and Andy. I remembered a day last summer. Jill was planting some red petunias in the garden. Andy was digging up worms with a stick. The afternoon sun filtered through the pear tree and onto the hammock where I was lying. Soon I was fast asleep.

—

Someone was shouting. I sat up and looked around. Wyn was still sleeping, his mouth half-open, a frozen ribbon of drool coming off his lip. Hoar frost covered the albino-white whiskers around his mouth.

"Wyn!" I heard from below the tent. "John!"

Dressing quickly, I went outside. "Al, is that you?"

"Yeah," he bellowed, his voice muffled by the snow.

By this time, Wyn was up.

"Al, you okay?" I shouted.

"Okay!" Al answered enthusiastically. "Okay!" His words trailed off into the wind.

We waited, shivering, as they climbed the last hundred feet to camp, post-holing up the new snow. Al came into view first. His glasses were fogged and his lips were blue. With his head, face, and purple parka shellacked with ice, he looked like a giant, purple Popsicle. He grinned fiercely and collapsed on the snow.

Wyn tied him into the anchor while I helped him off with his day pack.

"You made it." I slapped him on the back. On this vast indifferent face, it was a huge lift to have their company again, despite the earlier arguments.

Lane came next, patiently rest-stepping up the route. He chugged like a locomotive, pressure breathing slowly and regularly. He kept his shoulders erect, his actions unhurried. With his red parka, red pile hat, beard, and face covered with snow, he looked like a disheveled Santa Claus. His blue eyes were fierce and bug-eyed, but he smiled wearily as I grabbed his rope and clipped him in. Wyn helped him off with his pack.

"Freight Train!" Wyn held his hand up for a high-five. Lane missed his hand. "Let's get you guys inside our tent."

We hustled Al in first. Taking off his crampons, boots, and clothes, we put him in Wyn's sleeping bag.

Lane didn't want any help. "I can do it myself," he said, sitting down at the entrance to the tent.

While he unbuckled his crampons, we dug a platform for their tent. By the time we set up their tent and anchored it with ice screws, my hands were numb. Wyn helped me put their sleeping bags in the tent. Then we went back to our tent.

"We made it!" Al crowed.

Lane nodded dumbly.

Wyn helped them over to their tent while I brewed up some tea for them. By the time I brought it to them, Al and Lane were asleep. Al slept on his side in a fetal position, reminding me of Andy in his crib. It was hard to feel any animosity toward him when he was sleeping. Lane lay on his back with his arms across his chest, snoring. I nudged him awake. "Drink this," I ordered.

He sputtered awake, nodded, drank the tea, and promptly fell back to sleep. Then I went back to our tent. It was a relief to have our group together again. If we could get through this next section it might bring us together as a team.

In the night, the wind stopped. It looked like we were on for tomorrow.

At 2 a.m., I started the stove. My headache had disappeared. My breathing had calmed. My fingernails were still blue, but I ignored them. Feeling my bicep, I noticed I was losing muscle mass. My arms were becoming as knotty and stringy as Wyn's. I was itching to get moving. I wanted to finish off this mountain. The clock was ticking.

I melted a pot of water for instant coffee and oatmeal. The coffee was almost gone, so I put in half a teaspoon and filled the cup with water. I used only one packet of oatmeal, not our usual two. Wyn woke up, scratched his beard, and sat up in his sleeping bag. He ate the oatmeal slowly, making it last, then scraped every last bit off his blue plastic bowl. After we finished our coffee, we woke Al and Lane and told them about the plan. Lane propped himself up on his elbow, while Al stayed burrowed in his sleeping bag.

"We're going to check out the conditions," Wyn said matter-of-factly. "If they look good, we'll head up the Spiral Couloir. Then across Dartmouth Meadows to the base of the rock buttresses."

Al coughed and squinted skeptically at us. He looked haggard and withdrawn, his face ashen, his lips blue. "Will you guys wait for us?"

"We will at the top," Wyn said, looking at his watch.

"I'd like to lead the couloir," Al said.

"You're still in bed," Wyn said.

"I can be ready soon," Al said, adjusting his glasses. "What do you think, Lane?"

"I think you're out of your mind," Lane said. "You're only carrying a day pack. I'm carrying that pig." Lane pointed to his pack, which looked like it weighed seventy pounds. "Besides, we're running low on food."

"Exactly," I said. "We have to move quickly."

"This is just like Boeing," Al said, shaking his head.

"No it's not," Wyn corrected him. "It's not a job..."

"It's an adventure," I said. "And I want to survive it."

Al sank back into his sleeping bag.

"We'll follow you," Lane said, intervening. "If we're feeling better, we'll take the next lead. Okay, Al?"

"Yeah, right." Al sighed.

"Get moving as soon as you can," Wyn said. "We'll meet you up top. If for some reason you can't make it, call us at 8 p.m. Got it?"

Lane nodded.

On the way back to our tent, Wyn muttered. "Sanity prevailed."

"Maybe they can lead the rock buttress."

"We'll see," Wyn said, stuffing his sleeping bag into his pack. "We need to get up and over this thing."

"You don't need to tell me that," I answered. "I want to knock this sucker off."

"That's the spirit." Wyn laughed.

We loaded our packs and collapsed the tent. I checked the knots in my rope, locked the biner. Shouldering our packs, we started up toward the couloir like mules bowed beneath enormous burdens. We punched through wind slab until reaching the base of the couloir. Wyn fitted a Camalot into a crack in the granite on the right. It was solid.

We exchanged looks. The couloir spiraled upward several hundred yards, a forty-five-degree gully of new snow and patches of hard, blue ice. We both knew there was a chance of an avalanche. We should probably wait another day for the snow to firm up, but our supplies were running low.

"What do you think?" he said.

"Let's give it a shot," I said. "We can always retreat."

He nodded eagerly. We were both in sync now. He started moving up the couloir. For every step up, he slid half a step back. The snow was light and unbonded, like powdered sugar. Wyn wiggled and squirmed and clawed his way upward. Finally he reached a good belay point on a rock outcrop and pounded in a piton.

"Off belay!" he shouted, his words echoing down the couloir.

I moved up. Slipped back. Moved up. It was exhausting work. I tried to establish a rhythm, but then a step would collapse. It took me a good fifteen minutes to get to Wyn. Still, it was progress.

Taking the rack from him, I led out. Thirty feet above him, I sank a picket into the soft snow, more for psychological aid than any real protection.

Pressure breathing, I tried to calm my hammering heart. Keep cool. Take it easy. One step at a time. All the climbing mantras ran through my head. Moving up, I felt the slope around me settle with a whump. I froze, waiting for it to release. It held, allowing me to clear away enough snow to get into the ice. Unclipping an ice screw, I torqued it into place. It wasn't the best placement, but it would have to do. Speed was at a premium. "Belay off!"

Wyn started up, following my footsteps, which collapsed under his weight.

"This snow is a pain in the ass," Wyn said when he reached me.

"Did you hear how it settled? I just hope it doesn't..."

"Don't even say that," he said. "Don't even think it."

Wyn kept climbing. He found a section of well-bonded snow that chirped, squeaked, and protested as he climbed up it. It sounded like it was about to sheer off.

I didn't like this at all. Fear replaced the feeling of euphoria. "Further to the right!" I yelled as he headed up a slope that looked unstable.

"What?"

"Go right!"

"Are you sure?"

"Positive."

"Okay."

I had a good view of the upper part of the couloir. We had a hundred yards to go. Stomping my feet to keep them warm, I watched him kicking steps. Each one seemed to weaken the slope.

"Careful!" I yelled.

Gingerly, he danced his way to a rocky outcrop. Taking out his hammer, he drove in a piton. The ting, ting, ting sound calmed my nerves. A few minutes later, he brought me up.

I moved up delicately, trying not to kick my feet too deeply into the slope. I was congratulating myself on my ability to do this when my right foot lost its purchase.

"Falling!" A jolt of panic shot through me. Then I was hanging on the end of the rope, five feet below where I'd fallen. I stood up, readjusted my pack, and kept going.

"I've got you," Wyn said.

I didn't even look up at him. I just concentrated on my steps. When I reached his stance, I stopped and caught my breath. Then I reached for the rack.

"Are you okay to lead?" he asked.

"Why?"

"You're shaking."

I looked at my right hand, which trembled uncontrollably. "I just want to get the hell out of here."

"You and me both," he said, wiping the sweat from his forehead. "Go."

The slope creaked and protested as I moved up the last hundred feet, alternating axes, watching my feet. Below the final lip, I drove in a picket and clipped into it. Ten feet to go. Above me, the snow rose in a frozen wave, a tricky formation to climb. Remembering the slip, I vowed to be deliberate. Moving up, my left crampon found ice. I kicked it in harder. I kicked in my right foot but found only powder. Flicking my left ice axe, I landed a good placement. I tried to get a similar one for my right axe. Nothing. My left crampon and axe shook from taking so much weight.

Pivoting off my left leg, I lunged upward and hooked my right axe over the lip. It looked as solid as meringue, but it held. Now I was committed. I threw my right leg upward and over the top, a Hail Mary of a climbing move. Flailing desperately with my left axe, I managed to sink it into some scree, giving me just enough purchase to throw the rest of my carcass over the top. My cheek landed in the gravel. I lay there hyperventilating, trying to get my wind back. It was an ugly but effective lead. My chest heaved as my lungs fought for air. Then I looked around for a placement. I settled for a picket hammered into the soft snow. Not very secure, but screw it, I was too tired to look for another.

After setting up the belay, I called to Wyn. I heard his muffled reply and brought him up, keeping him on a tight leash. I didn't trust the picket. I didn't want to have a millimeter of slack in the rope if the slope gave way. He moved up quickly and stopped below the lip. I heard him sink his axes and crampons. Then he swore, grunted, and hacked away ice. One ice axe appeared over the edge. Then another. The axes searched for a solid placement. Nothing. He poked his green helmet over the lip. His eyes bulged as he scanned the snow and gravel. He cursed, sank the axe into the gravel, and lunged forward. His momentum carried him over the top. He lay like an insect pinned beneath his huge, blue pack.

Then he crawled forward and slowly stood up. "Jesus!" He spat gravel and snow from his mouth. "That was sick."

"Did you get a photo?" I asked.

"Your butt is going to be famous."

"I'm just glad to get my butt out of there."

"Let's go up a little higher," he said. "I don't like that picket."

"Best I could do," I said, ignoring the criticism.

"Sure," he said. "Looks like a better stance up higher."

He led the way toward a rock bench. I waited until he'd set up a belay and then followed him. Dumping my pack, I sat down to admire the view. We had a panoramic perspective on the entire of the Alaska Range, a dazzling array of serrated peaks like the jaw of an immense prehistoric beast. I stared at Mount Foraker in the distance, its steep, icy slopes changing from pink to apricot as the sun rose. Joy welled up in me. Now I knew why I'd come back to climb this peak.

Far down the glacier, I spotted a tiny red dot—our base camp tent. It was a concrete measure of how far we'd come. Immediately below us, our footprints zigzagged up the couloir, as tiny and sketchy as the tracks of a sparrow.

Above us, the jagged, wind-blown face rose toward the summit, which was obscured by clouds. But I knew it was up there. I could feel it. We were getting close. I envisioned that long, white pathway up the ridge, and then the wind-whipped mound of snow at the top of North America, the place where everyone planted their flags, left their mementos, snapped their photos, and fulfilled their dreams.

Small flakes of snow drifted down. The next section of the route rose in a magnificent series of granite buttresses, the last technical challenge of the ascent. Getting to the base looked easy—ice and snow slopes thirty to forty-five degrees and only a few steep rock steps. It seemed tantalizingly close.

"Should we keep going?" I asked Wyn.

"Let's have something to eat," he said. "I'm starved."

I broke a couple squares off a bittersweet chocolate bar. We were down to half rations now. The chocolate shattered in my teeth. I wanted more, but forced myself to put the bar away. We only had three left.

Feeling dizzy and lightheaded, I drank as much as water as I could. I didn't want the vise back on my head. I didn't bother to check my fingernails. Taking off my mittens would just make things worse.

Looking down the couloir, I noticed a slab of snow crack and release near the top of the chute. It broke off and raced down slope, setting off a chain reaction. The upper couloir avalanched, sending blocks of ice as big as refrigerators tumbling end over end.

"Holy shit." Wyn dropped his chocolate.

We watched in horror as the slide rumbled down the couloir. When it finally stopped, Wyn grabbed the radio.

"Al and Lane, can you hear me, over?"

Nothing. He tried several times over the next five minutes. He paced, swore, paced, called again. It was hard to avoid the obvious conclusion. Finally, Al came on the air.

"Jesus H. Christ," Al said, an edge of panic in his voice. "You guys okay?"

"Yeah. What about you?"

"I thought you were toast," Al said, panting.

"We were above the couloir when it released. How about you?"

"It came down right past us," Al said, breathing hard. "It sounded like the Concorde taking off."

"Any damage?"

"It snapped one of the tent poles," Al said, shuddering. "Man, I'm getting too old for this."

"Are you guys coming up?" Wyn said.

"For once, I'm glad I slept in," Al said, laughing.

"The couloir might be unstable."

"We're coming up," Al said, clearing his throat. "We've come this far."

"Okay," Wyn said. "We're going to keep moving. We'll meet you at the base of the first rock buttress."

"That's a long way to go," Al said.

"Our food is running out."

"So is ours."

"Got another suggestion?"

"I just hope we can make it."

"Your call."

There were several seconds of silence. Finally, Al responded. "We'll see you up there."

"Okay." Wyn turned off the walkie-talkie. "Let's keep moving."

TWELVE

The buttress soared into the blue-black sky, as pure in its ascension as the steeple of a cathedral. A series of vertical cracks bisected the orange-gray granite, providing the key to the route, the last technical difficulty before reaching the long undulating ridge to the summit. We seemed so close to the top that I tingled with anticipation. But I forced myself to put a damper on my enthusiasm. We still had a long way to go.

Through the morning and into the afternoon, I labored upwards toward a long, ragged cleft that split the first of the buttresses. It was a chimney and would be tough to tackle with a fifty-pound pack. The rock would be plastered with ice and snow. The footing would be treacherous. The pack would throw me off balance. But it did no good to psych myself out in advance. If I'd learned anything on this climb, it was to compartmentalize my thoughts. Only worry about things I had some control over. So, I simply slogged upward through the fresh snow, a machine, a beast of burden, with no extraneous thoughts to interfere with hauling myself up the peak.

As I moved through the fresh snow, I had to force myself not to stare at the buttress ahead. If I did, I'd get frustrated at the slowness of our pace. If we reached it by nightfall, we'd be on track. If we didn't, I didn't want to think about it.

Last night's storm had dumped a blanket of dry, light, unstable snow. Above me, Wyn took a step upward and slid back down. He kicked in his crampons and managed to reach ice. Wading through the waist-deep snow, he made little progress. He placed an ice screw, attached a sling, and clipped into the rope. Then he kept moving. The rope pulled taut around my waist. I started up, following in the swath he had plowed through the snow. I hoped Al and Lane would make it up today. It would be so much easier if they had the benefit of our trail.

As we moved upslope, I kept my eye on the buttress. There was supposed to be a wide flat area at its base. It would be a luxury to walk around without wearing a harness. It would be great to set up the tent without having to hack a platform out of blue glacial ice. If we could just get there.

Wyn set up a series of running belays, putting in one picket or ice screw per pitch. He was taking a chance, but the angle was only forty degrees, and the clock was running. When I took the lead, I also ran it out, putting in two pieces of gear per rope-length. I worried about what would happen if I fell, but we had no choice. We *had* to move fast.

We made good time until clouds came up in the early afternoon. They playfully swirled around us, providing a welcome relief from the intensity of the high-altitude sun. The buttress appeared and disappeared in the mist. I got a compass bearing on it before it vanished. The temperature dropped, and we were plunged into a solipsistic fog of exhaustion and anxiety. I zipped up my parka, put up my hood, and clenched my fingers to keep them warm. As I moved up, I took out the photo by famed Denali photographer Bradford Washburn and kept my eye on the trembling red needle of the compass to make sure we were on track. I'd gotten a good bead on the buttress. I was confident of my navigational ability. But in the absence of visual proof, doubts crept in.

When we switched leads, Wyn asked, "Are you sure you got the right bearing? I think we're going too far to the left."

"I'm positive," I said. "And it jibes with the photo."

"It doesn't seem right."

"What do you suggest?"

"Heading to the right."

"I don't think so."

"I'm going with my hunch."

"I'm going with magnetic north."

"Well, okay," Wyn said, spitting. "You're probably right."

"I am right," I said.

Wyn exhaled and picked up his pack. "Okay, amigo."

Fog and snow swirled around us. The falling snow obscured a series of narrow crevasses. Wyn punched through one, but I self-arrested and stopped his fall. It was draining to be on high alert all the time; the higher we climbed, the more dangerous things became. Despite my weariness, I stayed vigilant. I didn't want to let my guard down.

"Watch me!" Wyn said.

"Got you!"

He moved carefully upward, kicking his crampons into the slope to test it. The ground was easy, but the snow was loose. We moved slowly but steadily. Each step was one I wouldn't give back.

Then Wyn lunged forward. I shoved the ice axe into the snow, anticipating a fall.

"Shit!" Wyn yelled.

"Are you okay?" I yelled back.

"Fuck!" he yelled.

"What is it?"

More swearing. "Keep going!"

"Okay!"

Wyn moved slowly, favoring his left leg. Finally, he stopped, set up a belay, and brought me up.

"What's wrong?" I said, breathing hard.

He sat on his pack and held his knee. He winced as he tried to move it. "I wrenched it when I fell into that damn crevasse."

"How did it happen?"

"The crampon's front-points caught on the ice and jerked my leg back," he said, grimacing. "It hurts like hell."

I sat down on my pack and put my head in my hands. We'd be lucky to make it to the base of the buttress tonight if both of us were moving fast. Now that seemed impossible. But I kept the doom and gloom to myself.

Grabbing his arm, I helped him up. Wyn stood, tested his left leg, grimaced, and hobbled around in a circle. He downed a couple ibuprofens and shouldered his pack. "Okay."

"I'll lead," I said, starting up the slope. The snow gave way. Kicking my crampon deeper, I put my weight on my right foot. The soft snow collapsed. I tried again; the snow wouldn't hold. I pounded the snow, cursing the mountain, the weather, Wyn's injury. We weren't going to make it. We might as well just sit here until the food ran out and rigor mortis set in. Flailing in frustration, I screamed, "This sucks!"

"Take it easy, John," Wyn said as if dealing with an ill-mannered child. "Don't waste your energy."

"Why should I take it easy?"

"Because we're not dead yet."

I stood up and turned around. That was an old joke with us. Whenever things had gotten really, really, really bad, we'd told ourselves, we're not dead yet. This had gotten us through some hairy climbs. "We're screwed."

"We're toast," Wyn agreed, "but we're not dead yet."

Shaking my head at our predicament, I laughed until tears came from my eyes. What the hell? I could give it one more pathetic try.

"We're going to make it," he said in a voice that mimicked the pitch of a used car salesman. "I *guarantee* it."

I laughed, took a deep breath, and kept going. Venturing off to the right, I found a patch of snow that just managed to support my weight. I moved up and pounded in a picket. Wyn hobbled along behind me, breathing hard, his face creased with pain.

At 2:10 p.m., we reached a granite outcrop, which according to my calculations should have been near the top of the Dartmouth Meadows. We were over halfway there.

I stopped, dumped my pack, and took a break. Despite the cold, my feet were sweating from the exertion. But I didn't want to change my socks; it would take too much time. So I drank some water and ate my ration of two squares of chocolate. When a high-altitude migraine started boring into my skull, I popped some ibuprofen and vowed not to let it bother me. Wyn massaged his knee. The clouds swirled around us, parting once to reveal a massive lenticular cloud squatting over Mount Foraker.

"Look at that," I groaned. "Heavy weather."

"Nothing we can do about it," Wyn said matter-of-factly. "We just need to make it to the buttress."

I asked him how his knee felt.

He dismissed my concern with his hand. "Keep going. I don't want it to tighten up."

My legs wobbled as I stood up, but I caught myself and then strapped on my pack. Each action required conscious effort, a small triumph of will. I headed up the slope, temples pounding, my heart hammering. Step by step, I shuffled through the tattered remnants of clouds. The clouds opened, and I caught a glimpse of the buttress. We were on track.

Through the late afternoon and into the early evening, we kept going. When I reached a large granite boulder, I stopped and took out my water bottle. When Wyn caught up with me, his face was gray and haggard. His knee barely supported his weight.

"You okay?" I asked.

He nodded but said nothing. Taking out his water bottle, he drank deeply and then stomped his feet. "Let's go."

I craved a rest, but if Wyn wasn't going to stop, I certainly wasn't either. There was plenty of daylight, even though it was now 9:23 p.m.

My eyelids started to close at the belays. Rubbing my face with snow, I forced them open. Wyn made agonizingly slow progress, hopping along on his right leg. As soon as he reached the belay, I was off.

The angle of the slope eased. Above me, the dark tower of the buttress reared up. We'd made it. Winding my way around large granite boulders, I found a flat campsite near the base of the wall.

I dumped my pack and collapsed on the snow. Wyn followed me, a carapace of snow and ice covering his face and parka. I helped him off with his pack and handed him his down parka. Then I shook the tent out of the bag, spread it out on the snow, and inserted the poles. My hands were so cold I couldn't get the poles into the grommets. Swearing, I tried again. Wyn looked at me blankly, too tired to help. Pinning one corner of the tent with my elbow, I managed to get one pole into the grommet. Then another. After five minutes of cursing, I got the tent up. I didn't bother to anchor it. Screw it. If it blew away, it blew away.

"Get inside," I told Wyn.

He nodded dumbly. Unzipping his Gore-Tex coat, I put his arms into his down jacket. Then I got him into his sleeping bag. I fell asleep next to him and woke with my teeth chattering. Where was my sleeping bag? My foam pad? Rummaging through my pack, I took them out, spread them down, and tried to take off my crampons. My hands were so cold, they wouldn't work. Nearly weeping from the effort, I shoved my fingers into my mouth, warming them enough that I finally could release the black plastic buckles. I sank into the sleeping bag, whispered a prayer of thanks, and fell into a long, dark tunnel of sleep.

—

"Wyn! John!"

I was onstage with an orchestra, surrounded by musicians wearing black tuxedos. The red-faced conductor was waiting for me to clash the cymbals. I tried to anticipate the precise moment to do this. Not too soon. Not too late.

"Wyn! John! Where are you?"

The music built toward a crescendo. The well-timed bash of the cymbals would put the perfect finish on the symphony. My palms sweated. My hands shook. The conductor glanced over at me. Ready?

"Wyn! John!" The shouts came louder now. I sat up in bed. Where was I?

"Wyn? John?" Pulling on my over boots and down parka, I stepped outside the tent. The wind was blowing hard. It was just after midnight, but a dull glow lit the horizon. Below, two dark shapes staggered upward.

"Over here!" I yelled.

Al was in the lead, his glasses fogged, his parka covered with ice. He seemed punch-drunk, barely able to keep from tripping over his feet. Lane brought up the rear, swaying back and forth, barely staying upright.

As relieved as I was to see them, it was disturbing they had pushed themselves so hard. I'd have to help them off with their packs. I'd have to set up their tents. If this became a pattern, it could put all of us in jeopardy. Then I chided myself for my lack of charity. We too had pushed hard. They would have helped us if we needed it. This was what you did; you helped your teammates when they were in trouble.

"We made it," Al croaked.

"Let me take your pack." I brushed off the ice-covered buckles and managed to release them. The pack peeled off him. It was little more than a daypack. I felt envious; my pack weighed three times as much.

Lane stumbled forward as if he were sleepwalking. Grabbing his pack, I carefully lowered it to the ground. It must have weighed seventy pounds; he was more than pulling his weight.

By this time, Wyn was up. He helped Al into our tent and took off his crampons, over boots, boots, and socks.

"You've got some frostbite," Wyn said, massaging Al's left big toe. He put the socks back on.

Lane sat in the vestibule of the tent, his head thrown back and his mouth agape, staring blankly at his feet. Then he pressure-breathed, bent over, unlaced the crampons, and took off his boots.

"Socks, too," Wyn ordered.

Lane slowly pulled them off his feet. He had a purple nail on his right big toe.

"Did you have this before?" Wyn said, examining it.

Lane nodded. "But it's getting worse."

Wyn grimaced. "You guys take our tent. We'll set up yours."

Lane didn't bother to reply. He simply crawled into the tent.

Al went in after him. He was getting so thin that he looked like a cadaver, but his eyes glittered like a maniac. "We made it," he said, giving me a thumbs up. "We made it." Whatever he ran on, I wanted some of it.

After I handed them their sleeping bags, I helped Wyn pitch their tent. The surface was flat; there was no need to dig another platform. But the broken pole made it difficult to erect. By the time we finished, we were too tired to talk. We grabbed our bags, shoved them into their tent, and tried to fall back to sleep.

The last of the mountain's technical defenses loomed ahead. The rock buttress would likely present the most sustained climbing of the entire route. With our battered bodies and frostbitten limbs, I doubted we were up to the challenge.

The wind howled throughout the night. By morning, it gusted so hard that the tent fabric rattled like a machine gun. The wind caught the fly and violently whipped it back and forth. The nylon seams were stretched to the breaking point.

Wyn roused himself and sat up in bed. His blond hair was twisted and knotted like some kind of exotic bird's nest.

Despite my fatigue, I couldn't help laughing at it.

"What's so funny?"

"Your hair. It's sticking straight up."

He smoothed it down with his hand, but the strands sprang back up. "Is that better?"

I nodded.

"Report me to the fashion police," he said, unzipping the door to the tent. "God, that wind is brutal." He put on his down parka. "I'm going to see how those guys are doing."

I got the stove going. Despite my tiredness, I wanted to keep moving. We needed to get up this route quickly.

Wyn came back in a few minutes later. "They're wiped," he said, taking off his parka. "My knee's bothering me. I think we should take a rest day."

"But our food's running low," I argued. "We need to give it a shot."

"Be my guest," he said, pointing outside. "But the wind is blowing about sixty."

Sticking my head outside the tent, I saw that he was right. My face went numb after a minute. I zipped the tent shut and got back into my sleeping bag.

"The wind will clear things out," Wyn said. "We'll be good to go tomorrow."

"I hope you're right," I said, sighing. I poured hot water into our cups and put in tea bags. We were out of coffee. I drank one cup, squeezed the tea bag, and drank another, determined to get every last bit of flavor out of it.

Huddling around my cup of tea, I forced myself to sip it slowly. I hated cutting things so close. Since my foot was asleep, I massaged it, but the numbness remained. I peeled off my sock to see that a dark, purple bleb of frostbite had blossomed on my right big toe. I should have changed my socks. The sweat had caused this. Now I'd really have to watch myself. Little things snowballed on a peak like Denali.

I spent the rest of the morning eating, drinking, resting, and worrying about my toe. At noon, I put on my parka and went over to their tent. Al coughed like a tubercular as he contemplated his purple toe, which looked worse than mine. He poked, prodded, and admired it, as if the frostbite were a badge of courage. Lane helped him wrap it in gauze. Lane pressure breathed constantly, but his color was good, and he seemed to be recovering.

"How are you guys doing on food?" I asked.

Lane frowned. "We're almost out. How about you guys?"

"We've got some Top Ramen tonight. We'll cook that up if you guys want."

"I'll cook dinner," Lane said. "It's Al's birthday. I thought I'd make something special."

"What did you have in mind?"

"You'll see," he said, winking.

I noticed a foil hood on his hanging stove. When I tried to examine it, he shooed me away.

While Lane worked on dinner, I went back to our tent to rest and hydrate. Wyn didn't want to play chess, and I couldn't concentrate on my reading, so I watched a small bug crawl over the tent fabric. How could it live up here? How could anything live up here? How could *we* live up here? I flicked off the bug with my finger and immediately regretted it, imagining the finger of God flicking us off the side of the peak.

I slept off and on throughout the day. I woke in a panic. Where was I? Was the food gone? Why had we wasted the day? But when I got up to pee, I nearly fainted. I had to stop, bend over, and breathe to clear my head. Once I calmed down, I realized it was good we'd rested. We needed to regroup before the last push up the buttress.

When I came back into the tent, Wyn was sitting up in his sleeping bag, poring over the map and photo. He looked at the map so often he had rubbed the ink off the creases.

"What are you thinking?" I asked.

"Just trying to find the easiest way up this thing," he said, biting his lip.

"We could go around the buttress and up the snow, couldn't we?" I said.

"We could." Wyn scratched his beard. "But then we couldn't claim the credit of doing a new route."

"Screw the new route," I said. "I just want to get up and off this thing."

Wyn bit his fingernail. "It's not that simple."

"Why not?"

"The plan was to do the complete route, including the buttress," he said, tapping his finger on the map.

"Plans change," I said, shrugging. "Why are you so committed to the buttress?"

"I'd like to complete it," Wyn said, frowning. "It's what interested me about the route in the first place."

"Does this have anything to do with the Everest permit?"

Wyn looked at me as if caught in the act.

"I suppose it's the 'purity of the line,' something like that."

"Something like that," he said defensively.

"You're so transparent," I said, laughing. "You could never be a politician."

"Why not?" Wyn's mouth was a tight line.

"You're a lousy liar."

"What do you mean?" he said, trying to sound injured.

"You want the cred," I said. "That's what you're after."

"That's how I make my living," Wyn said, shrugging. "If I back off from it, the sponsors will disappear. You know how things work."

"But you have to know when to say when. Your knee is in bad shape."

"It's been worse." He patted his knee affectionately as if it were an old friend. "It'll get me through. What about your toe?"

"I can walk," I said. "But I'm aware of the clock."

"It's always this way on expeditions," he said, smiling. "It never comes easy. Just wait till you see that summit ridge. You won't care what it takes. You'll just want to tag the top."

I looked away from him. "I hope I have enough sense to turn back if it's dangerous," I said. "The summit is optional, coming back is mandatory."

"A worthy thought," Wyn said, shaking his head. "That's certainly the decision you made last time."

"Yeah, and I'm still here," I said.

"And you've spent the last five years regretting that decision," Wyn said.

"No, I haven't," I protested, but of course he was right. It had eaten at me like a weevil, boring into my confidence, eroding my sense of myself. Was I just a husband and father? Store manager? Or was I fundamentally a climber? Was mountaineering rooted in my DNA, like the color of my hair and eyes, or was it optional, a dangerous illusion? Would getting to the summit answer these questions? I didn't know, but I had to find out. I'd always been good with a map and compass; too bad navigating other parts of my life wasn't so simple.

"I'm not blaming you," Wyn said. "But after that climb I learned that the margin is often wider than you think. You have to push yourself to find it."

"But what if you push too hard?" I said. "Then you die. Game over."

"Of course," Wyn's voice cracked. "But it's not so easy to decide. Many other climbers, safe climbers, have thought they were making the right decision, the safe decision. But they were wrong. And they paid for it."

"Yes, I know some. Your partner, Hans, for example."

"Yes, Hans." Wyn tensed. "He made a mistake, and he paid for it—with his life. But he's not representative. Other climbers have calculated their limits, done great climbs, and gotten away with it."

"So you think you're invincible."

"I didn't say that," Wyn said, annoyed. "I said I was calculating."

"But calculations can go wrong," I said. "There are too many factors." I shook my head. "The weather, the fitness of the group, the objective danger—it's hard to assess all that. You need a margin for error. That's why I think we should bypass the buttress."

Wyn shook his head. "We need to climb the buttress. What did Mallory say about Everest? 'Because it's there!' Sure, it will help my reputation, my slide shows, but ultimately it's a kind of test. I want the mountain to throw its worst at me, and then I want to overcome it." He stared at me fixedly, his eyes looking slightly maniacal. "It's a test. Will I pass? We'll see."

Later in the evening, the storm seemed to be blowing itself out. Spindrift still obscured the distant peaks like Foraker, but the buttress stood out clear and imposing. A chimney split the buttress, making an obvious line of attack and a good reference point for the route. The climbing looked hard and steep. It would be a real grunt with our packs.

We went over to Lane and Al's tent for dinner. Lane insisted that we wash our hands and faces. This seemed fastidious, but he was adamant. "This is a quality establishment," he insisted.

We took a pan of water and some dish soap and scoured the last three weeks of dirt, sunscreen, sweat, and filth off our hands and faces. It was a chilly if liberating experience, as if we'd shed an old skin. What I wouldn't give for a long, hot shower and an evening with Andy and Jill. I imagined the look of relief on her face when I'd tell her that we'd climbed the route.

Lane passed around a plate with crackers and cheese. "Go easy," he said. "That's the last of them."

Al handed the plate to me. "Boy, am I looking forward to getting back home," he said. "You're a great cook, Lane, but there's only so much you can do with noodles."

"What do you mean?" Lane said, stirring a batch of what he called his "seafood surprise." "You're going to miss my cooking."

"Right." Al's eyelids drooped and his complexion was sallow, but he still laughed his he-haw laugh. "What's the first thing you're going to eat when you get back?"

"I'm going to dinner at Giorgio's," Lane said. "I'm going to order veal osso buco and mushroom risotto with a glass of Barolo. What are you going to have?"

"A Foster's lager for starters," Al said. "Then a New York steak—very rare—a baked potato, and Caesar salad."

"I'm going to barbeque a salmon," Wyn said. "I'll serve it with French fries, a green salad, and a bottle of pinot noir."

"I'm going to eat a bowl of Top Ramen casserole," I said. "With a mug of mint tea."

Wyn threw his hat at me. I whipped it back. He threw it at Al, who threw it at Lane. It landed in the seafood surprise.

"Who wants to eat Wyn's hat?" Lane said, picking it up. "Anyone that hungry?"

We laughed uneasily.

"Forget it." Wyn grabbed it back.

"This is ready," Lane said, spooning the "seafood surprise" onto our plates. It was a can of tuna fish divided four ways, mixed with a package of noodles and seasoned with the last of Lane's oregano.

We ate slowly, savoring the dinner.

"Now for the grand finale," Lane said. He reached behind his pack and pulled out a plate covered with a lid. He pulled off the lid. "Ta-da!"

It was a chocolate cake, with a sparkler stuck in the middle of it. It read: Happy Birthday Al! There was a summit with a flag planted at the top, all done in red icing.

"How did you cook that?" Wyn asked, incredulously.

"Simple," Lane said, licking a piece of frosting with his finger. "I made an oven with aluminum foil and baked the cake inside."

"And the icing?"

"I brought this." He proudly displayed a crumpled plastic tube. "It wasn't in my pack when you did your little inspection back in Talkeetna."

Wyn tapped his forehead to acknowledge Lane's smarts. The cake was exactly what we needed.

"Let me get my camera," Wyn said. "This will be great for the slide show."

As Lane cut it in pieces, we leaned over it like a pack of wild dogs around a sheep carcass. He lit the sparkler in Al's cake and we sang "Happy Birthday." Lane's bass voice boomed loud and deep and carried the rest of us. Wyn's tenor fortunately drowned out my singing. Al squirmed in the spotlight, grinning slyly.

Wyn snapped photos as we pumped our fists and yelled, "Al, Al, Al!"

It was the Fourth of July. We'd been on this peak for three weeks. With a little luck, we could get up this thing. My spirits soared.

"So how old are you, Al?" Wyn asked.

"Forty," Al said, shaking his head.

"Forty?" Wyn said. "You don't look that old."

"Thanks," Al said, "but I'm feeling it today." He wiggled his toe. "I really want to knock this sucker off."

"We all do," I said, eating a bite of cake.

"For my fortieth birthday," Al said, looking back and forth between Wyn and me, "I'd like to lead tomorrow."

"Are you sure?" Wyn stopped his fork in mid-bite. "You guys pushed pretty hard getting up here."

"I want a piece of that buttress," Al said, coughing. "We've been feeling like donkeys for most of this trip. We want to get out front."

Wyn laughed. "I'd love to give you a shot at it, but every time I do, you guys blow it."

"That's a crock," Lane said. "We deserve a chance out front. You guys just want to get hero photos for your slide show."

"It's not that," Wyn said, raising his voice.

"What is it?" Al asked. "So that John can publicize his store?"

"What are you talking about?" I asked, putting down my plate. "That's not why I'm up here."

"What is it then?" Al asked, the distrust in his eyes magnified by the glasses.

"To climb the peak," I said. "Publicity for the store is way down the list."

"Really?" Al said, his face reddening. "You don't want to burnish your bonafides? Won't that help your business?"

"Yes," I said tightly. Al had a point, but I was surprised at the hostility behind his remarks.

"Case closed," Lane said, wiping the cake crumbs from his hands.

"Listen," I said. "We're not trying to relegate you guys to the rear. We're only trying to climb this peak in the safest way possible."

"In that case, we should lead," Al said. "Wyn's knee is hurt. You've got frostbite. Overall, we're the healthier team."

Wyn smiled as if amused by the whole thing. He went out the door, took a pee, and came back in.

"If you guys want it that bad you can have it," he said, looking at Al and Lane. "But we're running low on food. Your tent is falling apart. Al lost his pack. We don't have much of a margin left."

"I understand that," Al said.

"I hope you do," Wyn said, fixing him with a stare. "Because I'll hold you to it."

THIRTEEN

During the night, I checked and rechecked my altimeter, watching the small, black arrow tremble across the liquid, crystal face as it registered the barometric pressure, indicating the likelihood of a storm and serving as a kind of electrocardiogram of our chances for survival. I couldn't help but think of the Wilcox Expedition of 1967, the worst mountaineering disaster in Alaska history. Seven of the twelve members died on the upper slopes of Denali when a severe winter storm pinned them in camp for days. Rescuers found one of their tents shredded by wind. Inside they discovered a corpse huddled around a tent pole, its partially decomposed flesh frozen to the metal. The climber had apparently been trying to steady the pole when he died. His gloveless hand and face were swollen, cracked, and covered with purple frostbite blisters, not unlike the one on my toe.

The black arrow fluctuated throughout the night. Then it began to drop in the early morning. The wind picked up. At 3 a.m., I heard Al and Lane rousing themselves to begin the slow, laborious process of getting ready to withstand temperatures of twenty degrees below zero. Grunting and cursing, they donned pants and pile jackets. In my sleep-deprived state, I saw with uncomfortable clarity the ridiculousness of what we were doing.

Trying to fall back asleep, I burrowed into my sleeping bag, but its stench disgusted me. Over the last few weeks, it had degenerated into a dark, evil-smelling hole. The smell had so saturated the nylon fabric that there would be no way to wash it out. I fantasized about pouring white gas over it and burning it back in Talkeetna.

My anxiety about the buttress made it impossible to sleep. I kept thinking about the plan for the route ahead. We needed to get up the first and second buttress today, 1,000 feet of tough, technical climbing. Normally, this would be a reasonable objective, but at 17,000 feet, in subzero conditions, with heavy packs—we'd be lucky to knock off even the first buttress.

From the other tent I heard Al mutter, "I'm getting too old for this shit."

"Me, too," Lane said.

"What do you mean?" Al said. "You're a kid."

"No, I'm not. I'm almost thirty."

"Just wait till you hit forty," Al said, coughing. "Your body will really fall apart."

"I'll take your word for it," Lane said. "Boy, that buttress looks like a bitch."

"Don't worry," Al said, clearing his throat. "We'll nail it."

"I hope so," Lane said. "I want to get off this rock pile."

"Why? You miss Stacey?" Al pronounced her name with a long, slow, sarcastic emphasis.

"What about it? Aren't you looking forward to seeing anyone back home?"

"My ex-wife? Ha. She's probably screwing some other guy, now that she's screwed me out of my house."

There was grunting and swearing as they put on their crampons.

"Boy, Wyn can be a prick," Lane whispered.

"Yeah, but he gave us the buttress."

"But will he let us keep it?" Lane said. "He'll probably give it to John so he can brag about it to his customers."

I cupped my ear, quietly fuming. Did they think I was that selfish? I wanted to give them the benefit of the doubt but the words stung.

"We'll just move fast," Al said off-handedly. "That'll keep them off our butts." There was a rustling of Gore-Tex. "Ready?"

After they headed out, I unzipped the tent door to watch them. Al went first, his bandolier of ice screws tinkling. Lane cursed softly as he shouldered his pack. It was 3:30 a.m. From here, at 16,800 feet, they'd head up through a cleft in the first buttress and, depending on how fast they were moving, would continue up to the top of the second buttresses at 18,400 feet, where we hoped to spend the night. The climbing would be hard mixed ground—steep granite, with ice and snow in the cracks. They'd place fixed ropes; we'd jumar up them. And if they were moving too slow, we'd pass them. Period. This was no time to worry about hurting their feelings, especially after what they'd just said about me.

Once we got to the top of the second buttress, we'd set up camp and prepare to climb the third and last buttress to gain the summit ridge at 18,960. From there, it should be a short, cold sprint to the summit at 20,320 feet—or so I hoped—and then two days to descend. We had three days of food left and a dwindling supply of gas for melting water. If we didn't make the summit soon.... I didn't want to think about it.

Al trudged forward, coughing and wheezing but making progress. Lane rest-stepped and pressure-breathed like a steam-engine. Above them, the buttress shot steeply into the sky. The wind had died down, but wisps of clouds and vapor swirled around the dark rock, making it look mysterious and malevolent.

Al's purple parka and Lane's red shell stood out against the granite of the lower buttress. I heard the whump, whump, whump as Al hammered in a picket for an anchor. He exchanged words with Lane, laughed about something, and then he set his ice axes and started moving up the snow. He threaded his way up a section of steep ice toward a break in the buttress. This narrow couloir split the buttress vertically, making it the most direct way to the top. Even with the marginal weather conditions, it should be easy to stay on route.

I shivered and zipped the door shut.

"Wyn? Are you awake?"

"Yeah," he said, yawning.

"They're on schedule."

"Good." He extended his knee up and out of the sleeping bag. He massaged it and moved it side to side.

"How does it feel?" I asked.

"Sore." He winced and drew his leg back into the sleeping bag.

I tapped my altimeter watch. "I've been watching the barometer. I think we're in for another big blow."

"You're probably right," he said, shuddering.

"I've been thinking," I said. "Why don't we bypass the second buttress on the snow slope to the left?"

"Naw." He sat up. "It won't be that hard."

"Look," I said, unable to conceal my irritation. "You've got a sore knee. Al and I have frostbite. Lane is teetering on the edge of total exhaustion."

"Let me worry about my knee, John," Wyn said, dismissing it as if it was none of my business. "Your and Al's toes aren't that bad. I've seen worse. Just change your socks once in a while."

"Thanks for the grooming tips," I said. "And as for your concern about my toes. It's touching, really."

He started to say something but then seemed to think better of it and leaned forward in his sleeping bag. "How many times do I have to tell you," he said, speaking slowly and distinctly as if explaining something to a retarded child. "Expedition climbing is a war of attrition. The winners are the survivors." He picked up his dirty socks and flung them at me.

I threw the socks back at him. "But what if conditions get worse? What then? At what point do we say, enough is enough?"

"We'll know," Wyn said, as if this was obvious. "We can always reassess. But for now, we need to stick to the buttress."

"Why are you so committed to the buttress?"

Wyn examined the back of his weathered, mahogany-colored hand. "A new route on Denali wouldn't hurt my chances of sponsorship for Everest," he said, looking away from me. "An Everest permit costs at least $15,000 per person. I don't have that kind of cash. But I'm in a position to get sponsorship..."

"If you do a new route." I said, nodding. "That's the bottom line, isn't it?"

"Of course," he said. "You know the way things work. Sponsorship would be a lot easier if we did a *new* route. A new route is a lot sexier than repeating an established one, especially with our retrograde tactics. We've been sieging the hell out of this route. There will be a lot of grumbling in the climbing magazines."

"So what," I said. "Alpine style without fixed camps may be the standard, but sieging a route with fixed camps like we're doing still has its place on new routes."

"I'm just saying there will be criticism."

"I don't give a shit what they say about our tactics."

"You don't care about the publicity for your store?" Wyn asked incredulously. "Wouldn't business improve if you could say you'd done a new route on Denali?"

I shook my head. "I don't care at this point. I just want to climb Denali and get back to my family."

"That's touching." Wyn smirked. "You could be the founding member of the Father's Climbing Club of America."

"Listen," I said, glaring at him. "I just want to get back alive."

"Who says we're going to die?" His eyes were large and staring. "I'm sure as hell not planning on it."

"Neither am I." I sunk back into my sleeping bag. "But we're cutting things way too close."

"Trust me, John," he said, sighing. His eyes were tired, bloodshot, but unwavering in their intensity.

"I'm trying," I said.

"Good." He knocked me awkwardly on the shoulder. "We've been through a lot together."

"You're right."

"Don't worry," Wyn said. "Despite what you've heard, I don't want to kill any more of my partners. Bad publicity."

"That's not true," I countered. "It's good publicity. Any buzz is a good buzz, right?"

"Give me a break, John," he said. "I'm not that sick."

"I hope not."

"It was a joke. Got it? Now let's get something to eat. What's on the menu?"

We split a bag of instant oatmeal, eating in silence. Wyn's admission that our route was a stepping stone to Everest raised troubling questions. Was he using me and the rest of us to get to the top? Would he cast me aside if I got in his way of the new route? Wyn's ambition was legendary. He'd stepped over more than a few bodies in his time. I'm sure he wouldn't hesitate to do the same here. But as Al put it, Wyn was our ticket. His drive and skill would boost all of us to the top, assuming his knee didn't worsen.

At 9:15 a.m., we headed for the base of the route. I led out. Wyn hobbled behind me. At the foot of the buttress, I stopped and examined the tattered black static line that snaked upward. It looked as if they already had notched several pitches, which boded well for getting up the second buttress today.

Despite his sore knee, Wyn placed his jumars on the rope and started up behind me. The jumaring seemed to put less stress on his knee than walking, and if he moved more slowly than usual, he made steady progress, grunting as he rose up the rope. His crampons scraped against the orange granite, past a ledge covered with ice and snow and footprints, signs of Al's and Lane's passage.

By the time he finished with the first rope, I was at the top of the second rope. We jugged three more pitches and then caught up with them as Lane led a small patch of ice. We stopped, tied into their anchor, and waited for Lane to finish his lead.

He drove his axes into the ice, retrieved them and drove them in again. He worked carefully, showing a deftness he'd lacked earlier but moving too slowly. He had performed well on the lower stretches of the route but dawdled on the technical pitches. Reaching an alcove at the top of the ice field, he spent five minutes before driving in a piton. It took him another five minutes to set up the belay. By the time he brought Al up, Wyn and I were shivering.

Wyn glanced from his watch to the clouds below us. "Hey guys!" he yelled, cupping his mittens over his mouth. "Stop there!" He led out, stepping around the fixed rope they'd trailed behind them. He front-pointed up to them, clipping into their gear as he moved up. When he reached them, he brought me up to the crowded alcove.

"Nice work," I said. "You guys moved well."

"Thanks," Al said guardedly, adjusting his fogged glasses. He coughed, cleared his throat, and leaned against the rock. His eyes were blank and glazed, as if he were in a trance. "I led most of the pitches, but Lane needed a shot out front, too."

Lane nodded, spat, and crossed his arms. He rolled his shoulders and placed his feet apart. He stood a good half a head taller than Wyn and me. But he kept his eyes and intentions concealed behind mirrored sunglasses.

"Mind if we play through?" Wyn asked, looking up at the next pitch.

"You told us we had the buttress," Al said, racking his gear.

"I never said that," Wyn said, turning to him. "I said you had a shot at it as long as you moved quickly."

"We're moving quickly," Al said. "Ask John."

I tried to say something but Wyn broke in. "It's not fast enough," he said, hands on his hips. "We've got to get up this thing. Take a look at those clouds." A bank of black clouds were creeping up from below, obscuring the lower part of the face.

"We're going as fast as we can," Lane said, his voice cracking. "What do you want?"

"Velocity," Wyn said. "Speed is safety."

"What makes you think you can climb it faster than we can?" Lane said hoarsely. "Your knee's hyper-extended."

"Let me worry about my knee." Wyn gave him a pained smile. "I don't want to argue about this. John, are you ready?"

"Okay." When I tried to move past Lane, he blocked my way.

"Nothing doing." He lowered his hands to his side.

"Listen," I said, looking at him. "Save your energy for climbing."

"I don't believe this," Al said, shaking his head. "First you guys say we've got the buttress, then you fucking take it back."

"Hey," Wyn said, putting his hand out as if to stop Al. "Let's keep it civil. You guys are dogging it. Lane looked like a damned Girl Scout on that last pitch."

Lane tensed. He balled up his gloves. "A Girl Scout?" He moved toward Wyn.

I put myself between him and Wyn.

"You just want the glory," Lane shouted, spittle flying from his lip. "You don't give a damn about your climbing partners. Well, I'm sick of being a good Sherpa. Yes, sahib. No, sahib. Whatever you say, sahib."

"I don't give a fuck about the glory," Wyn said with total conviction. He could be a good actor when he wanted to be. "I just want to get off of this thing with no casualties. That's it. Bottom line."

They stared at each other, seeing who would look away first.

Al muttered and shook his head. "Go ahead and lead if you're in such a hurry," he said, disgustedly. "I'm freezing."

"Yeah," Lane said, turning away. "We'll watch the great climber and see how it's done."

"You could learn a few things," Wyn said, keeping his eyes fixed on Lane. "John, am I on?"

"You're on," I replied. I just wanted to get the hell out of there. The tension between our teams was becoming unbearable. Wyn needed a lesson in diplomacy, but Al and Lane seemed to be acting increasingly irrational. Swinging leads was a common practice. Al looked wiped, his face white, creased, and haggard. Lane still seemed tentative on vertical ground, which was a serious liability on a route like this. Was it the altitude or simply the growing tensions that led them to believe they'd become the persecuted minority on this expedition?

Pivoting from hold to hold, Wyn worked his way up through the steep granite. He moved steadily even though burdened with a large pack and a sore left knee. He pounded in a pin, clipped into it, and kept moving. He reached a stance and put in another couple pins. Then he brought me up.

"See you up there," I said to Al and Lane.

Al muttered and adjusted his glasses. Lane mock-saluted me.

I moved up above the alcove, eager to put some distance between us. The climbing was hard—steep granite steps interspersed with small ledges covered with snow and ice. Reaching a vertical section of rock, I contemplated the sequence. A good ledge lay just beyond my grasp. Under other circumstances, I would have worked my way up to it. But I wanted to move fast. There was no way I wanted to relinquish the lead. So I pivoted off my right crampon and lunged for it. The front-points slipped and sparked against the rock. The world blurred past me. I found myself dangling from the rope.

"You okay, John?" Wyn asked.

"Yeah," I said, disgusted with myself. My right hand throbbed painfully. I took off the glove and saw that blood oozed from the knuckle of my right index finger. Wiping it off with a bandana, I examined the gash. Not too deep, but up here even small cuts took a long time to heal. Putting the glove back on, I kept climbing, forcing myself to concentrate and find small cracks in the rock where I could insert my crampons. The angle eased as I approached Wyn's stance.

"Good lead," I said, panting.

"Thanks," he said. "You okay?"

I nodded sheepishly.

"Don't rush it. Remember, unhurried haste."

"Thanks," I said, irritated with his condescension. "I just want to stay ahead of those guys."

"I know what you mean." He cleared his throat and spat. "I wish we were doing this on our own. I hope those guys don't end up killing us as well as themselves."

"A comforting thought," I said, bending over to catch my breath. "But we've got to stick together. We owe it to them. Afterwards, we can go our separate ways."

"We don't owe them anything," Wyn said. "We should cut them loose. Let them move at their own damn pace."

"We can't do that," I said. "They're still part of the team."

"In name only." Wyn handed me the rack. "Your lead?"

"Sure," I said hesitantly. "What the hell."

"That's the spirit." He smacked me on the shoulder. We wouldn't let the other two ruin our trip. We were over halfway up the first buttress and beginning to see some serious air. The views spread out on both sides of us. I took in the dizzyingly steep rock walls smeared with snow and ice and stole one vertigo-inducing glance down the face we had climbed. Then I moved up as quickly as I could, clawing my way up the mixed ground of ice, snow, and hard granite. With crampons on my feet and gloves on my hands, it was hard to get a good purchase on the rock. I moved awkwardly, grunting and sweating despite the cold. My stomach growled and turned over. Our dwindling food supply was rapidly becoming an obsession. This made it all the more imperative to get to the top.

Spotting what looked like a good line, I started up, trying to imitate Wyn's style and experimenting to see where the crampon points would hold, often slotting the points into small crevices in the rock.

It was full-on mixed climbing at altitude. It demanded my entire repertoire of climbing techniques, hooking tiny ledges with the pick of my ice hammer and working my feet up. Lunging for a granite knob, my gloved hand slipped off. Trying not to panic, I caught myself with my right foot. Then I retreated back to my previous hold and removed my mitten. I tried the move again. This time I grasped it easily.

"Good job!" Wyn's disembodied words floated up the face.

We were almost through the rock band. It was steep climbing, but if I was patient, I could climb it safely. I began to enjoy the freedom of moving over steep rock and ice, entering that magical zone where every move seems logical and predetermined.

At the top of the pitch, I drove in a piton and set up a belay. Looking back down over the route, I felt exhilarated at what I'd just ascended—a steep pillar of orange granite near the top of the tallest mountain in North America. I'd done it at altitude, and with a pack weighing fifty pounds. The old mastery was returning.

"Off belay," I yelled to Wyn.

No response.

"I'm off!" I shouted, cupping my hand.

"Okay!" His reply floated up to me like a scrap of mist.

He untied from the anchor and got ready to move up. Beyond him I could see all the way back down the immense face—the huge avalanche chutes, the broken rock ridges, the top of the Spiral Couloir, and the sea of clouds right below them. Wyn's crampons scraped over rock. He cursed, held his knee, and then kept climbing. Wisps of his breath rose up the rock.

"Nice lead," he said, tying into the anchor.

"How's your knee?" I asked.

"Sore," he said grimly. "I bashed it on a rock down there."

"What about Al and Lane?" I asked.

"They're pissed," he said, tying the fixed rope into the anchor. "But they're making progress. I told them they should jumar this pitch. That'll make it easier on them."

"I thought Al wanted to climb it all free."

Wyn laughed. "That was for the first pitch or two. Then he changed his mind."

"How's Lane?"

"Angry, but I hope not totally delusional. On belay?"

"You want me to lead?"

"You don't trust peg-leg?" Wyn winked. "I think I can handle it."

I nodded and payed out the rope. I watched him grind his way up the steep snow and ice of the couloir. He lacked his usual finesse, but he toughed it out. After moving a good thirty feet above my stance, he took a nut off his rack and slotted it into the rock. He clipped into it and kept moving above it. After another twenty feet, the nut fell out of the crack and came sliding back down the rope.

"Wyn," I yelled. "Get another piece in!"

He turned and looked back in alarm. He glanced left and right, searching for a placement. Then he kept climbing, not satisfied with the rock. He was now some sixty feet above me. If he slipped, he would fall 120 feet, accelerating so fast that he likely would rip me out of the anchor. I prayed that he'd get something in soon.

Wyn kept his cool. He moved to the left, found a crack to his liking, and drove in another knife blade. The ting, ting, ting echoed down the couloir. Teetering on the points of his crampons, he calmly clipped into the pin and attached the rope.

Wiping a trickle of sweat from my forehead, I looked back at the anchor and glanced anxiously up at him. Those were the sorts of chances I'd told Jill I'd never take, and yet here I was doing it. Thank God Wyn was so practiced. It didn't seem to bother him at all.

Feeling the tug of the rope against my harness, I untied from the anchor and moved up. The climbing wasn't hard, but there were few places for protection. Panting, I reached Wyn and tied into the anchor. "You really ran it out back there!"

"Gets your blood pumping, doesn't it?" Wyn said, grinning.

"I wish you'd protected it better."

Wyn shrugged. "We need to move fast."

"Not that fast," I said. "I've got dependents."

"Don't we all," he said, dismissively.

Choosing to ignore this remark, I looked at the route ahead. The wind had picked up, blowing tattered bits of clouds over the ridge and giving us a clear picture of our proximity to the top of the first buttress. Two more buttresses loomed above us, but the summit ridge didn't look that far away. Below, the entire Alaska Range spread out in a chaos of snow, ice, and rock, with Mount Foraker standing directly across from us, its broad triangular summit rising above a thick layer of clouds. Far off in the distance, the silver ribbon of the Talkeetna River shimmered amid the million small lakes scattered across the Alaska tundra. Somewhere down there was Talkeetna—beer, showers, and bacon cheeseburgers. I thought of Andy and Jill and the tremendous distance between us. I hoped that getting to the top would quench my appetite for hard climbing. I hated it—this terrible need for stimulation, an addiction to adrenaline. Was it a simple chemical equation? If only someone could invent a pill that would suppress it. It would be a hell of a lot cheaper and safer.

"Let's finish it off," I said, moving up.

"It's all yours, John."

I wormed my way up through a squeeze chimney. It was an awkward, strenuous, desperate move. My pack slipped out of the chimney. I shoved it back in. A strap got caught on a rock. I backtracked and freed it. Shoving a Friend into a crack, I moved up. I didn't care about style. I only wanted to get up the damn thing. I blundered upward, closing in on the top of the buttress. After hauling my sorry ass over the last rock step, I collapsed onto a patch of snow. Then I breathed deeply to clear my head and brought Wyn up.

"See, it wasn't that bad," Wyn joked. "We'll get the first ascent after all."

"We'll see," I said warily. "Let's take a break. I'm starved."

Putting on my down parka, I sat on the boulder and unscrewed the top of the water bottle. I shook it to break the skim of ice and then drank deeply, avoiding a bloated noodle and particles of dirt at the bottom. Taking out some crackers, I put my last piece of salami onto it. The salami smelled odd, but I ate it anyway. I needed the protein. I limited myself to one square of bittersweet chocolate. We were on quarter rations now.

Several minutes later, Lane poked his head over the top of the couloir.

"Freight Train!" Wyn yelled.

Lane ignored him but kept jumaring. As he reached the belay stance, Wyn started to help him with his pack.

"I'm okay." Lane waved him off.

Wyn shrugged and sat back down. A few minutes later, Al's hangdog head appeared. He was coughing almost continually now but somehow made progress. We had knocked off the first buttresses, and it was just past noon. We were moving very well. With luck, we'd be on the summit ridge in another day or so.

"Ready, John?" Wyn said, getting up.

"Okay," I said, even though my stomach felt queasy. We didn't want to fall behind them again.

"How's it going, Al?" I asked.

"It's going," he said, still fighting for breath.

Lane sat on his pack and ate on a bagel, avoiding eye contact with me and Wyn.

"We'll see you up there," I said, trying to sound cheery, even though my stomach continued to grumble.

Al nodded barely. Lane kept chewing like a steer at a feed lot.

Hoisting his pack, Wyn crossed the short snow slope to the base of the second buttress. As I followed him up, the salami sat in my stomach like a lump of congealed fat. I tried to ignore it and keep pace with

Wyn. We were on our way to the top. Nothing was going to stop us now. Not Lane's belligerence. Not the steep ice and rock. Not even the weather, or so I hoped. The clouds were still below us. The storm had not moved in yet.

At the base of the second buttress, Wyn drove in a pin and moved upward. The bright yellow dot of his parka moved up and away from me. A few minutes later, he banged in a pin and set up a belay.

We swung leads up through the lower half of the second buttress. My throat burned and my temples pounded, and as my hip belt bit into my churning stomach, I felt like I was going to explode. Finally, I couldn't take it anymore. After tying into the anchor, I bent over and barfed up all of my lunch and breakfast. It splattered all over my boots and the rope.

"Take it easy," he said disgustedly. "You okay?"

I wiped my mouth with my sleeve. Then I vomited some more. Weak and light-headed, I slumped over on the ledge. A pit of misery opened up beneath me.

After helping me off with my pack, he clipped it into the anchor and took out my blue down parka. Shivering, I put it on.

"Let's take a break," he said, sighing. He handed me a water bottle. I tried to drink but couldn't choke it down.

Then he handed me a square of his chocolate.

I waved it away. I sat hunched over, my head pounding like a drum. "Pepto Bismol," I managed to say. He got some out of his pack. After swallowing it, I put my head on my knees and just hoped the world would go away.

"What's going on?" Lane bellowed from below.

"Come on up," Wyn said.

Lane jumared up to our stance. "Shit," he said, trying to step around the vomit.

"You guys keep going," Wyn said. "John needs to rest."

Now I really felt like hell. Not only had I lost my lunch, but I had allowed them to pass us. The summit ridge, which seemed so close an hour ago, now seemed impossibly far away. I felt like a total loser.

"You're sure?" Lane said, scratching his head.

Wyn nodded forlornly.

Al arrived at the crowded stance with his glasses askew and a dazed look on his face. Everyone was trying to avoid stepping on the remains of my lunch.

"Al, are you up for leading?" Wyn asked.

"You bet," Al said, seeming more than a little pleased at my misfortune. He took a sling from Wyn, broke into another spasm of coughing, and then started up the rock pitch.

"We're going to climb this bastard after all," Lane said, paying out the rope.

"As long as we move quickly," Wyn said bitterly, as if in a parody of himself. He kicked at the ground with his crampons.

"How long are you going to wait here?" Lane asked.

"Till he recovers," Wyn said. "You guys set up camp at the base of the third buttress."

"Roger," Lane said excitedly. His anger seemed to have dissipated now that they were back in the lead.

"Belay off!" Al shouted from above.

"Okay," Lane answered. He got ready to go. "See you up there."

Wyn nodded and put a hand on my shoulder. "How are you feeling?"

I flicked a piece of vomit off my boot. I tried to stand up but nearly fell over.

"Whoa." Wyn helped me back down. "Drink some water."

After sipping the water, I felt a little better. Then I managed to choke down a square of chocolate. My body desperately needed fuel, but I didn't want to risk vomiting again. "Okay," I said, wobbling as I managed to stand up.

"You go first," Wyn said. "I'll follow you."

I took out my jumars. We had been in the lead for so long that it took me a minute to get the hang of them. Then I stepped up and began the tedious process of hauling myself up the rope. But at least I didn't have to think—I simply needed to keep moving.

The rest of the route was a blur. By the time I reached the anchor, they had gone on. I clipped into the next rope, tested it, and kept going. Finally, I reached the anchor at the top of the second buttress. The slope eased. I saw them moving up the ice field above us.

Wyn came up behind me, coiled the rope, and gave me a drink of water and a square of chocolate. Then he led out, impatient with my slow pace. He kept moving, slower at first, but then faster. Soon the rope was pulling against my waist.

"Slow down!" I yelled.

He didn't respond. He seemed to be taking out his frustration on me, punishing me for my stupidity. I resented the way he was dragging me along. I'm sure he considered me dead weight, a piece of cargo he'd prefer to jettison. Who did he think he was anyway? Why didn't he just stop to rest for a while?

I looked at my watch. Then I understood. It was 10 p.m. The sun was going down. Snow was starting to fall. First small flakes. Then large, fatter ones. The start of the storm? I didn't have time to think about it. Wyn kept moving, still favoring his left knee. I stumbled, and the rope pulled against me. He turned and gave me a long, exhausted look. Bastard. He was probably as sick of me as I was of him. I got up and kept trudging. The slope seemed endless. The clouds closed in. The rope kept pulling me along, goading me forward, a constant reminder of my stupidity.

Then the rope halted. I bent over to catch my breath and tried to see what was happening. It started moving again. Could we be at camp? I wouldn't allow myself to believe it. I trudged upward, rest-stepping, barely able to stand upright. Through the snowflakes I spotted the bright yellow half-circle of Al and Lane's tent.

"We made it," he said. Through the cowl of his parka, I saw that his face was grey with exhaustion. He helped me off with my pack. I slumped onto it, too tired to be angry at him.

"I'll set up the tent," he said. "Can you get your parka on?"

I nodded and collapsed onto my pack.

"Hey, can you guys help us here?" Wyn said to Al and Lane.

Lane stuck his head out the door. "I'm pretty beat. Al's totally wiped."

"Thanks a lot," he said hoarsely.

"Sorry," Lane said, zipping up the tent again.

I couldn't believe it. We'd saved their butts twice, and they couldn't even bother to get out of the tent to help us. Limping a little, Wyn cleared the site. I held a corner of the tent as he wrestled the poles into it. Then I shoved our gear inside. For a full minute, I stood at the door of the tent wondering how I could get inside while wearing my crampons.

"Take off your crampons," Wyn said, as if I was a total idiot. "They'll rip the tent to shreds."

Chastened, I sat dumbly down at the door and managed to get the crampons off my boots. Getting to the top had seemed such a sure thing; now I doubted I had any realistic chance at the summit. If the storm broke, as it seemed to be doing, we'd be lucky to get off this thing alive. Weeping at the unfairness of it, I unlaced my boots and shoved them inside. My hands were like blocks of wood. It was all I could do to take out my sleeping bag and crawl into it.

FOURTEEN

Polish alpinist Voytek Kurtyka called high-altitude climbing the art of suffering. When I woke at 3:30 a.m., I knew exactly what he meant. My head felt as tight as a drum. My breathing was fast, erratic, and shallow. Propping up my head with my elbow, I breathed deeply for five minutes before I could get enough oxygen.

Slowly, I began to remember where I was. My watch read 18,800 feet. We were at the foot of the last buttress. The black arrow of the barometer flickered downward, signaling the onset of another low pressure system. Wind attacked the tent, hammering from all sides. There was something malicious in its ferocity, as if it were taunting us before blowing us off the mountain. It didn't help that our duct-taped tent pole bent at an awkward angle, compromising the aerodynamic design and making it even more vulnerable to the gusts. Not only had Al and Lane refused to help us last night, they had neglected to take back their damaged tent. It was a simple fix—sliding a sleeve over the broken pole—but they hadn't bothered to do it. The team was coming apart.

As I looked around the tent—hoar frost on the walls, gear strewn everywhere, Wyn snoring in the corner—it seemed like a bad dream. Sticking my head out of the tent door, I breathed deeply, trying to overcome a wave of nausea. I didn't want to throw up again. We had so little food left.

Above us, the granite pillar rose into the blue-black sky. We were *so* close to the top. The summit was right over the ridge. If we could just keep it together another day or so, we'd have it in the bag.

I zipped the door closed and began priming the stove. It was so cold that my fingers stuck to the metal. I managed to start the stove and began the long, laborious process of melting water. This was the hardest part of the day. Simply getting up, getting dressed, eating, and drinking required an enormous effort. Back home, it would be such a luxury to simply turn on the tap.

Once the water was boiling, I emptied the last package of instant oatmeal into our bowls. It tasted like puree of cardboard, but I made myself eat it. I'd need every ounce of energy today.

As I poured water into my cup and squeezed a teabag to get every last bit of flavor, Wyn roused himself and called base camp on the radio.

"Base camp. This is Razor's Edge."

"Roger, Razor's Edge." It was Kim.

"How's the weather look, over?"

"High pressure system breaking down. Front moving in from the Gulf of Alaska."

"When is it due?"

"Probably a day. Two at most."

"How does it look?"

"High clouds, high winds, snow at higher elevations."

"Thanks, Kim."

"Are you descending?"

"Are you kidding? We're going for the top."

"You are?" The note of concern in her voice was palpable. "How far are you from the summit?"

216

"We're close," Wyn said. "Very close."

"Be careful, Wyn." Her reply was long and slow and doubtful. "A team was killed yesterday on the West Buttress. They slipped on the way down from Denali Pass. We couldn't do anything for them."

The words hung in the air. The radio crackled and hissed with static. Wyn punched the send button. "We'll see you in a few days, Kim."

"We've got our window," he said, snapping the case of the radio shut. "Let's get ready to go."

"We'll bypass the buttress," I said. "We'll make good time on the snowfield. We'll be up and on our way back down before the storm hits."

He stopped eating his oatmeal. "We're *doing* the buttress."

"Are you nuts?" My voice broke. "Didn't you just hear the weather report?"

"We have at least a 24-hour window," he said, starting to pack. "That's plenty of time."

"No, it's not," I said, enunciating each word. "I'm fried. You're injured. Those other guys are exhausted."

"We have to finish it off!" He made a pistol with his hand. "Pull the trigger."

"No, we don't. We can bypass it and come back alive."

"Look," he said, shoving his clothes into his pack. "I'm going up the buttress. You can come with me if you want. Or you can bag out—like last time."

"What are you talking about?" I said, lowering my voice so the others couldn't hear this. "The weather was bad."

"*The weather was bad,*" Wyn mimicked my voice. "*The weather was bad.* The weather's always bad, John. You have to push through it."

"That's how people die."

Wyn shook his head.

I shoved him.

He tensed as if he was going to hit me but then relaxed. "Look, John, I want that buttress." He stared me down. "It's about success—and failure."

"So you're calling me a failure." I felt like hitting him.

"Calm down, John," he said, raising his hands. "Give me a fucking break. I don't want to die either." He shook his head. "I know you think I'm crazy." His high, nervous laugh sounded like a horse whinnying. "But I *know* we can do it. It'll be a total coup. I'll get my first ascent. You'll get your summit. Everything will be cool." He gave me his biggest conspiratorial grin as if that would seal the deal. "Otherwise, I'll have to get a real job. I'll have to go to work for you."

I breathed deeply, uncertain whether he was borderline or just totally psychotic. "But what about the other guys? What if they can't make it up the buttress?"

Wyn held out his hands. "We'll fix the ropes. They can follow us."

"Let's see what they think," I said, putting on my parka. I hoped they would side with me. With three against one, Wyn might reconsider. I unzipped the tent door. Wisps of clouds obscured the lower part of the buttress, but the upper part stood out clear and distinct in the arctic twilight.

"How are you guys doing?" I asked, unzipping the tent door.

"We're alive," Lane replied, groaning. "That's something."

"We need to get moving," Wyn said, kneeling down next to me. "There's a front coming."

"I need to rest," Al said deliriously. "I'm baked."

"Al pushed pretty hard coming up here," Lane said.

"If you rest now, you might end up resting a *long* time," Wyn said, drawing out the word. "How are you doing, Lane?"

"I'm fine," Lane said curtly. "Thanks for asking."

"Do you guys want to do the buttress or the snowfield to the left?" I asked.

Wyn gave me a look out of the corner of his eye as though I'd betrayed him. I didn't care. Safety was more important than Wyn's approval at this point.

"I just want to get up and down," Lane said, scowling. "I don't give a shit about the buttress."

"We have to do the buttress," Al said, with crazed ferocity.

"Are you sure?" I asked. "In your condition?"

"I just need to rest," he said, and then erupted into a spasm of coughing.

It was hard to know what to think about Al. In some ways, he seemed to be living in a dream world. He sat back in his sleeping bag, a thousand-mile stare in his eyes. And yet he had led all the way up here yesterday. He burned to climb the route. It was impossible to discount his intensity.

"I don't think it's safe for Al to move right now," Lane said. "We'll rest and then start behind you."

"It's almost 5 a.m.," Wyn said, pointing to his watch. "The window's closing."

"We can see that," Lane snapped. "We don't need your advice."

Lane's hair was greasy and plastered over his head. His jaw was set. With his upturned nostrils and bloodshot eyes, he looked like a large pig. Al was as thin and gaunt as a predatory bird, his eyes shining with a steely determination.

"I'm sorry you feel that way," Wyn said. "But the fact is if you guys don't move fast you'll die up here." He looked back and forth between them. "It's now or never."

"Thanks, asshole," Al said, squinting through his glasses as if finally seeing Wyn's true nature. "We don't need any help from you."

"Okay," Wyn shrugged. "If you want to be that way."

"We'll put fixed ropes up the buttress," I said to Al. "Use them."

"Your conscience bothering you, John?" Al said, with a sickly grin on his face. "Don't want a death on your hands?"

"No way," Lane said, laughing. "It would ruin his slide show."

"It would probably *make* the slide show," I said pointedly and closed the tent flap. It was a relief to be rid of them. How had things gotten this bad? I couldn't help but think that if we were at sea level, we could have worked all this out over a beer at the 5.10.

Walking away from their tent, I stared at the route ahead. To the left, the snow slope looked easy and fast. But Wyn had ruled it out. Instead he wanted to climb the last buttress, giving us indisputable bragging rights for notching a first ascent. My stomach turned over. It looked hard and steep. I cursed Wyn under my breath. If I wanted to climb the peak, I had to go with him. There was no way to team up with the others. Wyn and I would just have to climb it as fast as possible, leaving a ladder of fixed ropes for them.

When I got to our tent, Wyn was stuffing his sleeping bag into his pack. "Now they're really pissed at us," I said.

"Good," Wyn said. "I *wanted* to make them angry. Get them fired up."

"I think you accomplished that," I said dryly.

After we finished packing, I sat down on my pack and psyched myself up for the route ahead. Cradling the ice hammer in my lap, I stared at it as if for the first time. The short, stubby tool looked like Exhibit A in a murder trial—a long, serrated pick on one end and a blunt hammerhead on the other. The ice hammer was a masterpiece of design, the hammer head for bashing in pitons, the sharp pick made of high carbon steel for penetrating the hardest ice. Despite all of the abuse it had taken, it was bent but not broken, scarred but still sharp and durable. It felt good just to hold it in my hand.

"Ready?" He looked over at me.

I stood up, shouldered my pack, and tied into the rope.

Wyn checked the route ahead against a Washburn photograph. "New ground," he said, grinning. "We're fucking pioneers."

"Sure," I said. "Just like the Donner Party."

"No worries." Wyn laughed dismissively. "We'll cruise it. On belay?"

"You're on."

And then he was off. He seemed to climb with particular relish today, despite the altitude that left me breathless. Wisps of clouds swirled around the buttress, but Wyn kept moving, putting in an occasional piece of protection.

Jumaring up the fixed rope, I looked back at Al and Lane's tent. There was no sign of activity. As I rose higher, their tent became small, forlorn, diminished by the immensity of the south face. I regretted leaving them behind, but there was nothing I could do about it. I just hoped they had enough sense to get moving quickly.

At the belay, we exchanged gear. I led the next pitch. Despite the quality of the rock, I found nothing attractive about the climbing. I simply bashed my way up it, pulling on gear, driving in pitons when I needed to, slogging my way up. Wyn yelled that I should try to climb it free rather than relying on aid, but I ignored him. Screw him. If he was going to drag my ass up this buttress I'd climb it any way I felt like. It was a grunt. Drive in a piton, move up a few feet, drive in another, and hang off it. There was another three feet I wouldn't give back. It wasn't sport, it was engineering.

Slowly, inexorably, we rose up the last buttress. While he led, my mind seemed to separate from my body. It floated above me like a balloon tethered to a string. I climbed the fixed rope like an automaton. My left toe went numb. The coarse granite had shredded the outer shell of my mitts. I didn't care. I felt strangely indifferent to my fate. I tried to keep telling myself that this was important, that everything was at stake here, but I felt as if I were surrounded with cotton wool.

Wyn waved at me, trying to get my attention. A rock whizzed past. I didn't even bother to duck. The rock skipped off the side of my helmet. I kept climbing as if nothing had happened. Finally, I caught up with him at the belay.

"Sorry about that!" he yelled. "I kicked it loose accidentally."

I nodded but didn't bother to reply. I'd save my breath for climbing. Wordlessly, I took the rack.

"How's your hand?" he said, pointing to the mitts.

I shrugged.

Wyn grabbed some duct tape from his pack. "There," he said, wrapping it around the mitten. Then he glanced back down toward the slope toward their tent. "Hope they get going."

"I wonder if we should have waited for them."

"Naw," he shook his head. "They didn't want our help."

"Maybe if we were more patient."

"There are limits to patience." Wyn frowned. "I'm worried about Al. He looks like he has the symptoms of mountain sickness. I just hope it doesn't get worse. I don't want to have to haul him off this thing."

"Me neither," I said.

"We've put in fixed ropes for them," he said. "We've given them a good chance. It's up to them now. Your lead?"

I took the rack and started up. As I neared the top of the buttress, the ice and rock gave way to steep snow. We simul-climbed it, putting in a picket or ice screw, clipping the rope into it, and then moving beyond it without setting up a belay. This was faster than setting up fixed belays, and since the ground was relatively easy, I gambled that neither of us would fall. Despite the lack of oxygen, I moved steadily upward until I was right underneath the cornice on the summit ridge, an ominous, overhanging wave of ice. It looked like something created out of confectioner's sugar, as if it could topple over at any moment.

Like an ant at the base of a boulder, I worked my way back and forth, looking for some way to get over or around it. Normally, I would never have stopped beneath such a large cornice, but in my oxygen-deprived state, I wasn't thinking clearly. Sinking in my ice axes, I moved upward until the roof of the cornice stopped me from going any further. Unsure of what to do next, I began tunneling into it with my ice axe. Ignoring the coldness in my fingers, I kept digging. Five minutes. Ten minutes. Fifteen minutes. I feared it would topple at any moment. My hands were numb with cold. Then a circle of blue appeared at the end of the tunnel. I enlarged the opening and tried to claw my way through. My pack kept getting stuck, pulling me backward, so I took it off and dragged it behind me. Finally, I managed to crawl through it and lay sprawled out on the summit ridge.

The horizon expanded around me. I couldn't take it all in at first. I'd been stuck on a vertical wall for what seemed like an eternity, and now I was standing on flat ground with a sweeping view of Denali and the entire Alaska Range. I marveled at an immense sea of peaks to the north, the sprawling glaciers that wound around them like vast, white highways. Clouds boiled up to the west. The wind picked up, buffeting me as I admired the view.

Dumping my pack, I hammered in two pickets and brought Wyn up. He grinned at me as he emerged from the tunnel. "That was sick!" he said. "Totally sick."

I laughed.

"You're a stud." He dropped his pack and gave me a high five. "Even I would have trouble climbing that." He turned round and round, admiring the view.

"What's going on with Al and Lane?" I asked.

"They were at the base of the fixed ropes," he said. "At least they were moving."

Slumping down on my pack, I put on my down parka, drank some water, and ate one of the last squares of chocolate. I chewed it slowly, savoring every bite.

The long, cornice ridge snaked upward to the summit. It didn't look that far, but I knew that this was an illusion. The wind was blowing hard. The snow looked unconsolidated. Still, if we left soon, we could beat the storm to the summit. But what about Al and Lane? And what about the descent route?

Below us, the southeast ridge curved down and around: our escape route. Clouds rose in the valleys but hadn't yet reached the ridge. I took a compass bearing on the edge of it, just in case.

It was 3 p.m. We couldn't wait any longer. It was time to make a decision. Would we make a dash for the top? Should we wait for them and then head back down the South Buttress? Would the storm hold or was it luring us into a trap? These questions crowded my mind. It all came down to a decision. A roll of the dice.

I figured that for Wyn it wasn't a real choice. Of course he was going to the summit. That's what he did. But I was different. I had choices. I had a wife and a family to go back to; at least I hoped so. I thought about this briefly, weighed it, but my mind wasn't working very well.

The blinders had formed. Without thinking, I'd made my decision and sealed my fate.

"What do you think?" I asked him.

"I don't know," he said. "The weather's coming in."

I nodded, surprised at his caution.

"We've done the hard climbing," he said. "The rest is just a slog."

I shook my head. We were so close. Had Wyn lost his drive? Was he thinking straight? I suddenly realized how much I wanted to get to the top. I wanted the summit, something I could hold in my memory, burnishing for years to come, like a trophy on a mantel. I wanted to be able to say that I'd climbed Denali, by a new route no less. After putting so much effort into the climb, I had to go for it. Looking back down the south ridge, I thought briefly of Jill and Andy. Then I put them out of my mind. I had to get this done.

"Let's go," I said, standing up.

Wyn pointed toward the west. "Don't you see the clouds?"

"We can make it."

Wyn stared at me but I could not see his expression, only my own face reflected in the mirrors of his sunglasses. He looked away from me and then back at the clouds. "Okay," he said, as the wind snatched the words away.

That was all I needed.

We left the packs down on the ridge and took only our ice axes, a water bottle, and a candy bar. The snow proved as treacherous as I suspected. It was a mindless, exhausting marathon of a slog, with my boots plunging through the crust of the snow. I kept the summit locked in my sights.

Though I was light-headed, I didn't want to relinquish the lead. I kept going. I wanted to make it far enough along the ridge that there would be no turning back. I wanted it more than Wyn did now. Desire made me stronger. I'd pull him to the top.

The wind burst wildly around us, assaulting us one minute, dying down the next. The surface of the snow held my weight and then gave way, plunging me up to my knees. It was frustrating, exhausting work. I had to stop and breathe every few steps. Wyn was right behind me.

The flapping of my parka sounded like machine-gun fire. I gasped for air as it rushed past me. Bending over, I stopped to catch my breath. I was so tired.

"My turn!" he shouted, moving past me.

The cold, glistening high arctic peaks spread in all directions. Mist crept up the valleys. Cirrus clouds crowded the western horizon. I glimpsed what looked like the top itself, crowned with bamboo wands and strips of orange surveyor's tape.

Putting my boots into his footprints, I kept going. Since I outweighed Wyn by twenty pounds, I still broke through. My lungs felt like they were going to burst. A gust of wind knocked me over and blew my hood over my head. I had to stop and pull it back down. I couldn't stand having my hood up, despite the wind chill. The wind roared in my ears.

As the ridge narrowed, the slopes dropped off steeply on either side. To the right, the Muldrow Glacier wound among a jagged sea of peaks. It looked like a scene from the South Pole—a world made of ice.

The immense south face loomed to the left. I couldn't see it, but I could feel it there, just over the summit cornice.

When Wyn stopped to rest, I took over breaking trail. I felt like a prizefighter, battered and punch drunk but still slugging away. We were getting close. A strip of orange surveyors tape flapped from a pole anchored to the summit. I put everything out of my mind—the coming storm, my frostbitten foot, Al and Lane, my family—and focused on the white triangle in the distance.

Fifteen minutes later, it didn't seem any closer. A wave of nausea overcame me. I had to stop and encourage myself. Take it easy. Don't get exhausted. Save something for the descent. I looked back at Wyn. Behind him, two tiny dots appeared on the summit ridge: Al and Lane! Now I was totally pumped. I turned around and kept going.

We fought our way up the last part of the summit ridge. I felt spacey, nauseous, utterly spent. I just wanted to sit down and rest. But I kept going. A thousand feet. Five hundred. Three hundred. Two hundred. One hundred. I ticked off the altitude on my altimeter watch. In a final burst, I passed Wyn on the way to the top.

Bending over, I knelt on the summit of North America. I uttered a silent prayer. Thank God, I'd made it. Then I turned and watched the tattered flags flapping in the wind. We had the place to ourselves. No one else had been foolish enough to make an attempt today. A profound sense of relief and gratitude welled up in me. We had snatched the summit from the dragon's mouth. No one could take it away from me.

A vast sea of peaks spread out beneath us. I felt a euphoria I hadn't felt in years. Tears welled up in my eyes. I felt invincible, as if there was nothing I couldn't climb. Such an attitude was dangerous, foolhardy, profoundly stupid, but I didn't care. It was worth all the trouble and anxiety and effort required to get here. I took out Andy's green plastic frog and left it on the summit—a token, a memento, a way of trying to bring the divisions in my life together.

Wyn stepped onto the summit a minute later. I tried to exchange a high five with him but missed. I bent over laughing and collapsed in a spasm of coughing. We tried again. This time we smacked gloves.

"Yes," he yelled above the wind. "We did it!"

"Way to go!" I said. "Way to go!"

We hugged and then snapped photos of each other, grinning like idiots through our ice-covered beards.

I drank some water and forced myself to eat a square of chocolate. Four squares to go. Shivering, I drew my down parka around me. With wind chill, it was forty degrees below zero. I couldn't feel my fingers. "Let's go," I said.

"I'll follow you."

FIFTEEN

It started snowing. The flakes were as light and insubstantial as particles of Styrofoam, but as we descended, they covered our tracks. Drunk with success, we stumbled downward, trying to put as much distance as possible between ourselves and the summit. Visibility dropped. The wind blew fiercely, forcing me to brace myself against the slope.

Leaning against my ice axe, I tried to keep it together and avoid a slip over one side of the ridge or the other. Gusts whipped and buffeted me, throwing me off balance. It took all my concentration to avoid getting blown over. Despite the precarious spot, I couldn't help grinning. We'd fucking done it! We'd climbed a new route on the south face of Denali!

Wyn plunged ahead, favoring his knee. As the snow fell harder, I lost sight of him. Taking out my compass, I made sure we were going the right way, even though it seemed impossible to veer off the ridge.

Where were Al and Lane? Were they still below us? Had they made it up the fixed ropes? If we could all get back safely, the expedition would be a success, even if we never spoke to them again. It was a huge relief to see the red and purple specks of their parkas coming toward me. As I got closer, I saw that they had dumped their packs. Despite the weather, they were heading to the summit. This was madness.

Wyn met them first. He gesticulated toward the descent route. Al and Lane stopped to listen, but they didn't seem to be turning around. By the time I reached them, they seemed ready to get going.

"How's it going?" I yelled above the wind.

"Okay." Lane grunted and hyperventilated as if he were going to throw a valve. His nose was burnt and blistered, his mouth gathered into a round O as he forced the thin, bitter air into his lungs.

Al nodded and pushed up his thick glasses with his gloves. His face was gray, his beard caked with ice. He looked like the marathon runner gutting it out to the finish line.

"It's suicidal," Wyn shouted. "There's no way you can make it."

"Listen," I said, putting my hand on Al's shoulder. "We barely made it. You've got no chance."

"You guys made it." Al shoved my hand aside. "We'll make it, too."

Lane stayed where he was. "How far is it?"

"Two hours—at least," I said.

"We're losing time!" Al said fiercely. "Let's go."

"It's crazy." Wyn said. "Turn around."

Al coughed, staggered, and kept going. Lane looked back and forth between us and Al, shook his head, and then fell in behind him. They climbed into the gathering storm, willing victims of what was about to unfold.

"Let's go!" I yelled.

Wyn stood with his hands on his hips, shaking his head as they disappeared into the storm.

I started down. Fingers of clouds closed in over us. This was no time to relax. We'd never seen the descent route. We had a topographic map and a Washburn photo of the route, but that would prove only marginal help in a storm. And we had so little food and water left that we couldn't wait it out.

A few minutes later, I reached the packs. Wyn arrived right behind me. I was so fatigued, I was starting to lose my balance. I wanted to set up camp right there, but the wind was too strong. Huddling behind our packs, we brewed up some tea. I ate a square of chocolate. I put on my down parka. We waited. And waited. No sign of Al or Lane.

"What should we do?" I asked.

"Let's keep descending," Wyn said. "We need to get off this damn ridge."

"But they may need our help," I said. "We can't just abandon them."

"We're not abandoning them," Wyn said dismissively. "They knew the risks."

He was already speaking of them in the past tense.

"Here," I said, handing Wyn the tent. "Set it up while I go back and look for them."

"What?" Wyn said.

"I can't leave them," I said, standing up. "Besides, the conditions are going to hell. It's not safe to descend."

He looked up the route and back down. "Here," he said, handing the tent back to me. "I'll go back for them."

"You kidding?" I said incredulously.

He snorted disgustedly.

"You do have a shred of humanity."

"Don't tell anyone," he said.

As he headed out, I began digging a shallow trench for the tent. I was so tired that I could barely stand up. After what seemed like an hour, I'd scoured a trench two feet deep. It would have to do.

I carefully removed the tent from the pack. The wind tried to snatch it away, but I knelt on it like a wrestler pinning his opponent. Unrolling it deliberately, I staked one corner at a time. The fabric flapped furiously, making it nearly impossible to get the poles in. Taking off my mittens, I managed to insert the poles into the sleeves.

Inside the tent, I saw that the fingers of my right hand were covered with black frostbite blisters. I'd have to be careful not to pop them. They could easily get infected. Then I'd lose my fingers. It was agonizingly slow taking off my crampons and boots with my almost useless right hand.

I wanted to collapse into my sleeping bag, but I made myself start the stove. Everything required a deliberate exercise of will. I made myself go back outside and dig up some snow. I put the pot on the stove. Flicking the lighter with my left hand, I started the stove. I had to hydrate. I had to take care of myself. I had to get back home.

A few minutes later, I heard shouts. Shoving on my boots, I ducked out of the tent and got hit in the face with a blast of windblown snow. A hundred yards above me, three figures staggered down the summit ridge—Wyn in the lead followed by Al and then Lane. Al fell, nearly knocking over Wyn. Lane helped Al to his feet. When they were just outside the tent, I grabbed Al and eased him inside.

Wyn handed me a sleeping pad. I took Al's parka off and got him in the bag. He coughed up a long ribbon of blood, a sign of high-altitude pulmonary edema. His face was pale, his breathing rapid and shallow.

"They got to the top," Wyn said breathlessly.

Al's head rolled back and forth as if he had no control over it.

"Lane," I yelled. "Al needs your help."

Lane slumped down on the floor of the tent, exhausted.

He grabbed Al's wrist and took his pulse. "It's fast," he said. Then he checked his fingernails. Sure enough, they were tinged with blue, likely the onset of edema. "Get me some Decadron," he said.

"Wyn, bring in the first-aid kit!"

"What?" Wyn's head appeared at the door of the tent.

"First-aid kit!" I yelled.

He nodded and brought it inside. "How is he?"

"He's in tough shape," Lane said, hyperventilating.

Wyn went over to him. "Al, you okay?"

Lane pushed him away. "I'll take care of him."

Wyn backed off. "Just trying to help."

Lane opened Al's mouth and slipped a Decadron between his lips. Then he handed one to each of us. "Here," he said. "Take these."

Lane explained they were supposed to aid high-altitude acclimatization. We needed all the help we could get. I passed around a water bottle. Lane handed it to Al, who spilled most of it over himself.

"Shit!" I yelled. "It took an hour to melt that."

"He's losing his small motor coordination," Lane fumed as if it was my fault.

"I can see that," I said. "Here, you keep track of him! If you're going to take charge, take charge." I'd had it with Lane and his bullshit posturing.

"It's not my fault he dropped it," Lane said, pressure breathing.

"You're right," I said. "I'm sorry."

Lane gave me a look, sipped from the water bottle, and then handed it to Wyn, who finished it off. I gave Wyn another pot to fill with snow. We had to hydrate. I cracked off another square of chocolate and ate it. Wyn sucked on one of his last lemon drops. Lane gave a piece of beef jerky to Al. It sat in the side of his mouth and then dropped out.

"We've got to get him down," Wyn said, putting the beef jerky back in Al's mouth.

"Not tonight!" I said, shaking my head. "I'm not going back out there."

"If we don't get him down soon he won't be able to walk," Wyn said grimly. He wiped the back of his hand against his mouth. "And if he can't walk..."

"I'll take care of him," Lane said, hunching his shoulders.

The four of us huddled together in a tent designed for two, Wyn and I at one end, Lane and Al at the other. None of us could lie down. Al gasped for breath like a fish out of water and hallucinated about being back to work at Boeing. "Tell the lead. Run the numbers," he mumbled. Lane cleared an endless supply of mucus from his throat. Wyn snored loudly. I resented how easily he could fall asleep.

The rattling of the tent fabric rose to a crescendo. Without the protection of the trench I'd dug, the tent would have likely blown away. I thought of the dead climber from the Wilcox Expedition who was found with his hands still clutching the tent pole. If we didn't keep the tent up we'd be like him—frozen meat in the morning. I drifted in and out of consciousness, thinking of Jill in bed back home, and then woke up in a bitterly cold tent crammed with three other guys.

The wind ripped and clawed at the tent. The gusts were savage, percussive. I'd never experienced anything like it. I understood why so many climbers feared Denali.

Around 2 a.m. the broken pole worked loose. I grabbed it, shoved the sleeve back over it, and held it in place with my foot so it wouldn't turn the tent into a huge sail that would blow us over the north face.

At 5 a.m., the sky grew lighter. I sat up in my sleeping bag. Al was still breathing, but rapidly and irregularly. There was blood and spittle all over the hood of his sleeping bag. His face was blue and ashen, set like a mask.

Peeling off my inner gloves, I saw my hands had gotten worse. Two black blisters had popped on my left hand, the blood and fluid sticking to my inner gloves. Wincing, I put the gloves back on.

Lane sat up in his sleeping bag. He massaged his feet for a good fifteen minutes. "Can't feel my toes," he complained.

Wyn blew on his fingers to get the blood circulating.

At 6 a.m., Wyn passed around a water bottle. I ate a square of chocolate. Wyn sucked on his last lemon drop. Lane ate a piece of beef jerky. I tried to get Al to eat one of my last squares of chocolate, but he spit it out. It was covered with blood and spittle, but I wiped it off on my pants and ate it anyway.

"How're you doing, Al?" I asked.

"Run the numbers," he croaked. "Tell the lead." The fluid in his lungs made a sickening gurgling sound as if he were drowning.

"Don't ask him any more questions," Lane said. "You'll just tire him out."

"I was just trying to encourage him," I said.

"Don't bother," he said, lacing up his boots. "I'll take care of that."

"Of course you will," I said, glaring at him. Lane could go to hell, but I suppressed the urge to tell him this. It would only make things worse. We had to keep the party together until we got off this thing.

"His pulse is 130," Lane said, pressing his hand to Al's wrist. "We've got to get moving."

Wyn took out the radio.

"Razor's Edge to base camp, over."

"We read you, Razor's Edge."

"We've got an injured climber, base camp. High-altitude pulmonary edema. Over."

"Can you get him down?" It was Kim.

"We'll try, but we may need help with the rescue."

"Where are you now?"

"Summit ridge, right above the south face, about 19,000 feet."

"Can you get him lower?"

"We'll try to get him to Face Camp."

"Where's Face Camp?"

"East Fork of the Kahiltna. Big red tent. About 11,200 feet."

"I'll see if we can get a helicopter up that high. Depends on the weather. It doesn't look good."

"We'll get him down."

"Good luck, Wyn. Take care…"

"Will do, Kim."

Wyn shut off the radio. "Let's divide up Al's gear."

"Listen," Lane said. "I'm in charge now. This is a rescue." Lane looked back and forth between us, slapping his gloved hands against his thighs to emphasize his points. "There's a procedure in place for these kinds of emergencies. There needs to be a clear chain of command. If not, everything breaks down."

Wyn looked at Lane as if he was out of his mind. "Of course there needs to be a clear chain of command," he snapped. "But your experience at high altitude is nil. I'll make the decisions."

"Look," Lane said, spitting the words out. "I'm responsible for Al. I'll do what it takes to get him off of here. You have nothing to say about it."

"Don't be an idiot!" Wyn's voice cracked. "Your climbing experience is pathetic."

"I've had a lot more experience than you in emergencies, buddy." Lane wagged his index finger at Wyn. "I've dealt with heart attacks, gunshot wounds, third-degree burns—you name it."

"At sea level!" Wyn said, the veins standing out in his neck. "We're at 19,000 feet—in case you hadn't noticed." He rolled his eyes and looked outside the tent. "We need to get going—if that's okay with *you*."

Lane worked his jaw back and forth, smacking one of his gloves into the other. The tension inside the tent became unbearable, but I'm glad Wyn didn't back down. He and I had way more experience than Lane. Everything was at stake here. This was no time to learn by doing. Wyn and I would make the decisions—not Lane. Wyn snorted disgustedly and went outside to begin packing. I finished lacing my boots. I started to help Al with his, but Lane pushed my hand aside.

"I'll do it," he said.

"We need to cooperate," I said, putting my hand on his shoulder. "Especially on the descent. If we don't, we'll be toast."

"You say cooperate," Lane said, turning away from me. "But you mean *dictate*."

I crawled over Al's legs to go outside. Despite the gusting winds and bitter cold, it was a relief to escape the claustrophobic tent. Ground blizzards scoured the ridge, but the clouds opened up enough to give tantalizing views of the Alaska Range and the tundra beyond. We had enough visibility to get down if we moved fast. After we got off the ridge, we still had to find our way down the south flank, a steep but considerably easier patch of ground than we'd just climbed.

We divided up Al's gear, putting most of it in Wyn's pack. Al crawled from the tent and tried to stand up. I helped him up. It was scary how easy he was to lift.

Lane came out and took Al's other shoulder. "Easy does it," he said gently. As much as I resented Lane's officiousness, I admired his devotion to Al, whose determination to get to the top at all cost had put all of us at risk. Lane didn't seem to hold this against him.

"I've got him now," Lane said. "Thanks."

Al's breathing was labored, the fluid gurgling in his lungs. Gone was the he-haw laugh, the thin determined lips, and the constant fiddling with his glasses. Al looked spent, as if he'd used it all up in getting to the top.

Wyn and I broke down the tent, struggling to keep it from blowing away. Wyn wanted to discard it, but I insisted we keep it. We didn't know how far we'd get tonight. We had 8,000 vertical feet to go over terrain we'd never traveled. Taking a photocopy of the route from my pocket, I poured over it, trying to figure out where to go. It was taken on a cloudless day by Washburn, the famous Denali photographer. I'd have to rely on it and the map and compass to get us down.

Wyn went first, breaking trail. I kept the compass out, making sure that we were on track. We followed the ridge, staying clear of the overhanging cornice on the right.

Al staggered behind me, his mouth agape, his head slumped back, like someone in a waking nightmare. Lane brought up the rear, reining Al in when he was about to fall. They moved slowly. Al had to stop often to catch his breath or pick himself back up. I marveled at Lane's forbearance.

The ridge seemed to go on forever. It was hard to tell what kind of progress we were making in the white, hissing mist. Wyn kept moving, probing the snow for cornices. I followed, keeping track of the compass bearing, wondering when we needed to turn right. Somewhere up ahead, the south ridge divided, with one ridge going east and the other going south. We wanted the one going south. If we made the wrong choice, we were hosed. We'd end up in Thayer Basin, far away from our base camp, and would become statistics in the American Alpine Club's *Accidents in North American Mountaineering.*

I kept an eye on my altimeter watch. The elevation fluctuated with the barometric pressure, making a precise calculation impossible. It read 18,900 feet, which, according to the map, should have been the terminus of the ridge. I scanned the slope for signs of a ridge to the right.

As I looked down to recheck the compass, my right crampon caught on a patch of ice. Before I could react, I was tumbling out of control. "Falling!" I yelled. I tried to jam in my ice axe, but my frostbitten hands couldn't hold the pick tight. I accelerated and hit a patch of snow. The rope pulled tight and stopped me. Wyn's self-arrest had held. Getting up, I dusted the snow from my jacket and pants. I slowly stood up and climbed back up the ridge, riveting all my attention on the slope in front of me.

"You okay, John?" Wyn shouted. "Why didn't you self-arrest?"

"I tried," I said lamely. "My hands wouldn't work."

He shook his head and kicked at the snow.

We kept going. Clouds raced by. Then they opened up. It looked like we'd reached the end of the south ridge. Working quickly, I got compass bearings on Hunter and Huntington, the two tallest peaks visible to the south. Triangulating from the bearings, I estimated our position on the south face. We needed to go straight. Of that I was sure.

"Let's keep going," Wyn said. "They can follow our tracks."

"We should wait for them," I said. "They're in bad shape."

"But we have to take advantage of this window," Wyn said, gesturing with his ice axe. "It's closing fast."

"Al can barely stand," I said. "Lane's not much better."

"They're going to get us killed if we're not careful," Wyn said.

I looked at my watch. Five minutes had elapsed since we'd arrived. That could be the difference between life and death in marginal conditions like these.

By the time Al and Lane arrived, the clouds had moved in again. Al stumbled but remained standing. He looked like a bowling pin that wobbled back and forth and wanted to fall but just couldn't do it. If we got him down, he had a shot at recovering. If we didn't, the edema would get worse. He'd drown in fluid from his own lungs.

Lane put an arm around Al and lowered him onto my foam pad.

"Tell the lead," Al mumbled. "Run the numbers."

After they drank some water, I stood up. I had to keep moving. My core temperature was dropping. Lane and Al sat there, mouths agape.

"Let's go!" Wyn said.

Lane shook his head. "We need to rest." His cheeks were blue, his goggles fogged, his blond hair matted with spindrift.

"We can't." Wyn braced himself against a gust of wind. "We need to get off this ridge."

Lane slowly got up, as if every movement took a deliberate effort of the will. He helped Al stand up. "Which way?" Lane asked.

"Straight," I yelled.

He walked around the perimeter of the ridge, probing with his ice axe. Then he came back over to us.

"We need to go to the right." He took the 200-foot static line from his pack. "I'll lower Al from here."

"No!" I yelled. "That's the south face!"

"Quickest way down," Lane said.

I shoved the map in front of him. "Look," I said, pointing out the gathered lines that indicated the nearly vertical drop. "It's way too steep. We need to go *straight* to the col."

"Where's Al's GPS?"

"He lost it in the avalanche," Lane said. "But if we had the litter..."

"The litter?"

"The litter, remember?" Lane said. "We left it back in Talkeetna. If I had it, I could follow you guys. Without it I have to lower him with the static line."

"That's suicide," I said.

Lane ignored me and put on his pack. "Come on, Al." He helped Al get to his feet.

"Lane!" I shouted. "You'll never make it."

"See you down there," he yelled, pulling on his pack.

Wyn ran toward him, plunge-stepping through the knee-deep snow, and tackled him from behind. Lane fell face forward, with Wyn on top of him.

"Don't do it!" Wyn yelled.

Lane stood up. He outweighed Wyn by at least fifty pounds. He pressure breathed to catch his breath. "Stay back," he warned. "Bringing Al down. Don't want you killing him."

"What?" Wyn yelled.

"Not like your other partners," Lane said, breathing hard.

Wyn lunged at Lane, hitting him above the right eye. Lane staggered backward. Then he came at Wyn. Wyn hit him again, bloodying his nose and knocking the goggles from his face. But Lane grabbed Wyn, picked him up, and threw him onto the snow. I got to him as he jumped on top of Wyn. Putting Lane in a half nelson, I managed to drag him off Wyn, but he was as strong as a steer. He twisted away, threw me down, and raised his cramponed foot above me.

"Back off," he said. "I know what I'm doing."

"Like hell you do," I said. "You're going to kill yourself and Al."

"Fuck you," Lane said and spat at me. "Don't need your help."

"Stay with us," I yelled. "You'll regret this!"

Lane stared at a spot in the snow midway between us. Then he put on his pack as if nothing had happened and moved to the right. He popped a dosage of Decadron into Al's mouth and gave him a sip of water. Then Lane headed toward the south face. The rope jerked tight. Al lurched forward.

"This way!" Lane yelled.

"Stop!" I shouted. "Wait!"

But they kept going. They had broken the cardinal rule of climbing: keep the party together. They had cut the invisible rope between us.

SIXTEEN

Wyn led out, plunging down the forty-five-degree slope. He zig-zagged back and forth, searching for a rock, a nylon sling, a wand—anything to indicate we were on route and not blundering down a side gully that would lead us to a cliff band. I kept my compass in my left hand. Watching the trembling red needle, I tried to keep us on track.

The slope steepened and the visibility dropped. I was flying on instruments now. In the absence of any other confirmation, I began to doubt the compass. Did I get the bearings right? Were we headed toward base camp or into Thayer Basin, named after an early climber who died of a broken back in a serac fall?

Wyn turned around. "Which way?"

"Straight," I yelled, pointing.

As he descended farther, I fought back a feeling of dread. We could easily be heading toward a cliff. After the fight with Lane I felt hunted, as if the mountain wanted to obliterate us. I was hyperaware of our vulnerability. Now that our party was down to two any accident or crevasse fall could be fatal. This area of the mountain was riddled with crevasses, though the recent snows seemed to have covered them. If Wyn fell into one, I doubted I'd be able to self-arrest with my right hand.

Constantly checking the compass, I made slow progress. Wyn tugged against the rope, turned around, and looked exasperated. I didn't care. We couldn't afford a screwup.

We passed a rock outcropping, a solid feature in a world of fog and flat light. Below it, I spotted something blue. It was a nylon sling threaded through a rappel ring. Yes! Relief flooded through me. "We're on route!"

He turned and looked up. "What is it?" He sounded annoyed. His face was red, tired, and weather-beaten.

"Look!" I said, pointing to the sling.

He bent over it. "It might have been placed by someone who was lost—like us."

"I doubt it," I said. "It's right where it should be."

"I hope you're right," he said. He untied from the rope, threaded an end through the ring, tied the ends together and then coiled the rope and threw it into the void. There was no going back now. I went first, rappelling down through a gulley swirling with snow and spindrift until I reached a rock alcove.

While I waited for Wyn, I searched for another rappel sling. After brushing the snow out of several cracks, I uncovered a sling made from the same blue nylon as the one above. It was tied to a piton driven into a thin seam. This didn't look like a desperate, amateur job but a deliberate, well-constructed rappel route.

Wyn released a small snow slide as he approached. As he came level with me, I pointed out the blue sling. He tugged on it and, satisfied, joined me in the alcove and got ready to pull on one end of the rope. The red perlon rope snaked through the snow, hissing as it went. I prayed it didn't snag on anything. The rope fell in loose red coils around us.

Several raps later, we were through the steepest section of rock. It was just steep snow and ice now, dangerous but manageable. A sense of relief washed over me. We were almost off this thing. Then I thought of Al and Lane. They were still up there somewhere. Guilt clogged my throat.

Taking my eye off the slope, I tripped on a patch of ice and tumbled forward. As I landed in a patch of snow, I plunged my axe into the slope. It popped out. I shoved it in again. It popped out. I was picking up speed. Then the rope caught me. I came to a stop, spread-eagled on the snow. Tension constricted my chest and shoulders.

"Are you okay, John?" Wyn shouted.

"Yeah," I said, brushing the snow off my parka.

"Pay attention!" he said angrily.

"Sorry," I said, angry at my own incompetence.

He gave me a look and then took off, plunge stepping downward. I followed, forcing myself to concentrate. I had no time for thinking about Al and Lane. We had to get ourselves down. Period.

The angle of the slope eased. The wind gusted, blowing scraps of cloud past us. As Wyn stopped and took off his pack, I did the same. Shivering, I took out my water bottle. I drank what I could and gave some to Wyn. My stomach felt as hollow and tight as a drum. I craved something to eat, but there was nothing.

Taking out the map, I showed him where I thought we were. "Camp should be that way," I said, pointing in the direction of a bank of clouds.

"I hope you're right." He looked tired, his face lined, bags under his eyes. I craved a rest, but I stood up and shouldered my pack. It was 4 p.m. The wind picked up, sending spindrift whipping past us, stinging the exposed skin on my cheeks. Then the clouds opened. I caught a glimpse of the top of the Japanese Ramp. We were on track.

"Look!" I yelled, overcome with relief.

"You're right!" He said, slapping me on the back. "Let's go!"

We kept heading down, but as we approached the top of the ramp, clouds moved in, obscuring the descent. Tired, hungry, running on fumes, we decided to set up the tent, melt some water, and settle in for a long, cold, miserable night. We sipped hot water, got into our sleeping bags, and shivered away the hours. By morning, I was cold, stiff, miserable, but still alive. We packed quickly and kept going.

As we descended, the slope steepened. I kept a careful watch on Wyn. My right hand was almost useless so I held the ice axe in my left hand, which would make stopping a fall that much more difficult. As we plunge-stepped down, we set off small slides of new, unconsolidated snow. To the right I spotted what looked like a safer, more gradual line. Why was he risking it by going straight down the slope? Why did he always have to push it?

"Watch it!" I said. "Head to the right."

"Don't worry!" he said, turning around. "We'll cruise it."

"It's too dangerous!" I said, but he ignored me, heading straight down the steepest section of the cirque. My nerves went on red alert.

One hundred feet. Two hundred feet. Three hundred feet. We were closing in on food, warmth, safety. I kept slogging, trying to keep my balance, doing everything I could not to fall.

Then I heard a loud crack. The slope below me fractured in a long, jagged line. Wyn turned, astonished, and pitched forward. The avalanche caught him from behind.

Suddenly, everything was in slow motion. I tried to self-arrest, but the rope ripped me out of my stance and pulled me into the churning cauldron. My mind went into overdrive. I remembered the advice from avalanche safety courses. Swim! I tried to swim to the side, but everything went white. Snow and ice overwhelmed me. I got my head into the air, tried to self-arrest, but a chunk of ice hit me in the forehead. Something pulled me under again. Clawing my way to the surface, I got a breath in before being buried by another wave of snow.

Tumbling over and over, I didn't know what was up and what was down. I saw Jill at my funeral, dressed in black. Her face was contorted with grief. She gushed tears and tore at her hair. "No," I shouted. "No."

A block of snow hit me in the stomach, knocking the wind out of me. I couldn't breathe! Stroking madly with my arms and legs, I broke through the surface. I sank my ice axe into the slope. The rope jerked tight around my waist, yanking me from the stance. I landed on my back heading downhill.

Shove the axe in! Pivot around it! My brain screamed out commands. It was all instinctive, the product of years of practice. Snow hissed around me, but my momentum slowed. I lay spread-eagled, waiting for another huge pull of the rope that would pop me from the stance. The pull came. I held it. Blocks of ice roared past.

Finally, the slide stopped. The rope came taut around my waist, so I shifted the axe to my right hand and took a two-foot aluminum picket out of the pack. Digging my boots into the slope for purchase, I hammered the picket into the slope. Then I took a sling off my harness, clipped it into the picket, and attached it to the rope. Slowly, I transferred the weight from the ice axe to the picket.

"Wyn!" I yelled.

No reply.

A hundred feet below me, the avalanche debris had set like concrete. I had to get down there fast. Seconds were crucial for burial victims. But why was the rope still loaded? It made no sense. In the mountains I'd learned to process things carefully, not to panic. If he'd fallen into a crevasse, he could be hanging in mid-air. Hence the weight on the rope.

Hammering in another picket, I secured the anchor. I untied from the rope, a risky move on an avalanche-prone slope but the only way to get to him. Picking my way through the debris, I followed the red perlon rope right to the edge of a yawning crevasse. Then I pounded in another picket, clipped it, and leaned into the crevasse.

"Wyn," I yelled. "Are you down there?"

"John!" Wyn's cry echoed like a voice from a tomb.

It was such a relief to hear him alive. "Can you climb out?"

"I don't think so."

My heart sank. "Why not?"

"My leg's broken."

A hot, sickening feeling washed over me. With my frostbitten right hand there was no way I could haul him straight up. And if I didn't get him out of there quickly he would die of shock or hypothermia. Trying not to panic, I ran through the options. They all seemed bleak except for the Z-pulley system, a rescue method that required turning the rope and pickets into an improvised block and tackle. It seemed simple when I practiced it years ago on a sunny glacier on Mount Rainier. It seemed anything but simple now.

Walking back to my pack, I set off a small slide. The slope was still dangerously unstable. I worked quickly, fumbling as I reset the pickets thirty feet away from the crevasse. I attached a pulley to them and another pulley to pickets at the foot of the crevasse. Then I ran the free end of the rope between the pulleys, allowing me a three to one mechanical advantage. Looking over the contraption, I hoped that I'd done it right. Wyn's life depended on it. Standing at the foot of the crevasse, I slowly took the weight onto the Z-pulley. Wrapping the rope around my body, I walked up the slope, trying to winch him out of the hole. The rope stretched but went nowhere. Shit! I pulled harder, this time putting all my weight into it. The rope came a few inches. Pulling it as hard as I could, I brought him up a few more inches. I repeated the procedure, getting desperate. I wasn't getting anywhere. Snow continued to fall. The slope could release again.

The pressure of the rope against my shoulder rubbed my skin raw. The rope came up another few inches. I stopped, tied into the anchor, and reset the prussik knot. I switched to my left side, leaned into the rope, and brought it up another foot. I repeated the process. I managed only a foot or two before I couldn't pull any more.

I knelt near the edge of the crevasse. "Wyn, can you hear me?"

"Yeah," he gasped.

"Can you climb up any farther?"

"I'll try."

"Wait till I start pulling." I went back to the Z-pulley. This time when I started hauling the rope came up a foot. Then another foot. The rope kept coming and then stopped. I secured it and walked over to the edge of the crevasse.

"What's going on?"

"The rope's cutting into the side of the crevasse," he said resignedly. He dangled ten feet beneath me, spinning slowly in the void. "I can't climb any farther." He breathed raggedly. He would slip into shock or hypothermia soon. There was only one thing left to try.

Going back to the Z-pulley, I took the free end of the rope, attached a rescue pulley to it, and then tossed it down to him. "Clip it into your harness."

"Okay," he said.

"When I give the word, climb!" I didn't add that if this didn't work, he'd be a goner. I stood back a few feet from the crevasse. "Climb!" The rope bit into my shoulder as I leaned uphill. My hands screamed with pain, but I kept going. There were muffled shouts and curses as he clawed his way upward.

My hands were bleeding, the frostbite blisters popped.

"Fuck!" he yelled. His progress stopped.

"Keep going!" I shouted, pulling harder. The rope threatened to slide through my frostbitten hands. "Keep going!"

My grip on the rope was slipping. I heard scraping, swearing, pressure breathing. His ice hammer rose over the lip of the crevasse. I managed one last tug with the rope.

His fluorescent green helmet appeared. Snow covered his beard and eyebrows. Bright red blood flowed from his nose. He got his arms over the edge of the crevasse. He sunk one ice hammer into the snow. Then the other. He worked his left foot up, mantled with his right hand. I pulled again, bringing him right to the lip. Then, in one last effort, he swung himself up and over the side. He landed on his chest and brought up his left leg. Then he dragged the right leg up. It collapsed under him, and he fell over, writhing in agony. I tied the rope into the anchor and went over to him. He lay on his side with his lower right leg bent back in a sickening manner, like the broken wing of a bird.

Working quickly, I took off his pack and pulled out his foam pad. Laying out the pad, I tried to roll him over onto it. Wyn couldn't have weighed more than 150 pounds, but my hands made everything difficult. I shoved him onto it, twisting his right leg.

"Watch it!" he yelled.

"It's okay," I said, but I knew it wasn't. His leg was badly broken. His eyes were dilated, his skin blue and purple. I checked his pulse: one hundred and weak. Shock was setting in. I knew enough about first-aid to realize I had to straighten his leg.

"This is going to hurt," I said.

His body tensed. Holding his right boot, I swung it back to straighten his leg.

"Shit!" he said, kicking me involuntarily. The front-points of his crampons ripped through the sleeve of my parka, but I eased his boot forward. Then I checked for other possible injuries. Wyn was delirious but coherent, telling me that a chunk of ice had hit him in the face, giving him a bloody nose. Probing around the back of his head, I found no fractures or bruises to indicate a head injury.

"Is your back sore?"

He shook his head. I sat him up, gave him some water, and wiped the blood from his nose. After helping him put on his red down parka, I gave him two Tylenol with codeine. This was about as effective as putting a Band-Aid on a gunshot wound, but I didn't have anything stronger. Lane had the Percocet in his first-aid kit.

Watching the snow fall, I considered what to do next. I could set up the tent here, but we desperately needed something to eat. We weren't far from camp. I could set out on my own, but I didn't want to leave him here. He was in shock and could go downhill fast. He might have internal bleeding or some other injury. No, I'd have to find a way to bring him with me. But first, I'd have to do something about his leg.

Unzipping his right pant leg, I had to look away to keep from gagging. The jagged tip of his tibia protruded from his leg like the end of broken stick. The calf muscles spasmed around it. Blood oozed from the wound, staining the snow bright red. I applied a compress bandage to stop the bleeding.

Wyn yelled, shoving my hand away. Finally, I got him to let me put the bandage around the wound. After several minutes, the flow diminished. His artery was probably still intact.

"I need to move you, Wyn," I said, kneeling beside him. "If I try to do it without setting the break it's going to hurt like hell."

"Okay," he said, breathing rapidly. "Whatever you think."

I was flying blind, but I followed the procedure in the first-aid manual. Gripping his boot, I straightened the leg. He grimaced and put his hands out to stabilize himself. Then I pulled and the tibia slid back inside the leg with a click. It was hard to believe that I'd actually done it. I sat back, breathing hard. The snow was still falling. I was running on pure adrenaline. It was now 8:20 p.m. Wyn couldn't survive a night out in the cold. I wasn't sure that I could, either.

"I'm going to splint your leg in a foam pad to protect it," I said. "Then I'm going to take you down to base camp. Okay?"

He looked at me, his eyes wide with fear. I'd never seen this look on his face before. He was the strong one, the cocky one, the one who had more than enough strength and bravado to make it through. Now it was up to me.

"Crevasses," he gasped. The word held new meaning for him.

I nodded and eased him back off the pad. Then I shoved it under his right leg, wrapped it around it, and secured it with duct tape. Wyn closed his eyes and gritted his teeth. Soon, the splint was in place. Then I wrapped him in the tent and handed him an ice hammer. "Use this to steer."

I coiled all but twenty feet of the rope and tied one end of it to my seat harness, the other end to the tent. Then I lifted the pack to my shoulders. Circling around the left side of the crevasse, I probed the snow with my ice axe.

"Careful," he said.

I nodded, taking bitter pleasure in the irony of him telling me to be careful.

Then I moved to the left of the crevasse, dragging Wyn behind me. He hit his leg and groaned. I kept moving.

The angle of the slope eased. It was harder to drag Wyn now, even though the tent slid easily over the snow. Face Camp was several hundred yards ahead. Then the wind came up, blowing snow over the surface of the glacier. I reached into my pocket to get a bearing on the tent. The compass was gone, lost in the avalanche.

Visibility fell to fifty feet. I felt like crying. We were so close, and now we were going to freeze to death. I just couldn't accept it. I remembered what I'd told Jill: I'm coming back. I *will* be back. It pissed me off that she doubted me. Well, I was going to prove her wrong. I've never been an especially religious person, but I needed help now. So I prayed, "Our Father, who art in heaven..." I kept going, hoping to spot the red triangle of our expedition tent. I caught a glimpse of it, no more than one hundred yards away.

The clouds closed in. Despair overwhelmed me. I cursed God. He was toying with me, raising my hopes just to dash them. I just couldn't take it any more—the weight of the pack, the difficulty of pulling Wyn.

Trudging into the arctic twilight, I put one foot in front of the other. The clouds opened and closed. The tent grew closer. I was standing outside the door. I was inside, dropping my pack. I was carrying Wyn and putting him into his sleeping bag. I was drinking water, spilling it over my parka. I was cramming a handful of Fig Newtons into my mouth. I was getting into my sleeping bag. I don't remember the rest.

SEVENTEEN

The thwack, thwack, thwack of the rotors rattled the walls of the tent and sent snow flying. Getting up to see what was happening, I watched the helicopter descend like an enormous metallic dragonfly. After it touched down, the copilot jumped out and gave me the thumbs up. Before I knew it, he had Wyn and me strapped inside. As the helicopter rose and banked, I turned to look back at the mountain. The immense south face of Denali grew smaller and smaller, suffused with the golden light of alpenglow. Everything was going to be okay.

When I woke from the dream, snow had drifted into the tent. In my exhaustion, I had forgotten to close it. Now snow covered my sleeping bag, pack, and the rest of my gear, and some of it had melted, wetting my bag and down jacket, making hypothermia that much more likely. Crawling over to the door, I brushed out as much of the snow as I could and zipped it shut.

Then I sat up in the sleeping bag, rubbed my eyes, and looked around. Clothes and gear were strewn everywhere. Wyn was curled up in one corner, breathing raggedly. Al's and Lane's duffle bags were neatly stacked in the other corner. A cloud of depression and disbelief hovered over me; they couldn't really be gone, could they? I shuddered and pulled my sleeping bag around me.

The wind beat against the red fabric of the tent. I was grateful to have reached shelter, but we were still a long way from safety. My pulse was rapid, my breathing labored. I felt hunted, as if it was my turn next. I'd heard plenty of stories about accidents but had never actually lived through one. Now Wyn's leg was broken. Al and Lane had disappeared. I had severe frostbite.

My thoughts drifted back to Jill and Andy. They were probably having breakfast now. What I wouldn't give to be back with them. But I was a good twelve miles from base camp. The descent was heavily crevassed. The line-of-sight radio was probably useless; we were out of sight of base camp and with the bad weather, it wasn't likely anyone would fly by and pick up the signal. The cavalry wasn't coming.

Peeling the glove off my right hand, I brought strips of blackened flesh with it. So I put the glove back on and decided not to look at it. It would only depress me.

I glanced over at Wyn. He was still wearing his yellow Gore-Tex parka but was halfway out of his sleeping bag. His lips were blue and cracked; his complexion was ashen. He breathed painfully and erratically, as if he were suffering in a world far distant from the one I inhabited.

"Wyn, are you okay?"

He coughed and shivered violently.

I put my hand on his shoulder.

He tried to sit up but lay back down and blinked his eyes. They were dull and glazed.

"Don't move," I said. "I'm going look at your leg."

With great care, I removed the sleeping bag from his leg. Then I unwrapped the foam pad. His windpants were sticky with blood, but the flow had mostly stopped. The wound had swelled up and turned an ugly purple and green color. Taking out some gauze, I lifted his leg to wrap it.

He yelled as if I'd branded him.

"Sorry."

"Careful," he said, gritting his teeth.

I tried again, this time lifting his leg slowly.

He pressed his hands against the tent floor and clenched his teeth. He shook with effort, as if he was doing everything he could to keep from crying out.

I wound the gauze around the wound and taped it in place.

"There," I said. "You okay?"

His eyes were closed.

"Wyn, are you okay?" I shook his arm.

No response.

Shit, have I killed him? I felt his pulse in his neck. It was faint but steady. Slowly, Wyn came to. He must have passed out from the pain. It was sobering to see how sick he was. His leg was infected. No doubt it would get worse. I had no antibiotics. No Percocet.

After I'd re-splinted his leg, I went outside to get some snow. Clouds still covered the upper and lower mountain, but they had cleared from the glacier. After scooping snow into the pot, I came back inside and started up the stove. It sputtered and then roared to life. The familiarity of that sound and the warmth it created raised my spirits. I got back into the sleeping bag and waited for the snow to melt. We needed to drink and eat and get our strength back. Then I could plan what to do next. I needed to think carefully to avoid making another serious mistake.

While Wyn slept, I rummaged through the duffel bags. I found mint tea bags, two cartons of soup, a package of Fig Newtons, a can of corned beef hash, and four packages of Top Ramen. Never was I so glad to see Top Ramen! I made a cup of tea and drank it so quickly I burned my tongue. Then I propped up Wyn's head with my pile jacket and put the cup to his lips. He sputtered and coughed but managed to drink a little.

Start with the small things, I told myself. *Finish them, and then move on to the big things.*

I spent the rest of the morning getting as much food and water into him as possible. Slowly, his condition stabilized. His breathing grew more regular. His cheeks gained some color. He shifted in the sleeping bag and sighed deeply.

"That avalanche..." he said, shuddering.

"Let's talk about something else," I said, trying to suppress the memory.

"I should have backed off," Wyn said.

"Too late now," I said. "Here, eat this." I handed him a cup of noodle soup.

Then I took out the radio. "Razor's Edge to base camp, over."

The hissing of static came over the airwaves.

"Base camp, do you read?"

More static.

I tried several times, with the same results. With the South Buttress separating us from base camp, the line-of-sight radio was useless. I would have to haul Wyn out by myself. I'd have to travel un-roped for twelve miles on a glacier slit by crevasses, dragging Wyn behind me on the sled. If I fell in a crevasse, there would be no one to stop me. No one to pull me out. No one to tell our story. Crossing a glacier un-roped violated all of my mountaineering training, but I could see no alternative.

"Here, let me help you with that," I said, tipping the package of soup so he could eat the last of the noodles.

"Thanks," he said, and he lay back down. "How's my leg?"

"Broken," I said.

"I know that," he said, annoyed. "How bad?"

"Do you really want to see it?"

"Yeah."

Helping him to sit up, I unwrapped the splint and unzipped his pant leg. Thick, red blood welled up through the gauze. Purple, green, and yellow bruises covered the rest of his leg.

He probed the wound with his finger, morbidly fascinated by it. He touched it and blacked out. After I propped him up against the pack, he shook his head and slowly regained consciousness. "So much for Everest," he said dejectedly.

"We don't need to worry about Everest right now," I said, covering up his leg. I didn't want to see it anymore. It was a reminder of all that had gone wrong on this trip.

He rolled his head back and forth. "Do we have any pain meds?"

"I gave you some Tylenol with codeine," I said, defensively. "That's all we've got."

"What about the Percocet?"

"It was in Lane's pack."

Wyn covered his eyes with his hand. "God, it just comes in waves. It builds and builds and builds…" He lay back down, breathing hard and clenching his teeth. Sweat beaded around his temples.

The pain seemed to be getting worse. I dreaded dragging him behind me on the sled. Every bump would be torture for him.

"Wyn, I'm going to look for Al and Lane."

"What?" Wyn looked up. "Don't do it, John. It's too dangerous." There was a quaver in his voice.

"I've got to try." I needed the Percocet and antibiotics and to see what had happened to Al and Lane. They might still need my help. They might be huddled in a snow cave, barely hanging on. It was a long shot, but I couldn't rule it out. I couldn't live with myself if I didn't try to find them.

It took me several minutes to lace my boots. I could only use the second and third joints of my right hand. It was even harder to put on my snowshoes, but I forced myself to do it. I'd be taking a big risk traveling un-roped on the glacier; the snowshoes would make it harder to punch through a snow bridge.

As I stepped out of the tent, the wind gusted, blowing snow crystals up my nose and making me sneeze. The clouds had lifted enough that I could see the base of the south face. The storm continued to dump snow on the higher elevations of the mountain, making avalanches a threat. Some of the south-facing slopes had already released their loads, including the one below the Milan Krissak Memorial Route, the one that Lane and Al had planned to descend. Great rivers of ice and snow fanned out across the upper part of the cirque.

As I started toward the face, a sharp crack made me jump. Terrified, I sprinted back to camp as fast as the snowshoes would allow. Glancing back over my shoulder, I saw the avalanche peter out below the south face in a large cloud of snow. It was ridiculously far away. I forced myself to turn around and started moving toward it. I studied the face, hoping to see the purple and red dots of their parkas. Could they have survived the descent? What if they'd fallen from the top of the south face? Where would they end up? I hated even thinking about it.

I moved above a crevasse field, watching for telltale signs on the surface that might indicate a crevasse. Probing carefully around a depression in the snow, I moved past it. My senses were on red alert. This hyper-attention fried my brain.

Coming to a patch of avalanche debris, I picked my way through blocks of ice. By the time I reached the other side, I was more than halfway across the valley. I could see more of the details of the south face, including the route we'd climbed. It looked dark, exposed, and dangerous. But we'd climbed it! The deed was done. No one could take that away from us. Then I thought of Al and Lane—the elation evaporated.

Whump! Another avalanche released from the south face. I tensed and watched the slide thunder down, taking the snow and debris below it. A cloud of finely grained snow drifted up the valley.

As I approached the base of the south face, I spotted a red stuff sack. A cracked water bottle. Al's blue pile hat. Scanning the avalanche debris in front of me, I saw a raven sitting on what looked like a red parka. I hurried toward it, then stopped.

A raven was perched on the back of Lane's head, pecking at a large patch of blood encrusted on his scalp. The bird glared at me, its eyes black, gleaming, malicious. Then it flew off, squawking across the valley.

My stomach clenched into a knot. Stepping closer to Lane's body, I saw he had lost his helmet in what must have been a tumbling fall down the south face. He and Al probably had gotten caught in an avalanche, judging by the debris surrounding him. A large gash had opened up in the back of his head. Purple blood oozed out of it. I knelt down beside him and touched his cheek with my glove. It was cold and rough, but not frozen. Then I rolled him over, hoping for some sign of life.

A white carapace of ice covered his face. It was hard and opaque, a death mask, obliterating his individual features. I tried to scrape it off, but it was as smooth as alabaster. I shrank back, shivered, and stood up. It all seemed so silly now, the arguments, the posturing, the fight. Of course, it was easy to think this way now, being off the ridge and out of the storm. Perspective seems like such a small thing, and yet the lack of it had cost them their lives.

My stomach started churning. Before I could stop myself, I vomited up all the soup I'd worked so hard to eat. After I'd finished, I sat down next to him on the snow.

"Lane, how you doing, man?" I asked him.

Only the wind answered me.

Another slide released on the south face. I felt so numb I almost didn't care. It cascaded over a rock buttress, hit the slope below, and gradually dissipated. It was a small avalanche, but it was a warning. Getting up, I covered Lane with blocks of snow to keep the birds away. I stood there for a moment, not knowing exactly what to do. I couldn't just walk away. I had to bring some closure to it. I remembered the priest using the sign of the cross at my father's funeral. Genuflecting on the snow, I clumsily made a sign of the cross over him—the Father, Son, and Holy Spirit. For many years the sign had seemed to me an empty exercise. Now it was charged with significance. This was the only burial Lane was going to get.

Then I stood up and began searching the rest of the debris. Following the shock cord tied to Lane, I made my way toward Al. After twenty feet the cord disappeared under the snow. I pulled hard on it, but the avalanche debris had set like concrete. Al was down there somewhere, but there was nothing I could do for him. I made a wide circle around the rope, looking for Lane's pack. I spotted something black. Al's glasses. I picked them up, wiped the snow off them, and put them in my pocket. Walking farther, I spotted a red cloth on the snow. I stooped to pick it up—Lane's handkerchief. At least I'd have something to share with their loved ones.

Trying to keep a grip on my emotions, I looked for Lane's pack, but I didn't see it. Then I took a photograph of the place. I wanted to memorialize this. I wanted to fix it in my mind so I'd never forget. I knew that Al's and Lane's relatives would want to know. And for better or worse, I was the one who would have to tell them.

Another slide cascaded down the face. I forced myself to walk away. I could not afford to take any more risks. I needed to concentrate on surviving.

I followed my tracks back toward base camp. Already the wind had started to erase them. The roar of avalanches echoed around the valley. My nerves were on edge. Keeping to the lower slopes of the valley, I gambled that the slides would stop before they reached me. It was hard to find any safe passage in a valley hemmed in on three sides by steep, rocky cliffs covered with ice and hanging glaciers. Even our base camp was vulnerable.

Scrambling up and over avalanche debris, I looked back up the slope where the avalanche had hit us yesterday. If only we had traversed along the side, we might have been able to descend safely. But it was too late for that now.

By the time I reached the end of the slide, my tracks had vanished. Snow had drifted over them. Working back and forth, I searched for a trace of my passage. Visibility dropped to one hundred feet. Scraps of clouds drifted across the glacier. Without a compass, I had to draw on my skills of observation and intuition. I kept on a rising traverse, hoping to cross my tracks at some point. Mist drifted up the valley. I kept going, trying not to panic.

A crevasse field came into view. Was it the one I passed earlier this morning? I wasn't sure. It looked like the same one, but perhaps I was fooling myself. I probed with my ice hammer as I made my way through it. Then I wove back and forth, hoping to pick up some trace of the tail. The large, faint tracks of snowshoes appeared up ahead. Were my eyes playing tricks on me? In the flat light it was hard to tell. I kept going and finally located the trail. The trail disappeared again, but I searched and found it. Soon I spotted the red expedition tent on a small rise and climbed up to it.

Wyn was curled up in the corner on his side. A pool of vomit—the remains of the soup—covered the tent floor near his head. Slowly unlacing my boots, I took off my parka and got back in my sleeping bag.

He stirred and looked at me. "What took you so long?" he said.

I ignored the question. "I found them. Lane at least." I let the statement hang in the air. Wyn could figure out the implications.

"Did you get the Percocet?"

I shook my head. "Couldn't find his pack," I said. "Most of their stuff was buried in an avalanche."

His expression went blank. "So they're both dead," he said matter-of-factly.

"Yes," I whispered hoarsely.

"Did you see them?"

"Just Lane. Al was buried."

"Shit!" Wyn grimaced again. "We shouldn't have brought them. They weren't ready for it."

I hung my head. "If it wasn't for me, they would never have come on this trip."

"It's not your fault," Wyn said. "It was *their* choice. They knew what they were in for."

"But I talked them into it." I remembered the whole thing so vividly.

"Don't blame yourself," Wyn said. "We all agreed to it."

"Do you know the story of Cain and Abel."

"Of course, Cain killed Abel."

"When God asked him, 'What happened to your brother?' Cain said, 'I'm not my brother's keeper.'"

"What is this, Sunday school?"

"Doesn't that mean anything to you?"

"What's it supposed to mean?" Wyn looked at me quizzically. "That we're responsible for them?"

"Yes!" I put my face in my hands to avoid blubbering.

Wyn shook his head. "*They* walked away. It was *their* choice. *I* tried to stop them. *You* tried to stop them. There was nothing more either of us could do."

"Yeah, but before that…"

Wyn cut me off. "Give up the guilt trip, John. If you don't, we're both going to die. Now get some sleep. You're going to fucking need it."

I spent the rest of the afternoon eating, drinking, sleeping, and brooding. I ate half the package of Fig Newtons and would have eaten the rest of them had I not forced myself to save a few for the trip out. The sticky sweet lump sat in my stomach, giving me indigestion and heartburn. Then it started to make me sick. I forced myself not to vomit. I couldn't afford to lose the calories. I sat in my sleeping bag, like a snake digesting a toad, and waited for the nausea to pass. Eventually I fell asleep and dreamt of the helicopter again. I was hanging to the tether below it. The tether rotated faster and faster and faster. I couldn't hold on. Just as I fell off, I woke up.

The wind had died down. Shoving aside my sleeping bag, I went outside to relieve myself. The skies were clearing. Patches of clouds scurried across the glacier. The storm seemed to be blowing itself out. The evening sun lit the tops of the surrounding peaks. They rose sharp and jagged in the cold, clear air, glittering malevolently like the snarl of a prehistoric beast.

I tried the radio one last time. Nothing.

EIGHTEEN

When my watch beeped at 3:30 a.m., I rolled over, unzipped the tent door, and looked outside. A cloud of spindrift hit me in the face. Visibility was zero. There was no way I could go anywhere in this weather. Depressed and anxious, I closed the door, set my watch for 4:30 a.m., and tried to go back to sleep. At 4:30 a.m., the weather was no better. At 5:30 a.m., it was worse.

Sitting up in my sleeping bag, I decided to write out the story of our expedition, in case I didn't make it back. As I ripped a sheet out of my stenographer's notebook, I wondered if I were being melodramatic. Then I put aside that concern. If Wyn and I fell into a crevasse, someone would find the note. I wanted our story to be told.

> *In the event I do not survive, Wyn Mitchell and I attempted*
> *to walk back to the landing strip on the Kahiltna Glacier*
> *after completing a new route on the south face of Denali.*
> *Al McKenzie and Lane Fredrickson completed the same*

route and died while descending the Milan Krissak Memorial route. May God have mercy on their souls. Please give my love to my wife, Jill Walker, my son, Andrew Hastings Walker, and my mother, Lydia Walker. Please follow the terms specified in my will regarding the division of my property to them.

I lingered over the note, wondering if I should put more emotion in the words, but in the end I kept it simple. It felt weird to be writing my own epitaph, but I needed to do it. Jill, Andy, and my mom would want to know what had happened. So would my partners' families. These details would matter to them. I prided myself on being the kind of guy who took care of the details, even if they were difficult and unpleasant. I signed the note, put it in a Ziplok bag, and placed it in the mesh side pocket of the tent.

While Wyn slept, I got ready for the descent. The plan was simple but dangerous. I'd drag Wyn behind me on the sled back to the airstrip. It would be a long, exhausting ordeal, but I didn't see any way around it. The radio wasn't working, and the weather made it unlikely any plane would spot us.

I brought the stove, water bottles, corned beef hash, tea, first-aid kit, camera, and snow shovel. Everything else I left behind. I hefted the pack; it seemed to weigh almost nothing. Then I went to work on the plastic sled we'd used on the approach. Laying my sleeping bag over it for padding, I examined the seat harness and the aluminum stays to make sure they would bear Wyn's weight. Using my Swiss Army knife, I tightened the nuts attaching them to the sides of the sled to keep it stable. If the stays twisted or broke, the sled would slide away from me, especially on the steep gradient down to the main fork of the Kahiltna Glacier.

By 7 a.m., I had the sled packed and ready to go. Outside, visibility had improved. I went back inside the tent and shook Wyn's shoulder. "Time to go."

He nodded groggily. Putting my arm around his shoulders, I eased him onto the sled.

He yelled when his right foot hit the snow. The pain punctured whatever dream world he'd been in.

"Sorry," I said, lifting his legs inside the sleeping bag. Then I took the climbing rope, cut it into short lengths, and tied him to the sled.

"Give me an axe," he said. "I can help steer."

"Okay." It was a huge relief. We were a team again, even if our partnership had radically changed.

Taking one last look inside the tent, I saw Al's and Lane's duffle bags stacked in the corner. I'd left a can of tuna fish and two tea bags on top of their duffle bags. I should have brought them with me, but I couldn't help myself. Maybe I was wrong. Maybe Lane and Al were just sleeping. If they woke up and came back to the tent, they'd want something to eat and drink.

Zipping up the tent, I put on my pack and struggled to buckle the harness. The scabs on my hands broke open and bled.

As I pulled against the sled, it slid forward. I was taking a chance by traveling at this time in the morning; the snow bridges would be softening up. But I had to risk it.

The sled skidded downhill. Moving quickly, I slowed its momentum. Wyn weighed about 150 pounds, much more than the fifty pounds of equipment I'd carried up here. I had to anticipate the sled's movements to keep it from throwing me off balance. Wyn swore as his leg hit the snow.

"Just another Bataan Death March," I said, hoping to raise his spirits. This had been one of our stock jokes over the years. Wyn didn't bother to respond, but he set his jaw and gripped the sides of the sled. The irony of the joke wasn't lost on either of us.

At the bottom of the slope, I veered to the right to avoid an enormous crevasse that smiled like a malevolent deity.

Probing the snow with my ice axe, I moved to the left, plunge-stepping through the soft snow, trying to keep the sled from sliding into the crevasse. As the slope steepened, the sled veered toward the crevasse. Sitting down in the snow, I tried to use my snowshoes to brake. The sled kept sliding.

"Watch it!" I yelled.

"Okay!" He tried to use the axe but couldn't get the pick into the snow. Turning, I plunged my ice hammer into the slope. Wyn stopped inches from the lip. It took a huge effort to pull the sled uphill and away from the crevasse.

Taking a deep breath, I wiped the sweat from my eyes. This was more dangerous than I imagined. Hoping to get down to the main fork quickly, I took a direct line to the bottom of the slope. This made it easier to keep the sled from sliding away from me, but it also meant that Wyn's leg hit me in the back, knocking me off balance and making him cry out.

Halfway down, I heard a muffled whump. Cracks radiated around me. Gingerly shifting my snowshoes back and forth, I felt the snow settle again. If I kept going I'd set off another slide. And yet I didn't know if I had the strength to haul Wyn back up. Listening to the eerie squeaking of the snow, I decided to reverse course. Slowly, I climbed back above him. The straps of my seat harness bit into my thighs as I dragged him back up the slope. I took a step. And another.

At the top of the slope, I made a long traverse to the left. The sled pulled sideways and threatened to flip. After an hour of this, the angle eased. The glacier spread out below me. The clouds moved in again, with the occasional black flank of a mountain appearing through the mist. The steep sides of the valleys, which once looked so magnificent, now looked dark and forbidding.

Avalanches released around me. I flinched at an especially loud crack to my right. It looked like the entire ice cliff had collapsed. It seemed in slow motion, clouds of snow boiling up around the snout of the debris. I watched it dumbly. I knew I couldn't outrun it. The clouds of debris stopped several hundred feet ahead. A gust of wind hit, dusting me with a fine, floury snow.

I bent over and breathed deeply. I had to keep the blinders on. *It's not far now*, I told myself. *You're going home. You're not going to die.*

The air felt thicker and warmer as I descended. The snow softened. I picked up the pace. I was covering ground in an hour that had taken us the better part of a day on the ascent. When the sled hit a bump, Wyn cried out.

"Sorry," I mumbled.

I slowed my pace. The light was fading by the time the glacier flattened. It looked like the main Kahiltna, but it was impossible to tell for sure. Then I saw them. "Ski tracks!"

Wyn said nothing. He was lost in a world of pain and delirium.

I pulled the sled up to them. I had seen no one outside of our party for two weeks. I desperately needed to talk to someone, to unburden myself.

"Look," I said. "They head for the landing strip."

"Sure," he said, moving his head from side to side.

I checked the map. Three miles to go. So close. But the snow had softened up. My snowshoes sank into the surface. Probing around with my ice axe, I satisfied myself that I was not standing directly above a crevasse. Then I took off my pack, put on my parka, and started melting some water.

I felt Wyn's forehead. It was burning, so I gave him some aspirin and water. "How are you doing?"

He shook his head.

In a few minutes, the water was boiling for tea. He spat out the first swallow but took the rest of the cup. I drank several cups of tea and ate the remaining Fig Newtons.

It was now 10 p.m. The clouds parted, revealing the steep, white flanks of Kahiltna Dome. The massive bulk of Mount Foraker materialized in the distance. To the left, Mount Hunter towered above the airstrip, a glittering pillar of ice, rock, and snow. I kept my eyes on Hunter. It became my goal.

Alpenglow lit the surrounding peaks in incandescent orange, softening the ridges, making the peaks seem warm and hospitable. But this was an illusion.

Wyn moved his head back and forth.

"How are you doing, Wyn?"

"Sure," he gasped.

"You're going to make it," I said. "We're both going to make it." I said it as much for my own sake as for his.

It was 10:30 p.m. The Kahiltna was deep in shadow. The surface had iced back up. I hoisted my pack and buckled the sled harness. Leaning forward, I strained against the weight of the sled. It lurched ahead, making Wyn yell.

I didn't even bother to say I was sorry. The sled glided across the surface of the glacier. Following the sled tracks, I homed in on Mount Hunter. The airstrip lay underneath it, a mile up from the main fork of the Kahiltna. As I trudged into the deepening dusk, the harness squeaked, the sled scraped, and the straps bit into my thighs.

Snow drifted over the tracks. Stopping the sled, I glanced around to get my bearings. The mist had moved in again. Working my way back and forth, I stumbled upon them again. They were even fresher than before. Perhaps a party was just in front of me! But then I noticed the telltale marks of the sled. I'd been walking in circles!

Slumping over, I stopped and dropped my pack. Covering my face with my gloves, I sat down on my pack and cried. My body trembled with fear and self-pity.

After a few minutes, I looked up. An image of Jill and Andy floated six feet above the surface of the glacier. They were sitting at our dinner table. The table was set with napkins, candles, and a white linen table cloth. Jill wore a black dress. Andy wore a flannel shirt.

"We're waiting for you," she said sadly. "The food is getting cold."

At the head of the table, a plate was piled with potatoes, string beans, and filet mignon.

"Are you for real?" I said.

"Of course," Jill said tartly.

"So you're not an angel?"

She laughed. "Not exactly."

"And I'm still alive?"

She frowned and put her arm around Andy. "We've missed you," she said, leaning toward me. "Come back home."

I stood up, put on my pack, and walked toward them. As the image moved forward, I moved with it. Then my right snowshoe punched through a snow bridge. Before I could react, my left snow-shoe crashed through, too. I was dangling in midair, my arms alone keeping me from falling into the crevasse. The sled pressed against me, pushing me in further. Adrenaline surged through me. Cursing, I levered myself up with my arms and pulled out my right leg, press-ing it against the other side of the hole. Then I pulled up my left snowshoe, twisted to my right, and rolled back away from the cre-vasse. For several minutes, I lay there panting.

"John," Wyn said. "You okay?"

I nodded weakly.

"Careful, John," he said. "I don't want to die."

"Shut up!" I yelled. "Shut the fuck up!"

I just couldn't stand him talking about death. It was hard enough to survive without listening to him moan about not wanting to die. I didn't need him bringing me down. Sitting up, I trained my headlamp into the hole. The polished, blue ice dropped down into the blackness. There would have been no way that Wyn could have pulled me out. I would have died a cold and awful death. No one could have done anything for me.

Walking to the left of the crevasse, I probed the snow and moved across it. The light was eerie and otherworldly, a perpetual twilight. The sun had gone down, but only below the rim of the horizon; light suffused the surrounding peaks while leaving the glacier in shadow. A yellow candy wrapper skipped across the snow in front of me. Never was I so glad to see trash. A few minutes later, I found the ski tracks.

They wound through a crevasse field and then headed left. Uphill to the airstrip. A mile left. I checked my watch. It was 5:15 a.m. I had been going continuously for almost twenty-four hours. Stopping to rest, I closed my eyes and nodded off. I wanted to sit, but I told myself to keep going.

Wyn was completely incoherent, babbling about dying, his leg, and his mother. He was lost in another world. I couldn't worry about him now.

The slope wasn't steep, but the effort to move uphill was excruciating. It felt like someone had driven nails into my hips. Without warning, my legs buckled. As I tried to get up, a circus clown ran up to help me. He blew up a balloon, twisted it into a dachshund, handed it to me, and patted me on the head. Then a fat lady wearing a Viking helmet sang a song from an Italian opera. Tears rolled down her cheeks until a dwarf on a unicycle chased her away. I closed my eyes and shook my head. When I opened them, I was alone on the glacier, the weight of the sled tugging against me. Slowly, I stood up.

The first rays of sun hit the top of Mount Hunter. It was 6 a.m. It seemed I was looking through the wrong end of a telescope. I noticed a yellow dot to my left. Then a red dot. Was this another hallucination? Or base camp? I didn't allow myself to hope.

A few minutes later, I spotted the outdoor privy. The details were so clear—cracked plastic seat, plywood box, wands decorated with fluorescent pink surveyor's tape. It had to be real. But I walked over and touched the toilet seat to be sure. Yes! It was little more than a hundred yards now. It seemed to take forever. Then I was in front of an orange tent. A climber was priming his stove.

Unbuckling my pack, I let it drop to the ground. I didn't know what to say. I felt embarrassed to ask for help.

"Are you okay?" A young, stocky, bearded guy looked up from his stove. He walked over to me for a closer look. "What happened?"

"It's a long story," I said, trying to control my voice. Emotion constricted my throat. "Two of my partners died." I gestured toward Wyn. "The third broke his leg."

He yelled into the tent. "Hey, Dave, get out here. I need some help!"

"What's going on?" his friend replied. He was a tall redhead with a wispy goatee.

"These guys need help," the first climber said, snapping his fingers. "Go tell Kim we need a doctor."

While Dave ran down to relay the news, his partner introduced himself as Justin. Climbing is a very tight-knit community, and when a climber is injured, fellow climbers spring into action, even if they don't know the victim personally. I felt immense relief having Justin help me.

"What happened to him?" he said, kneeling down next to Wyn.

"Avalanche," I said.

Justin felt for Wyn's pulse and anxiously looked back toward the base camp. "Well, he's got a pulse," he said, standing up. He noticed I was having trouble unbuckling from the sled. "Here, can I help you with that?"

"Thanks," I said. "My hands aren't working very well."

Justin dragged Wyn over to the tent and covered him with a sleeping bag. I staggered over to the tent, where Justin lowered me onto a foam pad and unbuckled my snowshoes.

Dave came bounding back with an emergency room doctor, a short, cheerful woman with red hair, freckles, and a sunburned nose. After spending several minutes examining Wyn, she popped some pills into his mouth and came over to me.

"Is he going to make it?" I asked.

"I hope so," she said. "But he's lost a lot of blood. He's got a broken tibia and a severe infection from it. He also may have internal bleeding. I gave him an antibiotic and a narcotic. We'll need to get him to a hospital. In the meantime, I'm going to have Kim take care of him. She'll set up a cot in her tent."

"Thanks," I said.

"Not a problem," she said. "I'm Dr. Rachel Parker. How are you doing?"

"I'm alive."

"That's a good place to start," she said. "Did you carry him all the way back?"

"I dragged him on a sled."

"That's amazing," she said, scrutinizing me. "You must be exhausted."

I nodded.

"Any injuries?"

Taking off my overmitts, I peeled back the blue inner gloves. The black skin of ripped blisters hung in shreds from my fingers. The flesh around the skin was red and angry with infection. My hands looked like pieces of badly barbecued meat.

"Wow," she said, taken aback. "We need to get you to a hospital, too. Dave, will you tell Kim these guys should get priority on the next flight?"

"Will do." Dave ran back toward Kim's tent.

Her upbeat, professional manner put me at ease. Lying back on the foam pad, I stared at my hands. I wouldn't be going climbing again anytime soon.

"Let's bandage you up." She unzipped a red nylon bag and took out a roll of gauze. After she finished dressing my hands, she gave me an antibiotic. "I'll be back to check on you in a little while."

"Thank you," I said. "Thank you so much."

Justin came over with a cup of hot chocolate and a bowl of granola. At first I couldn't taste the food; it was as if my taste buds had ceased to function. But as I kept eating, they roared to life. It was such an exquisite pleasure to chew something with taste and texture. I wolfed down the cereal.

Looking up at the fifty tents dotting the rise above the runway, I marveled at the strangeness of being back here.

Kahiltna base camp slowly came to life. Climbers emerged from their tents to relieve themselves and to fill pots with snow for boiling.

The smell of coffee wafted on the breeze. Stoves roared and hissed, filling the air with clouds of steam. Sitting on the foam pad, I drank in the sense of normalcy. Civilization and its contents. The sunlight spread down the northeast face of Mount Hunter. Another day was starting. Despite my injured hands and all that had happened, I rejoiced. I was alive.

I tried to stand up to get another bowl of cereal, but Justin waved me down. "I'll get it."

This small kindness stood out against the vast indifference of the peaks around me.

"Eat," he ordered, handing me another bowl of cereal. I shoved the food into my mouth like a wild animal. I was embarrassed by my manners.

"Lost some weight?" Dave asked, looking down at how my pants sagged around my waist. I tried but couldn't pinch any fat on my stomach. After a third bowl of cereal, I borrowed a compass mirror and looked at it. A gaunt and bearded stranger stared back. His skin was the color of dark leather. The lines in his face were hard and deep. His eyes looked haunted.

Sitting back on the foam pad, I tried to piece all of the fragments of the trip together. I felt an overwhelming sense of gratitude that I'd survived and a stoic pride that I'd gotten Wyn back, but a black hole of guilt lay in the pit of my stomach. I had to fight to keep from getting sucked into it. Al and Lane would *not* be coming back.

"So did you make it?" Justin asked.

"What?" I said, coming out of my stupor. "We got to the top, if that's what you mean."

"Was it an awesome climb?"

"It was a nightmare," I said, recalling the moment when Al and Lane disappeared into the mist. It played over and over in my head like a film clip. "A white nightmare."

Justin looked interested. "Do you want to tell me about it?"

I hung my head.

"How about a beer?" he said.

It was 8 a.m.

"Sure," I said recklessly. "Would you mind?"

"Not at all," he said. "You deserve it."

He handed me a Budweiser. I couldn't open it, so he did it for me. I drank it so quickly that it foamed up my nose and over my face. It tasted clean and sharp and good.

"So what route did you do?"

"A new route," I said, wiping the beer off my mouth with my sleeve.

"Really?" His eyes were wide with astonishment. "I didn't think there were any new lines left."

"Wyn found one."

"Who?"

"Wyn Mitchell."

"I thought he looked familiar," he said, squinting. "I've got to tell Dave. He'll be totally impressed." He glanced over at Wyn. "Now tell me what happened."

Sipping the beer, I scrutinized him carefully. He was probably in his late twenties, with the energy and enthusiasm of someone whose life revolves around climbing. I was hoping for sympathy, understanding. As a climber, perhaps he could give it to me. I recounted the story of the ascent, including the night on the summit ridge.

He waited for me to keep going. When I didn't, he asked. "What happened to your partners?"

"I don't know for sure," I said, staring down at the snow. "I found them at the bottom of the south face."

"That sucks."

"To say the least." I wondered how much I should tell him, but then I thought, screw it. "We had an argument. A fight." I drained the beer and tried unsuccessfully to crush the aluminum can with my mangled hands. The alcohol was making me dizzy.

"Want another?" Justin offered.

"What the hell?" I took another can from him. It felt good to get drunk. "They wanted to descend the Milan Krissak Memorial Route."

"Isn't that a steep face?" Justin asked.

"It's a fucking cliff."

"Did you try to stop them?" Justin asked.

"Several times," I said, slumping back on the foam pad. "Wyn tried to tackle Lane. It was like trying to wrestle a steer."

"That's crazy," Justin said doubtfully. "What were they thinking?"

"It's hard to explain," I said, shaking my head. "It might have been altitude sickness. Down here, it all sounds stupid. But up there..." I took another sip of the beer.

"I'm sure you did all that you could," he said, looking away. He was trying to be diplomatic. Did he think I was at fault? Should I have done more to keep the party together? I knew this was a dress rehearsal for meeting with Al's and Lane's families and the press. If I couldn't convince him, I'd have a hard time with the others.

"So you did a first ascent," Justin said. "What are you going to call it?"

"The McKenzie-Fredrickson Memorial Route."

"Cool." His steely exuberance reminded me of myself ten years ago. He didn't seem fazed at all by the dark side of climbing. "It must have been hairball."

"It was awful."

"It sounds classic," he said. "We were thinking of doing the Cassin Ridge. Your route sounds better."

"Too risky," I said, shaking my head.

He seemed encouraged. He couldn't get over the prestige of what we'd accomplished. "I'm going to talk to Dave about doing the second ascent," he said, starting up the stove. "Would you mind drawing me a topo?"

NINETEEN

Our wanded cache sat near the top of the hill above the landing strip, right where we'd left it. Lugging my pack up the last hundred yards, I had to stop and rest several times. Justin had offered to carry it, but I decided to do it myself, to get a break from his endless questions about our new route and his relentless enthusiasm for climbing, even in the face of our own tragedy.

After dumping the pack, I went down to the Weatherhaven to borrow a tent, sleeping bag, and foam pad. I set up the tent and threw the gear inside. For the rest of the day, I dozed off and on, lost in a funhouse of yawning crevasses, steep ice cliffs, and suffocating avalanches.

Later in the afternoon, I woke tremendously hungry. I remembered that Lane had left a pot of stew buried in an aluminum pot as well as a six pack of beer. Using a snow shovel, I dug up the pot. I sat on my foam pad and ate the stew, not bothering to heat it up or even pick out the bay leaves Lane had used to season it. Washed down with the icy beer, it was one of the best meals I'd ever had, despite knowing that Lane had cooked it for all of us.

Having eaten myself almost sick, I walked down to the Weatherhaven tent to see how Wyn was doing. I knocked tentatively on the aluminum door. Kim met me at the door and gave me a hug, which almost undid me. I'd been suppressing my emotions for so long I felt like a dam about to burst.

"Sit down," she said. "You must be exhausted."

I sat down on her cot.

She brought me a cup of peppermint tea. "What happened to your hands?"

I ignored the question. "How's Wyn doing?"

"Better," she said, looking over at him. He was in a blue sleeping bag, with an IV drip attached to his arm. His cheeks were slightly less pale than the last time I saw him.

"Can I talk to him?"

"He's pretty sedated."

I took a sip of my tea.

"We got your call from the summit," she said, sitting down next to me. "There was nothing we could do. The choppers wouldn't fly in that kind of weather."

"I understand," I said, looking at the floor. "It's not your fault."

"What happened up there?" She put her hand on my arm. "Tell me about it." Her eyes were wide, green, and empathetic. She wasn't a climber herself, but being around them all the time she might understand. I told her the whole story, including the descent. She didn't criticize anything I'd done, but she had questions.

"They just walked away?" she asked. "You didn't try to stop them?"

"Of course we did," I explained. "They wouldn't listen."

She nodded sympathetically. She seemed to have doubts about my story but was protective enough of my emotional state not to ask them. I asked her if I could use the phone. I dialed my number back in Seattle. Jill's voice came on the line, instructing me to leave a message.

I told her that I was okay. That I loved her. That I would call again. In a way it was a relief that she wasn't home. I still needed to prepare myself mentally for telling her about the climb and the accident. After I hung up and left the hut, I heard Kim send out a radio call about an "incident" on Denali.

Snow fell the rest of the afternoon, preventing planes from landing. I went back to the tent to be alone. I ate the stew, drank the beer, and eventually fell asleep.

The next morning, I sat outside and ate the stew for breakfast. Despite my appetite, I was starting to get a little sick of it. I watched a stream of climbers returning to camp, hoping Al and Lane might be among them. They'd have an amazing story to tell. They'd laugh about it over a beer back in Talkeetna. They'd write a book and become famous. Putting my fork down, I spotted a pair of climbers wearing a purple and red parka. As they drew closer, I saw that it was a man and a woman. I couldn't believe the intensity of my disappointment.

Then I heard droning in the distance. Far down the vast, white Kahiltna Glacier, I spotted a small orange dot. Then another.

"Planes!" I yelled at no one in particular. I stood up and watched as they approached. I felt both relief and dread at their arrival. One ordeal was over. Another was about to begin. Everyone would want to talk about it—Al's and Lane's families, the media, Jill. They'd all want to hash and rehash it. Some would blame us.

Quickly gathering my equipment, I hobbled down to the Weatherhaven and put my head in the door.

"The planes are coming," I said. "Is Wyn okay to go?"

"He's stabilized," Kim said. "Round up some folks to help carry him to the plane. We need to get him on a stretcher."

"Will do."

Wyn's eyelids flickered and his eyes opened.

"Wyn, how's it going?"

He moaned but said nothing. His eyes were glazed and unfocused. He didn't seem to recognize me.

"He's on Percocet," she said. "I wouldn't try to talk to him now."

Justin and Dave were eating breakfast outside their tent. They were almost too willing to help. Wyn's celebrity was too much to pass up. Inside the Weatherhaven, we carefully lifted Wyn onto a litter. Once outside, he blinked and shielded his eyes from the brightness. I put glacier glasses on him and covered him with a blanket.

An orange Cessna 185 banked around the side of Hunter. Then another. The planes made one pass to check out the runway, then came in, skis fishtailing across the surface of the snow. The planes taxied on the runway and kept their engines running.

Justin and Dave carried Wyn to the first plane. The pilot pulled back the seat. He grabbed Wyn's pack, stowed it, and then cleared an area so that Wyn could lie down in the plane. I ran back to get my pack, but Justin waved me off. "I'll get it, John."

Two climbers clambered out of the second plane. They gazed around at the scenery, grinned at me, and then stared at my bandaged hands. Dave helped them unload their gear.

"Move it," Miles yelled above the engine noise.

Justin loaded my pack into the plane.

"Thanks again," I yelled as I climbed in.

"No problem," Justin said.

"Are you going to repeat our route?"

He gave me the thumbs up.

"Be careful." I waved with my damaged hand.

"We will," he said, looking away.

Miles reached over and slammed the door. "What happened to Wyn?"

"Broken leg," I shouted.

He shook his head and muttered to himself. As he waited for the other plane to take off, he checked and rechecked his instruments. Then he revved the engine, making it snarl louder and louder. Waving to Kim, he opened the throttle. The plane lurched forward, accelerating past the black plastic garbage bags lining the landing area. The plane bumped and skidded along the snow. Then we were airborne.

Miles banked the Cessna to the left and followed the broad expanse of the Kahiltna Glacier.

As we gained elevation, the glacier resembled a vast white highway, broad and smooth in the middle, with a curving pattern of crevasses on either side. It seemed so innocuous now.

We soared over the landscape, covering terrain that it would have taken days to walk. Our speed seemed unreal. Then Miles veered left and headed for One-Shot pass. The Cessna labored to climb higher. Miles pointed the plane toward the notch. He pulled back on the stick, nosing it higher. We cleared the pass by a good hundred feet. No jokes this time. Immediately we entered a large, black cloud. Rain pelted the windshield. The visibility was three feet.

We burst out of the cloud and back into the world again. The Cessna banked over the brilliant, green carpet of the tundra. I feasted my eyes on the verdant colors of high arctic summer. I felt like I'd been living in a sensory deprivation tank for the last month. The color was so intense it hurt.

A rainbow arced above the Susitna River near Talkeetna. Miles turned the plane back to the left, giving me a full view of Denali in all its terrible majesty. The mountain glistened malevolently in the high, bright arctic air like an immense angry deity. Then Miles headed for Talkeetna. The tiny settlement grew closer. Brown dots became buildings with corrugated metal roofs, yards filled with old washing machines, rusting cars, and flocks of chickens.

We glided over the Fairview Inn, just clearing the telephone wire and streetlight. Miles brought the plane down smoothly on the gravel runway. Up ahead, a team of paramedics carried Wyn out of the other plane.

Miles taxied the Cessna over to the edge of the runway and parked it in front of the hangar. I got out of the plane slowly, trying not to break the scabs on my hands. I jumped to the ground and inhaled deeply. The smell of the earth returned like an exotic perfume—a heady mixture of gasoline, fireweed, and tree pollen.

One of the paramedics came over to the plane. "We'll get you in the next ambulance," he said.

"I'd really like to wait till tomorrow," I said. Things were moving too fast. I needed to collect myself before I called Jill and faced Al and Lane's families back in Seattle. "I want to get something to eat. I need to decompress."

"You sure?" he said. "Your hands must be painful."

"They are," I said, wincing, "but I think I'll be okay."

"Let me give you some codeine." He handed over some tablets. "We'll pick you up here in the morning."

"Thank you."

Miles took my bags from the plane and carried them to his hangar. Then he booked me a room at the Roadhouse. His son, Jake, helped me with the bags. I hobbled through the main street of town behind Jake, a teenager with short, dark hair, zits, and a low, bass voice.

As we passed a window, I stared at my reflection. I barely recognized myself. I looked like a mental patient—unkempt beard, gaunt face, haunted and cadaverous eyes, two bandaged hands, and a lame right leg. I looked nothing like the well-fed, clean-shaven version of myself from a month ago. I would have been stared at anywhere else, but in Talkeetna, no one noticed. The walking wounded were a common sight.

Jake took the bags up to the room. "Dad wants to buy you a drink," he said. "He'll be at the Fairview Inn around nine."

I nodded and shut the door. Sitting down on the bed, I undressed and dragged myself into the bathroom. Using two plastic bags to keep my hands from getting wet, I took a long, hot shower, washing all the grime, sunscreen, and anxiety off me. The water surged against my back. Its warmth flowed into me.

After toweling off, I put on clean underwear and got into bed. The coolness of the clean, linen sheets seemed like a fantasy. I reveled in being here and not freezing my ass off in our wind-battered tent on the summit ridge. Sleep came like a narcotic. I dreamed about climbing inexorably toward the summit. The wind burst around me, trying to rip me off the ridge. I couldn't get traction. With every step, I slid farther back.

I woke up with a start. I looked around the room. Where was I? I sat up in bed and looked at the clock. Eight p.m.: I had slept for seven hours. I got up and went to the bathroom, marveling that I could do this without pants, jacket, and boots.

Then I sat on the bed and put on a pair of blue jeans, a T-shirt, and running shoes. Combing out my long, stringy hair, I looked in the mirror. Grizzly Adams stared back at me.

It was 8:30 p.m. and broad daylight. Limping over to the Fairview Inn, I opened the screen door and stepped inside. I remembered our last meal here, all the hope and bravado of our expedition. Spotting the table where we'd sat, I moved to the other side of the room.

A waitress came over to my table. She had short, blond hair and wore blue jeans, a white starched top, and a small diamond stud in her right nostril.

I looked up at her, marveling at the strangeness of ordinary life. I would give her my order. The cook would prepare it. She would bring it back to me. An implausible, all-but-forgotten ritual.

I studied the menu as if it was a hieroglyphic.

"Can I help you?" she asked with an exaggerated upbeat lilt as if she was speaking to a simpleton.

"I'm sorry," I said, shaking my head.

"What happened to your hands?" she said, frowning.

"Frostbite."

"Did you climb Denali?"

"Yes."

"I remember you," she said, standing with her hand on her hip. "You were with three other guys."

"Yes." I cleared my throat.

"Are they...?"

"Two of them...died." I had trouble forming the words. "The other broke his leg."

"I'm sorry," she said, covering her mouth with her hand. "Can I get you something to eat?"

I ordered two cheeseburgers, two orders of French fries, and a chocolate milk shake.

She walked back to the kitchen and put my order on a metal spike. Leaning back into the booth, I looked around at the other diners. A table of four climbers joked and laughed and looked like they were heading for the summit. I hoped they'd feel the same way on their return.

When the waitress arrived with my dinner, I thanked her and ate like a starved wolf. Miles walked in as I ended my private orgy of eating.

"That's tough about your friends," Miles said, sitting down across from me. "Want to tell me what happened?"

As I told the story, he sucked on a cigar and blew smoke rings into the air. "Don't be so hard on yourself. You're a hero, for crying out loud."

"I don't feel very heroic," I said, crumpling a napkin.

"You saved Wyn's life," he said, leaning toward me. "If you hadn't pulled him out of the crevasse he would have been dead meat." He expelled another cloud of smoke.

"Yeah, but what about Al and Lane?" I asked.

He squinted through the smoke. "Did Wyn have anything to do with that?"

"He wasn't exactly Mr. Diplomatic."

"Doesn't surprise me," he said, tapping his cigar over an ashtray. "And the other two?"

I described their belligerence.

"That happens up high," he said philosophically. He wagged his head back and forth, as if weighing a decision. "You never want to split up a party, but..."

I leaned back in the booth, relieved that he didn't openly criticize my actions but wondering if he thought otherwise.

"I don't need to tell you this," Miles said, his eyes narrowing. "But this is going to be a big deal with the media. You did a new route. You brought your friend back alive. You're going to be a hero, whether you like it or not."

I stared at my hands. "Any news on Wyn?"

"No, but the trauma docs down there know what they're doing. They get a lot of practice." He ground out the cigar. "Let me buy you a drink." He went up to the bar and came back with two shots of whiskey. "Here's to your friends."

He downed his in one gulp.

I sipped mine slowly, letting the whiskey burn my throat.

"I'll contact the Park Service," he said, getting up. "They'll want a full report. Now get a good night's sleep. The ambulance will bring you into Anchorage in the morning."

TWENTY

The pneumatic glass doors opened with a rush of air, expelling a whiff of floor wax and disinfectant. After I filled out a form, a brisk, efficient nurse ushered me down a long, brightly lit corridor. An orderly wheeled in my pack on a gurney. Our footsteps echoed down a labyrinth of corridors to a tiny, windowless room. The nurse gestured to a table covered with a piece of paper. After I sat down on it, she carefully unwrapped my hands. She winced slightly and wrote down notes in her pad. "Dr. Graham will be with you shortly." She closed the door to the room.

I sat on the table and looked down at the raw hamburger of my hands now puffy with infection. The black skin of popped blisters hung in tatters from my fingers.

Someone rapped on the door.

"May I come in?" A thin, dapper man strode into the room. He wore tan slacks, a white lab coat, and a maroon bow tie.

"I'm Dr. Arthur Graham," he said enthusiastically. "How are you doing?"

"Okay." I started to offer my hand.

He waved it away. "We don't need to shake hands. Just let me take a look at them."

He bent over my hands, gently probed and pinched the tissue, scrutinizing them in detail. He was the first person to look at them that didn't shrink back in horror. "You certainly have a . . . good case here." His pager went off. "Sorry," he said, looking down at it. "Problem with your toe, too?"

Taking off my right sock, he examined the toe, which had a quarter-sized black blister on it. Then he scribbled out a prescription. "We'll get you some antibiotics to help with the infection. The physical therapist will show you exercises to increase circulation in your hands and feet. I may prescribe whirlpool baths as well."

"Will I lose my hands?"

He looked at me directly, his eyes gray and steady. "I don't think so. But we have to make sure the infection doesn't spread. If we stop it, you have a good chance of regaining the use of your hands."

"What about my fingers?"

"We'll know in time," he said, looking down at them. "You've suffered some deep tissue damage. We'll do our best to return them to regular function."

I slumped in my chair.

"Don't worry," he said, clapping me on the back like a high school basketball coach. "We're going to fight the frostbite."

I tried to smile. "Any idea when I can get back to my wife and family?"

He put his hand to his chin. "I want to keep you here for a couple days at least to see if the infection responds to the antibiotics. If it does, I'll refer you to Dr. Sweeney, a colleague of mine at the University Hospital in Seattle."

"I'd appreciate that," I said. "Have you heard anything about Wyn Mitchell, my climbing partner?"

"No," he said, patting his pager. "It's been a busy morning. I'll have the nurse check on that."

The heavy metal doors of the burn and frostbite unit slammed behind him. His nurse prepared a room for me, which I shared with several other climbers who had suffered frostbite, none as severe a case as mine. The others talked like heroes about their climb. They had attempted the West Buttress, the standard route on Denali. I said little about our route; I didn't feel like discussing it.

Later, an orderly brought in lunch, a starchy, glutinous lump he called chicken a la king. I ate it quickly and asked for more. After I'd finished two bowls of chocolate pudding with whipped cream, the nurse informed me that I could visit Wyn in the intensive care section of the hospital.

Shuffling down the corridor in hospital slippers, I opened the door to his room. Wyn was lying in bed with his leg in traction. He had a purple frostbite blister on the tip of his nose. He looked like a raccoon, the skin around his eyes white and the rest of his face deeply tanned.

"How are you doing?" I asked, placing my hand on his shoulder.

"John?" He tried to smile. "I feel like shit. They've got me on all these pain meds."

"It's about time."

"I guess," he sighed.

"How's your leg?"

"It's got so many pins in it I'll set off the metal detector at the airport."

I laughed, pleased he had the energy to joke. "Are you ready for the nursing home yet?"

"Get me a rocking chair." He laughed carefully so as not to move his leg.

"How about a case of diapers?"

He gave me a pained smile. "I hate to say it, but you were right—the slope was ready to go."

"You tell me that now." We both fell silent. The accident was too fresh a memory.

"Those poor schmucks," Wyn said, shaking his head.

"If only they'd stayed with us."

"They did what they did." Wyn shrugged his shoulders. "There's no changing that now."

The sound of the hospital air conditioning droned in the background.

"So I guess Everest is out of the question," I said.

"Not at all," Wyn said, trying to sit up.

"Are you kidding?"

"We'll have no problem getting sponsorship now." His eyes snapped into focus. "I've already started planning the trip."

"What about your leg?"

"It'll be okay," he said, a hint of desperation in his voice. "I'll train. I'll do rehab. I'll hop to the top if I have to. The March of Dimes climbing team does Everest."

I shook my head. His leg was in traction, his hair was wild, yet his eyes were wide with excitement. "You're something else, Wyn."

"What do you mean?" He winced as he shifted his leg.

"You're nuts," I said, getting up. "You should be in the psych ward."

"I'm just optimistic," he said, straining against the traction device. "Once all this hits the media, I'll get backing for Everest. Your shop will blow Mountain Mart out of the water."

"You never change, do you?" As I turned to leave, I finally understood the difference between us. His ambition burned as hot and bright as ever, no matter what had happened or who had died. It didn't seem to bother him to have lost Al and Lane; it was all part of the price for playing in his league. He would just keep pushing until he pushed too far. He didn't seem to have a choice.

But I did. I'd never accomplish what he would, but now I didn't care. I'd gotten what I wanted, even if it had come at a terrible cost. I'd climbed Denali via a new route. Maybe in the future I'd climb something else, but for now, I wanted nothing more than to see my wife and son. I had something to go back to. He just had another hill to climb.

"Think about it, John." He gave me a sly look. "The Big E would look mighty good on your resume."

There was a pay phone in the corridor outside my room. Shoving quarters into it, I dialed the numbers with my knuckle. For just a second, I had trouble remembering the last four digits. Jill picked it up on the third ring.

"Jill?"

"John! Where are you?"

"Anchorage."

"Thank God. Are you okay?"

"I'm okay, Jill. It's great to hear your voice."

"Christ, I've been worried sick about you. I got your call. What happened?"

"It's a long story. How's Andy doing?"

"He misses his dad. When are you coming home?"

"I've got to get out of the hospital first."

"What's wrong?"

"I've got frostbitten hands."

"What happened?"

"I fill you in later, but right now there's something I have to tell you. It's about Lane and Al."

"Yes?"

I tried to speak, but couldn't make myself say the words. Putting down the receiver, I leaned against the wall.

"John, are you there?"

"I'm here," I said, struggling to regain my composure.

"What about the other guys?"

"They're. Not. Coming. Home." I spoke one word at a time.

"Are they...?"

"Yes." I put my head against the wall.

Jill gasped. "How did it happen?"

"They fell." I finally gained control of my voice. "Down the south face."

"Oh my God!" Jill said. "How horrible!"

I didn't know what to say.

"John, are you still there?"

"Yes, I'm here."

"Look, let me notify their families. When my dad died, the squadron leader notified my mom first. It meant a lot to us. We were able to brace ourselves before the media onslaught. I'll call the families. What about Wyn?"

"He broke his leg."

"Should I call his parents?"

"Call his sister. Tell her that he'll be okay. He's in the Anchorage hospital with me."

"I'm so glad you're safe." She let out a sigh. "So did you climb it?"

"We did."

"Thank God," she said.

I told her I loved her and hung up. I was reminded again of the importance of our marriage. We were a team, or at least, I hoped we were.

The Alaska Airlines 737 rose steeply from the tarmac, banked to the right, and passed in front of the massive south face of Denali. The evening sun painted the mountain with an eerie incandescent light, making it look like a remote, mysterious world, beyond human comprehension.

As the jet headed south, Denali faded into the background. I looked out at the vast spine of mountains running down the southeast coast of Alaska. There were huge glaciers, timbered valleys, and jagged peaks as far as I could see. As we flew further south, the sky darkened for the first time in a month. Lights came on in the small communities along the coast. Then I spotted the San Juan Islands. Anacortes. Everett. Seattle. As the plane approached Sea-Tac, I marveled at the condos and apartment houses ringing the airport. It was a pleasure to see a place so clearly designed for human beings. Even the traffic backed up along the I-5 corridor looked strangely beautiful.

I hobbled up the Jetway like a soldier coming home from the war. Jill and Andy were waiting at the terminal. Andy had his summer buzz cut and his goofy grin. Jill wore a red flower print dress, black sandals, and an expression of relief and bemusement. She shook her head at my long hair, beard, and bandaged hands. Andy didn't recognize me until she pointed at me. He dropped his frog and jumped into my arms. I held him tight, despite my hands. Jill hugged us both.

"It's great to see you," I said, overcome with emotion.

She buried her head into my shoulder.

"I'm so glad to be home."

We kissed, long and hard, and then I released her. "Did you notify the other families?"

She nodded. "There's a memorial service next week."

"Thank you," I said, dreading the firestorm ahead.

"Let's get you home." She picked up my carry-on bag and took my arm. "You look like hell."

When we arrived back at the house, Andy danced around me, unable to contain himself, grabbing and pulling on my beard, convinced it was a fake. He lifted his shirt for me to tickle him, but I couldn't without injuring my hands, so I hugged him instead, incredibly grateful to be home.

Later that evening I put him to bed and cracked a bottle of merlot. I sat on the living room couch with Jill and told her the whole story.

"That's incredible," she said, shaking her head. "I'm so sorry for their families."

"Me, too." I stared at my hands, still trying to comprehend all that had happened.

"I'm so glad you're back," she said, putting her arm around me. "I can't imagine losing you."

"So you're not going to divorce me?" I asked.

"I probably should," she said. "You're barely husband material."

"Why not?" I laughed.

"You lack balance," she said. "You're not the solid, stable type."

I'd always thought of myself that way, but my hands said otherwise. "No, I guess I'm not."

"But I love you anyway," she said, leaning into my shoulder. "I couldn't stand that type of guy."

We both laughed. We'd been through hell—me on the climb, her waiting for me here, worrying I might not come back alive.

"You're a hero," she said. "They should give you a medal."

I shook my head. "I just wish I could have gotten them back down."

"You did all that you could."

I drew her closer and put my hand on her breast.

"I was so worried, honey," she said. "I know what can happen."

I nodded and stared at the city lights, comforted by the pinpoints of light in the surrounding darkness.

We held each other and listened to the rain drum on the roof and drip into the bucket in the kitchen. Later, when Andy fell asleep, we went upstairs. Jill lit a candle and turned out the bedroom lights. We lay next to each other, not saying anything, holding each other tightly. Then we kissed and made love, slowly and carefully to avoid breaking the blisters on my hands, with an avidity I hadn't known in years, beginning to heal the distance between us.

The service took place at Camp Long, a large, wooded park in West Seattle. The Reverend Robert Williams, a Baptist minister and friend of Lane's family, set up a simple wooden altar in the middle of a meadow near the practice rock where Al and Lane had begun climbing. Friends and family sat on folding wooden chairs around the altar. It seemed surreal to be talking about death on such a beautiful summer afternoon, but the grief on the faces of Al's and Lane's families was frighteningly real.

Lane's father, a large, bluff man with piercing, blue eyes, looked like he'd imploded. His dark, charcoal suit hung from his shoulders like clothes on a scarecrow. The creases in his weather-beaten face had deepened, his cheekbones had gone hollow, and his eyes had sunk into the sockets of his skull.

Al's mother, a petite, blond woman, wept loudly. Her nose was red. Her mascara was running. The tightly wound bun on the top of her head had toppled over. In her eyes, I read the appalling suffering I could have inflicted on my own family.

When the minister concluded with a final prayer, I steeled myself for the gauntlet of friends and relatives. I'd already spent the last week visiting their families, recounting the story again, trying to bring some closure to the tragedy. It was a long, exhausting process, but it was the least I could do. After paying my respects to everyone else, I spotted Lane's father. It took my last ounce of strength to walk up to him.

"Thank you for being here." He wore aviator sunglasses, making it difficult to read what he was thinking.

"I wish I could have done more."

"It's too late for that now."

"Can I do anything for you? I'd like to do something."

"You've already done enough," he said bitterly.

"I'm sorry."

"You should be." His lips trembled. Then he nodded curtly and walked away.

EPILOGUE

Three months later, Dr. Michael Sweeney removed the first joints of the ring and pinky finger on my right hand and the ring, middle, and index finger on my left hand. At first my hands were numb, just like the rest of me, but eventually I regained the use of my fingers. The skin around the ends of them has yellowed and callused, making it hard and unyielding. At first I was self-conscious about this and avoided shaking hands. Now I take perverse pride in it. It's a sign the mountain has marked me.

Dr. Sweeney said the effect of frostbite on tissue is much like that of a burn, which seemed appropriate, because a part of my life has been cauterized by the tragedy. I no longer need to push the limits. I know what lies beyond them. I've obtained a dark knowledge I could not have obtained any other way. I've gambled and won.

If I'd learned anything from the climb it was about commitment. When you tie into the rope, you commit yourself. When you marry, you commit yourself. I couldn't do anything about Al and Lane now, but I could do something about my marriage. I'd been on the verge of walking out on Jill before the climb, but now I understood her importance. Without the vision of her and Andy willing me forward, I would not have made it back.

As Miles predicted, the tragedy generated an enormous amount of publicity. In the sensational way the media covers mountaineering, most of the stories concerned the deaths of Al and Lane, hashing and rehashing it, second-guessing my and Wyn's actions, and spending little if any time on the boldness of our ascent or my success in bringing Wyn back alive. The attention did nothing but help the store. Sales doubled over the next year, allowing Hal to retire and me to buy him out.

Despite my reconciliation with Jill and the store's success, my failure to help Al and Lane still haunts me. Hardly an hour goes by when my thoughts don't return to Denali, as if the storm and its aftermath have still not worked themselves out. Often, I wake in the middle of the night and replay that final scene over and over in my head, like a rerun of a movie I am doomed to see again and again, knowing exactly what will happen, and knowing I can do nothing to stop it.

The wind is howling. The clouds are closing in. Lane bends down, takes a dosage of Decadron from his pocket, and pops it in Al's mouth. Al's Adam's apple bobs as he swallows the pill. He pushes up his glasses. It's an ordinary, insignificant gesture, but it's caught in my memory. Al waits patiently, then the rope comes taut and he moves off.

"This way!" Lane shouts, beckoning us with his gloved hand. He takes one, long look over his right shoulder, his bug eyes visible through the yellow lenses of his goggles. Then he turns toward the south face.

"Stop!" I shout. "Wait!" I start toward them, but Wyn stops me.

"Let them go!" he yells. "There's nothing we can do!"

The red Perlon rope snakes along behind Lane. Al follows, stumbling along in a hypoxic stupor. He coughs and hunches against the wind, his limbs moving jerkily as if attached to puppet strings. Shreds of clouds swirl around them. They pass through a wall beyond which it seems we can't reach them. Then the clouds part and they reappear like an apparition. Al falls to his knees. Lane helps him up. Al stands, wobbles, and staggers forward. The mist closes in again. There's nothing left but swirling clouds, icy wind, and the vast, white nightmare of Denali.